"Awesome! Sarah Castille ripped my heart out with this book. It is a vivid and powerful story of love, loyalty, lust, and redemption."

—*Night Owl Romance* (A Top Pick) on *Sinner's Steel*

Also by
SARAH CASTILLE

Rough Justice

Beyond the Cut

Sinner's Steel

Chaos Bound

Nico

Available from St. Martin's Paperbacks

Praise for Sarah Castille's Sinner's Tribe series

"The exploration of the hardcore society of a motorcycle club (MC) is fascinating and chilling. Strong personalities populate this world and take no prisoners. Crafting a love story out of this combination is admirable."

—*RT Book Reviews* (4 ½ stars) on *Rough Justice*

"A sexy and dangerous ride! If you like your bad boys bad and your heroines kicking butt, *Rough Justice* will rev your engine. A great start to a new series!"

—Roni Loren, *New York Times* bestselling author

"Put your helmet on and hold tight for the ride of your life!"

—*Romance Reviews Today* on *Beyond the Cut*

"Castille continues to raise the stakes in her visceral, violent series, offering her biker heroes plenty of pulse-pounding action, and giving readers the compelling romance they crave."   —*RT Book Reviews* (4 ½ stars) on *Beyond the Cut*

"Castille takes the MC genre and lights it on fire! I want my very own Sinner's Tribe Motorcycle Club bad boy!"

—Julie Ann Walker, *New York Times* bestselling author

"Castille emphasizes the darkest aspects of motorcycle gangs in the gritty Sinner's Tribe Motorcycle Club [series] . . . for the reader who doesn't believe bad boys need redemption and hungers for the story of a couple whose love survives despite dangerous times."

—*Publishers Weekly* on *Sinner's Steel*

"Raw, rugged and romantic . . . you'll feel the vibration of the motorcycle engines in the pit of your stomach, smell the leather, and fall in love . . ."

—Eden Bradley, *New York Times* bestselling author

LUCA

SARAH CASTILLE

St. Martin's Paperbacks

This is a work of fiction. All of the characters, organizations, and events portrayed in this novel are either products of the author's imagination or are used fictitiously.

LUCA

Copyright © 2017 by Sarah Castille.
Excerpt from *Rocco* © 2018 by Sarah Castille.

All rights reserved.

For information address St. Martin's Press, 175 Fifth Avenue, New York, NY 10010.

ISBN: 978-1-250-10405-2

Printed in the United States of America

Our books may be purchased in bulk for promotional, educational, or business use. Please contact your local bookseller or the Macmillan Corporate and Premium Sales Department at 1-800-221-7945, ext. 5442, or by e-mail at MacmillanSpecialMarkets@macmillan.com.

St. Martin's Paperbacks edition / July 2017

St. Martin's Paperbacks are published by St. Martin's Press, 175 Fifth Avenue, New York, NY 10010.

10 9 8 7 6 5 4 3 2 1

To Laura,
For your friendship, pizza dinners,
and your knowledge of romantic Italian phrases.

ACKNOWLEDGMENTS

My tremendous thanks to Danielle for her incredible artistic skills, and for keeping everything running behind the scenes, and to Casey for her keen eye, attention to detail, and enthusiasm for my stories. Thanks also to my editor, Monique Patterson, and to Alexandra Sehulster and the St. Martin's Press team for making this story shine. Thanks to my agent, Laura Bradford, for having faith in all my ideas. And a huge thanks to my fabulous street team and the bloggers who help me spread the word about my books. You guys rock!

ONE

It began like every other day in Vegas.

Luca Rizzoli had rolled out of bed just before noon, showered, shaved and groomed. There was nothing more important for a Mafia capo than *la bella figura*—looking good in the eyes of society. Once his knives were strapped to his body, he dressed in a new Italian wool suit, crisp white shirt, and red silk tie. He holstered two Glocks across his chest, an S&W500 and a Ruger GP100 around his waist, and a Walther P22 beside the knife on his ankle, just above his Salvatore Ferragamo shoes. After meticulously checking his appearance, he walked back into the bedroom, ready to start his day.

That's when things had started to go wrong.

First, the woman in his bed didn't want to leave. When his usual charm and soft smiles failed to encourage her departure, he had to yank the covers off the bed and toss her money on the dresser, shattering the illusion that she was anything other than the high-class escort she pretended not to be. Luca always tipped well so her feigned indignation lasted only as long as it took her to count the cash and wobble her way out of his pent-house suite on her four-inch stilettos.

After that, it had been one broken leg after another as he called in a few business loans from scumbags who didn't want to pay up. As a senior *caporegime* in the Toscani crime family, he could have delegated the job to his crew of soldiers, but he had welcomed the opportunity for a little stress release.

Unfortunately, his day had continued its downward slide when he visited a new convenience store down the street to offer them his "protection", only to discover that the Albanians had muscled in on his territory.

Whacking Albanians was never a good way to break in a new suit, but the Toscani crime family didn't waste time when there were lessons to be learned.

Luca had called up Frankie De Lucchi, a top-level enforcer. Together, they sent the Albanians back to their home country via the fiery pit of Hell.

And wearing cement shoes.

Shoes were Frankie's specialty. He was a mean SOB who had once dabbled in the concrete-pouring business. He never gave up the opportunity to practice his trade, and the depths of Lake Mead boasted many examples of his handiwork.

After Luca had changed his clothes, washed off the blood, and dropped off his suit at the dry cleaners, his day had gone from bad to worse.

He got cocky.

And cocky had led him here. To this hospital bed. With a bullet in his chest.

It was his own damn fault. Luca knew better. He had let overconfidence blind him once before, and it had almost destroyed his life. His hand clenched on the bed rail as memories flooded through him, adding an emotional bite to his physical pain.

When Gina got pregnant after their one-night stand, he hadn't hesitated to do the right thing. After all, Gina ticked all the boxes for a desirable Mafia wife. She was pure Italian, well versed in the culture, easy on the eye, and a good cook. Love wasn't part of the Mafia marriage equation, so he had felt no guilt about spending Friday nights between the sheets with his sexy *goomah,* Marta, engaged in the extra-curricular activities expected of a senior Mafia capo. A wife was a symbol of status. A mistress was a symbol of power. Gina understood how things worked and as long as the money rolled in, she had no complaints. Life was good.

And then one afternoon he came home too early.

Too early for Gina's lover to escape.

Too early for Gina to hide the needles and packages of white powder her lover brought her every week.

Too early to clean up their son, Matteo, so Luca didn't find him crying and hungry in a shit-covered crib.

Too early to avoid having his heart ripped out of his chest by the devastating revelation Gina made before he kicked her out of the house, and her death by over-dose late that night in a bathtub in the Golden Dreams Hotel.

Luca had been totally unprepared for the emotional trauma of Gina's death. Sure he cared for her, enjoyed spending some time with her, and they had a two-year-old son together. But he hadn't loved her—had never pretended to love her—and her accusations that their empty marriage had turned her to drugs and other men had almost destroyed him.

Almost.

It was her parting shot that had done the real damage. His cocky overconfidence had blinded him to what was going on right under his nose.

Reeling from shock, and unable to share the depths of Gina's betrayal with even his closest friend, Nico Toscani, now self-appointed boss of the Toscani crime family, he'd gone off the rails. He sent Matteo to live with his mother, and dedicated himself to numbing the pain. He lived fierce. He lived large. He lived for the moment. Women. Fights. Booze. Craps. He took on the most dangerous jobs, and set up the most daring rackets. His attitude to risk became almost cavalier as he dedicated himself to his lifelong quest of restoring the family honor—destroyed by his father many years ago—by proving himself the most loyal of Nico's *caporegimes*.

Hence the mistake, which had led him to his current confinement.

Gritting his teeth, he shifted in the uncomfortable hospital bed. Pain sliced through his chest, and he bit back a groan. When he'd thrown himself in front of the bullet meant for Nico's heart, Luca could have saved himself a whole lot of pain if he'd worn a bulletproof vest. But sometimes, in the pit of despair, down was a hell of a lot more attractive than up.

A pale-yellow glow flickered in the doorway, and his pulse kicked up a notch, pulling him out of the sea of regret.

Nurse Rachel visited him every night to give him pain relief of another kind. Even bruised and broken, his dignity ruffled by the continual poking and prodding of his person, his life at rock bottom, he hadn't had to put much effort into convincing the young nurse to get down on her knees and wrap her plump lips around the only part of his body that didn't ache.

Luca had a gift for seducing women. Sweet words flowed easily off his tongue. His smile could sink one thousand ships. He was a lean, mean, fighting machine, but it was his dick that always brought them back for more.

When the door opened, he smoothed down his blue shirt and adjusted his belt. With a constant stream of family and crew coming to his room, he had made it clear to the medical staff that he would not suffer the indignity of a hospital gown. Every morning, he washed, shaved and dressed with the assistance of his sister, Angela, before greeting visitors from his hospital bed. His mother brought food every day to ensure he didn't "succumb to starvation". As with most Italian mothers he knew, there was her food or there was no food. That was her way.

"Rachel, sweetheart." His smile faded when an orderly followed Rachel into the room pushing a hospital gurney in front of him. Luca's gaze narrowed on the sleeping woman in the bed. Her long, blonde hair tumbled over the pillow, gleaming reddish-gold like the first autumn leaves. Her skin was pale in the harsh light, and her hospital gown gaped open at the collar, revealing the beautiful curve of her neck and the gentle slope of her shoulder.

Rachel gave him an apologetic smile, and he watched as they settled the woman in the cubicle near the window, wondering what the hell had happened to the wad of cash he had slipped the head nurse to ensure he had a private room.

After the orderly left, Rachel leaned down and brushed a soft kiss over Luca's cheek. "I'm sorry, Mr. Rizzoli. I know you like your privacy, but there was a big shootout in the Naked City, and the ER is swamped. We don't have enough staff or rooms to accommodate everyone, so the head nurse ordered us to ensure these double rooms were filled. She put you two together because you've got the same kind of injury."

Despite his irritation at losing his privacy, he graced her with a smile. He liked Rachel. She was a sweet girl, willing and compliant, and very skilled with her mouth. There was no point taking out his frustration on her. The Toscani crime family had friends everywhere. No doubt a few more bills and a word in the right ear in the morning would restore the status quo with a minimum of fuss. In the meantime, he'd have the company of a beautiful woman who had, apparently, like him, been shot in the chest.

After Rachel left, Luca's gaze drifted over his new companion. She had turned to face him in her sleep and the thin blanket dipped into her narrow waist and up over the curve of her hip. Her features were delicate, her cheekbones high, and her nose slightly turned-up at the tip. She was the opposite of everything that attracted him to a woman: blonde instead of brunette, curvy instead of slim, soft instead of hardened by the years of rough living that made it easy for him to limit his encounters with his escort companions to just one night.

Angelo. For the last four years, he had been lost. Now, he was found.

"You're staring."

Her warm, rich voice slid through him like a smooth Canadian whiskey that finished the palate with a whisper of heat.

"I was just wondering, *bella.*" He lifted his gaze to soft blue eyes framed in thick golden lashes. "Who would shoot an angel?"

Gabrielle couldn't remember the last time a man had looked at her with such open admiration.

Well, except for David. But David was gone.

Her hand drifted to her neck where she usually wore

a locket containing the last picture of her and David together. But the nurse had removed it when she went into surgery, and now it was buried somewhere in the plastic bag that held all her clothes.

Miss you.

Her heart squeezed in her chest, and she focused her gaze on the smartly-dressed man who sat on a hospital bed across the room. His eyes were the color of sunlight streaming through the pond behind her childhood home in Colorado. He had thick, blond hair, neatly cut, and rugged features that suggested Nordic descent.

But *bella* was an Italian word.

He'd called her an angel.

It was the kind of line she heard in the bars her bestie and roommate, Nicole, dragged her to on the weekends, hoping to pull her back into the world of dating so she could find another "happily ever after." But coming home at the end of her patrol one night to find her husband of only one year brutally murdered in their new home had ended Gabrielle's belief in fairy tales. And since they were definitely not in a bar or anywhere that remotely resembled a place where two people might hook up, the man across the room couldn't possibly be trying to seduce her. Although he was wearing street clothes, he was hooked up to the monitors just like her, and his bedside table held the kind of personal items one expected to see in a hospital room—shaving bag, magazines, flowers, and, disconcertingly, a holster.

"I've made you uncomfortable." His warm, sensual voice wrapped around her like a thick velvet blanket and she felt a flicker of awareness deep in her chest.

"I'm no angel." Her male colleagues in the Las Vegas Police Department (LVPD) Narcotics Bureau had other names for the most junior and only female detective in their squad, none of them flattering. She was a poor replacement for David, who had worked his way through the bureau from officer to detective, and from sergeant to lieutenant. Even after two years proving herself in an investigation into the rise of the Fuentes drug cartel in the city, she received little respect.

Not that she cared. She had pulled every string she could to get into the bureau and assigned to the Fuentes case with the sole goal of avenging David and bringing his killer to justice.

The Mexican-based Fuentes cartel had been traced to the supply of heroin, methamphetamine, and cocaine that came through Death Valley from Arizona and California. The drugs were stored and used in Las Vegas, and transitioned to other cities across the country by a vast network of smugglers extending from Canada to Mexico. Gabrielle's squad had been tasked with dismantling the Las Vegas cell of the cartel and capturing the man in charge, José Gomez Garcia, one of the biggest drug lords on the West Coast. And the man who had killed David.

"You look very angelic to me." His eyes dropped, slid slowly from her face to the embarrassing white-and-blue hospital gown with its gender-neutral graphic pattern. With the gaping neckline, and her semi-reclined position, it exposed just enough to make her flush as he perused her body. She tugged on the gown, but the instant his gaze flicked to hers she knew he'd had a close and personal view.

And for some reason, that made her tremble. Men like him didn't give heated looks to women like her. At least not now. Two years after David's death, she didn't recognize the woman she saw in the mirror every day. Revenge might have pulled her out of a year-long depression and given her a reason to get out of bed in the morning, but it hadn't done anything to put the spark back into her eyes or fill the black hole in her chest that got bigger every day that Garcia walked a free man.

She studied him as he studied her. Seated, his legs almost reached the end of the bed. She guessed he was taller than David who had dwarfed her five-foot five-inch frame by a good seven inches. Her roommate's shoulders were broad beneath his fine shirt, unmistakably powerful. He was the kind of man who would walk into a bar and instantly attract attention. She couldn't imagine a woman who wouldn't be swayed by his rich, soothing voice, soft lips, or the wicked sensuality that oozed from every pore of his taut, toned body. Even the scars along the curve of his chiseled jaw just added to his rugged charm. From the pressed pants he wore, to the wrinkle-free shirt, and the perfectly trimmed hair, he was breathtakingly gorgeous, and utterly magnetic.

"Luca Rizzoli," he said into the silence. "And you are . . . ?"

"Gabrielle Fawkes."

The faintest hint of a smile spread across his face. "Suits you. Gabriel was one of the archangels. And you remind me of Carlo Dolci's *Angelo dell'annunciazione* that now hangs in the Louvre. Emotional intensity translated into physical beauty . . ." He sighed. "Such a tragedy. Italian paintings should remain in Italy. Don't you agree?"

Gabrielle didn't know anything about art. She'd spent her first nine years in a small town in Colorado, and when her mother died, she and her older brother, Patrick, had been dragged to Nevada to live with her father's new wife in a lower-class suburb of Vegas. She also didn't know how to talk to handsome men who knew about art, dressed in expensive suits in the hospital, and spoke in a language that was so beautiful, musical, and vivid it made her knees weak. No wonder they called it the language of love. And in that deep, liquid voice . . . For a moment, she almost forgot the pain.

But movement reminded her. She grimaced as she tried to push herself up on the pillow, tugging the bandages that covered her chest.

His brow furrowed. "You're hurting."

"I'm fine," she lied. The physical pain from the gunshot wound was nothing compared to the utter despair of knowing she'd not only failed to catch Garcia tonight, but she'd compromised a two-year investigation into the cartel. If her stupid mistake got her kicked out of Narcotics, or even the LVPD, she would never have the chance to catch the man who killed her husband.

No. Not just David. Garcia was responsible for taking two lights out of her life. Not just one. Her stomach clenched at the memory, and she fisted the covers. She'd thought nothing could be worse than losing the man she loved. She'd been wrong.

"I'll call Nurse Rachel," Luca said, frowning.

"You don't need to call her. It only hurts when I move."

"Don't move," he commanded, jabbing his finger on the call button. "Rachel will be able to do something for the pain."

"It was a joke," she said lamely. "I mean, it hurts, but it's not unbearable."

"A joke?" His beautiful eyes narrowed, their rich hazel depths hidden beneath a thicket of lashes.

She laughed at his puzzled expression, startling herself with the sound. When was the last time she had laughed out loud? Even the perpetually upbeat Nicole hadn't been able to drag a spontaneous laugh out of her in a long time. "I guess being shot isn't something to joke about. I turned down the painkillers. I don't like drugs, especially if they fuzz up my brain."

He gave a soft grunt of approval. "We have that in common," he said. "As well as the bullet wounds we share. Pain is the body's way of guiding us how to heal."

She wished that were true and that there was some purpose or end to the relentless emotional pain of loss, a new universe on the other side of the black hole in the center of her chest. Revenge was all that sustained her now, and she didn't know what would happen when revenge was gone.

"You were a shooting victim, too?" She cut herself off when he glowered at her, sending a chill down her spine. How could he be so attractive and so terrifying at the same time? She'd dealt with criminals every day on the beat, the kind of men he likely never encountered in his life. Now that she was a detective, she dealt with criminals of another sort—ruthless, violent drug lords who followed no laws, respected no boundaries, and wouldn't let anyone stand in their way of spreading their poison as far and as fast as possible. They didn't scare her, but something about this man made her shiver.

"I'm sorry. If it's difficult to talk about . . ."

He stiffened his spine, puffed his chest. "I got in the way of the bullet by choice."

"Ah." She wanted to know more, but his tight expression made her wary of prying. "Well, we differ in that respect. I didn't put myself in front of my bullet. In fact, I didn't even see it coming. I was ambushed. It went right through me, but missed my internal organs. The doctor said I was the luckiest person he'd ever met."

"It was a good day for luck." He tapped his chest, and Gabrielle forced a smile. She didn't feel lucky. When the bullet hit her chest, she'd felt a profound sense of relief, knowing that there would finally be an end to the pain, and she would find peace and be with David again.

Waking up in the hospital, realizing it wasn't over, had almost destroyed her.

Luca must have seen something in her expression, because his brow creased in a frown. "Who shot you, *bella*? You don't look like the kind of woman who should be on the wrong side of a gun." He winced ever so slightly as he turned to her and she wondered how he'd managed to convince the hospital staff to let him wear his regular clothes. Except for the wires protruding from the neck of his shirt, he didn't look like he'd been shot at all. She admired him for his refusal to accept not only the label and the gown, but also the pain. A rebel after her own heart.

"Wrong place at the wrong time." She didn't know if the botched drug bust had hit the news, or if the top brass had tried to keep it quiet. It had been the largest investigation in the department's history, involving officers and detectives from multiple bureaus including the SWAT team, Homicide, and even Organized Crime. What they had thought was a small-time drug operation, turned out to be a massive drug cartel crossing state and country lines, and the day of reckoning had turned into a PR nightmare when a junior detective hell bent on revenge had inadvertently allowed the drug lord to escape.

"How about you?" she asked, to deflect any further questions. "Are you in law enforcement?"

"I'm in the restaurant business." He pulled a card from his wallet and gingerly reached over to place it on the table beside her bed. "If you ever want a good meal, come to *Il Tavolino*. Ask for me. You won't find better Italian food in the city. Even my mother has eaten there, and that's saying something."

She was in too much pain to reach for the card, but she managed a smile. "I didn't realize the restaurant business was so dangerous."

"Life is dangerous. Where was your man to protect you?"

God, not another one. Twenty percent of the sworn officers in the LVPD were women, and yet she had to deal with this kind of traditional attitude every day. Although the younger officers gave her professional respect, most of her more established colleagues struggled to accept the concept of a woman with a gun. "The men I was with didn't need to protect me. I can protect myself." Although in this case she hadn't done a very good job.

"Then they are not real men."

The door opened and the nurse came in. She checked Gabrielle's vital signs, made sure she was comfortable, and then pulled the curtain separating the two cubicles.

Gabrielle heard murmurs from the other side of the curtain, the lilt of flirtatious laughter, and the rumble of Luca's deep voice as he bid the nurse goodnight before she left the room.

She sighed, stared out the window at the city lights twinkling in the distance. Luca was very obviously a real man—and one who loved his women young, slim, and pretty.

It was definitely not a lucky day. But then, luck had never been on her side.

TWO

"Get the good mozzarella. The wet one," Luca's mother shouted through the phone.

"Ma. I got the mozzarella." He waved to Roberto behind the counter at Bianchi's Deli, the only place his mother would buy the ingredients for her Sunday dinner.

"It's not enough. We're going to have a big thing. Everyone is coming over. Nonna Cristini and Peppe are coming over. Josie's coming over. Rosa's coming over. Lele's coming over—"

"Ma. I've got enough mozzarella to feed all of Sicily. It's only Thursday. If it's not enough, I can come back."

He heard a crash and groaned inwardly. Turning, he saw his six-year-old son, Matteo, standing by a broken flowerpot.

His mother stopped mid-tirade. "What's that noise?"

"Matteo broke a flower pot. I thought you were teaching him good behavior. Everywhere we go, he gets into trouble." He gestured to Paolo to go deal with the mess. Tall and lanky, with dark hair cut to the side that constantly fell over his face, seventeen-year-old Paolo had been helping out with Matteo, running errands, and making deliveries for the last few years in the hopes that one day he would be accepted as an associate in Luca's crew.

"He's a boy," his mother said. "Boys run. They get dirty. They break things. They get in fights. You ran all over the place."

Luca's younger brother, Alex, used to run, too, until he started snorting powder up his nose, and then his running days were over. Yet another victim of the scourge that had killed Luca's wife and threatened to destroy the city he loved.

"Tell him not to run in stores." He watched Paolo wipe away the big fat tears streaking down his son's face and felt a twinge of guilt that he had not gone to comfort his own son.

"You tell him. You're his father. You never see him. Maybe once a week and on Sunday. That's not enough."

"Ma. I don't have time. Protecting and supporting the family is my job. Discipline. Manners. Not running indoors. Those are your job. You did okay with me. I'm standing here. Not running. Not breaking things."

His mother huffed into the phone. "Since you're standing there, tell Roberto to save the end of the *bracciole*. I'm going to make *pasta e fagioli*. Alex loves it. He's working hard now and he's got a big appetite. I cook him breakfast, he asks what's for dinner."

Luca didn't have the heart to tell her that Alex, still living at home at the age of twenty-four, was spending his days working in a coffee shop to earn money for crack, and his nights sneaking women into the bedroom they'd shared until Luca left home at the age of eighteen.

He covered the phone and sent Paolo out to watch the vehicle. Frowning at Matteo, he pointed to a chair by the door. "Sit over there and don't move." The boy was the spitting image of Gina—dark hair, deeply tanned skin, and a round, soft face. The constant visual reminder of Gina's betrayal was another reason why Matteo now lived with Luca's mother.

Frankie and Mike snickered by the deli counter as his mother talked. Neither of them had to contend with their mothers living close by. Not just mothers, but all the cousins, aunts, uncles, and grandparents that encompassed his family—the family Luca's father had dishonored when he became an FBI informant. Luca had been trying to prove that he was not his father's son ever since.

Frankie had no family to worry about. Orphaned when he was young, he had been taken in by the De Lucchi Crew, the enforcement arm of the New York Gamboli crime family and trained as a Mafia enforcer— the kind of man who made even the meanest, most ruthless killers tremble with fear.

Named after one of the most powerful New York Mafia bosses of all time, the Gamboli crime family was one of the most powerful *Cosa Nostra* families in America with factions in many key cities. The Toscani family ran the Gamboli's Vegas faction, although the recent death of the Toscani boss had split the family in two with both Nico and his cousin, Tony, claiming the title of "don". Nico had appointed Luca and Frankie as his closest advisors.

"Alex is bringing a girl over after church on Sunday," his mother said. "I don't know why she can't come to church with him. What kind of girl doesn't go to church?"

"Maybe she's not Italian." Although he and Alex were expected to marry Italian women, there were no restrictions when it came to girlfriends and mistresses. Marta, his *goomah* when he'd been with Gina, was half Spanish and half Portuguese. She knew a few Italian words and a little English, but he hadn't been with her for the conversation. Marta liked her sex rough and dirty and Luca had been able to let go with her in a way he'd never been able to do with his wife.

Still, life was easier with a woman who had been raised in a Mafia family. Mafia women understood the culture and hierarchy. They wouldn't insult him by trying to pay for a meal, opening a door, or leading on the dance floor. Although they were accorded the utmost respect, they knew the man's job was to provide and protect, and the woman's job was to look after the children and the home.

"I want more grand babies," his mother continued. "I have Matteo and that's all. Rosa has two grandchildren already, and two more on the way."

Luca braced himself. He knew where this conversation was headed.

"Rosa's daughter is going to be in church on Sunday. You can meet her. She just moved back to the city from New York. She's an accountant. Good with money. She has braces to straighten her teeth, but they're the kind you don't see right away, and your sister is going to fix her hair. She tried to bleach it blonde and burnt half of it off. Angela says it will grow back, so don't worry."

"Ma, I've got to go. Matteo's disappeared." He wasn't interested in a future with anyone. One night and then he moved on. No attachments. No regrets. No betrayal. No fucking discovering the person you married was not the person you thought she was.

Unless God sent him another angel. Then he might be tempted to break his own rules.

"Don't forget the *bracciole*," his mother continued. "And buy something for Matteo. He got a good mark on his math test. He's a smart boy, just like his father."

Luca's stomach tightened as he searched the deli for Matteo. His mother used to say that to him before his father wound up dead after trying to exchange his honor for a cushy life in witness protection. There was nothing the Mafia liked less than rats, except maybe the police.

"Matteo!" He grabbed his son's hand out of the aquarium in the front window just as it was closing in on a fish.

"Nonna always cooks fish for dinner on Friday," Matteo said, his mouth turning down at the corners. "I wanted to bring her Nemo."

"She doesn't want that kind of fish." He looked out the window and froze.

If his mother had been there at that exact moment, she would have said God had led Matteo to the fish. She was a strong believer in signs, portents, and omens. God regularly visited her home, rustling leaves to remind her that the door was open or making her drop her clothespin just before the neighbor's kid hit a softball into her yard.

Since his mother wasn't there, Luca figured it was just good luck that Matteo decided to go after the fish in the window just as three of Tony Toscani's soldiers stepped out of their vehicle with automatic weapons in their hands. The same luck that had saved him when he stepped in front of the bullet that had Nico's name on it. The same luck that had sent an angel to warm his heart in the hospital.

Time had not been on his side when he'd attempted to hunt down his angel after being discharged from the hospital. Duty had called him away, and nothing was more important to him than duty. Only by doing his duty to his crime family, and proving himself the most worthy of capos, would he be able to redeem the Rizzoli family name in the eyes of *Cosa Nostra*.

"Down!" He flipped over the nearest table and threw

Matteo to the ground, covering him with his body as the first bullet shattered the window.

Another fucking day in the war for the City of Sin.

"Hello and good-bye, Fawkes."

Gabrielle ignored the sarcastic comments from her fellow detectives as she walked into the department meeting room for her disciplinary hearing. Seated around the table were the bureau commander, her union representative, her supervising sergeant, and an unfamiliar man in a dark suit and blue tie whom the commander introduced as Special Agent Palmer from the FBI.

"Have a seat, Gabrielle. Glad to see you're up and around." Bald and red-faced, the sergeant was a big man with a big attitude. Although he came across tough, he had always been supportive of Gabrielle, and had pushed through her application to Narcotics the year after David died.

"Thanks." Heart pounding, she sat at the end of the table, twisting her hands in her lap as a ray of afternoon sun worked its way through the reinforced blinds, sending hopeful light in her direction. Maybe she would just get a slap on the wrist or a suspension for jumping the gun on the SWAT team with her early infiltration of the warehouse where Garcia had allegedly been hiding. "The bullet went right through, so it's been healing quickly."

"Good to hear."

The first part of the hearing went as expected. Her union rep ran through her record of achievements, the good work she'd done both as a beat cop and then as an investigator on the Garcia case. He talked about her marriage to David and her devastation after he died. If she'd really wanted to play the sympathy card, she could have told them what happened a few days after David's death, when she'd discovered losing her husband wasn't the worst of the pain she would have to bear. But that was a secret she had shared only with her friends, Nicole and Cissy, and with David's best friend, Jeff.

"You okay?"

She startled, realizing too late she'd inadvertently opened the door to her greatest pain, and it had reflected on her face.

"Yes, I'm fine." Slamming the mental door closed, she forced her fingers apart and tried to relax them in her lap, embarrassed at the show of emotion, however small. Her union rep continued with his submission, glossing over the strings that had been pulled in contravention of policy to get her on the Garcia case by emphasizing her understandable need to be part of the team that had been tasked with bringing Garcia to justice.

Bring him to justice. He emphasized those words again and again, making it seem that Gabrielle's intention when she entered the warehouse prematurely had been simply to ensure Garcia didn't escape, when in fact, she had hoped for an excuse to kill him.

She had only been three months pregnant when she returned home after a late shift one night to find David hanging upside down, stripped and tortured, his throat slit, his blood a red sea across their new cream carpet.

Stress-induced miscarriage. The doctors had a clinical name for what had happened a few days later. But she couldn't get beyond the fact that she had lost her last and only link to David. Proof that he had lived and loved on earth. She had wanted the baby so much, to give her all the love she never had, to be the mother she so desperately missed.

She suspected everyone in the room, except the mysterious Special Agent Palmer, knew she wouldn't have hesitated to pull the trigger if she'd seen Garcia in the warehouse. They were all seasoned cops, and David had been their friend as well as a highly respected and well-loved lieutenant. They all knew that true justice—Garcia spending his life behind bars—was less likely than Garcia hiring a good lawyer, making bail, and disappearing again to sell the drugs that were destroying countless lives, or at best doing a few years for some minor charge for lack of evidence of his more serious crimes.

The union rep closed his submission by emphasizing the fact that no one had established the identity of Gabrielle's shooter, and it was very likely Garcia had not, in fact, been in the warehouse at the time of the raid. After all, the facility had clearly just been vacated, with only the drug-packaging equipment left behind and no sign of the thirty-strong team that was allegedly at the heart of Garcia's local distribution operation. And if that were the case, the raid would have failed in any event and not because Gabrielle had entered the warehouse too early and had the misfortune of encountering a lone straggler who shot at her in a desperate attempt to escape.

His arguments were convincing. However, she was well aware that she should never have been allowed to work on the case. Although everyone had turned a blind eye to her promotion from beat cop to Narcotics detective, the shooting had forced the issue into the light, and the bureau had to be seen as taking action. Her hand went to the locket that she had held after the bullet hit her, believing she was about to see David again, and she gave it a squeeze for luck.

"We'll have a decision for you before the end of your medical leave," the commander said by way of wrapping up. "But before you go, I want to let you know that the FBI are taking over the Garcia case. Special Agent

Palmer will be on site for the duration of the investigation. He's reviewed the file, and he knows how hard you've worked on this case for the last two years." The commander hesitated. "He's going to make some changes, shake things up a bit." He looked away, and Gabrielle had a bad feeling about what those changes were going to be.

"Ms. Fawkes." Special Agent Palmer gave her a cold smile and she disliked him right away. He was tall and lean, with dark hair, angular cheekbones, and a pointed chin that narrowed his long face. He looked too thin to be imposing, but she had a feeling that under that suit he was all ropey muscle and a whole lot of nasty.

"You've done some solid work, and I'm sure everyone in the department is grateful for your contribution . . ."

Oh God. She swallowed past the lump in her throat. *Here it comes.*

"I've brought in my own team," he continued. "They have extensive experience dealing with drug lords like Garcia. And, of course, experience dealing with multistate and international drug-trafficking rings like the Fuentes Cartel. We first became interested in Garcia when he was in Los Angeles. He wanted to be a kingpin in the drug world, and he made that happen with the help of his cartel connections in Mexico."

"I know everything about him since he came to Vegas." No one in the bureau knew more about Garcia than her.

Agent Palmer gave her another cold smile. "I understand how much you have invested in the case. And I also understand that Garcia was responsible for the death of your husband, Lieutenant David Roscoe, a well-respected member of the LVPD. I was surprised, however, that given the incredible conflict of interest, you were allowed to work on the case. There is no way you can be impartial when you're a victim."

"I'm not a victim," she said firmly. "David was the victim, and I wanted to be part of the team that made Garcia pay for his crime." Not that being part of the team meant anything. As the junior detective on the case, she'd been given the task of managing the paperwork, inputting information into databases and sitting at her desk doing research. No one took her seriously. She was too young, too green, and everyone thought she'd been given the position because of the bureau commander's high regard for David, despite the fact she'd passed her exams, putting her on an equal footing with the other bureau candidates.

"He will pay," Special Agent Palmer said. "We have experience catching violent felons like Garcia, and the groundwork your team has done will be an invaluable resource. Your continued participation, however, is dependent on the outcome of this hearing, and my personal assessment of whether your emotional involvement would compromise the investigation or bring the administration of justice into disrepute."

Her mouth tightened and she fought back a wave of nausea. She'd come into the hearing hoping for a slap on the wrist. Never had she considered that they would boot her off the team. And there was nowhere else she wanted to go.

Until the death of her older brother, Patrick, she had never considered police work. With her love of puzzles and solving mysteries, her interests had leaned toward science and investigative pursuits. But she'd joined the police academy after graduating from high school, hoping that living Patrick's dream would pull her father out of the depression that had consumed him since Patrick died. He'd been so proud when Patrick talked about becoming a police officer, and so utterly devastated when Patrick overdosed only days after his third stint in rehab.

Gabrielle could barely remember the days when Patrick's addiction didn't rule their lives. He'd turned to drugs after their mother died and their father had moved them to Nevada to live with his new wife, Val, and her two sons. After the move, her good memories about Patrick were lost beneath all the shouting and fighting and lying and stealing. Her father lost his job as a bricklayer because of the time he had to take off for hospital visits and court hearings, bailing Patrick out of jail, or driving around the streets looking for him when he was so high he didn't even know his own name.

When she first joined the police academy, Gabrielle believed she could make a difference by becoming a police officer. She thought she could clean up the streets so other families wouldn't suffer, and she prayed that her dad would find some happiness in her attempt to keep Patrick's memory alive. Her rude awakening came first, when her father didn't bother to attend her graduation ceremony, and then when she walked the beat and realized that the war on drugs could never be won. If she hadn't met David, an instructor in one of her classes, who encouraged her not to give up, she would have walked away after her first year.

What would she do if they pulled her off the case? How would she fulfill the silent promise she made to David when she held him for the last time on the blood-soaked living room carpet? How would he rest in peace if he didn't have justice? How would she?

After thanking her union rep, she quickly made her way down the hallway, desperate to get out of the building before anyone saw her and asked about the hearing.

She hit the button for the elevator, and prayed for a quick escape.

"Gaby!"

Jeff Santos caught up to her just as the elevator door slid open, and followed her inside. She had known David's best friend, now a lieutenant in Narcotics with her, as long as she had known David. After David died, Jeff had been an incredible comfort and support, helping her with everything from selling the house to making sure someone was with her on weekends when she most felt David's absence in her life.

"You okay? What happened?"

She turned to face him, noting the lines of worry creasing his broad forehead beneath his buzz-cut black hair. Jeff was dark where David had been fair, deeply tanned with the blackest eyes Gabrielle had ever seen. He was six feet of solid muscle, with a carefully groomed moustache and a chinstrap beard. He had a wide, barrel chest and the beginning of a belly that had only just appeared after David died.

She stared at the bronze medallion he always wore on a leather chain around his scarred throat, thinking back to the day she and David had given it to him. He'd kissed her in thanks while David poured drinks in the kitchen, his lips lingering a moment too long on her cheek, his whisper just too close to her mouth. She'd brushed if off as imagination, but last year he'd let her know that he wanted to take their friendship to another level and he was prepared to wait as long as it took for her too feel comfortable. She didn't have the heart to tell him it would take forever.

"The FBI is taking over the Garcia case," she said. "The agent in charge isn't happy about my involvement because he thinks I have a conflict of interest. I'm pretty sure he wants me off the team." The elevator door slid open, and she stepped out into the reception area, a cacophony of noise from an eclectic mix of people, most of whom didn't want to be there.

Of course, Jeff followed her. He was always there, even after they'd had an awkward conversation one night six months ago, when he tried to kiss her, and she'd explained she wasn't interested in having a relationship ever again.

It's not you; it's me. Trite but true. She was broken inside. Damaged. She had nothing to offer anyone but her pain.

He sucked in a sharp breath. "The FBI? God, Gaby. I know how much this means to you, how much you wanted to make Garcia pay for what he did to David. But maybe it's for the best. You can move on."

"I don't want to move on," she snapped. "I want justice. That's all I lived for over the last two years. It's Garcia or nothing for me."

The doors slid open, and she stepped outside into the blazing heat of an unnaturally warm Nevada fall.

"Don't be rash," Jeff said, leading her into the shade beneath a Chinese hackberry tree with a firm hand on her lower back. "There are other options. I can talk to people, help you get into another bureau. What about Homicide? Garcia has been linked to dozens of murders in the city . . ."

"I know you're swamped with your own investigations. And after David, I couldn't deal with Homicide."

He put an arm around her and gave her a hug. "You just have to be creative. What if you transfer into Theft? I'm sure he's stolen at least one thing in his life."

She gave a half-hearted laugh. Jeff was such a nice guy. A police lieutenant. Respected in his bureau. He was fun to be around, and he'd been a good friend to both David and to her. And yet she didn't feel an attraction. He was the dark to David's light. Where David had been laid-back, Jeff was intense. He laughed too hard, talked too loud, moved too fast. Where David had an easy charm, Jeff's smiles sometimes seemed forced, like he had to work at the face he presented to the world. But more than that, he was almost like a brother to her. And his kiss six months ago had just felt wrong.

"I'm not leaving you alone tonight," he said. "I'll take you for dinner. I can't stand the thought of you alone at home after you've just had the carpet ripped out from under you."

"You make me sound pathetic." She sighed. "I'm not going to sit at home in the dark looking at old pictures and crying over a bottle of wine. I'm going for a run and then I'll hit the gym and work on getting my arm and shoulder back into shape. I also have to pick Max up from the dog sitter . . ."

She'd found her precious beagle after checking out several rescue centers on the advice of her therapist. It had been love at first sight, and after she sold her house, she rented a small bungalow in Henderson with a big back yard so Max would have some space to run. When she discovered Nicole was struggling to make ends meet as a casino dealer on the strip, she invited her to live with them. In turn, Nicole had helped Gabrielle through her first terrible year without David.

"You have to eat," he insisted. "How about I stop by later with a pizza and a bottle of wine and we can just kick back and watch TV?"

Gabrielle's chest tightened at the thought of being alone with Jeff, something she had tried to avoid since that awkward kiss. Why couldn't she take that next step and be with him the way he wanted her to be? He was David's best friend and they shared many interests; it would be easy and fun. And yet it wasn't fair to him. She couldn't even contemplate being in a relationship with anyone. She was broken, and he deserved to find someone who needed all the caring he wanted to give. "Thanks, Jeff. But I've got stuff to do, and I promised I'd hang out with Nicole tonight. She's off early from the casino. Maybe another time."

"I'm always here for you whenever you need me." He leaned in and brushed his lips over hers. It happened so quickly, she didn't have time to react. And then he was gone.

Her hands closed into fists and she pressed them against her head. Why couldn't she feel something when he kissed her? She was tired of being numb. Tired of going through the motions every day. Tired of pretending she loved her job when she was only there so David could rest in peace. Tired of feeling nothing when a good, decent man touched her. She wanted to scream. Run. Shout. She wanted to escape from the suffocating life she had built out of the ashes that held her in limbo between a future that scared her and a past that consumed her. God, she just wanted to feel something. Heat. Fireworks. Passion.

She wanted to feel the way she'd felt when she'd woken after surgery to see a handsome, impeccably dressed man studying her from his hospital bed. She had *felt* something then. Curiosity. Wonder. Excitement. Desire.

Everything about him: his looks, his demeanor, and his sheer utter rebelliousness in refusing to accept he had been shot and was in a goddamn hospital had taken her breath away. And his voice, that accent . . . Even now her knees went weak just thinking about it. What would it be like to kiss a man like him? Someone so utterly confident and in control. A rebel. A man who could seduce an injured woman in a hospital bed with just the sound of his voice and the heat of his gaze.

She pulled out her phone and flipped to the card image she had stored in an app.

Luca Rizzoli, Manager
Il Tavolino
Finest Italian food in Las Vegas
Just like nonna used to make . . .

Why had she kept it? She couldn't even bring herself to go on a date with a good friend, a man who wanted her despite the fact she was shattered inside. How could she even contemplate trekking across the city to the restaurant of a man she barely knew simply because of the way he made her feel?

Then again, what did she have to lose?

THREE

Il Tavolino

Gabrielle studied the swirl of gold letters above the restaurant across the street. She'd eaten at many Italian restaurants in Vegas, but hadn't heard of *Il Tavolino*. But then she didn't usually come to this part of the city. She didn't usually chase after mysterious restaurant owners either, but here she was, standing on the sidewalk, waiting for Nicole and Cissy to arrive.

Of course, Nicole had been all over the idea of checking out a new Italian restaurant when Gabrielle phoned her at the casino. Not only that, she'd called up Gabrielle's childhood friend, Cissy, and they'd convinced Gabrielle to try out the new nightclub that had opened across the street after the meal. But then Nicole had seen Gabrielle at her worst, when she couldn't breathe for the pain, and not even Max could pull her out of the darkness. Now, if Gabrielle even opened the door a crack, Nicole dove right in.

Gabrielle dropped her gaze from the sign to the restaurant exterior. With its bright-red awning, cheerful yellow paint, and fancy stonework, it had a warm, welcoming feel. Through the huge brightly lit windows, she could see tuxedo-clad waiters, plush banquets, and memorabilia and photos on the walls. It was Old Vegas-meets Old Hollywood and it fit in perfectly with the revival decor.

Laugher. A giggle. "Luca. Stop."

Gabrielle's head jerked up and she recognized the man from the hospital right away. She had thought him handsome then, but seeing him now—strong and able-bodied, a fitted suit hugging his powerful frame, his blond hair artfully mussed—her heart sped up and her mouth went dry.

Even from across the street, Gabrielle could see that the woman he was with was beautiful. She wore a tight green dress, four-inch heels, and loads of bling. Her long, dark wavy hair reached almost to the small of her back. She had olive skin and high cheekbones, ruby-red lips and matching nails. Over her shoulder, she carried the kind of designer handbag that Gabrielle could never hope to afford, even on a detective's salary.

The woman stumbled on a crack and Luca turned, swiftly putting one hand around her waist to steady her, before he pulled her into his body with practiced ease. She laughed loudly, without inhibition, and leaned up to kiss Luca's cheek.

Damn. All her silly fantasies about seeing him again shattered with that kiss. Of course, a man like that would be with a glamorous woman. Still, she couldn't tear her eyes away. There was something about the way he held her, confident and controlled, protective and demanding. She imagined his deep rich voice whispering filthy words in liquid Italian, telling her what he was going to do when he got her home.

She felt her loneliness like a sharp ache in her chest after Luca escorted the woman into the restaurant. David had held her like that. He had made her feel like she was the most beautiful woman in the world. She'd never have that again, and she missed it so fiercely her stomach twisted in a knot. Even if she could drag herself through the dating mill again, she'd never meet a man who loved her the way David did.

So why bother?

"Gaby!" Cissy waved from down the street, just as Nicole rounded the opposite corner. A lawyer, from a family of lawyers, Cissy was one of the first people Gabrielle had met when her father relocated the family to Vegas. Forgotten in the never-ending drama of living with a teenage addict, Gabrielle spent most of her time at Cissy's house where she could pretend for a short time she was part of a normal family.

As they walked toward her—Cissy in a green pleated-style wrap dress, and Nicole in a bright pink lace overlay dress that matched the pink streak in her light brown hair—Gabrielle immediately regretted her decision to wear black. But her halter-style form-fitting dress edged with sequins was the only dressy thing in her wardrobe that hid the scars on her chest from the bullet that had almost brought her to David again.

"Oh my God," Cissy shrieked, her voice surprisingly loud for someone with such a tiny frame. "I haven't seen you in a dress in forever. And your hair! I love it down. I'm so used to seeing you with a ponytail that I sometimes forget how long your hair is. And those shoes . . ." She pretended to pant over Gabrielle's three-inch rhinestone-encrusted T-straps. "We're definitely going to get you hooked-up tonight."

"I just saw the restaurant owner," Gabrielle said, trying to hide her disappointment. "He was with someone. I think he's got a girlfriend, or even a wife. Maybe we should just skip dinner and grab something else before we go to the club."

"He invited you for a meal, not to bed." Nicole gripped Gabrielle's shoulder as if she were afraid Gabrielle might run away. "And good-looking guys have good-looking friends. After such a terrible day at work, you deserve a little fun. Maybe he can introduce us to his friends and we can all have a good time. Lord knows I need it, too."

"She had a bust-up with Clint this morning after you left for work," Cissy said, in response to Gabrielle's puzzled frown.

Gabrielle stopped mid-stride. "Why didn't you tell me when I called? I wouldn't have asked you—"

Nicole groaned, cutting her off. "I didn't want you to know. This is supposed to be your night. And it's the same old same old. I looked on his computer and saw he had a couple of windows open: 'Big Wet Tits,' 'Ass Good Ass It Gets,' and my personal favorite, 'Office Lady Love Juice.' It's hard to believe he respects me when he spends his days wanking off to that shit, so I left."

"He doesn't respect you, honey." Gabrielle gave her arm a squeeze. "You've got to stop going back to him. You need to set boundaries."

"Yeah, well . . . sometimes I'm just not there for him the way he needs me so he has to release some steam. But he's always sorry after he . . ." She hesitated, stumbled over her words. "After I catch him, and then we make up. I'm just not ready to start all over again with someone else." She trailed off when Gabrielle opened the door.

Gabrielle understood Nicole's reluctance to find someone new. She'd had a few hook-ups since David's death, but they left her feeling sad and alone. It wasn't that the guys were unattractive or unkind, but she just didn't feel anything for them. She didn't feel at all.

"Where's the guy?" Cissy whispered as they walked inside.

"He probably won't remember me." Gabrielle ran a hand through her hair, finger-combing the waves that she could never get straight. "I'd just been shot, and had come out of surgery. I wasn't really looking my best."

"You're not easy to forget." Nicole's mouth dropped open when they walked into the restaurant, and even reserved Cissy gasped as she took in the décor.

Over the top didn't even begin to describe the sensory overload of *Il Tavolino*. Gabrielle felt like she'd re-entered the city's Golden Age—from the tuxedoed waiters doing tableside presentations, to the magnificent plush banquets, and from the Vegas memorabilia on every surface to the elevated stage where a Frank Sinatra impersonator was singing "My Way." On the walls, framed pictures of old movie stars sat alongside famous Mafia gangsters—Bogart beside Bugsy Siegel, and Frank Sinatra beside Anthony Spilotro. Glass cases containing old 45s and sparkly shoes, an old-fashioned revolver, and a top hat and cane gave the restaurant an old-school elegant feel.

Gabrielle approached the polished-wood reception desk and inquired about a table.

"I'm sorry, ladies." The maître d' gave them a sympathetic smile. "Reservations only. We're fully booked tonight."

"You didn't make a reservation?" Cissy frowned at Gabrielle. A control freak, Cissy never went anywhere without having planned out every detail first.

"I thought it was a casual place." Gabrielle had considered calling ahead, but she hadn't been sure what to say. Did she tell the person on the other end of the phone that she knew Luca? How awkward would that be? And what if Luca answered the phone? He'd told her to stop by, not call.

At once relieved and disappointed, Gabrielle smiled at the maître d'. "Thanks anyway." She made a move for the door, desperate to leave in case Luca saw her, hesitating only when her friends didn't follow.

"She's a friend of Luca's," Nicole said, turning on the charm that encouraged people to keep placing bets at her tables in the casino. "He gave her his card. Her name is Gabrielle Fawkes. Show him the card, Gaby."

"It's okay. We'll come back another time." Mortified, Gabrielle reached for the door.

"A friend of Mr. Rizzoli?" The maître d' gave them an appraising look. "If you could wait just a moment ladies, I'll let him know you're here." He disappeared into the packed restaurant, and Gabrielle groaned. "This is going to be so embarrassing. I think we should just go."

"He wouldn't have invited you if he didn't mean it," Nicole countered.

"Maybe he was just being polite. Or doing what business people do. Everyone hands out cards. It doesn't mean anything."

Nicole tipped her head back and groaned. "How many times have you done something like this for me? I'm paying it back, okay? At the very least, we'll have a nice dinner before we go out and drink and dance our sorrows away."

Gabrielle touched her locket. "I don't know. I saw him with that woman and it made me think of David."

Nicole looked up and over Gabrielle's shoulder. Her eyes widened at something behind Gabrielle, and she gently unclasped the locket, catching it before it fell. "I think you might want to consider leaving David behind, just for tonight."

Gabrielle turned and caught her breath when she saw Luca walking toward them. He had removed his jacket, and in his elegant, blue shirt and navy dress pants, he looked like he'd stepped out of a men's fashion magazine. His partially opened shirt revealed deliciously tanned skin dusted with gold hair, and the hint of a tattoo. His blond hair was longer than she remembered, and there was a sexy hint of stubble shadowing his square jaw.

Her pulse kicked up a notch, and she had to remind herself that he was taken, and by a beautiful woman he obviously adored.

"Oh, my God," Cissy whispered. "My ovaries just exploded."

Dio mio.

She had come to him.

His breathtaking, incandescent, golden-haired angel.

Luca drank in the long, loose tumble of her hair, the long legs that he could easily imagine wrapped around his waist, the slight flush on her beautiful face. She wore a tight black dress that exposed her shoulders and clung to her generous breasts, teasing him with a hint of the treasure that lay beneath. Her soft curves begged for a man's touch. Hell, his angel was built to be fucked.

She licked her plump pink lips, and his imagination went into overdrive, assailing him with a vision of those sensual lips wrapped around his cock. Their gazes met and held. Hunger shimmered in the depths of her Siren eyes, luring him forward until he could think of nothing but covering her body with his.

Christ. This was fucking crazy. He didn't go for

blondes or women who would blush beneath the appraising gaze of a man. He liked his woman dark, bold, loud,
and brash. The kind of woman who loudly demanded
a man's attention, not unassumingly drew it in with a
quiet confidence and a sensual smile.

"Gabrielle. You look well." He leaned down and
kissed her on both cheeks, eschewing the conventional
handshake for the intimacy of an Italian greeting simply because he wanted to get closer, touch the bloom
on her skin. Her scent—wildflowers, bold and sweet—
intoxicated him. He could get lost in that scent, in the
softness of her hair, in the cornflower depths of her beautiful eyes. His body brushed against hers, and he felt
her tremble, sending another wave of hot lust coursing
through his body.

"So do you," she said softly. "How is your injury?"

"A distant memory." He waved a dismissive hand. "It
doesn't trouble me."

"These are my friends, Nicole and Cissy." She gestured to the two women behind her, both pretty and no
doubt already the talk of the table of wiseguys in the
corner. Of all the nights she had to come, it had to be
the same one Nico had chosen for a dinner meeting at
the restaurant with his top *capos* and soldiers.

"I should have called ahead," she continued. "But I
didn't realize we needed a reservation. I understand
you're booked tonight."

They were fully booked, but there was no way he was
letting his angel walk out the door. "I always have a table
free for my friends." With a hand on Gabrielle's lower
back he escorted her toward one of tables he reserved
exclusively for members of his crime family who had
made his restaurant their permanent home.

"Luca, darling, the girls and I have been waiting for
our drinks for *evah*." Marta, who had been seated with

her friends at a table in the center of the restaurant, intercepted them and wound her hand around his arm, digging her long red nails into his bicep. She had been his mistress when he and Gina were married, but he'd stopped seeing her after Gina died, unable to disassociate her from that terrible period of his life. They'd remained friends, but Marta never stopped trying for more.

"I'll be there in a moment after I settle these guests."

Marta's gaze narrowed on Gabrielle as if she sensed she was no ordinary customer. "Who is she?"

"A friend." His curt tone caused her eyes to widen, but she knew him well enough to let the matter drop.

"I didn't mean to cause any trouble," Gabrielle said quietly after Marta returned to her table.

"You didn't." His gaze lingered on her a moment too long and she blushed.

Fuck. He wanted to make her blush for another reason, and one that didn't involve them wearing any clothes.

Lennie, the assistant manager and *maître d'*, arrived with the menus after Luca seated Gabrielle and her friends.

"They won't need the menus," Luca said, waving the leather-bound folders away. "Bring some *antipasti*, a little *prosciutto e melone, salame* and *formaggi*. After that they'll have some *linguine di mare,* and *pasta al forno.* Then a little *agnello* and *polpettone, insalata mista* and *pepperoni al forno.* For dessert, they can have *pasticcini* and a little *babà.* I'll select the wine myself." He looked over at Gabrielle who was watching him rapt. "How does that sound?"

"Beautiful." She reddened and glanced down. "I mean . . . the food. The food sounds good, but we can't—"

"On the house, *bella,*" he said firmly when he saw her gaze drop to her purse.

"Thank you." Her voice was as sexy as her fucking gorgeous face, and he wondered how he'd get through the rest of the evening staying away from her table.

What the hell had gotten into him? He'd been around beautiful women before. Hell, he'd made a point of being surrounded by beautiful women. So why did being near Gabrielle make him feel like an awkward teenager all over again?

He heard a disturbance at the door. Nico and the *capos* had arrived. Although Luca had been expecting them, he was almost annoyed to have business intrude on what could have been an entirely pleasurable evening.

After attending to Nico's table, Luca selected some wine and returned to Gabrielle's table.

"You don't need to spend all your time with us," she said, glancing over at the now rowdy table of wiseguys in the corner. "I'm sure you've got better things to do."

Puzzled, Luca frowned. "This is what men do. They look after their women. They keep them safe and provide them with food."

Her lips quirked, amused. "Maybe in the Stone Age. Women today can look after themselves."

Luca twisted the cork out of the wine bottle. "Shame. Things were easier in those days. You see a woman you like, and if she gives you the okay smile, you grab her by the hair, drag her to your cave, and have your way with her."

"I'll be sure not to smile around you." Her lips quivered at the corners.

Luca laughed. "Too late, *bella*. Your smile lights up the room."

She blushed again, her cheeks turning a delightful pink, and he was greedy for more. He wanted to know who she was, what she did for a living, what she was afraid of, how she got shot, and which of the dishes he'd presented to her she liked best. It didn't make sense. He didn't usually take the time to get to know the women he wanted to fuck. There was no banter or light conversation, no risk of falling for a woman who might betray him. Until this moment it had been a satisfactory existence, but now he felt a longing for something more.

He lifted her hand and brought it to his lips." I wonder, would you blush so prettily if I took you to my cave tonight?"

Usually, that's all it took. Seduction came as easily to him as breathing. He couldn't remember the last time he had been denied. So he struggled to contain his shock when she shook her head. "You'll never know."

"We're clubbing at Glamour tonight," Nicole added. "Have you been there? It's right across the street."

"I haven't had the pleasure." He had no interest in nightclubs where everybody was drunk or high and the music was so loud conversation was next to impossible. He preferred to socialize in places with a more intimate feel—bars, cafes, and restaurants, the Toscani clubhouse or family gatherings. Maybe it was his Italian heritage that made him value the warmth of intimacy over cold anonymity, but if his angel was going to be at Glamour, he could get over his issues for just one night.

"Too bad." Nicole sighed. "We haven't heard much about it. I hope we're not wasting our time."

Guaranteed, they wouldn't be wasting their time because the minute they walked in the door, they'd have half the men all over them and the other half wishing they had the balls.

He reluctantly left them to join Nico and the *capos*, although no actual business would be conducted until the meal was done.

"Which one do I get?" Frankie asked as Luca took his seat. The dark-haired enforcer rarely hooked up with women, at least to Luca's knowledge. If he did have a girlfriend, he kept it very quiet although Luca couldn't imagine any woman who would want to spend time with someone as cold and hard as Frankie. Nico's enforcer put even icebergs to shame

"None."

"I'll take the blonde. She looks like a screamer."

Fucking Frankie was pushing his buttons. Far too astute, there was little that Frankie didn't see, and Luca had made no effort to hide his interest in Gabrielle. Usually, he would just brush it off, but something about Gabrielle set off his possessive instincts and before he even realized he'd moved, he was halfway across the table with Frankie's jacket collar in his fist.

"Fuck you."

Frankie's eyes turned black as pitch, and his lips peeled back in a snarl. Luca didn't need to look down to know Frankie's gun was pointed at him under the table.

"What the fuck are you doing?" Nico barked from the other end of the table. "Let him go."

Luca released Frankie, pushing him away.

"This is why we have ten fucking commandments." Nico's sharp gaze settled on Frankie. "One of which is not to look at the women of our friends."

"She's kinda hard to miss." Frankie leaned back in his chair, his leather jacket creaking as he folded his arms across his chest.

Luca's blood started pumping when he looked over at Gabrielle's table and realized she and her friends were about to leave. He gave his excuses to Nico, and intercepted Gabrielle on her way to the door. He couldn't remember the last time he'd had to chase a woman, and the thought of pursuing Gabrielle made his heart pound.

"Thank you for a lovely evening." She turned to face him in the entrance, and his hand instinctively curled around her waist as if he could stop her from leaving. "The food was amazing. It was so nice of you to comp us the dinner." Her body trembled under his touch, and he tightened his grip, drawing her gently forward, his adrenaline still pumping after his altercation with Frankie. Their eyes held, heat filling the space between them.

"Luca." She breathed his name, nibbled her bottom lip.

He wanted to kiss her, hold her, feel her soft, sexy body pressed up against him. With his free hand, he cupped her jaw, stroked his thumb over her cheek. *"Non posso fare a meno di pensarti."*

He wasn't lying. He hadn't been able to think about anything but her since the second she walked in the door.

Her face softened, and her body swayed toward him. "What does that mean? Everything you say in Italian sounds beautiful."

"You are beautiful." He leaned down and kissed both her cheeks, his lips lingering on her soft skin. "I want to kiss your beautiful lips," he murmured.

He expected her to laugh or blush, definitely pull away. Instead, she turned her head just enough that his lips brushed over hers, and the taste of her set him on fire.

Desire spiked through his groin, that whisper of a kiss as potent as if she had wrapped her hand around his cock. His arm slid around her waist and he pulled her in to his body, sealing his mouth over hers the way he'd wanted to do since the moment she walked in the door.

The world disappeared. Nico and his *capos* sitting at the table near the stage. Lennie running around with the meals. The waiters and servers. The hostess. The customers. The band. Everything faded away when she moaned his name into his mouth and melted against him, her generous breasts pressed soft and warm against his chest. If they hadn't been in the middle of the restaurant, he wouldn't have stopped with a kiss. Hell, he was of a mind not to stop anyway.

"Luca." This time his name was tinged with warning, and when she brought up a hand between them, he retreated with a low groan.

"This is crazy. I barely know you," she said quietly.

"Then stay. Get to know me."

"I can't ditch my friends." She leaned up, her lips grazing his ear. "And I'm not that easy."

His breath left him in a rush. It was a challenge and all the more erotic because he hadn't expected it. He'd thought her sweetly submissive, but she was something else entirely.

A mystery to be solved.

FOUR

Glamour screamed Vegas.

From the huge chandeliers, to the private balconies, and from the multi-colored dance floor, to the sparkle and shimmer, the hidden gem of a nightclub clearly had aspirations of grandeur, and Gabrielle had to admit they were doing it in style.

With a decent DJ in residence, the massive dance floor was heaving, making it easy to find a table in the seating area near the bar.

"My God," Cissy said. "I've never seen so many beautiful people. Why didn't I know about this place?"

"It's a bit out of the way." Gabrielle dug her bling out of her purse. She'd thought it was too much for dinner, but in this place, even with her long, sparkly drop earrings, rhinestone bracelets, and matching necklace, she felt underdressed.

"I have a feeling you'll be coming to this part of town more often." Nicole gave her a nudge. "We held back in the bathroom as long as we could to give you some time alone with your Mafia prince."

Gabrielle laughed. She was still feeling the buzz from

the cocktails and wine Luca had sent to their table. And oh God, that tease of a kiss. Her hand flew to her mouth as she remembered the softness of his lips, the sensual rumble of his voice . . .

I want to kiss your beautiful lips.

"He's not a Mafia prince. Just because he's Italian, doesn't mean he's in the Mafia."

"Did you see his friends?" Cissy waved down a passing waitress and ordered a round of tequila shots. "They looked exactly how I always imagined mobsters would look. One of them was even wearing a tracksuit and he had gold chains around his neck. And the tall, handsome one at the end of the table had bodyguards."

"Don't be ridiculous."

"You need to be careful around Italian men," Nicole continued. "They are born to seduce, raised to seduce, and they die seducing the nurses in the hospital. I'm not making it up. My brother-in-law is from Rome, and he says it's true."

"Even if he isn't in the Mafia, I think you need to be careful around him," Cissy said. "He's got a temper. After he sat down with his friends, the biker dude said something and Luca grabbed him, and hauled him halfway across the table. I seriously thought he was going to start a fight. And that woman in the green dress was staring daggers at you all night. Two strikes against him right there."

Nicole reapplied her lipstick. She'd gone with nude lips to set off her new smoky-eye look. "Where was I when the fight happened?"

"It was an almost fight, and you were flirting with the sommelier."

"I liked the sommelier." Nicole tucked her lipstick away. "A guy who knows all about wine isn't going to spend his days jerking off to 'Big Dicks in Hot Chicks' or 'Whore of the Rings,' and it would be cool to introduce him to my parents. They'd think I finally got my act together."

Cissy shook her head. "I think it's scary how you remember the names of all Clint's porn films."

"I think it's scary how fast Luca moved in on our girl," Nicole said, beaming. "I thought they were going to go at it right at the door."

"I told him I wasn't that easy." Gabrielle grinned when Nicole's mouth dropped open in shock. "I can't believe I said that. I'm not really the *femme fatale* type. But there's something about him that makes me want to push back. He strikes me as a man who likes a challenge."

"Ahhh . . . that might be because he had *Alpha Male* written all over him," Cissy said. "I'm surprised he didn't actually grab your hair and drag you to his cave after the chest-beating show of dominance he displayed at the table for his friends."

"I thought you were a lawyer, not an anthropologist," Gabrielle said, but Cissy was right. Luca oozed power and dominance. He was the kind of man who went after what he wanted, and would let nothing stand in his way.

"Did you give him your number?" Cissy pulled out her wallet when she saw the waitress approaching the table.

"No." Gabrielle shrugged to hide her disappointment. "He didn't ask, and after I told him I wasn't easy, I couldn't ask for his number either."

They polished off their tequila shooters and made their way to the dance floor. Still buzzing from her encounter with Luca, Gabrielle put aside her worries about work, the fading pain of her injury, and her lingering sorrow about David, and lost herself in the beat of the music. She couldn't remember the last time she'd gone dancing. Ten years older than her, David's party days were long gone when they got together, and she'd given up clubbing with her friends in favor of accompanying David to police functions and dinner parties, or spending evenings with him relaxing in front of the TV. At the time, it hadn't bothered her. David offered her the love and security she had longed for since her mother died, and the comfort of his presence was worth any price.

Unlike most overly packed Vegas clubs, Glamour had enough of a crowd to energize the dance floor but not so much that they didn't have room to move. For the next hour, Gabrielle and her friends danced to DJ-spun hip hop and rock while fending off overly friendly dudes looking for a hook-up, and checking out some of the crazy club wear of the slightly younger crowd.

"I think it's time to hit the bar again," Nicole shouted when the DJ dropped a bass heavy house mix.

Still lost in her buzz, Gabrielle wasn't ready to leave. She opened her mouth to protest and closed it again when her skin prickled with awareness. After a quick visual sweep of the rapidly clearing dance floor, she looked up at the private balconies overhanging the dance floor.

Luca.

A thrill of excitement shot through her body when she saw him casually sipping his drink, his lazy gaze stroking lightly over her body. He was watching her with the same acute interest he had shown from the moment she'd walked into his restaurant.

Gabrielle trembled under the intensity of his stare. Power emanated from him. Controlled power. Not because he was the only man in the club wearing a suit, but because of the way he wore it: jacket unbuttoned, shirt without a tie, the neck open to reveal his corded throat and the dark lines of a tattoo. Luca unleashed. There was something wild beneath the surface that his suit couldn't hide. He had the cocky arrogance of a man who broke the rules with impunity. A man who feared nothing. A very, very dangerous man.

Tremors of awareness rippled through her body, awakening her darkest desires, needs she had never expressed, even with David. She had no idea what was happening between them, why she was letting herself get carried away, but with her body fueled by liquid courage, the deep bass pounding a primal beat, she threw caution to the wind and danced for him, sensual and uninhibited, letting the music sweep her away.

Crazy thoughts spun through her mind. Images of clothes tearing, lips and teeth and tongues, firm hands on her breasts, her hips, her ass, sweat slicking across her skin. She imagined he'd kissed her in the restaurant, devoured her, taking everything she had to give, and demanding more. He would have slid his hand under her skirt, pressed the hard ridge of his desire against her stomach. And then he would have dragged her into an alley, ripped off her clothes, and fucked her hard and rough against the cold, brick wall, while he whispered beautiful Italian words in her ear.

An ache formed in her gut and spread to her fingers and toes. She'd never felt desire like this before. Never wanted a man the way she wanted Luca now. David had been a gentle, careful, conservative lover, who never got jealous and wasn't interested in toys or games or making love anywhere but in bed. Although she accepted him for who he was, a tiny, betraying part of her wanted more. Deep in her most secret places, she wanted to be owned and possessed. She wanted to be desired by her lover so utterly and completely that nothing would stand in his way.

Luca was that kind of man. She had seen it in the way he touched the woman outside the restaurant, the way he filled the room with the force of his presence alone, the way he watched her. He was all raw feral power, liquid sex, and she wanted him to see that just below the surface, her blood ran hot and wild, too.

Cissy shrieked and waved her hand in the air. She disappeared into the crowd and returned with a man in tow.

"This is Ron, a friend of mine from law school," she shouted over the music. "He's here with a couple of friends. They're over at the bar."

Gabrielle looked up, her shoulders dropping the tiniest bit when she saw the balcony empty. Luca was gone.

"Sure. Let's go."

They headed to the bar, and Ron introduced his friends, but Gabrielle couldn't focus on the conversation. She kept glancing up at the balcony, wondering if Luca would reappear. Had he come to check the place out or was he somewhere in the crowd looking for her? But why would he come for her? He had his woman in the green dress and a restaurant to run.

"You don't look like you're having a good time," Ron said as his friends chatted with Nicole and Cissy by the bar. His eyelids were at half-mast and he'd clearly had too much to drink.

"I thought I saw someone I knew." She forced a smile. "It's hard to see clearly with all the lights."

"Cissy said you were looking to have some fun tonight." He slid an arm around her waist. "I'm an expert at getting into briefs."

She snorted a laugh and tugged his arm away. "Not the kind of fun I'm looking for."

"*Buonasera*, Gabrielle."

Gabrielle's heart skipped an excited beat at the deep

baritone of Luca's voice. She looked over her shoulder, her smile fading when she saw him glowering behind her. This wasn't Luca as she'd seen him in the restaurant. His eyes were cold, dark, and focused not on her, but on the man beside her.

"Is there a problem here?" Luca asked.

"Nothing I can't handle." She smiled at Ron. "This is the friend I thought I saw."

Ron's gaze flicked over Luca and he backed away, clearly not willing to challenge a man who looked like he was just waiting for an excuse to wrap his hands around Ron's throat.

Luca chuckled softly watching him go. "Yes, I remember. You told me in the hospital you can look after yourself, and yet somehow you got shot."

"I'm pretty sure Ron didn't have a gun."

Luca slid his hand around her waist and pulled her into his body, an overtly possessive move that sent a delicious shiver down her spine. "And if he did?"

Pumped with adrenaline that he had come to find her, she boldly leaned up and whispered in his ear. "I have one, too."

Far from being surprised, he gave an approving rumble. "Girls with guns are high on my fantasy list."

"I'm a woman, not a girl."

His gaze dropped to her breasts and she felt her nipples harden. "Yes, you are a woman. *Sei una donna molto bella.*"

"I don't know what that means, but it sounds sexy when you say it."

"You think I'm sexy." It was a statement, not a question and she laughed when a slow, satisfied smile spread across his lips.

"Yes, I do, but I suspect you already knew that. You could seduce a woman without even opening your mouth."

His hand dropped lower, curving over her ass. "Am I seducing you?"

"Do you want to seduce me?"

"I want to fuck you," he said bluntly.

Caught off guard by his bold statement, she didn't respond right away. If he'd been any other man telling her he wanted to fuck her after meeting her only twice, she would have laughed him off. But she'd learned to trust her instincts on the job and her instincts told her Luca wouldn't hurt her. For some inexplicable reason, she was deeply attracted to him. And after two years of feeling numb, the emotions and sensations coursing through her body were an incredible rush. Why not have one night with him? One night where she could let go of the sorrow of the past and the stress of the present. One night where she could do something she'd never had the courage to do before. One night where she could live, feel, breathe again. One night of passion.

"What about the woman I saw kissing you outside?"

He lifted a dismissive hand in the air. "It was a friendly kiss. We're not together anymore."

"Then I guess your wish is going to come true." She tilted her head to the side in invitation, and he feathered kisses along the curve of her neck sending a current of need straight to her core. Who was this sexual, brazen woman and where had she been hiding all Gabrielle's life?

Luca slid his hand over her hip, brushing his thumb over her stomach. "My car is outside."

His arrogance amused her, but in the end, he was still a stranger and her willingness to take a risk only went so far. "When I go out with my friends, I leave with my friends."

He didn't miss a beat. "Balcony. Upstairs. There's a private room attached."

"Let's go." Before she could lose this newfound confidence, she clasped his hand and, after a few reassuring words for Nicole and Cissy, led him across the dance floor. Or, at least, she tried to lead him. But he swiftly moved beside her and pulled her against him amidst the throng of heaving bodies.

"Go to the restroom," he murmured in her ear. "Take off your panties."

She lifted an eyebrow, shook out her hair as she collected her thoughts. She'd never been with such a dominant man. Part of her warned that there was only so much bossiness she could take, but the other part, the part that had awakened when Luca first appeared in the club, wanted to know just how much that would be. "Why don't you do it?"

His eyes blazed and he yanked her against him so hard, she lost her breath. "Because once I get you where I can fuck you, I'm not going to hold back. You care about those panties, you'll go take them off. Otherwise, I'll tear them to shreds."

God, he said the most thrilling things. It was like he'd been plucked right out of her fantasies and made real. She slid one hand around his neck, leaned up and whispered in his ear. "Tear away."

"So fucking hot," he muttered as he grasped her hand and half-pulled, half-walked her toward a gilt-glass elevator.

The elevator whooshed them up to a long, narrow corridor with six curtained alcoves. Luca led her to the curtain farthest from the elevator, then brushed it aside to let her go through.

Decorated in purple and gold, the alcove had a small wet bar in one corner and a couch in the other. Thick, purple carpet covered the floor. A separate curtain led to the balcony. She pushed it aside and saw Nicole and Cissy dancing with Cissy's friends near the stage.

"Do you feel safe, *bella*?"

She looked from one set of curtains to the other. No doors. Nothing to prevent someone from walking right in except the gold rope that he'd put across the front curtains indicating the balcony was in use. But she sensed that wasn't really the question he was asking. He wanted to know if she felt safe with him. A virtual stranger. Even if her police training hadn't given her the skills to defend herself in dangerous situations, the answer would have been the same, simply because he thought to ask the question.

"Yes."

"Anyone can come in here. Are you okay with that?"

Her teeth scored her bottom lip. Technically, what they were doing was illegal since the alcove would be considered a public place, and even in Nevada, public sex was a criminal offence. Gabrielle had never broken the law, although she'd been prepared to pull the trigger when she entered the warehouse looking for Garcia if he had offered even the hint of resistance to arrest. She'd also never had dirty, rough sex in a public place with a man she barely knew, but she was almost drugged with awakened sensation and nothing could stop her now.

"Yes."

"Lift your dress."

Her entire body jolted to attention. No one had ever spoken to her like that before, but she wanted more.

With her gaze locked on his, she slowly eased her dress over her hips as he closed the distance between them.

With his gaze locked on hers, he tore away her panties. She gasped as the cool air rushed over her pussy, but it only fanned the flames of her desire. Fear and excitement sent a chemical surge through her brain, almost like a high. There was no going back now, and her mouth watered in anticipation. She couldn't remember the last time she'd been with a man. Her few attempts at sex after David's death had been an unmitigated disaster—from the off-putting pictures of David around the house, to her feelings of guilt at betraying him, and her lack of attraction for the men she brought home.

But she felt none of those things now. David wasn't here. She'd given herself permission to enjoy a night out. And she'd never been as fiercely aroused as she was now, her pussy slick and throbbing, her body burning with a heat that had nothing to do with the light overhead.

Luca shrugged off his jacket, letting it drop to the floor. One hand snaked around her hip to cup her ass, while the other fisted her hair, twisting it tight. He yanked her against him and tugged her head to the side, positioning her for the descent of his lips.

She wanted this, wanted him. Gabrielle curled her hands around his neck pressing herself against his hot, muscular body.

He kissed her hard, stealing her breath away, his tongue sweeping through her mouth like he wanted to claim her. There was no softness in his kiss, no touching of lips or whispers against her skin. His kiss was raw and wild with a hunger that matched her own.

Gabrielle had learned early how to be tough and self-reliant, the only benefit of having to look after herself when her brother's addiction consumed every moment of her dad's and stepmother's time. But sometimes she just wanted to let go, to let someone else take control.

Body humming with anticipation, she reached for his belt. His hand covered hers, holding her fast. "You sure this is what you want, *mio angelo*? 'Cause I like it dirty. So dirty you'll never get back to heaven."

She liked it when he called her angel. It was like he saw through her shields to the girl she had been before her mother died.

"I've never been to heaven." She eased the belt free, rubbing the backs of her fingers over his erection, hard beneath the fine wool fabric. "Maybe you can take me there."

"Temptress." His lips curved in a smile. "I am more than up for the challenge." He clenched his fingers in her hair, hissed out a breath as she yanked down his zipper. His cock, thick and hard, strained against his boxers.

"Take it out," he gritted, the veins in his neck standing out in sharp relief.

She freed his cock from its restraint and rubbed her fingers slowly up and down his length. He was hot in her hand, firm, but his skin was soft. She ran her thumb around the crown, and released him when he let out a feral growl.

"I'm going to work my fingers into your pussy, until my hand is dripping with your juices. And you're going to slide those naughty little fingers into your dress and pinch your nipples while I do." With one hand beside her head, he caged her against the wall. "Open for me." He kissed her, his lips soft and gentle as he roughly kicked her legs apart.

Every coherent thought trickled from Gabrielle's mind as she tried to reconcile the dual sensations, but when his fingers slicked between her legs, she stopped trying to think and allowed herself to feel.

God, she could feel. Everything. Her thumb circling her nipple. The thrust of his thick finger inside her, the stroke of his tongue in her mouth, the pounding of her heart, the rush of blood in her veins, life pulsing beneath her skin.

His pumped his finger, working it deep. "You're so wet. So hot. I don't need to get you ready for me, but you can take more. Tell me."

It was an effort to find the words, but she found one. "Yes."

"Good girl."

Good girl. Usually the phrase made her cringe. It was a power play, pure and simple, implying at its basest meaning that she wasn't an adult. It was used to reduce, demean, and de-legitimize, and she heard it far too often at work. And yet here, now, with this man who had done nothing but pleasure her so far, it sent an erotic thrill through her body. Accepting those words meant accepting that she was giving up control in this situation. Not only that, she was attracted to the idea of being with a man who could completely dominate her in a sexual way.

He added a second finger, stretching her, filling her as he feathered light kisses down her throat. "Pinch your nipple for me. Nice and hard."

She did as he asked, and he rumbled his approval. His fingers slipped away, and he added a third, easing them inside her with a rocking motion that brought his fingertips in contact with her sensitive tissue. Her arousal spiked, and she arched her back, grinding against his fingers seeking more than a fleeting pressure.

"Squeeze my fingers," he murmured. "Show me how you can take me. I want to feel that pussy all around me. I want you to come all over my hand."

She moaned softly, his dirty talking sparking a primitive response.

When he pressed his palm against her clit, circled it over the swollen nub as his fingers pounded into her, she climaxed in a rush of white-hot heat. Her body jerked and she slammed her head against the wall with a cry she was certain could be heard over the music.

Luca leaned forward and kissed her, swallowing the sound, but his fingers continued to move inside her, preventing her from coming down from the ride.

"No. I can't . . . not again."

"Yes, you can. I can feel it right here." His fingertips glided over her sweet spot, and arousal coiled low and heavy in her womb.

"Oh God." She leaned against the wall, panting her breaths, her nipple forgotten beneath the fierce onslaught of need.

"Give it to me. I want to feel you come again." He pulsed his fingers inside her as his palm ground against her clit, and she soaked his hand in liquid heat as she shattered, pleasure consuming her like forest flames.

"*Così bella,*" he whispered dropping kisses over her neck, her throat, and along her jaw.

She reached out, pressed her hand against his chest, felt his heart thudding as wildly as her own. Despite the release she'd just had, her body was tight, and she felt empty inside. "More," she whispered.

"Beg."

Gabrielle stiffened for the briefest of moments. She had to fight so hard for respect in her job, his demand struck at her very core. And yet, she had made the decision to leave Officer Fawkes behind when she agreed to come here. For this one night, in this room, she could be anyone she wanted to be. She could indulge her deepest fantasies. She could let go of everything and just be Gabrielle.

"Please."

He gave an approving grunt. "Please what?"

"Please fuck me." She'd never asked a man to fuck

her before, and the words were sinfully delicious on her tongue.

"Makes me hot when you beg so sweetly, *bella*." He reached into his back pocket and pulled out a condom. One tear with his teeth and the wrapper dropped to the floor. He sheathed himself quickly, and then his hands were under her ass and he was lifting her against the wall.

"Legs around me."

She wrapped her legs around his hips, and he pushed inside her with one hard thrust, working himself deep into her wet heat, filling the emptiness inside her.

He stilled, rasped in a breath. "Take it all. Feel me."

Oh God. She felt him. Not just in her pussy, but everywhere.

Gabrielle dug her nails into Luca's shoulders and lifted her hips as he surged forward. His muscles bunched beneath his cool cotton shirt, his powerful body driving forward, possessing her inside and out.

She loved his dirty talking, his rough touch, the heat of his body, the scent of his cologne, the utter abandon with which he fucked her, the way his hips slammed against her clit, driving her relentlessly toward an orgasm that hovered just out of reach. Everything.

Blood pounded in her ears, and she gave a hoarse moan and jacked up her hips, trying to get that last bit of friction that would take her over the edge.

"You need something, you ask me." He stilled, stared down at her, his eyes as wild as the need inside her.

"My clit. God, Luca. Make me come." She was so close, she would beg again if she had to.

His eyes blazed, and he reached down between them to rub his thumb gently over her clit as he thrust forward, driving deeper. "Come for me," he growled. "I want to feel your pussy squeezing my cock."

Her climax was a sweet burn that flared around his hard length. She clamped her legs around him, heels digging into his ass, head braced against the wall as she arched against him, her pussy clenching around his thick, hard cock.

Luca plunged into her over and over, hard and rough, raw and violent. His fingers dug into her ass, hips hammering back and forth, until he stiffened and came, groaning as he pumped his release inside her.

Reality hit her as she came down, panting her breaths. She'd just had a sordid, illicit encounter with a man she barely knew simply because he'd come up to her in a club and told her he wanted to fuck her. *No.* He hadn't said he wanted to. He said he would. Like he knew she would say yes. Like it was a foregone conclusion. And maybe it was.

She shuddered and turned her head, looked over at the mini-bar with its crystal glassware, the neatly lined bottles on the shelves, the mirror on the wall that showed them both sweaty and disheveled, her lips swollen from his kisses.

"You okay?" Luca feathered kisses over her shoulder, the tickle of his lips sending a delicious shiver down her spine.

"I think so."

A curious tension thickened the air between them. He pulled out and lowered her to her feet. She wobbled and he steadied her with two broad hands around her waist, a curiously tender gesture for a man who'd just fucked her so hard she knew she'd feel it for the next few days.

"I'm good. Thanks." She pulled away, yanked down her dress, trying to reconcile how she could feel electrified and embarrassed both at the same time. And what were they supposed to do now? Sit on the purple couch and have a drink? It was a little too late for a "get to know you" chat since they'd skipped that part of fore-play when they dove into the main event. What was the protocol for the end of what had been effectively a booty call?

Gabrielle swallowed past the lump in her throat. "I . . . um. I guess I'd better get back to my friends."

While he straightened his clothes, she scooped her torn panties off the floor and tucked them into the evening bag she didn't even remember dropping when she entered the alcove.

"It was nice to see you again," she said into the awkward silence. She reached for the door, suddenly desperate to get back to the familiarity of her friends, and an ordinary evening of drinking and dancing and having a good time that didn't involve clandestine rough sex in a private suite with a man who radiated power and oozed sex. A man who aroused her for the same reason he scared her. A man she couldn't control.

"This isn't the last time." He leaned against the bar, his eyes disconcertingly dark in his tanned face.

"It's the only time." She stepped into the hall and caught the elevator just as the door was closing.

FIVE

Gabrielle's phone alarm sounded at eight in the morning, startling her awake. Even after a night of drinking, she had to get up to take Max for his morning walk or he'd be in her room, tugging at the covers with his teeth.

She rolled to her side, feeling a delicious ache between her thighs as she reached to turn off the alarm. What had she been thinking last night? Or had she been thinking at all? She'd had sex with a virtual stranger in a public place. Officer Gabrielle Fawkes had broken the law. If anyone had caught them, she could have been charged with "open or gross lewdness" and "indecent exposure." Hysterical laughter bubbled up in her chest. She hadn't even thought about the greater risks of her illicit activity—being kicked off the Garcia case, or even worse, losing her job.

And yet the crazy thing was, if she could go back in time, she would make the same choice again.

She sat up, pushing aside her pink-and-white duvet. She'd never had sex like that in her life, never imagined sex could be so raw, wild, and uninhibited. His dirty talking had made her wet, but not as much as the way he took control.

Take off your panties. Lift your dress. Beg.

Just the thought of the things he said sent her arousal spiraling. She slid her hand between her legs, imagined it was Luca touching her. His fingers. His body. His words.

I want to fuck you.

Who said that and expected it to happen? Did he even know what he did to her?

She slicked her finger over her clit, and need ricocheted through her. He'd given her a year's worth of fantasies in that one encounter. And it wasn't just his dirty talking. It was everything about him: the way he looked, the way he moved, his magnificent body, his deep voice, his sheer and utter dominance . . .

For the first time in two years, she felt alive, and she wanted more. More naughty whispers in her ear. More rough hands on her body. More walking on the edge with a dangerous man. More than just a fantasy.

You need something, you ask me.

But she couldn't ask him. Even if he'd wanted her number, she'd run out the door before he had a chance to ask, and he hadn't pursued her. Returning to the restaurant was out of the question. She'd initiated that encounter, but she wasn't doing it again or he would think she was desperate and pathetic. He might have held the power last night, but she had power of her own.

With her palm against her clit, she slid two fingers inside herself, remembering every detail of last night. The intoxicating scent of his cologne, the ripple of his shoulders beneath his shirt, the heat of his body, his thick fingers deep inside her . . .

Come for me.

She came with a gasp, her pussy tightening around

her fingers, pleasure rippling out to her fingers and toes. If just the thought of him made her horny, what would it be like to be with him every night?

She rolled out of bed and surveyed the bedroom. Sunlight streamed across the fluffy white area rug from the edges of the blinds, poking lazy fingers over the wrought-iron bed frame, and reclaimed furniture, painted in pastel green and pink. David's house had been all chunky dark wood furniture, hardwood floors, and bold colors. Manly. Solid. Stable. Built to last—the way he was supposed to be. She put her hand to her neck, but her locket was sitting on the dresser where Nicole had left it after they got home.

She followed the rich scent of coffee to the living room, where Nicole and Max were curled up in front of the television on the overstuffed red couch. Gabrielle and Nicole had furnished the small fifties-style bungalow with an eclectic assortment of furniture from charity and thrift shops. Gabrielle had sold all David's furniture along with the house because the memories they elicited were too painful to bear.

"Morning." Nicole gave Gabrielle a wave as she headed over to the kitchen. "I took Max out already. Mrs. Henderson was already up and watering her garden. She mentioned yet again how happy she is to have a police officer living next door. You'd think she'd be happy to have a casino dealer next door, too. If she ever wanted to have a night on the town, I could show her some tricks."

Gabrielle poured a cup of coffee and joined Nicole on the couch. They had a good relationship with their elderly neighbor, who was always happy to watch Max, and in return they kept an eye on her place and ran errands for her if she couldn't get out.

"You don't look like you're suffering too badly from

last night." Nicole looked up over her cup and grinned. Gabrielle had told Nicole and Cissy a very condensed version of what had happened with Luca upstairs in the nightclub, and they had mercifully not pressed her for details.

Max moved over to lay his head on Gabrielle's lap. He had been found sleeping on an old mattress beside a dumpster after his family moved away and abandoned him. Loyal Max couldn't be coaxed away from the mattress because it smelled like his owners, but when a shelter worker offered him food and water, starvation finally overrode his need to be loved.

"So when are you seeing Mr. Sex on a Stick again?"

"I'm not. It was a crazy, one-time thing. I just needed to get him out of my system." She sipped her coffee, letting the bitter liquid slide over her tongue as her lie hung in the air.

Nicole stretched out, putting her feet on the worn oak coffee table. "You don't get guys like that out of your system. They ruin you for all other men. Trust me."

"Are we talking about Luca or Clint?"

"Clint." Nicole worried the already frayed edge of the Cubs nightshirt she wore to bed. "I'm seeing him tonight."

"Oh, honey. No." Gabrielle's heart squeezed in her chest. "Don't go. He's probably watching 'Pornocchio' or 'Great Sexpectations' right now. And he probably spent the night with someone else. You always hate yourself after you go over there. You can do so much better than him."

"I'm not strong like you." Nicole stood and crossed the hardwood floor to the kitchen. A small breakfast bar separated the two rooms, and she poured her coffee on the other side. "And it's not easy for me to find guys. Everyone I meet turns out to be a dud. At least with

Clint, I know what I'm getting. And he was very sorry about last time. He says he wants to make it up to me tonight."

Gabrielle didn't feel strong. After David died she'd just gone through the motions, trying to get through each day, until she'd managed to get into Narcotics, and since then she'd been living solely for revenge.

At least, until last night when Luca had awakened something in her that made the world seem bright again.

Gabrielle eased Max off her lap. "We didn't exchange numbers, so it won't happen. Plus, he'd probably be turned off if he found out what I do for a living. He was very much a man's man. He's the first guy who has ever made me feel feminine. I haven't felt that way since my mom died."

"I guess living in a house with three brothers didn't give you many opportunities to indulge your girly side." Nicole picked up her mug and a blueberry muffin from the container on the counter.

"Not the way I did with my mom." Gabrielle sighed. "My stepmother wasn't into traditional girly stuff. And David was very practical. He liked my hair in a ponytail so it didn't get in the way, and he thought heels were silly. If I bought lingerie, he'd tell me it was a waste of money because he was just going to take it off me. Luca is almost his total opposite. He loved my hair loose. He thought my dress and heels were sexy. I shouldn't have liked him calling me angel or whispering beautiful things in Italian, but I did."

Nicole laughed. "Maybe you're right. Seducing women is like breathing to Italian men. The only way you know if they're serious is if they bring you home to meet their mother."

Max whined at the door, and Gabrielle went to the kitchen to rinse out her cup. They always went for a walk at this time on the weekends, and even though he'd gone out with Nicole, he apparently didn't want to break tradition.

"I've also got Jeff to think about," she said. "He's been so good to me, but until I met Luca I thought I couldn't reciprocate his feelings because I wasn't over David. Now I'm pretty sure that it's because he's just not the right guy. I need to have a talk with him and be up front about how I feel so he stops expecting something to happen."

If that was the case, she'd made a mistake not giving Luca her number. Maybe she'd just let the right guy get away. Or had she?

This isn't the last time.

"So where did you disappear to on Friday night?" Mike hefted his baseball bat as Luca knocked on Glamour's steel door. Paolo and Little Ricky, a soldier in Luca's crew, stood back in case things got rough. They had come to the nightclub in the light of day to convince Glamour's owner, Jason Prince, that he needed the Mafia's "protection," and sometimes protection conversations didn't always go as planned.

"I came here to check the place out." Luca had seen the opportunity for easy money as soon as he walked in the door the other night. And easy money was what the Mafia was all about.

A pretty young waitress answered the door. Luca charmed his way in, and she led them through the club to the manager's office. Luca counted four bars on the main floor and two more on the second floor outside the private balcony suites where he'd had the most incredible sex with a woman who'd disappeared like a goddamn fucking Cinderella. Except she hadn't even left behind a damn shoe so he could find her.

After the waitress was out of sight, he walked into Jason's office. No knock. No warning. In the protection business, establishing dominance and instilling terror in the customer were key.

"Who are you?" Jason jumped up from his desk, surprisingly nimble for a middle-aged man whose considerable paunch was straining the buttons of his shiny red shirt. "Who let you in?"

"How about a little respect? You're speaking to Mr. Rizzoli." Mike tapped the bat against his palm as Little Ricky closed the door behind them, his gold chains jangling against the zipper of his tracksuit. Soft and doughy, Little Ricky always dressed like he was on his way to the gym, although it was the last place he would ever be.

"Who the fuck is Mr. Rizzoli?"

"Your new guardian angel." Luca settled on the soft leather chair in front of Jason's desk.

Jason groaned. "I'm not stupid. I know what kind of help you have to offer. But I'm already paying the Albanians for protection. Arbin and Jak. You know them?"

"I do know them." Luca smirked. "But I'm afraid they won't be able to help you anymore. They've gone on a permanent swimming vacation." Damn Albanians had moved deeper into his territory than he had realized. He'd never been so glad of Frankie's penchant for concrete shoes. "Feel free to give them a call. I have all the time in the world. Little Ricky will look over your shoulder to make sure you're calling the right guys."

Relaxed now that he knew he had unintentionally dealt with the competition, Luca put up his feet. He had on a new pair of monk strap Salvatore Ferragamo's that he'd shined up for the occasion although he wasn't sure if he liked the strap or not.

"Mike. What do you think of this buckle?" He tilted the shoe so Mike could take a look while Jason made a call to a cell phone at the bottom of Lake Mead.

"I like it, boss."

He glanced over at Jason, who was still on the phone, and removed one shoe. "What do you think the heel is made of, Mike? Give it a tap."

Mike knew the drill. He took the shoe and used it to knock a fancy glass bowl off its pedestal, a warning to Jason to hurry it up.

Jason froze when the bowl shattered on the floor. "Oh, my God!" he shrieked. "That was a Chihuly. I paid fifteen thousand for it."

"You got ripped off." Luca took his shoe from Mike and slipped it on his foot. "My mother has nicer bowls, and she got them at the thrift shop for fifty cents each."

He lifted a finger and Little Ricky reached over Jason's shoulder and snatched the phone from Jason's hand.

"Hey! Give me my phone!"

Luca shook his head. "This is a dangerous area you're living in. You were right to look for protection, but you got it from the wrong guys. I'm here to make sure that you get the protection you need at a good price."

Jason's face tightened. "I can't afford your kind of protection. The nightclub isn't doing well. It was a struggle to pay the Albanians. If I have trouble I can't handle, I'll call the police. They'll come out for free."

"He's going to call the police." Luca signaled with two fingers, and Little Ricky smashed Jason's phone under his shoe. "That's going to be hard without a phone."

Luca slowly lowered his feet, and leaned forward, a

prearranged signal for everyone to start trashing the room.

Within seconds, he heard a crash behind him. And then another. Little Ricky smashed a few statues before he positioned himself behind Jason, ready for the next bit of fun. Even Paolo, who was often reluctant to get involved in the more destructive aspects of the business, grabbed a framed poster off the wall and smashed it on the floor.

"No. No. Stop. Please." Jason jumped out of his seat and his voice rose to a whine. "Those are irreplaceable."

"So are fingers," Luca said.

Little Ricky grabbed Jason from behind and forced him back into his chair. Luca leaned across the desk and grabbed Jason's hand, splaying his fingers out on the smooth mahogany surface. "We're offering you a good deal: whatever you were paying the Albanians plus ten percent. The way this works is you say yes and keep your fingers. Anything else that comes out of your mouth raises the price by twenty percent and one finger. We'll start with the baby one so you get a feel for how it goes."

Little Ricky pulled out his knife, and a grin spread across his face. He was sick when it came to persuasion.

Sweat beaded on Jason's forehead and his body trembled. "Yes. Yes. Okay. I'll do it."

"I think we're going to work well together." Luca released Jason's hand. "Little Ricky will be coming by every week to collect the payment. We'll take the first one now. You got cash?"

Jason paled. "It's in the safe. I can't open it, though. It's time-locked."

"Not a problem. Paolo specializes in safes." Luca patted his young apprentice. "What else do you have in there?"

"Security tapes, contracts, jewelry and phones we find on the dance floor . . ."

Something niggled at the back of Luca's mind. A mystery to be solved. "Do you have footage of everyone who comes into the club on those tapes? How about ID records?"

"The tapes are hard-copy backups of digital files," Jason said. "We've got ID records, too. The computer system checks IDs against the ANGEL database held by all the nightclubs in the city so we can identify trouble-makers who've been kicked out of other clubs."

"Looks like your angel didn't guard you too well 'cause she let me in last night." Luca grinned. He'd spent a few months in jail as a teenager after being caught driving a stolen car through the window of a jewelry store with a weapon in his jacket for which he didn't have a concealed firearm permit. With a few other Mafia associates to keep him company, the time had passed quickly, and he'd come out with the criminal record that was a rite of passage for a made man.

Angel. Christ, he wasn't superstitious, hadn't put much stock in his mother's belief in signs, but how could he ignore it? He crossed himself, the way his mother always did when she felt she'd been blessed, and made a mental note not to skip church this Sunday.

"I want to see the security records." He leaned forward, trying not to let his excitement show. "I'm looking for a girl . . ."

Mike snorted a laugh. "You're always looking for a girl, boss."

Luca smiled. "This girl is special."

SIX

Paolo parked his car in the parking lot of the Journey's End Care Home in North Las Vegas. For six years, he had been running errands and doing grunt work for the Toscani family, but mostly, he worked for Mr. Rizzoli and his crew. He delivered packages, picked locks, carried messages, kept a look out, trashed offices, and picked up Italian pastries from Roberto's Deli for the hungry wiseguys who could never have a meeting without food. But he'd never been given a real job—a job only Mafia associates or soldiers did.

Until today. Mr. Rizzoli, had asked him to do surveillance work tonight, and he was so excited he had to tell his mother.

He walked into the dull gray building, noting the stains on the worn carpet, the wallpaper peeling in the corners, and the dirty glass window in front of the reception desk. He waved to the receptionist, and she buzzed him inside. Paolo knew everyone at the rest home and they knew him because he'd been coming here once or twice a week for the last ten years.

When he reached the common room, he spotted his

mother right away. She sat in her wheelchair by the window staring out over the concrete parking lot. His stomach twisted as it always did when he saw her. One day he would have the money to move her to a nice care home with the trees and flowers she missed from her childhood home in Oregon.

"Hi, Ma." He stood in front of her because she didn't respond when people talked, but he knew she saw him because her eyes widened ever so slightly.

"How are you?" He frowned when he saw goose bumps on her arms, her body trembling under her pale pink nightgown. She was hunched over like an old person even though she had only just turned thirty-six, and her long blonde hair was so dull it looked gray. "Where's the dressing gown I bought you? Did you leave it in your room?" He patted her arm. "I'll go get it. Be right back." He made his way through the sea of wheelchairs, freezing when saw her dressing gown on a woman playing cards.

"That lady's got my mother's dressing gown," he said to the nurse supervising the common room.

"It happens a lot." She gave Paolo a sympathetic smile. "She doesn't know it's not hers. There's nothing we can do. Taking it off her would be against the rules."

Paolo could feel his temper rise, so he quickly walked away. His father, a Falzone crime family enforcer, also had a temper, and Paolo didn't want to wind up like him. He'd been thrown in jail when Paolo was seven years old for beating on Paolo's mom so badly she'd suffered irreparable brain damage. It was the last of many times and he'd finally gone to jail. Paolo's mother had been put in a care home, and Paolo had gone to live with his Aunt Marie.

For the first few years, he'd been passed around among relatives when Aunt Marie was away working as a flight attendant. But when he turned eleven, she decided he could look after himself, and he wound up on the streets after school and on weekends, running errands for the mob until someone brought his lock-picking skills to Mr. Rizzoli's attention.

"I can't find it, Ma." He unzipped the new hoodie he'd bought this afternoon after Mr. Rizzoli gave him the surveillance job, not wanting to embarrass his boss by wearing his worn T-shirt and jeans on official Mafia business. "You can wear this until I get you a new one." He placed the hoodie around his mother's frail shoulders, and shivered in his T-shirt. The air conditioning was going full blast even though it was fall. Were they trying to freeze the residents to death?

"Things are finally looking up." He sat on a chair across from his mother. "Mr. Rizzoli gave me an important job today. He even let me use a car." He hesitated, waiting for her to say something, but she never did, so he kept talking. "He's a good guy. He looks after his crew, and he protects people in his territory. And he treats his women real good. He says you gotta respect the ladies. You don't shout at them, and you never hit them. Not even with a flower."

It was Mr. Rizzoli's attitude toward women that had lured Paolo away from his father's Falzone crime family and over to the Toscanis. His loyalty had been secured the week after he told Mr. Rizzoli about his parents when his father was mysteriously beaten to death in jail. Mr. Rizzoli never said anything about it, and Paolo didn't ask, but there was nothing Paolo wouldn't do for Mr. Rizzoli after that.

He leaned over to give his mother a hug. Then he slid to his knees and buried his face in her lap, ending his visit as he always did—in tears. "I miss you, Ma, but things are going to be better now. I promise."

After his visit, he drove to the address Mr. Rizzoli had given him and parked down the street. He didn't know much except that Mr. Rizzoli was interested in a woman named Gabrielle, and he wanted Paolo to check out her place. The small bungalow stood on a corner lot surrounded by a thick hedge. From the dark windows and the absence of a vehicle parked in the driveway, he assumed no one was home.

Ten minutes of staring at the bungalow later, a sleek silver Audi TT turned into the driveway. Paolo pulled out his phone and videoed the woman and man exiting the vehicle. He recognized Gabrielle from the security tape footage they had watched at Glamour. He wasn't sure what Mr. Rizzoli had meant when he told Paolo to check out the house, but he figured Mr. Rizzoli would want to know about the man Gabrielle was with. He slipped out of his car and dashed across the street, taking up a position on the sidewalk behind the hedge, trying to look casual like he was playing Pokémon Go.

He positioned his phone at a gap in the hedge. Gabrielle was very pretty, but not his type. Paolo had his eye on Michele Benni, the daughter of one of Mr. Rizzoli's soldiers. She had long, thick dark hair, deep olive skin, big tits, and a curvy body. Of course, her father wouldn't let her date a civilian, but once Paolo became an associate in Mr. Rizzoli's crew, he was going to ask her out on a date.

He heard footsteps, keys jangling, the rattle of a screen door, and a dog barking in the back yard. Quietly, he moved closer so he could hear.

"Thanks for dinner, Jeff," Gabrielle said. "It was good to get out. It wasn't a total shock to find out they were transferring me out, but it was still incredibly disappointing, and to just get the decision in a memo . . ."

"That's what I'm here for, babe."

Paolo pushed his phone farther through the hedge and stared at the screen. Jeff was a big, muscular guy. Dark hair. Tanned skin. Thick neck. He had one meaty hand on the open screen door and he stood facing Gabrielle in the doorway, like he wanted to go in. Paolo knew the feeling. The first time he'd walked Michele home after school, he'd had an erection that wouldn't quit. He would have given anything to go inside with her, but her father had come to the door, putting a quick end to the problem in Paolo's pants.

"I'll come in and make sure the house is secure, and we can talk some more." Jeff took a step forward, and Gabrielle put out her hand.

"Thanks, but Max has been alone all day, and you know how he is around men. I just want to take him for a walk and then sit with him in front of the TV and chill."

"I thought you told me Nicole was at Clint's place tonight. You shouldn't be alone." Jeff leaned in and touched his mouth to hers.

Paolo hissed in a breath. He hoped Mr. Rizzoli's interest in Gabrielle wasn't the kind of interest that could get Jeff killed for stealing a kiss. Made men were very possessive about their women. One of the ten Mafia commandments was not to look at the wives of friends, which was a hard one to follow if a wiseguy had a beautiful woman—much harder than the prohibition against associating with cops.

"I won't be alone. I have Max."

As if he heard his name, the dog barked louder, the sound close to where Paolo stood.

"That's not what I mean, Gaby." Jeff's voice took on a cajoling edge that grated on Paolo's nerves. "You bottle everything up. You need comfort. You need someone to hold you. I'm here for you. I've been here for you for two damn years. I've been honest about my feelings, and I never pushed you." Jeff took another step forward, but Gabrielle didn't move from the door.

"It's been long enough," he continued. "You have to move on. I hate to say it, but I'm glad they transferred you. It's time to look forward not back. And I want to be part of that future."

"I'm not giving up," she said. "I can't. If I don't have that file, I have nothing to live for."

"You have me." He tried to kiss her again, and she backed away.

More barking from the dog. Paolo wished he could bark, too, and scare Jeff away. Should he do something? Gabrielle clearly wasn't interested, and Jeff wasn't backing down.

Paolo always tried hard to do the right thing, but he was either the unluckiest guy on the planet or he just made piss poor decisions. He was the guy who pulled a prank in the school restroom just when the principal walked by, or the guy who was caught doing dope around the only crime family that had a ban on drugs. Mr. Rizzoli was a one-warning guy. He'd beat Paolo black and blue and told him not to show his face until he was clean. Mortified that he'd let Mr. Rizzoli down, he'd gone into the first detox program that would take him and he'd stayed clean since.

"Jeff—" Gabrielle's voice had a warning edge that made the hair on Paolo's neck prickle. He zoomed the camera, trying to adjust for the fading light. Gabrielle's arms were folded over her chest, and Jeff was looming over her in what Paolo thought might be a threatening way for a woman her size.

"I've never led you on," she said, her voice wavering. "You've been a good friend to me. I don't think I would have pulled myself out of the darkness without you. But that's all I feel for you. Friendship. I'm sorry, Jeff. I've been thinking a lot about it, and I don't want you to get the wrong idea about where this is going to—"

Jeff cut her off with an angry bark. "You've been with other men, Gabrielle. Why not me? No one cares about you the way I do." His voice rose so loud Paolo's heart thudded in his chest. This was no way to speak to a woman. Mr. Rizzoli would be appalled.

The dog clearly felt the same way. His barking was loud and frantic now. Paolo heard the scratching of paws on the gate near where he stood.

"No one will take care of you like I will." Jeff's voice grew louder still. "No one understands what you've been through the way I do. Forget about the damn file. I want to be there for you, Gaby. Give me what you gave to strangers. Give me a chance to show you a future without revenge." He put one hand on the door and leaned in.

"God, Jeff. Don't do this." Gabrielle's voice cracked, broke. "Not now. Not today. You're like a brother to me. I care about you a great deal, but not that way."

"Fuck." Jeff smashed the screen door against the house so hard it broke off its hinges, and the glass shattered.

The dog went crazy. Paolo could see his head and paws as he tried to jump over the gate, and then his nose as he tried to squeeze underneath. And the barking . . . anyone with a dog would know something was wrong. Paolo was surprised no one had come out to see what was going on.

His heart thudded in his chest. Was Jeff going to hit her? If Mr. Rizzoli was interested in her, she was under Mr. Rizzoli's protection, and that meant Paolo had to act on his behalf. But what could he do? Although he was filling out fast, physically, he was no match for Jeff who had to outweigh him by at least one hundred pounds.

"I want you to leave. Right now." Gabrielle's voice, now cold and firm, cut through the air. She sounded more annoyed than scared, but Paolo knew just how much damage an angry man could do.

"I'm coming in, Gaby, and we're going to talk this through."

"I said no." She blocked the doorway, hands up in a warding gesture, face tight, legs apart. She looked fierce and determined, and Paolo couldn't help but admire her. Jeff was a very big man and he clearly had no intention of walking away. Gabrielle had no chance against him, but she didn't back down.

He had to act now. Frantic, he shoved his phone in his back pocket and grabbed the biggest rock he could find. Taking aim, he threw it as hard as he could, hitting the windshield of the Audi with a loud crash.

"Jesus Christ. What the fuck was that?" Jeff spun around and Paolo took off at a run.

"I see you little motherfucker," Jeff shouted. "You better run because when I catch you, I'm going to beat you black and blue. I'll give you so much pain, you won't even be able to beg for mercy."

Paolo looked back over his shoulder and stumbled on the curb, falling to his knees. He jumped up and was shocked to see Jeff behind him and gaining fast. But if he'd learned one thing as the kid of an abusive dad, it was how to run. He was a full block away when he realized his phone had fallen out of his pocket when he tripped. Going back wasn't an option. He could only hope Jeff didn't find it. And if he did, Paolo prayed Jeff wouldn't find him.

SEVEN

Gabrielle startled awake. She sat up, shaking off sleep, trying to figure out what had woken her. Then she heard Max barking.

She threw a sweater over her pajama top and shorts and raced down the hallway. A hard knock rattled the door, and she hesitated. Max would never bark at Nicole. So who was outside? Jeff? God, she didn't want to have to deal with him again tonight.

Heart thudding, she peered through the peephole, her breath catching when she recognized the man on the other side of the door.

"Luca?"

"Gabrielle. Open the door."

Holy crap. Her fantasy man had found her.

With one hand tight on Max's collar, she pulled open the door.

Without so much as a hello, Luca brushed past her and stalked into her house. He was a wearing a fitted dark gray polo shirt, perfectly pressed dark pants, and shiny leather shoes. He was too rough to be beautiful, but his raw masculinity was so utterly compelling, she couldn't look away.

"What are you doing here?"

"I came to check on you."

Max barked and strained to get at Luca.

"It's okay." Gabrielle struggled to hold Max back, patting his head with her free hand. "He's a friend."

"Let him go." Luca bent down with his hand extended. Gabrielle released Max and he sniffed Luca's fingers. A moment later, her betraying guard dog stopped barking and wagged his tail.

She gave an irritated huff. "You must have a dog."

"I had two growing up," Luca said. "Now I live in a penthouse, and I didn't think it would be fair. They need somewhere to run." He stood, his brow creasing in a frown. "Are you alone?"

"Yes. Nicole's at her boyfriend's place." She lifted an eyebrow. "How did you find me?"

His eyes darted around the house as if he expected to see someone jump out of the shadows. "I have a friend at Glamour who gave me your information from the database."

"But that's illegal."

Luca shrugged. "I wanted to find you."

Such simple words, and yet loaded with meaning. No matter that he had broken the law. He wanted to find her, and he made it happen. End of story. What she wouldn't give to have such a cavalier attitude.

"Why? Is this another booty call?"

"I thought you were in danger." He stalked past her and into the kitchen. Without asking permission, he checked in the broom closet and peered out the back door.

"What are you talking about? What danger?" She followed him back to the living room and watched as he rattled the broken screen door.

"How did this happen?"

The skin on Gabrielle's neck prickled, and she marched over to him and poked him in the chest. "Were you outside watching when Jeff was here?"

"I only arrived a few minutes ago." Something in his expression changed, his hazel eyes sharpening, darkening, turning feral. "Who is Jeff? Is he the one who broke your door?"

"I work with him, and yes, he broke the door. He was . . . agitated."

Luca's eyes narrowed. "I was agitated when you walked away in Glamour, but I didn't break your fucking house."

"He broke a door, not the house," she countered.

"It was disrespectful."

She supposed it was, but she hadn't really given it much thought. Jeff was upset, and his behavior, while unacceptable, was uncharacteristic of the man she knew.

"So is showing up at my home at eleven o'clock at night," she said, frowning at Max as he pushed his ball toward Luca's feet. "Normal people call during daylight hours and arrange to go for coffee or have a drink."

"You didn't give me a choice. You ran away and didn't give me your number."

Her cheeks heated and she dropped her gaze. "I was a little . . . overwhelmed."

"As was I," he said softly. He scooped up Max's ball and rolled it across the living-room floor. Max gave a delighted yip and raced across the room. It was hard to stay annoyed with a man who was so good with Max, especially because it became clear after the vet checked Max out, that her precious beagle had had little joy in his short life.

"He likes you," she said lamely. "He's usually wary of men. When the shelter found him, he wouldn't eat if there was a man in the room. I rarely bring men home because it upsets him."

Luca gave a satisfied grunt. "I'm glad to hear I don't have any competition except for Jeff, the door breaker."

"You didn't seem to be too worried about competition on Friday night," she teased.

"Gabrielle." He breathed her name, and her knees went weak. "The way you looked on Friday night, you were lucky we even made it upstairs."

A soft *oh* escaped her lips, but before she could respond he was halfway down the hallway toward her bedroom.

Why was she allowing this? She hadn't even let Jeff in the door, and she didn't have a problem asserting herself in any situation. But some part of her wanted him here. She was glad to see him, touched by his concern, and no small bit amused by his insistence on checking out her place for imaginary danger. For goodness sake, she had a gun and she knew how to use it.

"Wait."

Of course, he didn't wait. He pushed open the door and walked right in.

Gabrielle's cheeks heated as she followed behind him. Other than Jeff, who had helped her assemble the bed, she'd never brought a man into her bedroom, and it was very unlike the public face she showed the world.

"It's kind of girly," she said, her cheeks heating as he looked around at the pastels and lace.

"It's beautiful," Luca said. "It's you."

A lump welled up in her throat, and she bent down to give Max a pat, hiding her face. It *was* her. The *her* no one but Nicole and Cissy and her mother knew.

Luca studied the framed pictures on her dresser. "Are these your parents?" He picked up the only picture of Gabrielle and her parents together. Her mother had been in a wheelchair by then, but strong enough to want to go for a drive in the mountains.

"Yeah. My mom died when I was nine. Breast cancer. It spread before they caught it. She loved pink and purple and sparkly pretty things. We lived in Colorado. At the time, I didn't appreciate our town, but it was beautiful with forests and lakes all around it. My dad remarried two years later to a woman who had two sons, and we moved here with my brother."

She pointed to the next picture in the row. "That's my husband, David. And the picture beside him is my brother, Patrick. He died from a drug overdose."

He lifted the picture of David and her sitting together at a pool party a friend had thrown one summer. "You've suffered through a lot of loss."

"It's life, I guess. Just sucks when all the bad things seem to happen to you."

He studied her for a long moment, and lifted the last picture in the row, taken only a few weeks before David died. "Who is this?"

"That's Jeff with David and me. He was David's best friend."

"Jeff who broke your door?" His jaw tightened and he put the picture down with a firm thump.

Gabrielle sat on the edge of her bed and toyed with the lace edging on her duvet. "Things are complicated between Jeff and me."

"Are you fucking him?"

"You're being very crude," she shot back. "And not that it's any of your business, but no. I'm not fucking him. He's my friend. He helped me through a difficult time after David died—"

"Because he wanted to fuck you."

She gave an irritated groan. "Luca. Seriously. Do you have to be so direct? It wasn't like that." At least she hadn't thought so. And the first time he kissed her, she felt curiously betrayed. What she'd thought were selfless acts of friendship turned out to be a means to an end.

"What happened tonight?" He leaned against the dresser, folded his arms.

She shrugged. "I told him I wasn't interested in a relationship with anyone. I can't go through losing someone I love again. Three times was enough. And you don't know my whole story, but I have nothing left to give someone. I'm broken. He could do so much better than me."

"So he broke your door," he said impatiently, as if she wasn't understanding the importance of what Jeff had done. "A man who does not respect you is not worthy of you." Luca cupped her jaw in his hand and tipped her head back, whispering in Italian.

Her tension left her in a rush, her body heating all over. "What does that mean?"

He leaned down and kissed her, his lips warm and soft. "Roughly translated, it means you are my angel. Heaven is in your eyes. I am dazzled by you."

"Oh." Her breath left her in a rush and she kissed him back.

Born to seduce. Raised to seduce. Live to seduce. Nicole's words danced in her head, but she didn't care if he gave the same line to every woman he met. His words made her feel beautiful, happy, and so good inside she wanted to burst. Even if he walked away now, she would remember the sound of his voice and how his words made her feel.

Fuck.

She was so damn sexy, Luca could barely think. He deepened the kiss and Gabrielle melted against him, crushing her soft breasts against his chest. Her hips ground against his cock, painfully erect beneath his fly, and he groaned. Taking her kiss as a sign his intentions were welcome, he lifted her easily and carried her to the bed.

"Wait."

Fuck. No. He didn't want to wait. Couldn't wait. Something about this woman drew him in a way he couldn't understand. He didn't do relationships or even repeat hook-ups. Burned once. Scarred forever. He gravitated to women who understood the meaning of *one-night stand*. Mindless sex. And there's the door.

Gritting his teeth against a tidal wave of need, he stopped near the bed. "What's wrong?"

"Max. He's barking. Something's wrong outside."

He lowered her to the ground, listening to Max's frantic yelps. Even though he'd never had a beagle, he knew a warning when he heard one.

"Stay here." Luca put out his hand, gesturing her back.

"You stay here. I have a gun." She pulled a weapon from her nightstand and shoved in a magazine. Alarmed, Luca yanked his own weapon from his holster.

"I'm also armed, *bella*. Stay."

He frowned when she kept moving. He was used to obedience. Not used to strong, rebellious women pushing him aside to get out the door.

But when the first shot ricocheted down the hallway, he didn't think. Throwing himself on Gabrielle, he brought her down to the floor, just as the house shuddered from the rhythmic thud of an automatic weapon.

"What the fuck was that?"

"AK-47 from the sound of it." She heaved in a breath. "Max is out there. I have to get him. He'll be scared."

"He'll be hiding. He's safer where he is. And you're

safer where you are." Luca shifted his weight to one arm, trying to keep her body covered while he aimed his weapon down the hallway.

"Let me up. He might be hurt." Gabrielle struggled against him, but he dropped his weight, pinning her to the floor.

"If it's an AK-47, then he's almost out of bullets. Standard magazine capacity is thirty rounds." Adrenaline pounded through Luca's veins so hard, he could barely hear. Rarely was he in a situation where he had so little control.

She twisted beneath him, and shoved her knee between his legs. Stars exploded in his head. No need for condoms ever again. That part of his anatomy was no longer in working order.

"Max!" She wriggled away while he was still wondering if this was the end of the Rizzoli family name.

"Gabrielle." Groaning, one hand on his groin, the other on the gun, he followed her down the hallway. She was clearly experienced with this type of situation. She kept low, her back to the wall, gun ready. He had a vague memory of a discussion with her about guns at the hospital, and an overwhelming sense of disgust that the men she'd been with hadn't protected her.

But she hadn't told him why she was carrying a gun. Or how she'd been shot. Or what she did for a living that meant she'd been in a position to be shot in the first place. He regretted skipping the important questions the last time they met and diving right into dessert. Regardless, he was a man. This was his situation to deal with. His woman did not risk her life when he was here to defend her.

"Gabrielle. Stop."

But, of course, she didn't stop. She worked her way across the living room in a crouch, trying to coax Max away from the corner where he was hiding. With no choice but to cover her, he raced out, putting himself between the shattered windows and the courageous woman on the floor.

Sweat beaded on Luca's brow. He looked out the window and saw two shadowed figures on the street. Was it Jeff and a friend? What kind of crazy fucks would shoot up a house like this? It made no sense, but if they weren't leaving, then they were reloading, and that meant Gabrielle didn't have much time.

"Max." He stared the dog down, pointed at Gabrielle and used his dominant voice, the tone that kept his soldiers and associates in line and let the world know he was not a man to be trifled with. "Go to Gabrielle. Now."

Max shot across the room and into Gabrielle's arms. Luca felt a small amount of satisfaction that, although he could not get his woman to obey, he could at least command her dog.

"Back to the bedroom, *bella*." He stayed in position, keeping watch as she scooted across the floor tugging Max by the collar with one hand and holding her weapon in the other. "Who would shoot at you? Is it Jeff?"

"Jeff?" She snorted a laugh. "No. He's a police officer, and a friend. He was upset, but he's not going to come to my house with an AK-47 and try to kill me. I'm pretty sure it has to do with the case I just got pulled off. The one that landed me in the hospital where I met you. We were after a very bad guy."

Police officer. Friend. Case. Bad guy. Luca read between the lines and didn't like the story. He also knew a lot of "bad guys." Very bad guys. He understood how they thought and how they operated. He couldn't think of any "bad guy" who would come to a residential area at night and try to do a hit with an AK-47 from outside a house. The risk of getting caught was too high. And it was stupid. There was little chance of hitting her while she was inside. And if it was a message, why risk killing her?

Another round of gunfire shattered the silence. Gabrielle threw herself down, covering Max with her body. Seconds later, Luca was behind them, urging her back to the bedroom while he covered them from behind.

Glass shattered, wood splintered, and a rogue bullet sailed through the hallway and thudded into her door.

"Get in the bedroom," Luca shouted over the noise.

"I'm not playing victim while someone shoots up my house." She released Max and gave him a push toward the bedroom. "You call 911, and I'll go out the back door and circle the block so I can come up on them from behind."

"No. You call 911, and I'll go out the back door."

She gave an irritated groan. "I have a gun, Luca. This is what I do for a living."

"What do you do for a living?"

"I'm a police officer."

He froze, his body going rigid on the floor, and in that moment, she wished she hadn't told him. He'd seen Gabrielle the woman. Now he'd only see the Gabrielle everyone else knew: the public face that she used to fit in and mask the pain inside.

"You're a cop?"

"Detective. How did you think I wound up getting shot?"

"I thought you were the victim of a robbery." He thudded his fist against the floor. "Jesus Christ. Why didn't you tell me?"

She bristled at his anger. "You didn't ask. You were

too busy fucking me. Now, call 911. My phone is in the living room. I can't get to it."

"I'm not calling 911," he said emphatically. "I'll call some friends of mine."

She stared at him aghast. "What kind of friends are going to scare away guys with automatic weapons? They didn't shoot six hundred rounds of ammo into my house because they want to steal my spare change. And your friends aren't going to get here faster than the police."

"Stay calm." He put his phone to his ear. "I'm handling this."

What the fuck was wrong with him? He was going to kill them with his macho bullshit. "Stay calm? Are you serious?" Her voice rose in pitch. "Do you see me screaming and running around? No. You're the one who needs to stay calm."

"Trust me, *bella*."

"Trust you?" Her voice rose in pitch. "You illegally procured my ID from a database and showed up at my house in the middle of the night. And now you're phoning a friend instead of dialing 911. This isn't *Who Wants to Be a Millionaire*. If the guys outside don't put a bullet through you, I will."

Another round of bullets thudded through the house. She lay on the floor holding onto Max until the round was done.

"Luca." She lifted her head, stared down the hallway. Luca lay still on the floor surrounded by shattered glass.

Silence.

She had a flashback to the night she found David and her blood ran cold. "Luca? Are you okay? Oh God. Say something."

"You said you wanted to put a bullet through me earlier," he said dryly, looking up. "I thought I'd just lie still and make your wish come true."

"Fuck you." She released a ragged breath. "That wasn't funny."

Sirens wailed in the night, and she sank back against the bed. "Someone finally called 911."

"Too bad." He holstered his gun. "I would have enjoyed dealing with the bastards myself."

No doubt. He was the most self-assured, confident man she'd ever met, and she worked in an environment where confidence and machismo were in abundance.

The police arrived a few minutes later. After they confirmed the area was clear, two officers escorted Luca, Max, and Gabrielle out of the house.

"Gaby!" Jeff jogged toward her and she steeled herself to hide her shock. What the hell was he doing here?

"I was on duty and I heard your address on the police scanner. Lucky I was nearby. Are you okay?" He wrapped his arms around her and hugged her tight. "I came as soon as I could."

Something that sounded suspiciously like a growl came from deep in Luca's chest. Alarmed, Gabrielle pulled away, putting some distance between her and Jeff. "I'm fine."

"I should have been here." Jeff reached for her again. "I could feel something was wrong. I shouldn't have let you push me away."

She took a step back and into the solid heat of Luca's body. Before she could move, he pulled her to his side and dropped his heavy arm over her shoulders.

It was a purely possessive move, primal in nature. Warning bells jangled in her head, but they were drowned out by the inexplicable thrill of being so overtly claimed despite the fact she was a police officer and clearly able to look after herself. She never had any doubt that David loved her, but he had never chased other men away.

Jeff's face tightened. "Who is he?"

"Luca." And then because Jeff looked so taken aback, she said the first thing that came into her head. "He was in the bedroom with me when the shooting started."

Wrong thing to say.

Jeff's face darkened. Tension thickened the air between them. Max pressed himself against her legs, and growled.

"So that's why you didn't want me to come in?" Jeff spat out. "You went for dinner with me, but you spent the night with him?"

"It's not like that."

"Well, what is it?" he shouted. "I hope to hell it's a one-night stand because you said you didn't want a relationship with anyone. You said you'd never get over David. Was that a lie? Did you just mean me? After everything I did for you? You owe me, Gaby."

Luca's body went rigid beside her, and when she looked up, she saw his scowl darken to something dangerous.

"Is this Jeff who broke your fucking door?"

"Yes, but—"

Luca's fist shot out before she even realized he'd moved. Jeff's head snapped to the side with the force of the blow, but he was quick to retaliate with a hard uppercut.

Gabrielle threw herself on Luca's back, wrapped her arms around his chest and shouted in his ear. "Stop, Luca. He's a police officer. I don't want you to wind up in jail."

He shuddered, and she could see his pulse pounding in his neck. "He broke your door, threatened you, disrespected you, claimed you . . ."

Two of the attending officers helped her drag Luca and Jeff apart. Gabrielle's brain went into overdrive as she tried to think of a way to ensure Luca didn't leave her house in the back of a police car.

"What were you thinking?" She dabbed at the blood at the corner of Luca's mouth with a tissue.

"He disrespected you."

"Violence isn't the solution." She said it because she had to, but a small betraying part of her whispered that Jeff had been out of line, and now justice had been done. And yet another small part thrilled that Luca had stepped up to defend her knowing who she was and what she did for a living.

"He wants what's mine."

He was still pumped from the fight, she realized. Vein pulsing in his neck, thick arms folded, his gaze still tracking Jeff who was with one of the recently arrived medics, holding an ice pack to his jaw.

Deliciously, brutally, mouthwateringly masculine.

"I'm not yours," she said, keeping her voice low so only he could hear. "We had sex. Once. That's all. I'm not interested in anything else. I didn't think you were either."

His eyes blazed with feral heat, and his hand shot out, twisted in her hair. He tugged her head back and claimed her mouth in a fierce, hard, dirty kiss with a message behind it no one on the lawn could ignore.

"You thought wrong."

What the fuck was wrong with him?

Luca leaned against the police van, arms crossed, glaring at Jeff as a police officer took Gabrielle's statement. He'd started a fight with a fucking cop. In front of other fucking cops. Over a fucking cop.

Every made man pledged to uphold the ten commandments that were guidelines for good, respectful and honorable conduct for a mafioso. Many of the guidelines were not followed and sanctions were light. Wiseguys regularly went to pubs and clubs, lied, disrespected their wives, and showed up late for appointments. Some even had affairs with the wives of other men of honor, although justice in those cases was meted out by the aggrieved party and generally resulted in death. But the rules preventing associations with cops were more serious. They existed to protect the crime family and to ensure that potentially harmful information was not passed to the police.

Family was everything.

Luca didn't know what would happen if anyone found out he was with Gabrielle, but he was pretty damn sure he wouldn't just get a slap on the wrist. There were only three punishments for a made man who broke the rules. First, he could be "broken," which was a demotion of rank. In this case, Luca would be demoted from capo to soldier, lose his crew, the respect of his men, and his privileges in the family administration. Second, he could be "chased," a form of banishment in which he would be barred from doing business with any made men, and a punishment that was considered merciful because the third option was death.

And what of his quest to restore the family honor? *Like father, like son,* the family would say, and the Rizzoli name would be scratched off the *Cosa Nostra* books forever. Luca didn't have a real son to carry on the Rizzoli family legacy handed down over the generations from first son to first son. Although no one knew Matteo wasn't really his son, Luca would die knowing that the Rizzoli bloodline ended with him and in dishonor.

So why wasn't he walking away?

After texting Mike and Little Ricky to stand down, he'd given his statement like the good citizen he pretended to be. Gabrielle had managed to smooth things over and convince Jeff not to press charges. Watching her in action was the only good thing about the experience. She was confident, assertive, and she didn't take shit from anyone. Luca was a civilian, she'd said, a restaurant owner unused to violence and traumatized by the shooting. He'd overreacted. Surely Jeff could understand, and if he didn't, maybe he would understand when she pursued charges against him for breaking her door.

Traumatized. Unused to violence. Luca had to fight back a laugh. If only she'd seen what he and Frankie had done to those two Albanians a few weeks ago. Now that was trauma—for the Albanians, not him.

So now she was talking to three male cops. Luca didn't like how they were checking her out. But she was safer with them than with that fucker, Jeff.

As if he knew what Luca was thinking, Max growled beside him. Smart dog. Luca bent down and stroked his head. He had learned early to rely on his intuition, and his intuition told him something about Jeff was off, and it wasn't just about how badly he wanted Gabrielle.

And man, he wanted her bad.

Almost as bad as Luca wanted her. But it could never be. She was a cop. He was Mafia. Time to forget about his beautiful angel and return to Hell. But for the life of him he couldn't get his damn feet to move.

Someone had shot at his woman. At him. A made man. A fucking *caporegime*. A member of the Toscani crime family.

Revenge was now a matter of honor. Despite Gabrielle's unfortunate choice of profession, he had a duty to protect her. No honorable wiseguy would walk away from a woman in danger, even if she had her own gun. He would keep her safe until the streets ran red with the blood of the bastards who had dared shoot up the house. And then he would walk away.

If he could walk away.

He liked that she didn't take shit from anyone, and that she didn't expect her man to lay the world at her feet. She was fiercely independent, ridiculously competent, highly intelligent, and the hottest piece of ass he'd ever seen.

And a fucking cop. Of all the women in all the professions in the world, he had to fall for the one woman he couldn't have. He should leave. Right now. Turn around and never look back.

Out of the corner of his eye, he caught Jeff leaving the paramedics and making his way over to Gabrielle.

Decision fucking made. It wasn't like he and Gabrielle were going to be together forever. He would find the bastards who shot at her and keep her away from all the wiseguys in the city. By then, she would be out of his system, and he would be able to get back to his normal life of multiple women, single times.

Holding Max's leash, Luca pushed away from the vehicle and made it to Gabrielle with only seconds to spare.

"Come, *bella.* I'll take you and Max to my place." Luca held out his hand to her, although his gaze was fixed on the man with hatred in his eyes.

"Gaby, my couch is free." Jeff returned Luca's stare, his hand also outstretched to the woman between them.

Luca's heart pounded as the seconds ticked away. Gabrielle knew he had little respect for the law. Would she cross the line and come with him? Had he managed to tempt her to the dark side?

After a long moment of hesitation, she placed her hand on Luca's arm. "Thanks, Jeff. I appreciate it. But I think I'll stay with Luca tonight."

Luca gave a soft satisfied grunt and put an arm around her shoulders so there would be no misunderstanding who was the victor tonight.

"You need any help with the insurance or repairs?" Jeff persisted. "I set you up with my insurers when we found the house. I could give them a call."

Luca hissed in a mental breath. Outwardly, Jeff appeared contrite and accepting of the situation, but the words he chose, his reference to their time together, told Luca he hadn't given up the fight.

"I should be okay," she said.

"What about Nicole?" Jeff's voice rose almost imperceptibly and he dared take a step toward them.

"I called her," Gabrielle said. "She's going to stay with Clint until the house is safe again." She tugged on Luca's arm. "Come on. Let's go."

"Who the fuck is he?" Jeff called out as Luca walked her away with a protective arm curved around her body.

Unable to resist, Luca looked back over his shoulder and sent a silent message with his smile.

I'm the one she's going home with tonight.

EIGHT

"Wake up, *bella*."

Gabrielle came awake out of a delicious dream where she was being stroked and petted, warm hands on her breasts, her stomach, and down between her . . .

"Stop it."

"Stop what?" Luca lay on top of the covers beside her, his head propped up on one elbow, his other hand innocently on her shoulder.

Embarrassed by the erotic dream that had left her wet and aching, she ducked her head to hide her burning cheeks. "Nothing. You startled me. What are you doing in my bed?"

"It's my bed." His fingers feathered down her bare arm making her tingle.

"I thought this was your guest room." Gabrielle turned to face him, pushing the duvet away. Last night, she'd set up Max's basket in Luca's ultra-modern kitchen and unpacked her bag in a bright, airy bedroom decorated with dark gray walls and soft white carpet. The bed sat on a low-rise platform made of gray padded leather with two floating night tables on either side. Navy blue covers and pillows on the accent chair gave the room a cool, calm, masculine feel.

"It's a room for guests who I want in my bed." He pushed her hair back, exposing her rosy cheek. Only then did she notice that his chest was bare, his lower half covered by a pair of pajama pants that did nothing to hide his arousal.

"What time is it?"

"Ten. You said you didn't have to be at work until Thursday."

"Ten?" She jerked up. "I've been asleep for nine hours? I need to get back to secure the house, call the insurance people, get a quote for getting everything fixed . . ."

"You needed to sleep." He rubbed his knuckles over her cheek. "I've taken care of everything. There's a construction crew on site. I had a friend who owed me a favor, so you won't need to call your insurers. Unfortunately, your front window is a special order and even with my connections, they won't be able to replace it for a few days. They've boarded that one up, but you will be safer if you stay here until it's fixed."

For a moment, she was at a loss for words. She'd learned self-reliance early in life, and even David had expected her to handle most things herself because he'd been so busy with his work. Only after he died had she leaned on friends, and then just until she was able to move on from the trauma.

"You didn't need to do that. It was my problem."

"Now, there is no problem." He shifted on the bed, melting her with the warmth of his gaze.

"Thank you. But that's a lot of trouble to go to for someone you barely know."

An almost dangerous smile curved his sensual mouth. "I think I got to know you very well in Glamour.

Burn cheeks burn. "That's a different kind of knowledge," she protested. "Not the kind that would get you out of bed early in the morning to pull in favors from friends to fix the house of a woman you've only met a few times."

"Unless those few times left an unforgettable impression." His hand slid up and over her hip and down into the curve of her waist, leaving her in no doubt about his intentions. He smelled of body wash, fresh and clean, and in the semi-darkness of the closed blinds she could see a few drops of water glistening in his hair. She pictured him in the shower, his lean, muscular body, the powerful thighs, broad shoulders, and the ripple of his abs as water sluiced down to his thick, hard cock . . .

Her nipples tightened, and she swallowed hard, regretting her decision to wear only an easy-access nightshirt and panties to bed. "What about Max?"

"Max has been walked and fed. There is no reason for you to get up. In fact, I would be delighted if you would continue to enjoy the comforts of my bed." His hand splayed over her lower back, just above her ass and he pulled her forward until she could feel his erection pressed against her stomach.

"Luca . . ." Heat flooded her body, his touch kindling a fire she had no idea how to manage. She'd never felt anything like this with David. Their lovemaking had been sweet, nice, and pleasant. Luca was all raw sensual power, wild, an unstoppable, irresistible force.

"Tell me to stop." His fingertips grazed the bare skin under her nightshirt as he took her mouth in a long, slow kiss. "And I will. But I've thought of nothing all night except your beautiful body tucked between my sheets only a few rooms away."

Her pulse throbbed between her legs. What was it about this man that turned her legs to jelly and fuzzed her brain with lust? "Your workers might not be safe. I'm pretty sure I know who sent those guys to my house and he's dangerous. Very dangerous."

"So am I." Luca slid one hand under her neck and cradled her head in the crook of his arm, his other hand holding her still as he ravaged her mouth, manhandling her like she was a toy that existed solely for his pleasure.

"God, Luca. I can't think when you touch me." It was a struggle not to give in, not to rock her hips against his, not to meet every thrust of his tongue with one of her own, not to pull his hand between her legs to soothe the ache.

"Don't think. Just feel." His hand curled between her thighs, fingers stroking her panties, a light touch over her needy clit.

With a defeated groan, she parted her legs, giving him better access. "I feel like you're manipulating me with sex, except I don't know what you want."

"I want you." He stripped off her panties and night-shirt and then pushed her back on the bed, pinning her wrists against the pillow with one firm hand.

She gasped as her body responded to his rough hand-ling, heart pounding, blood running hot through her veins. "We keep doing this backwards." She arched her back in response to the pressure on her wrists, offering her nipples up for the pleasure of his hot, wet mouth. "It's supposed to be talk first, sex later."

"There is no 'sex later' when I'm with you." Luca licked and sucked one nipple, then the other, until she was writhing on the bed.

"Spread your legs for me," he said sharply. "Don't close them again."

Gabrielle moaned. "When you talk to me like that you make me—"

Luca didn't wait for her to finish. He pushed one finger inside her and rocked the heel of his hand against her clit.

"Wet." He finished her sentence for her. "Hot. Greedy for my cock."

Her body clenched and she rocked her hips against him, giving in to the arousal he had so easily awakened. "Yes."

His eyes blazed with feral heat. "Tell me what you want."

"I want your cock." She said the words without hesitation, savoring the illicit thrill of being so bold in bed.

"Not yet." He released her wrists and withdrew his fingers, kneeling back on the bed. "Up, *bella*. On your knees in front of me."

Curious, Gabrielle knelt in front of him, so close their knees were almost touching. His erection tented his pajama pants, but when she reached to touch him, he stopped her with a bark.

"You do that and this will be over before it begins."

She gave him a coy smile. "I thought it had begun."

"It begins when you come all over my hand." He reached down and eased two fingers into her pussy, muttering a curse as he pushed inside. "So fucking wet."

"Wouldn't you rather—"

"Spread your knees." His pulse pounded in his neck, and she widened her legs to accommodate the width of his hand.

"Good girl." He withdrew his fingers and slowly pumped inside her, stealing her breath away. He bent to kiss her breasts, swirling his tongue around her right nipple as his fingers thrust in a slow steady rhythm that drove her wild. She clung to him, fingers curling into his biceps when his thumb teased her clitoris, drowning in sensation, pleasure and pain and the white-hot heat of coiled desire.

"That's it." His voice dropped husky and low. "Ride my fingers. Take your pleasure from my hand."

Her thighs quivered as she ground shamelessly against his hand, hips rocking, body hot and aching, nails digging into his skin. She felt at once dirty and desired as she drove herself to a climax using his hand for her pleasure.

He groaned and hardened this thrusts, his fingers moving inside her as he sucked and licked her nipple. She met his every thrust with a rock of her hips, until she was breathless and dizzy, gasping for air with every sweep of his thumb over her clitoris.

When his fingers brushed over the sensitive spot inside her, her world shattered in a rush of wet heat, her vagina clenching around his fingers as pleasure rolled over her in a molten wave.

Luca gentled the pressure on her nipple, licking the peaked tip as his fingers slowed inside her, drawing out her climax until she sagged against him.

"Oh God." She panted. "I wet the bed."

Luca slowly withdrew his fingers and licked his lips, his eyes dark with hunger. "It's not that kind of wet. It's the kind of wet that tells me you're more than ready for my cock." Without warning, he flipped her over to all fours, shed his pajama pants, and sheathed himself with a condom he had tucked into his pocket.

"Shoulders down. Ass up." With a firm hand between her shoulder blades, and a tight hand on her hip, he positioned her for the firm thrust of his thick shaft.

She moaned softly as his hard length sank slowly inside her. "You feel so good."

Luca twisted her hair in his hand. "You feel fucking amazing. You want my cock?"

"Yes." She swallowed hard when his thrusts roughened. "Please."

"Like it when you beg."

Gabrielle had never begged for sex before meeting Luca, nor had she ever allowed a man to dominate her so completely in bed. But she was fully on board now as she sought to explore the part of her that responded so eagerly to his erotically charged commands.

His hands curled around her hips, firm fingers digging into her flesh. So strong. So powerful. He was like a drug, and she wanted more, and for the first time she wasn't afraid to ask. "Luca. Please. Fuck me."

He growled and pounded into her so hard her teeth clacked together. But the feel of his cock moving inside her, his hands on her hips, and his balls slapping against her ass, tipped her over the edge into another climax that rocked her very core. Luca followed her over with a shout, his cock hardening as he pumped deep inside her.

He panted his breaths as he dropped over her body, holding his weight on his arms. "Christ. You don't know what you do to me."

"Hopefully the same kind of thing you do to me." She dropped down, rolled to her back so she could look up at him. His face was flushed, and sweat beaded his brow. "You're like a whole new world of sex."

Luca smiled as he gazed down at her. "I'm just getting started."

She dropped her head to the pillow, stared up at the ceiling where he'd hung spherical glass lights that looked like stars in the dark sky. "How about a short commercial break so my heart doesn't break through my ribs?"

He laughed and left her to dispose of the condom. When he returned, she'd pulled up the duvet and he climbed into bed beside her.

"You have about twenty minutes to talk before I'm ready for you again." He turned to face her, one hand tracing the curve of her hip.

"I thought I had twenty minutes," she protested as his fingers slid to the soft down at the apex of her thighs, and then up again.

"I can only talk if I'm touching you." His fingertips grazed the undersides of her breasts, still sensitive from his rough attention.

Gabrielle pressed her lips together in mock reproach. "Touch is not the same as fondle."

"I like to fondle you," Luca said, grinning. "I like how your body responds, how wet you always are when you're with me. You've already wasted a minute, maybe two."

"Fine. Fondle away." She sighed. "I don't know that much about you. What do you do other than give mind blowing orgasms and run a restaurant?" Unable to resist, she ran her hand through his thick, golden hair, brushing away the last little droplets of water.

"A little of this and a little of that." He shrugged. "I have interests in several businesses."

She rolled slightly to face him, her legs coming together as she stroked her hand along his jaw, rough with a five o'clock shadow. "And what do you do for fun?"

"This."

"Sex?" Her eyes widened. "This is your recreational pastime?"

Luca smiled as his hand roamed her body. "It is right now."

Gabrielle threaded her fingers through his, holding him still. "Other than sex, what do you like to do? Do you like movies?"

"Comedy, but not slapstick. I like something intelligent. And Noir. Gumshoe detectives. That kind of thing. If I have time, which I usually don't."

She studied his face for a long moment, trying to see beyond his casual tone. "So you like detectives?"

He chuckled and twisted his fingers away, only to curl them around her breast. "Fictional detectives. And there's this blonde with the sweetest, wettest pussy . . ."

"No dirty talking," she warned. "I won't remember all the questions I wanted to ask you if my brain is addled by lust. What about your family? Are they around?"

"Yeah, everyone's here. I grew up in Vegas. My dad passed away when I was a teenager. He had an . . . insurance policy so my mother got by and I helped out when finances ran low. I have a younger sister, Angela, who's a hairdresser, and a brother, Alex, who's fucking his life away doing nothing except smoking dope and getting into trouble. Ma still holds the family together, makes everyone go to church on Sunday, meet up for family dinner . . ."

"Church?" Her lips quivered with a smile, even though her heart ached to hear about his brother. She knew just how difficult it could be to have an addict in the family.

"You don't know my mother."

"I still miss my mother," she admitted.

His hand stilled and he wrapped his arm around her and pulled her close. "How about your stepmother? Was she evil? Did she make you sleep in front of the fireplace?"

Gabrielle laughed. "She was okay, but she just didn't seem to have time for me when her whole life was taken up driving my stepbrothers around to practices and sporting events, and helping my dad deal with my brother. I wasn't a priority, if that makes any sense. I learned to take care of myself, but I was very lonely. I don't know what I would have done without Cissy and her family."

"And David?" he prompted.

"I met him when I joined the police academy. He was

one of my instructors. He was ten years older than me. Very stable. Knew what he wanted and where he was going in life. It was hard to resist someone who focused all his attention on me, someone who cared. He wanted to change the world, too." She traced a finger along the ridges of his pecs, careful not to touch the healing scar from the bullet wound that had brought them together. He hadn't said anything about her scar, and she wasn't sure if that was good or bad.

"Does it hurt?" His scar was larger than hers and the surgery had left a long gash across the tattoo on his chest, probably because they had to dig out his bullet. But it was round and dime-shaped like hers, and both were slightly raised and pink.

Luca shrugged. Just like a guy. Too tough to admit any pain.

"What about this tattoo?" She traced the edges of the incredible piece on his chest, a skull with wings and a crown, surrounded by roses, flames and swords. It encompassed so much, and yet the scroll-like banner beneath it was blank.

"My commitment to family and honor, life and death, love and friendship. At least that's what it used to mean."

"And the scroll? What are you going to put on there?"

His face tightened. "It's for the name of my first born son."

Gabrielle opened her mouth to ask more, but he leaned down and pressed a kiss to the scar just above her breast. "What about you? You picked a dangerous profession. Why police work?"

"I wanted to try and clean up the streets, get rid of the drug dealers so other families didn't have to suffer like we did," she said. "But I couldn't really make a difference. Not even when I became a detective. I guess I was a bit naive."

His body tensed and he eased away the tiniest bit. "What kind of detective?"

"Narcotics. Same as Jeff and David." She frowned when he released her and rolled to his back. Had he had a bad experience with the police? Or was he still angry about what happened with Jeff?

"I applied because I wanted to find David's killer," she continued, trying to fill the uncomfortable silence. "I like the investigation side of it, but the administrative side can be overwhelming. Sometimes opportunities pass you by while you're crossing your T's and dotting your I's." Opportunities like going after Garcia when the tip came in, instead of waiting four days for the paperwork to clear.

Luca folded his hands behind his head, and stared up at the ceiling. Even though he was right beside her, he suddenly seemed to be far away. It made her ache to feel his hands on her again, but she didn't know him that well yet, wasn't sure how he would feel if she breached the space he had very deliberately put between them.

"I'm done in Narcotics now," she said softly. "I was booted out because I messed up big time. We had organized a big raid with the SWAT team to catch the guy I've been after and take down a big drug distribution center. I didn't want him to slip through our fingers, so I went early to the warehouse." She sighed. "They knew we were coming. The warehouse was almost empty when I got there, but someone was in the building. I think he must have been clearing out the last of the stuff. He shot me and escaped out a side door. I took the fall for the failed raid even though no one knew for certain our target was there. I lost my place on the team and was transferred to Theft. I start on Wednesday."

She didn't mean to guilt him into touching her again, but when she finished, he turned to face her and stroked a finger over her cheek. "You lost your chance for vengeance."

"Yes. But now it looks like he's decided to come after me, although I have no idea why. I didn't see the face of the shooter or fire my gun in the warehouse, and I was one of the most junior people on the case. What was the point of sending two guys to shoot up my house? I just hope they don't come back one night when Nicole is home."

His eyes darkened almost to black. "You won't have to worry about them ever again."

"So protective." She laughed softly. "I appreciate the sentiment, but it's not like you can do anything about it. I don't even know who they were or if they were hired by the guy I was after. And you don't even know who that guy is, and I can't tell you."

He lifted an eyebrow, the clouds that had darkened his face only moments ago disappearing beneath his sensual smile. "Maybe I should manipulate you with sex again and you'll tell me what I want to know." His hand curled around her ass and he gave her a squeeze.

"More sex? Don't you have to work?" She nuzzled his neck. He smelled of body wash and sex. He smelled of her.

"We don't open until noon," he said, caressing her backside. "My staff handles the afternoon shift unless there's a delivery or I have to sample the food. When I'm not busy, I spend time with my son after he's out of school."

She stiffened, but when she tried to push away, he held her fast.

"You have a son?"

"Matteo. He's six."

Her heart thudded against her ribs. "Are you married?"

"I was." He rolled them until she was flat on her back,

pinned in place by his hard, muscular body. "My wife died when Matteo was only two years old."

Her hand flew to her mouth. "Oh, Luca. I'm sorry. You've suffered so much loss, too. At least you have him. Does he live with you?" She hadn't seen any children's toys lying around or anything to indicate a child lived in the penthouse with him, but at least now she understood the banner under the tattoo. He must be intending to ink his son's name on it.

"He lives with my mother." He feathered kisses down her neck to her shoulder, his stubble a delicious friction over her skin. "I work long hours, and I want him to have a stable life and a good role model. I see him once or twice a week."

"That must be hard." She tipped her head to the side to give him better access, parted her legs to accommodate his growing arousal, her interest in conversation waning beneath the flames of desire.

"It's all he's known."

"I mean for you."

He lifted his head, a frown creasing his brow. "I want him to have a good life. Letting my mother raise him is the best way to achieve it."

"Don't underestimate the importance of being in his life," she said softly. "I don't know how it was for you, but after my mother died I felt scared and alone. My father was already involved in his new relationship, although no one knew he'd been having an affair, and after we moved to Nevada, Patrick's addiction consumed our lives. My stepmother eventually left us, and after Patrick died, my dad fell into a severe depression. I joined the police hoping that seeing me live Patrick's dream of becoming a police officer would help him recover, but he didn't show up for my graduation. He didn't even send flowers." She mentioned the flowers in a joking tone, but Luca frowned.

"Beautiful women should have beautiful flowers." He toyed with her hair, his eyes unfocused, as if deep in thought. "Next time you have something to celebrate—"

His eyes were more green now than brown. Curious. When he was passionate about something, his eyes darkened, but when he was thoughtful or teasing, they were green.

"I didn't tell you that story so you'd run off and buy me flowers."

"I would have bought them anyway." He pushed back and knelt between her spread legs, his erection jutting up from its nest of curls. "And you'll thank me by wrapping those sweet lips around my cock. I'm ready for you again, *mio angelo.* You're like a drug. I can't get enough."

Neither could she. And it was a dangerous road to travel because Luca had flipped a switch in her that made her feel beautiful and brave and bold. She could see herself with a man like Luca—a man without boundaries, a man who took risks, and thought nothing of fucking her in a public place, tracking her down, or beating on Jeff because he considered him a threat. He took her breath away, and it scared her.

What if she fell for him?

And what if she lost him?

She couldn't afford this indulgence, giving herself over to the easy way he manipulated her body, to the pleasure of his touch, to her insatiable need to know everything about him. She needed to set boundaries. For her and for him.

But later. When she could think coherently again.

She lifted an eyebrow. "You just killed all the sweetness by being your usual arrogant self."

He slid his hand up her thigh, one thick finger gliding between her folds. "You like my arrogant self."

"I like your arrogant self's fingers." She moaned, and his eyes darkened.

"Ask more questions." His lips quirked in an amused expression as he pushed a finger inside her. "I enjoy watching you try to talk when I've got my fingers in your pussy."

She closed her eyes at the delicious sensation. "How soon before you fuck me again?"

Luca laughed. "Not soon enough."

NINE

Luca played his last hand, his body thrumming with the need to get the damn card game with Nico finished so they could move on to business. After dropping Gabrielle off at her house, and checking to make sure the contractors were doing their job, he had picked up Little Ricky and Mike and just made it downtown in time for the meeting in the private salon of the high-limit gaming room of Nico's Casino Italia.

Poker wasn't Luca's game. He was a decent poker player, but craps was his addiction—a game of chance that gave the illusion of control. He had also been avoiding Nico's casino since leaving the hospital, and particularly the private salon where he'd been shot. But when the boss wanted to talk over cards, you hauled ass, shut the fuck up, and tried not to look at the new plush carpeting that covered the spot where you'd almost bled out on the floor.

Exquisitely decorated in rich purple, gold, and brown, the ultra-exclusive private gaming salon was contemporary in a classic way, with expensive lamps, walls of books with neutral-hued spines, dark wood furniture and velvet sofas. On the other side of the stained-glass doors, the less-exclusive high-limit room boasted crystal chandeliers, rich, red leather furniture, and five-hundred-dollar-minimum slot machines.

Frankie glared as Luca drummed his thumb on the table. "You got a problem?"

Yeah, he had a problem. He had a lot of fucking problems—Albanians in his territory, a cop who wasn't happy he'd stolen his girl, two bastards who had dared shoot up her house, and a beautiful, sexy woman who had become a bigger fucking addiction than the craps that had almost wiped out his savings the year after Gina died.

"No, dickhead. You got a problem?"

"Christ, what the fuck is wrong with you, two?" Nico threw his cards on the table and gestured to his new casino manager to clear the room. "You got an issue, work it the fuck out before you come to a meeting."

Luca didn't know why Frankie was on his case, but Frankie was one of those guys who was always hiding in the shadows, and if he even suspected Luca had something going on with a cop, he wouldn't hesitate to act, and in the most brutal of ways.

He ran a hand through his hair, trying to get his emotions under control before Frankie picked up that something wasn't right. His gaze fell on the spot where Nico had held him on the floor, trying to staunch the blood spilling out of Luca's chest. At the time, Luca had almost been glad it was over. Gina's betrayal had ripped him apart, and he was tired of the anger and the guilt and the pain, tired of resenting Matteo for being another man's son.

He isn't yours, Gina had said smugly, before she walked out the door. But damned if he could leave Matteo with her sorry excuse for a family after she died.

He'd held Matteo when he was born, named him after his grandfather, shown him off to his family, taken pride in the fact that the Rizzoli family name would carry on and had the banner inked on his skin, ready for his son's name. Matteo was his son in all but blood, and he was the only person alive who knew the truth.

"Luca."

He looked up, saw the sympathy in Nico's eyes and knew that he thought Luca was lost in the moment the bullet had sliced through his chest.

"It's in the past," Nico said.

"Yeah." He lifted the glass of whiskey that had sat untouched for the last hour.

"I brought you all here to discuss the situation with Tony." Nico looked at each of the five capos sitting around the table in turn. There was no love lost between Nico and his cousin, Tony, especially after Tony tried to force Nico's girlfriend—now his wife—into marriage to gain an alliance with her family.

"Tony has allied with the Fuentes Cartel led by José Gomez Garcia," Nico said. "He has been desperate to get involved in the drug trade, and this is his way in. Garcia was operating independently until he became the subject of an intense police investigation. He had to go deep underground, taking many of his senior lieutenants with him. He's been using the Albanians for muscle and distribution, but, as we know, the Albanians are messy, uncontrollable, and unpredictable. They don't respect territory." He gave a brief nod to Frankie and Luca. "And they pay the price."

Mike snorted. "You give them a new pair of shoes, Frankie?"

"Heaviest ones I could find."

Nico lifted a hand for silence. "Tony is now providing the muscle, and in return Garcia is giving him distribution rights over key areas of the city. Garcia is flooding the market with a new kind of dope. It's highly addictive, and people are paying double or even triple what they'd pay for the regular stuff. It can also be lethal, and two nights ago two of Sally G's soldiers overdosed on Garcia's new product and died."

Sally G, a senior capo who had been a good friend of Nico's father, and was now a staunch supporter of Nico's claim to lead the family, stood and declared a vendetta against Garcia. The room exploded in a cacophony of curses and shouts, calls for revenge and promises to slit Garcia's throat. One of the benefits of becoming a made man was that the entire *Cosa Nostra* could be called upon for vengeance. And when that happened, there was nowhere to run. Nowhere to hide.

"They were both friends of ours and they will be avenged," Nico said. "Their deaths and the shoot-out at Roberto's Deli also give us another reason to go after Garcia. Not only is it a matter of honor, but if we take down Garcia, we'll cut off Tony's main drug supplier and weaken his power base in the city. In short, we'll be able to take Tony out, reclaim our territory and get this fucking tainted shit out of our city."

Cheers and shouts followed his statement. Nico silenced the room by thudding his fist on the table, an uncharacteristic show of emotion from an otherwise self-contained man. "I want Garcia. Alive. And I shouldn't have to remind everyone in this room that drugs are not tolerated by *Cosa Nostra*. Drugs attract law enforcement, and we saw what happened in New York when the families broke that rule—wiseguys turning rat and selling out, empires crumbling, businesses lost, men in jail, and women and children left without support. That's not what this family is about. That's not what I'm about."

Luca's heart squeezed in his chest. The decimation of the American Mafia families had spilled into Las Vegas because of his father. His dad had broken the rule against dealing in drugs, lured by the huge profits and the promise of easy money. The feds had followed the drugs and caught his father in their net. Instead of honoring *omertà*, keeping his mouth shut, and doing his time, Luca's father had agreed to wear a wire and rat on his crime family in a plea deal that would have seen him abandon his wife and children for a new life in witness protection.

Like that was going to happen.

Less than one week after jumping ship, Luca's father was found in an FBI safe house wearing a Sicilian Necktie, the traditional Mafia punishment for rats His throat had been slit from ear to ear and his tongue ripped through the hole made in his neck, dangling as if it were a tie. Devastated and disgusted by his father's betrayal, Luca had never mourned his father's death, and he had been striving ever since to regain the family honor and clear the family name.

"Who's going to lead the hunt for Garcia?" Nico asked.

"I will." Luca didn't hesitate to volunteer. Catching Garcia would go a long way toward regaining his crime family's trust and reclaiming his blood family's honor.

Nico nodded his approval. "It's a big job, but you'll have all the help you need, and Frankie can do the heavy lifting."

Everyone laughed at his veiled reference to Frankie's love of concrete footwear. Everyone but Frankie, who was studying Luca as if he couldn't believe Luca had been given such an honor. Christ, was there nothing he could do to show Frankie that he wasn't his father? That he would never betray the *Cosa Nostra*? Over the years, he had tried to be the best damn associate, soldier, and now capo he could be. He worked longer, fought harder, and followed every rule. If everyone around the table was Mafia, Luca was Mafia Xtreme.

At least this cemented in his mind the folly of asking Frankie to help him hunt down and whack the two bastards who had shot up Gabrielle's house. He would have to handle the situation on his own, and with only the most trusted and loyal men in his crew.

And afterward, when he had avenged Gabrielle and ensured her safety, their relationship, such as it was, would have to end. There was no half way with the Mafia. You were in or you were dead, just like his dad. And he knew just who would be pulling that trigger. Not just on him, but possibly on Gabrielle, too.

"I heard Luca almost got arrested for beating on a cop last night," Frankie said, silencing the chatter around the table.

Luca's stomach tightened and he dropped one hand to his lap where it would be within easy reach of his weapon. Every Mafia family in the city had police informants—dirty cops, ex-cops, janitors, admin staff, or even just regular cops who'd made a mistake and wound up owing the Mafia a favor. Clearly someone had ratted him out to Frankie, and now he was being called to account. The question was, how much did Frankie know?

"Yeah?" Mike's eyes lit up. "What was that all about?"

"He threatened my girl."

Nico frowned. "Since when do you have a girl?"

"He always has a girl," Mike said. "He has a new one every day of the week."

"This one's different." He forced a smile, playing at

being the manwhore he had been until he met Gabrielle. "I had her twice."

Everybody laughed, which was what he wanted them to do. But Frankie didn't even crack a smile.

Access denied. Classified.

"Dammit." Gabrielle threw her mouse across her desk. She was locked out of the Garcia case. Even her personal hardcopy files where she had jotted down notes, thoughts, and random pieces of information had been moved to Agent Palmer's office where they were accessible only with his permission and after he opened the locked filing cabinet with his personal key. The security setup was unprecedented, and she wondered if Garcia was something more than just a drug lord with ties to the Fuentes Cartel.

She pulled down the first of a stack of slim manila files from the shelf in her cubicle. There were no offices in the Theft department. No windows either. Most of her new colleagues spent their days visiting businesses and homes to take down details of items that would only rarely be recovered. The Theft bureau hadn't gone high tech and her new case files were all paper records—everything from stolen jewelry to cars, and from casino winnings to a prize poodle with pink fur. Her heart sank. This wasn't a transfer; it was a punishment. And now Garcia was out there thinking he could intimidate her. How could they take her off the case?

With a sigh, she opened the first folder and stared at the thick bundle of police reports all documenting cases of lost, missing, or stolen phones. Her new supervising sergeant thought a crime ring was operating in the area, targeting phones that would be stripped of their SIM cards and shipped overseas. It was a "dog file," he'd said, with no hint of apology in his voice. Missing phones rarely turned up, and they were easy cash for any criminal whether linked to organized crime or not. Still, they had to make a token effort to track them down. She pulled out the most recent report and threw it across her desk.

No. She couldn't just sit here and pretend like it was all okay. For two years, she'd followed the rules while she worked on the Garcia case, and what had that gotten her? Nothing. No justice for David. No vengeance. No Garcia behind bars. No streets clean of drugs. She buried her face in her hands, catching sight of the faint bruises on her wrists from her night with Luca.

Luca who flaunted the rules with his cavalier attitude. Luca who refused to wear a hospital gown, had sex with her in a public place, illegally accessed the Glamour database to find her address, tracked her down, and then attacked a police officer on her front lawn. Luca was a rebel. Why couldn't she be one, too? She had said she was going to talk to Agent Palmer. So why not do it now?

She buttoned her suit jacket and made her way down to Agent Palmer's office. Part of her—the part that was sweating profusely into her shirt—hoped he wasn't there. But the other part—the part that had turned Jeff away in favor of a man she barely knew, a man with whom she had willingly committed "open or gross lewdness" and "indecent exposure"—was looking forward to the challenge.

Good thing. Because there he was.

"Do you have a minute?" She took a step into Agent Palmer's office, imposing herself into his space.

Agent Palmer looked up. If anyone had to guess his job, they would get it right away. Slicked down black hair, black suit, dark gray tie, white shirt, and bland face. All that was missing were the dark glasses.

"Ms. Fawkes. What can I do for you?"

"Garcia sent two of his goons to shoot up my house."

He nodded. "I heard about the shooting. How do you know it was him?"

She opened her mouth to respond, hesitated. How did she know it was him? After two years of investigation, she felt like she knew Garcia. He was a man who stayed hidden, sending others to do his dirty work so he could keep his hands clean. He was quick to react when he felt threatened, eliminating any opposition or competition in the most brutal way, which suggested he was ruled more by emotion than logic. David got too close, and he paid the price. And if she was right about the identity of the shooters, it meant she'd uncovered something in those files Garcia did not want her to see.

"Who else would shoot up my house? I haven't been working on any other case."

"You tell me, Ms. Fawkes. I'm not privy to your personal life."

She hadn't liked Agent Palmer when they first met, and she liked him even less now. He wasn't even like a real person. He didn't lean back, fold his arms, sigh, yawn, or twiddle his thumbs. Unlike Luca who was very expressive, he showed no emotion, no hint he was even alive. She wondered if he was even breathing.

"For the sake of argument, let's assume I haven't pissed anyone else off so that they would bring a couple of AKs to my house for a target-shooting party," she shot back. "We can't let Garcia think he intimidated us. I need to be on the case again, doing something visible so he understands we're not afraid of him."

"No."

"That's it? No?"

"That's it," he said evenly. "You've just proved to me that I made the right decision pulling you off the case in the first place. This is emotion talking. You're angry. Your home was violated. Just like when your husband was murdered, you are devastated and want revenge. Emotion gets in the way of an investigation, Ms. Fawkes. It prevents us from being objective, and if we're not objective, we can't do our job, which I believe for you now involves the retrieval of stolen property."

She folded her arms, pressed her lips tight together. "This is nothing like what happened to David. And I think you're making a mistake."

"Of course, you do." He waved a dismissive hand. "Unless Garcia has stolen something, I don't expect we'll need to talk again. However, a word of advice, Ms. Fawkes. For the sake of argument, if Garcia was behind the incident at your house, it would make sense to accept the department's offer of police protection until the shooters are caught. I understand you turned it down."

"I agreed to drive-bys of my house and non-work locations—the gym, bars, restaurants, places like that—for the deterrent effect. But I don't need a twenty-four-hour bodyguard. I know Garcia. If he wanted to kill me, I'd be dead. That was a warning. He feels threatened. And if you really wanted to catch him, you would try to find out what made him feel that way."

"Gabrielle Fawkes?"

She turned to see a department courier in the hallway, holding an enormous bouquet of delicate pink and white roses. "Yes?"

"Delivery. You'll need both arms. I've never delivered a bouquet this large."

Her cheeks flushed and she looked back at Agent Palmer as she took the bouquet.

"Personal life, Ms. Fawkes." His thin lips quivered in what she was sure was an FBI version of a smirk. "Also compromises our objectivity."

Gabrielle fought back the urge to retort. No point getting on the bad side of the FBI, if she wasn't there already. "Thank you for your time."

She stepped out into the hallway, closing Agent Palmer's door behind her. "Are you sure they're for me?" She couldn't imagine who would send her a bouquet of flowers. It wasn't her birthday or any special occasion.

"Card is stapled to the paper," he said. "Your name is on it."

Gabrielle returned to her cubicle and breathed in the delicate scent of roses. The soft petals brushed her cheeks and for a long moment she just drank them in. She counted at least forty, but she had a feeling there were more. She lay the bouquet down on her desk and pulled off the card.

Happy First Day of Theft.
Someone stole my heart. Maybe you can find it.
—L

A powerful wave of emotion swept over her. It wasn't just because the flowers were exquisite or that the size of the bouquet took her breath away, and it wasn't because he'd remembered the story she told him, or that he'd made good his promise to send her flowers; it was because in this moment, when she'd been feeling so utterly down and defeated, he'd lifted her spirits and made her laugh, without even being there.

"Gaby. You have to see what I found. I never got a chance to show you the other day." Jeff walked up to her cubicle and froze. "Who are those from?"

She stroked a finger over a soft pink bud. "Luca."

Jeff's jaw tightened. "I figured there had to be some reason you picked him over me. I saw the Maserati outside your place. What does he do? Billionaire? Business tycoon?"

"He owns an Italian restaurant."

Jeff snorted a laugh. "I guess pasta is in high demand these days."

She looked up and sighed. "Jeff. Please. Don't be like that. There's no need to be snarky."

"Would you look at me the way you looked at him if I sent you fifty roses?"

"Jeff . . ."

He held up his hands in mock apology. "I'm sorry. Okay? I'm sorry for what I just said, and I'm sorry for what happened the other night. I was way out of line, but this isn't easy for me. I care for you, and I really think we would be good together. And I'm worried. This guy . . . You never mentioned him before. He was fucking out of control. Maybe he had something to do with the shooting. He could even have been the target. How much do you know about him?"

"Enough." She folded her arms over her chest.

"Maybe not." He held up a phone. "I found this outside your place. I'm pretty sure it belonged to the guy who threw the rock at my windshield. It might have been him."

"You think Luca hid behind a bush, threw a rock through your windshield, ran away, and then returned a few hours later in a Maserati to knock on my door?"

Jeff's smug expression wavered. "Who else? He wanted you. He was in the area. He must have been stalking you and got jealous when he saw us together."

"He had his phone with him at my place. I saw it."

"Maybe he bought another one, or maybe he had two phones."

She looked at the beautiful bouquet of flowers on the desk and then at the phone in Jeff's hand, but she couldn't reconcile a man who could be so thoughtful with a man who would hide behind the bushes and throw a rock through Jeff's window. Luca wasn't the type to skulk around.

I want to fuck you.

He was direct.

Spread your legs for me.

When he wanted something, he let nothing stand in his way. Jeff pissed him off, and he punched him in the face. "That just sounds crazy," she said.

"Hey, I'm sorry." Jeff put a hand on her shoulder. "I wasn't going after him or anything. I was just trying to catch the guy who vandalized my car, and I found the phone."

"It wasn't him." She leaned forward and breathed in the fresh perfume of the roses.

Jeff shrugged. "Maybe. Maybe not. I've been trying to crack the password, but it's got six digits so I'm going to see if anyone in the crime lab can help. As soon as I find out who owns it, I'll let you know."

After he left, Gabrielle found a vase in the break room and arranged the flowers on her desk before texting a picture to Luca.

Gabrielle: I think someone raided every florist shop in the city.
Luca: You like?
Gabrielle: They're beautiful. Thank you.
Luca: Pleasure.
Gabrielle: They're my favorite colors.
Luca: I know.

She laughed. He could be smug even by text.

Gabrielle: Aside from having been in my bedroom, how did you know?
Luca: Your panties.

Her cheeks heated when she remembered that he'd watched her pack before she went to his place. She hadn't realized he was paying such close attention.

> Gabrielle: Did you lose your phone the other night?
> Luca: If I did, I wouldn't be texting you. Why?
> Gabrielle: I'll tell you next time I see you.
> Luca: I want to see you now.

She laughed again. So impatient, and yet it felt good to be wanted that much.

> Gabrielle: I'm at work.
> Luca: After work.
> Gabrielle: I'm going to the gym. I have to stay fit to apprehend the criminals who have stolen goods.
> Luca: What do you wear at the gym?

Hmm. Naughty Luca. She flipped through her photos until she found one of her at the end of a 10K she'd run to raise money for the local addiction center. Not her best picture, but her damp hair was hidden beneath a charity cap, and her sports bra top and spandex running shorts were her usual workout attire. She texted the picture, and his response came in a heartbeat.

> Luca: Hot. Don't wear in public.
> Gabrielle: Why?
> Luca: I'll have to come to the gym and fight the guys off. I know what they'll be thinking.

Her hand slid into her shirt and she undid the top two
buttons as she settled in her chair.

Gabrielle: What will they be thinking?
Luca: They'll want to fuck my angel.
Gabrielle: Your angel?
Luca: Sei il mio angelo.

God, even the things he texted made her hot. She
glanced around to make sure she was alone in her cubicle, and slid her hand farther into her shirt to caress
the top of her breast. Beneath her desk, she parted her
legs, imagining he was there, pushing her thighs apart.
If anyone came by, she figured she just looked like she
was hot and trying to cool off.
    Yeah, right.

Luca: Gabrielle? Are you still there?
Gabrielle: Yes.
Luca: What are you doing?

It was like he could see into her head. For a moment,
she thought about pretending his words hadn't affected
her, but she saw no harm in being honest with him. He
was direct, and as far as she knew, he had been honest
with her.

Gabrielle: Being naughty.
Luca: Naughty in your police uniform?
Gabrielle: No uniform. Is that a fantasy of yours?
            Women in uniform?
Luca: Gabrielle in uniform in her pretty pink
            bedroom.
Gabrielle: It's not an easy access uniform.
Luca: It will be when I get through with it.

Sweat beaded on her forehead, and she gave serious consideration to going to the restroom to relieve the throbbing ache between her thighs. But why get herself off all alone in a restroom stall when she could have the real thing?

Gabrielle: Are you free tonight? I'm usually
finished at the gym around seven.

Luca: Are you asking me out on a date?

A date? They'd slept together, been shot at together, and shared details about their pasts. That took them past date territory, but not into relationship territory. Maybe they could be friends with benefits, or fuck buddies. Something that didn't involve emotional ties.

Gabrielle: I'm asking if you want to have sex. I'm
not into the whole dating thing.

Luca: I want to take you on a date. I'll pick
you up at nine.

Gabrielle typed a few words into the search engine on her phone and ran them through an online translator. She didn't know if she had the grammar right but it looked like *sesso* meant sex and *fai* meant to do.

Gabrielle: No fai sesso?

Luca: Ti scoperò fino a farti esplodere di
piacere.

Gabrielle: What does that mean?

Luca: Something naughty.

TEN

"Thanks." Paolo smiled when the punk fairy dropped a few coins in his box.

He hadn't expected his disguise to be so profitable. If Mr. Rizzoli found out he'd lost his phone and "chased" him, cutting his ties to the mob, he would have to turn to alternate sources of income and begging held serious appeal. He'd been outside Vice, an underground bar in downtown Vegas, for the last two hours, keeping watch for Mr. Rizzoli, and he'd already made twenty bucks.

Not that he wanted to be chased. Paolo liked everything about the Mafia.

He liked the respect the wiseguys got from people in the know. He liked that they had connections so that they got the best tables in restaurants, and the best seats for shows. He liked that they drove classy cars, and wore nice clothes. They could get things done that normal people couldn't do. Someone fucked with a made man, his woman, or his family, that disrespect was paid back in a way that meant no one ever fucked with you again. Once you were made, you and your family became untouchable. No one dared mess with a made man.

More than the money or power or respect, Paolo wanted that protection. He wanted to walk down the street and know that no one could touch him. That his family, if he ever had one, would be safe. He had never felt safe at home with his abusive, bullying father. Even after he'd learned to defend himself, that sense of safety had eluded him.

Mr. Rizzoli could give him the safety he craved. He protected his family, his crew, and his girl. Look what happened after the incident at Gabrielle's house. Mr. Rizzoli had gone crazy. He'd called an emergency meeting of his top soldiers at six o'clock the next morning and ordered everyone to get their associates on the streets hunting for the shooters. With his vast network of contacts, Mr. Rizzoli quickly identified them as Albanian hit men, and within three days he had tracked down the bar where they offered themselves for hire. Paolo's job was to call the boss if they showed up at the bar tonight.

Except he didn't have a phone and no money to buy a replacement.

The door to Vice opened and closed again. Two men with green dread hawks walked by him without even acknowledging his presence. Men never seemed to notice him in this disguise, but women always did. He hoped it was because they saw something attractive beneath the grubby clothes he'd picked up from a thrift shop.

He pulled his hat lower on his forehead. Did Michele Benni think he was good looking? Despite her father's rules, she'd agreed to go on a date with him, and this time it wasn't going to be a walk home with her father waiting behind the door. He was going to take her to The Look Out at the top of Lake Mead Boulevard. They could sit in his car listening to music, and hopefully she'd let him feel under her clothes.

Paolo shook his head, trying to focus. He needed to

prove himself worthy so Mr. Rizzoli would invite him
to join the crew. His lock-picking skills were a big bonus, but his tendency to make stupid mistakes and his
issues with violence and blood were a major problem.
Paolo didn't know how to toughen up. Every time he saw
someone being beaten, he had visions of his mother lying on the kitchen floor. Every drop of blood became her
blood, and he was seized with the same abject terror he'd
felt that terrible night when he thought she was dead.

He heard a laugh, and dropped his head just as two
men passed by, conversing in a foreign language. Both
stocky, with short-cropped blond hair and thick, Slavic
accents, they matched the description Mike had given
him of the Albanian shooters. One of them tossed a
handful of change in Paolo's hat and he gave a mumbled
thanks as they pushed open the door to Vice.

As soon as the door closed, Paolo grabbed the change
and ran to find a payphone. If he screwed this up, he
wouldn't be "chased," he'd be dead.

"Is that them?"

Mike shouted at Paolo over the riot of The Ramones'
"Blitzkrieg Bop" and pointed out the two Albanians
Paolo had seen on the street less than an hour ago. They
were sitting at Vice's sticker-clad bar talking with a
woman who had half her head shaved and the other half
done up in a spiky blue Mohawk. Not that the dudes
cared about her hair. One had his hand under her skirt,
and the other had a hand on her breast. Man, Paolo
couldn't wait to be twenty-one for real. The bouncer
hadn't bought his fake ID, but Mike had handed him a
few bills and murmured a few words, and Paolo had his
first taste of heaven.

"Yes, sir." He desperately wished he knew what Mike

had said to the bouncer, or how much money had changed hands to smooth his way in. He needed to learn these things if he was going to join the crew, although he doubted he would ever be able to intimidate anyone with a look the way Mike did.

"I want you to go to the back door," Mike said. "You're gonna hold it open when Little Ricky and I come through with the Albanians, and then you're gonna make sure no one comes into the alley. Sally G was supposed to be here, but he got held up. You think you can do the job?"

"Yes, sir."

"Good, kid." Mike patted him on the shoulder. "Now go."

Paolo pushed his way through the crowd, drinking in the ambiance of the dark, seedy bar where anything seemed to go from drugs, to smokes, to a woman riding a dude's hips in the back hallway as he fucked her against the wall. He was hard by the time he made it to the door, his teenage hormones going crazy at the X-rated scenes happening everywhere he looked. It was too fucking much.

"Look out! This guy's gonna be sick," Mike shouted down the hallway, pushing one of the Albanians in front of him, one hand over the guy's mouth.

Paolo spotted a gun pressed against the Albanian's back as Mike shoved him past Paolo and out into the alley. Little Ricky followed with the second Albanian, and Paolo closed the door behind them once they were outside. He stood in the alley, one hand on the doorknob in case anyone tried to come out, his heart pounding at the scene unfolding in front of him.

Mr. Rizzoli leaned against a brick wall, arms folded, as the two Albanians were shoved to their knees in front of him. A few of his soldiers and trusted associates stood nearby. Paolo spotted two more guys at one end of the alley, and a white van parked on the street blocking the opposite entrance. The van told him everything he needed to know, and his stomach tightened. Although he'd been hanging around the mob for years, he'd never seen a man get whacked, and he prayed Mr. Rizzoli planned to do the hit off-site.

"Names," Mike demanded.

The taller of the two swallowed hard. "I'm Fatos. My friend is Besnik."

"Albanian?" Mike asked.

Both men nodded.

"I hear you're for hire," Mr. Rizzoli said to Fatos. "Is that right?"

Hope flickered in the dude's eyes. Did he seriously think the mob would ever hire out their work? The Mafia did everything in-house, working quietly and discretely unless there was a message they wanted to send, and then they did it with style.

"Maybe. Depends on the work." Fatos shrugged. "How do we know you're not cops?"

Mike slammed the butt of his gun into Besnik's head, knocking him sideways. Blood welled up on his temple, and he fell to all fours with a moan.

"Would cops do that?"

Fatos paled, his skin turning almost translucent in the poorly lit alley. "Who are you?"

"We're the guys who have questions you're gonna answer," Mr. Rizzoli said. "Monday night, did you shoot up a house in North Las Vegas with a couple of AKs?"

"What the fuck? Are you looking to hire us, or not?"

"Answer the fucking question," Mike said to Fatos. "Or I'll kick your friend until he coughs up a fucking rib."

"Yeah, we did."

Mr. Rizzoli grabbed the dude by the hair and yanked his head back. "Who hired you?"

"Don't know his name." Fatos's voice was strained. "We were in the bar, made it known we were looking for work, he came up to us, needed a rush job, offered to pay above asking, so we took it on."

"What did he look like?"

The dude shrugged. "Dark hair, dark eyes, big guy, kinda stocky. He looked Mexican if you ask me. Or maybe he was Italian."

"You can't tell the fucking difference between a Mexican and an Italian?" Mike's tone rumbled with warning, but Fatos clearly had had enough, or maybe he was just tired of living.

"What the fuck is this? If you're not looking to hire us, then stop playing fucking games."

"Games?" Mr. Rizzoli smashed his fist into the dude's jaw. "You want to play games? Here's one for you. Did you know who was in the house before you shot it up?"

"No." Besnik pushed to his knees. "It was a warning job. Wait until the lights were off in the back, then shoot up the front."

"No?" Mr. Rizzoli let loose on Fatos as he continued to talk. "A woman was in that house." Punch. "My woman." Kick. "And do you know who I am?" Punch. Punch. Punch. "Take a fucking look around."

The two Albanians looked around. Mr. Rizzoli was wearing an impeccably tailored suit, as usual. Mike was dressed casually in jeans and a short-sleeved shirt. One of the soldiers had a thick gold chain around his thick neck, a white T-shirt, and a worn pair of jeans. Little Ricky wore a tracksuit like he was on his way to the gym. There was nothing and everything about them that screamed Mafia, and Fatos looked confused.

"I don't—"

"Cosa Nostra." Besnik cursed in what Paolo assumed was Albanian. "They're in the mob. You took a fucking contract for a hit on the mob."

"Yeah? Well fuck them." Fatos spat, his saliva landing on the tip of one of Mr. Rizzoli's fancy shoes. "You don't fucking scare us. We're the ones who do the work the mob is afraid to do. Shakedowns, executions, warnings . . . you pussies think you're too good to get your hands dirty. You need us, so enough with this fucking game and let us go."

"Mike?" Mr. Rizzoli studied the saliva on his shoe.

"Yeah, boss?"

"Did he just spit on my shoe?"

"Yeah, he did boss."

"Did he just call us . . . pussies?"

Little Ricky kicked Fatos hard in the ribs and Paolo's stomach churned. Oh man. This was going to be bad.

"Yes, sir," Mike said. "He called us pussies."

Mr. Rizzoli removed his jacket, folded it neatly and handed it to one of his soldiers. "Better check his balls, Little Ricky. Anyone who would call us pussies must have balls of steel."

Little Ricky kicked Fatos between the legs and Fatos doubled over, howling.

"His balls seem kinda soft to me, boss. You wanna check it out?"

"I would but my shoe needs to be cleaned." Mr. Rizzoli undid his tie and handed it to the soldier, while Little Ricky forced Fatos's head down to the ground.

"You heard him," Little Ricky said. "Clean his shoe. Use your tongue or I'll blow your fucking head off right here."

Paolo's heart thumped so hard he thought it might break a rib. He mentally begged Fatos to stop acting like a dick and lick Mr. Rizzoli's shoe. Maybe if he was co-operative, Mr. Rizzoli might let him off with a beating.

Fatos licked the shoe.

Mr. Rizzoli carefully rolled up his sleeves. He gestured to Little Ricky to pull Fatos up and then he studied the glowering Albanian.

"You disrespected my girl. And when you disrespect her, you disrespect me. And when you disrespect me, you disrespect my family. No one disrespects my family." Mr. Rizzoli slammed his fist into Fatos's nose, and then he let loose showering Fatos with kicks and punches as if he'd been holding back all this time. "You didn't check who was in the fucking house? You don't know the guy who hired you? What kind of morons are you? Who the fuck shoots at a woman? And who the fuck do you think you are calling us pussies?"

"What do you want to know?" Besnik moaned. "We'll tell you. Whatever you want."

"We want to know how loud we can make you scream," Mr. Rizzoli said.

And then the beating really began.

Paolo understood the way the mob worked. He knew *Cosa Nostra* protected its own, and meted out justice for every crime to ensure they were never challenged. But tonight, he realized that Mr. Rizzoli had sheltered him from what it truly meant to belong to the mob. When someone crossed the line, the message that was sent had to be understood by everyone in the know.

Besnik screamed, but the noise was drowned out by the pounding of the music inside the bar, the laughter of happy people inside, and the constant hum of traffic on the street. Blood spattered across Paolo's shoes. Bile rose in his throat. Before he could stop himself, he doubled over and relieved the contents of his stomach on the ground. With one hand on the brick wall beside the door, Paolo retched and disgraced himself over and over again.

Little Ricky looked over, and his face curdled with disgust. "Jesus Christ. What the fuck? What kind of man are you?"

A fuck-up. A loser. Weak. Just like his father had said every time he beat up Paolo's mom to make Paolo pay for his mistakes.

Maybe Paolo would have been able to suffer through Little Ricky's insults, or the disappointment on Mr. Rizzoli's face, or the fact he wasn't as strong as Mr. Rizzoli's other associates. But he would never be able to make good the events that happened next.

Overcome by his weakness, he failed to carry out his duty of guarding the door. Too late, he heard the creak of hinges.

"Shit." Little Ricky raised his gun, moved to intercept.

"This is your fault." Papa kicked at Mama's lifeless body on the blood-splattered floor, his gaze on a Paolo, cowering in the corner. "She was covering for you. She paid for your mistake. You'll live with this for the rest of your life."

Assailed by visions of his mother's crumpled body, Paolo bolted, his feet thudding down the alley, strings of vomit hanging from his chin. It was one thing to have to witness the brutal beating of two hired hit men who had done a great wrong to the Toscani family. But he couldn't watch someone die because he had fucked-up again.

Paolo slowed to a walk outside the projects at the corner of East Searles and Northeastern, and dropped to sit on the concrete steps. He'd been in a daze most of the way back to the shithole he called home. It was over. His dream was dead. He would never be in the mob.

Elbows on his knees, he dropped his head and heaved in a breath, choking on the fetid scent of rotten garbage. This late at night there weren't many people out on the street and he could sit in the darkness and watch the few unbroken streetlights flicker overhead. He'd let Mr. Rizzoli down in a big way. He'd humiliated himself, and he'd forgotten to watch the damn door. If the unexpected visitor was a civilian, Little Ricky would have had no choice but to shoot him. Paolo's mother was in a care home because he'd screwed up. But this time, an innocent man might have died.

He didn't have the courage to call someone and find out what happened. And even if he did, he had no phone because he was a fuck-up, just like his old man said.

"Hey, 'bro. You looking for something special?"

Paolo recognized Crazy T, a member of the 22nd Street Boyz, and a local drug dealer. Before Paolo started working for Mr. Rizzoli's crew, he'd done a lot of dope and Crazy T had been his main supplier. Paolo liked how the drug made him feel—self-confident, good-looking, like he was at the top of his game.

After Mr. Rizzoli's warning the one time he caught Paolo using, Paolo had deleted Crazy T's name from his phone and stayed away from the parties and friends who were part of that scene, fearful of jeopardizing his future in the mob. The Toscanis had kept him busy enough over the last few years that he didn't miss the high, but he'd never been as low as he was now. He was done. Humiliated. Embarrassed. And, as soon as the mob caught up with him, he was dead. Why not go out feeling good one last time? Why not numb the pain?

"Yeah. What you got?"

Crazy T checked the street and came up to the steps. "I've got two bags on me. Just give me forty. Is that cool?"

"I've only got twenty so I'll take one." He handed over the money and Crazy T passed him a clear, plastic bag. It was about the size of a baseball card. Inside were two folded wax paper bags stamped in bold pink: "Pink Label." Even cocaine had a brand name.

"Gave you a bonus 'cause it's been a while and this is good shit," Crazy T said in answer to Paolo's unspoken question. "It's new stuff from Mexico."

"Thanks." He stuffed the bag in his pocket.

"I'm still around, yeah. Just find me if you need more."

"It's just one time," Paolo said. "Had a bad day."

"Sure bro'. Whatever you say. But everyone who's tried this shit has come back for more."

Paolo sighed. "I'm out of work."

"Yeah?" Crazy T cocked his head to the side. "You looking to make a few bucks?"

"I might be. What are we talking about?"

Crazy T shoved his hands into his overly large jeans, tugging them down until Paolo could see the waistband of his Calvin Kleins. "This new stuff is so fucking good I can't keep up. I could introduce you to my supplier and we can divide up the territory. I'd take a percentage of what you earn as a finder's fee and you get all the dope you want for free."

"For free?" His eyes widened. "Are you shitting me?"

"No, man." Crazy T shrugged. "There's rivers of the stuff coming in to the city, and the head guy is cool with us taking what we need as long as we're getting the product out there. He's been getting pissed with me 'cause I can't keep up with demand, so it would be good to have you on board."

Paolo had never dealt dope before, but how hard could it be? He wasn't a good salesman—hell, he wasn't a good anything—but when he was high, he had all the confidence in the world. And he knew a lot of guys outside the mob. He could spread that shit around and make way more money than he had with the Toscanis. He would be able to afford to put Ma in the kind of care home where rich people went, and he could buy a nice car so he could take the ladies out in style. He wouldn't have the respect the mobsters got, or the sense of family, and he wouldn't have one hundred guys chomping at the bit to avenge him if someone gave him shit. But that dream was gone, and if Mr. Rizzoli spared his life, he would have to find a way to survive. Maybe he'd turn out to be good at it. Maybe even better than Crazy T.

"If I'm around tomorrow, then I'm interested."

"Gimme a buzz." Crazy T waggled his phone. "It'll take about a week to arrange a meet."

"I lost my phone. You know someone who can hook me up?"

"Sure bro'. I know a guy. He buys stolen phones, packages 'em up and ships them overseas. You tell him what you want and he'll deliver. I'm heading that way."

Paolo glanced down the street. Maybe sitting on the steps waiting to be whacked wasn't the best way to spend what could be his last few hours on earth. A smart man was always prepared, Mr. Rizzoli said. Paolo wasn't smart. And he wasn't a man—not yet. But he could be prepared for the crushing blow to come. At best, he'd be able to get in touch with Crazy T and set himself up as a dealer. At worst, he'd be able to call his mother and say good-bye.

ELEVEN

"*Shut up and drink*." Cissy read the sign above the small stage as they walked into Red 27, a well-known dive bar in downtown Vegas. "Well, this is going to be an experience."

"I can't believe I finally got you here," Nicole shouted at Gabrielle over the pounding music. "You're going to love it." She smiled at the tall muscular dude beside her who had covered his shaved head with a gray knit cap that matched his gray T-shirt emblazoned with a howling wolf. "What do you think, Clint?"

Gabrielle shot Cissy an exasperated look as Clint, the Porn King, gave a bored shrug. Friday nights were supposed to be girls only, but for some reason Nicole had begged them to let Clint come along.

Gabrielle followed Nicole to the bar with a nervous Cissy almost plastered to her back, skirting around worn tables filled with Goths, ravers, and a smattering of punk fairies. Dread hawks, lazy hawks, and shark fins were the dominant hairstyles, the more brightly colored, the better. It was the polar opposite of the Vegas tourists came to see, from the tagger-decorated walls to the mobiles on the ceilings, and from the eclectic clientele to the X-rated shenanigans happening at the tables.

She'd resisted Nicole's previous attempts to drag her to the dive bar, uncomfortable with being a police officer in a place known for turning a blind eye to illicit activities and hosting a less-than-savory clientele of bikers, punks, tattooed mongrels, and the odd assortment of criminals.

However, with her life in a tailspin, she needed a distraction. Luca hadn't turned up for their date Wednesday night and she hadn't heard from him since. Not only that, Theft was proving to be a major bore and she had exhausted her options for trying to get reassigned to the Garcia case. Cissy had suggested going back to Glamour, but after pushing her limits with Luca, Gabrielle had decided to walk on the wild side and check out Nicole's favorite place to party.

An aging hipster in a green knit hat greeted Nicole with a kiss when they reached the bar.

"Welcome back, my friend."

"King! These are my friends I told you about. The ones I've been trying to get here for ages. And this is my boyfriend, Clint. Can you make them something special?"

King gave her a wink. "Anything for you, princess."

Gabrielle cut Clint a sideways look. He didn't seem bothered about King's kiss or the wink. She imagined King kissing her in front of Luca and had to bite back a laugh. Luca was the most possessive and protective man she had ever met. No doubt King's lips would never have made it near her cheek.

"You've got quite the eclectic clientele," Gabrielle said to King, grabbing a free stool at the bar while Nicole, Clint, and Cissy went to find a table.

"Keeps things interesting." He poured three different

types of alcohol, and what appeared to be random mixers in giant beer mugs and stirred them with a spoon.

Gabrielle grimaced as he put the brown frothy drinks on a tray for her. "What are those?"

"Dive bar special." King grinned. "Loosens people up."

She found her friends at a wobbly table precariously close to the dance floor where everyone seemed to be dancing to anything but the beat.

"What is this?" Cissy tasted the drink and shuddered. "It tastes like one hundred proof alcohol. Is it legal?"

"It doesn't have a name, but it'll give you a buzz in less than five minutes." Nicole took a big sip and nudged Gabrielle's glass. "Drink up and drown your sorrows. You'll get over him."

"Maybe I should have ordered two."

Luca's brush-off shouldn't have bothered her, but it did. Even though what they had was just supposed to be about sex, she'd been looking forward to seeing him on Wednesday night after her terrible day at work, especially since Nicole was spending the night with Clint. She'd stopped at a lingerie shop and bought something out of her most secret fantasies, something so pink and girly—all bows and ribbons and lace—that David would have laughed. She'd showered, shaved, and put on a little black dress over her garters, stockings, and bra, along with a pair of heels that Nicole had bought her the first time she'd ventured out after David's death.

Anticipation had been a luscious treat. Humiliation had been a hard pill to swallow.

Even now, she couldn't stop berating herself for getting carried away, for being the pathetic widow so desperate to find love again she'd sit in her house all dressed up waiting for a man who had no intention of coming.

They are born to seduce, raised to seduce, and they

will die seducing the nurse in the hospital. Well, from the giggles and low murmurs she'd heard from the other side of the curtain when she'd been in hospital, that wasn't far from the truth. He probably had the florist on speed dial.

"If it makes you feel better," Cissy said, "I thought he was too intense, especially after you told me how he tried to beat up Jeff. I mean, who does that?"

"Ah. Clint did." Nicole glanced over at Clint who was watching two punk fairies dancing together. Her weak smile made Gabrielle's stomach tighten in a knot. She'd only met Clint two or three times in the year Nicole had been with him, and each time she liked him even less than the last. She particularly didn't like how submissive Nicole acted around him. The Nicole she knew didn't do weak smiles or simpering gestures. She was bold and confident in a way Gabrielle had always admired, but that smile said something else.

"You never told us about that," Cissy said.

Nicole shrugged. "Two weeks after we started seeing each other, we went dancing with a friend of his who was staying with him on a visit from Australia. His friend hit on me and Clint punched him in the face and threw him out of the house. Didn't you, babe?"

Clint's gaze sliced to her and away. "Yeah. Fucker stole my amp."

"It wasn't just about the amp," she whispered. "It was me. He didn't want his friend touching his girl."

Gabrielle had a feeling it wasn't about Nicole at all; it was just about the amp, like Clint said, but she didn't contradict Nicole. Her friend had had a rough start in life and had spent most of her teen years in foster care. If she felt good about the story the way she believed it, then it wasn't Gabrielle's place to say otherwise.

For the next hour, they chatted over drinks, squeezed

onto the tiny dance floor when the tunes were good, and tried to drown their sorrows when the house punk band took to the stage.

"Punk rockers should never attempt shredding," Gabrielle said as she sipped the last of her drink. The alcohol had finally taken the edge off her tension, and she could breathe a little easier with Clint away at the bar. "Even if they're trying to be ironic. And the front man sounded nothing like Hendrix and everything like he was trying to bend Jimmy Kimmel."

"He was watching you dance." Cissy gave her a nudge. "He couldn't take his eyes off you."

Nicole choked on her drink. "Give her a chance to get over Luca. It's only been two days."

"I was really crushing on him for a bit." Gabrielle took another sip and realized half her drink was gone. "He was very different from David. Very protective and possessive. Dangerous and exciting." She put her hand to her neck and realized she hadn't put on her locket after Nicole had taken it off her in Luca's restaurant. It was still sitting on her dresser beside David's photograph.

Cissy lifted a manicured eyebrow. She always looked perfect, no matter where they went. Tonight, she'd dressed in elegant punk: a tight, form-fitting black dress with strategically placed lace panels, ankle boots and chain bracelets. "Are you excusing him for standing you up and not answering your texts?"

"No. I'm just saying I've never met someone with so much personality and presence. He's all out there. He does what he wants and fuck the rules. It's very refreshing after spending all my time with law-abiding types. He makes me want to be a little bit bad."

"You should be bad!" Nicole's eyes lit up. "We should be bad together."

"Then you'll need to ditch the deadweight." Cissy tipped her chin at Clint, now talking to King at the bar. "What's he really doing here? This is our girls' night out."

"He wanted to come and check out the bar." Nicole stared down at the table. "He wasn't really . . . interested . . . in hearing no as an answer."

Before Gabrielle could find out what was going on, she sensed a disturbance near the door. She looked up just as the crowd parted to accommodate six feet two inches of breathtaking scowling male and two of his equally formidable friends.

"Oh my god! It's Luca."

"How did he know where you were?" Cissy frowned. "He's either a stalker or he's keeping tabs on you, both of which are illegal, I might add."

"I don't think a guy like that cares too much about what's illegal and what's not." Nicole pushed back her chair, and gave Cissy a not-too-subtle head nod. "I'm going to help Clint at the bar. You want to come, Cis?"

Cissy hesitated. "His friends are . . . uh . . ." She licked her lips. "I just might stay and meet them. To be polite. Politeness is good."

Nicole's gaze flicked to the two men who stood at Luca's back, almost like bodyguards, and her lips quirked in a smile. "If Clint wasn't here, I would be polite, too."

Luca descended like a hurricane. A drop-dead gorgeous hurricane. Gabrielle liked him in suits, but she loved him in the worn jeans he wore tonight, along with a tight Affliction T-shirt and a beat-up leather jacket. He looked badass in the most delicious way.

"Luca." Just saying his name did strange things to her stomach. "What are you doing here?"

"You're here." He seemed curiously irritated even though he was the one crashing the party.

"I don't recall inviting you." She leaned back, played it cool like she hadn't had the equivalent of six drinks in two hours, and the music wasn't pounding through her body, people weren't sexing it up around her, and she wasn't thinking about getting him alone in the darkest corner of the bar, and reliving their Glamour experience all over again. "You always seem to crash our Friday Fun Night. I'm here with Nicole and her boyfriend and Cissy." She gestured to her drooling friend. "You remember Cissy."

Luca tore his gaze off her to give Cissy a nod, and then introduced his friends. "Mike and . . . uh . . . Rick."

"You guys thirsty?" Cissy asked. "I was just heading over to the bar."

They both looked to Luca and he gave another nod. "Go ahead. I'll let you know when we're leaving."

"Thanks, boss."

Gabrielle watched them go. The taller of the two had the body of a boxer, all thick, ropey muscle, his hair military short. His equally stocky friend shared Luca's dark features but not his sense of style. She remembered them from the restaurant, but at the time she'd thought they were friends.

"Boss? Do they work for you?"

Luca folded his arms across his chest. "In a way."

She sensed the topic was closed for further discussion, and moved on to the more-important question of his presence in the bar. "How did you find me?"

"Your neighbor." He held out his hand, but she made no move to take it. "I stopped by your place to check the work the contractors had done and I saw Max in the next yard. Went to check it out. Talked to Mrs. Henderson. She mentioned you were coming here."

"She's nosy that way." Relief flooded through her now that she knew he wasn't stalking her and his presence here had a rational explanation. "She likes to know where we are, even though we're contactable by phone. Nicole thinks she's reliving her youth through us."

"She cares about you," he said. "I think she was worried about you coming here."

"I seem to be undamaged so far." She shrugged, sipped at the dregs of the drink she'd drunk too fast. "And I think we both know I can take care of myself."

"Come." He made an abrupt motion with his fingers as if expecting her jump up and do his bidding. "I want to talk to you outside where I can hear myself think."

"I wanted a date the other night. I guess we'll both be disappointed."

Jesus Christ. He had to get her out of here. If they were seen together by anyone in the know, they could both be at risk.

The easy solution would be for him to leave. After all, he'd promised himself that he would end it with her after he caught the two Albanians who shot up her house, and now they were lying in the desert at the side of the road, a message to the fucking Albanian mafia that they had messed with the wrong girl. He felt like a bastard for standing her up, and worse for not responding to her texts, but it was for the best. Safer. For both of them.

And yet tonight, he had found himself in his car, driving down her street, telling himself he was just there to check the work the builders had done on her house. When he saw Max in the yard next door, he felt compelled to investigate. And when he found out she'd come to Red 27, he'd texted Mike and Little Ricky and told them to meet him there.

Red 27 was not a good place for cops to be.

"Something came up," he said quickly, in response to her admonition.

"Was it something that paralyzed your fingers so you couldn't call or text?" Her lips thinned and she sighed. "Never mind. It wasn't supposed to be anything serious. You wanted to end it, and it's over. I'm good with that."

She wasn't good with that. He could see it in the way she dipped her head to mask the disappointment in her eyes. And, if he was honest with himself, he wasn't good with it either. He pulled up a chair beside her when it was clear she wasn't going to leave with him. "It was work."

"The restaurant?"

"My other business operations. And, to be honest, I was being an ass."

She tipped her head to the side, studying him. "Is that an apology?"

"I've never admitted to being an ass before."

Her lips tipped up at the corners. "You missed out on something special at my house."

"Every moment with you is special." Taking a chance, he threaded his fingers through hers and squeezed her hand. "Let me take you out of here and make it up to you."

She shook her head, but her face had softened and she didn't pull her hand away. "I'm here with my friends."

Luca hauled her off the chair and into a straddle across his lap. "Do I get the pleasure of looking after you until you're ready to go?"

"I have a feeling that's not the only pleasure you want tonight."

Heat sizzled between them, and he pulled her tight

against his hips. "I could pleasure you right here and no one would notice."

"Hmmm." She looked over at a couple barely concealing their illicit activities in a shadowed corner of the bar. "It does look like our kind of place."

Dio Mio.

His cock was hard in an instant. He had to get her the fuck out of here. Not just because of the risk of being recognized, but because he was only moments away from taking her up on her offer.

Did he want to go down that road again? What would she do if she found out that he had made good his promise to ensure the shooters never bothered her again? Or if she connected him to the two dead Albanians in the desert? Where did her loyalty lie? Would she choose Luca or would she choose the law?

Maybe he'd been too quick to trust her. She hadn't revealed she was a cop until she had to. For all he knew, her story could be just that—a story—and she had been undercover from the start. In his business, they couldn't be too careful. It was why they had a rule about associating with cops, and why associates couldn't become made men until they'd been with the family for ten years. Few cops would give up ten years of their lives to bring down the mob, although former trusted associate, Big Joe, had been one of those few. How much easier to send in a woman undercover, especially to the wiseguy most likely to fall for her charms.

"Luca?"

Her soft voice pulled him out of his dark thoughts, and his body responded to the sweet angel in his arms, the woman who twisted him in knots, challenged him, aroused him, and dragged him back for more. Desire sparked deep in his gut. He had never thought he would be attracted to an assertive woman, but the more he got to know about her, the more he wanted her. Gabrielle would never be crushed by his demands and needs. She would never give in when he was wrong. She was strong in a way he needed a woman to be strong. She'd fight to the death for the people she loved, and she wouldn't be scared to use her gun.

For the years after his father's death, Luca had struggled to prove himself worthy. Worthy of the boss's trust. Worthy of *Cosa Nostra*. Worthy of the family he wanted to protect. But when he was with Gabrielle, he didn't have to try.

She was a rule follower, open and honest, courageous and strong. There was no pretense with Gabrielle. And he felt his self-worth in her forgiveness, understanding, and acceptance. She saw the essence of who he was, untainted by his father's legacy or Gina's cruel betrayal, and gave him courage to be that man—a man who could do what it took to protect his woman. She made him wonder if, all these years, he'd been trying too hard. Maybe he had only to see himself as worthy to get others to accept him. Maybe he needed to trust himself, believe he was not his father's son, and others would, too.

"What are you thinking about?" She ground her hips against his shaft, rock hard beneath his jeans.

"You." He kissed her lightly on the lips.

"So honest," she teased. "You don't need to think about me. I'm right here."

Would she be right there when she discovered the truth? He hadn't been honest with her—not about who he was or how he lived his life. Could he be honest with her now? Would the punishment for breaking *omertà* be worse than the punishment for associating with a cop? Could he trust her? He'd trusted Gina, and she'd almost destroyed him.

I've been snorting this shit for years, right under your nose

I fucked him in exchange for dope.

You never loved me.

Matteo isn't yours.

Lost in a maelstrom of emotion, Luca wrapped his arms around the woman who kept him anchored to the ground.

"I guess here is good." She settled against him, her breasts pressed up against his chest, as she ground her hips against his shaft.

Lust beat away the last of his thoughts on matters that didn't involve stripping off her clothes and burying his cock deep inside her. "This is highly inappropriate behavior for a public place, Detective Fawkes," he murmured.

She looked up and gave him a sly smile. "Then we'd better find somewhere private. I think I saw just the thing we need down the back hall. It even has a door."

TWELVE

"Hmmm." Luca looked around the dusty storage closet in the back hallway of Red 27. "I think we should fuck in the bar like everyone else."

"I've never had sex in a closet before." Gabrielle pressed herself up against him. "And this way we'll be legal." It was the middle-of-the-road solution that catered to her need to follow the rules and his need to break them.

His hand curled around her waist and he pulled her closer. "The things I want to do to you aren't legal in any sense of the word."

Gabrielle grinned, studying his handsome face in the dim light. "I'm a closet virgin. Be gentle." She nuzzled his neck, nipped his earlobe, and curled one hand around his nape until his thick hair teased her fingers. Even the musty smell of the closet couldn't mask his scent— whiskey and cologne with a hint of danger.

"I won't." He lowered his head and took her lips in a demanding kiss, his tongue tangling with hers, pushing deep, taking control as his fingers dug into her ass. God, he could kiss. Her panties were wet and getting wetter the rougher he got.

"Fuck, you're a hot piece of ass." His crude words inflamed her. Beneath the civilized veneer, he was raw and wild and she wanted more. More dirty talking. More rough handling. More bruising kisses. She wanted to be manhandled. She wanted his hard body between her thighs. She wanted to ache tomorrow so that every time she moved she would remember him inside her.

She wanted to hurt, to feel, to live. And this man could give it all to her.

With one hand, she gripped the buckle of his belt, intending to pull it away, but before she could move, Luca captured her wrists, pinning her arms behind her back, making her arch and offer her breasts up for his pleasure.

"I like to see you like this." Holding her firmly, he pushed her against the wall and rubbed his chest against her breasts making her nipples peak beneath her clothes and her clit throb.

"How?" The word came out in a panted breath.

"Wet. Wanting. Doing what I tell you to do." He plundered her mouth, his tongue sweeping inside, tasting, testing, claiming. With her hands secured, and her mouth ravaged by his kiss, her insides liquefied, and she let out a moan.

"You can do better than that." He released her hands to unzip her dress, letting it fall to the floor. "Take off your bra and panties. I want to fuck you in just those boots."

Gabrielle's gaze flicked to the door behind him. He'd locked the old-fashioned door knob when they came in, but if someone outside had a key, there would be no hiding what they were doing, no quick straightening of the clothes. Even in the semi-darkness, the only light a faint flicker through the cracks in the door, she would shine like a beacon if she were nude. And wouldn't that just bring the police force into disrepute.

"Now, Gabrielle."

At his soft command, she startled. This was the side of Luca that frightened her. Not because she thought he would hurt her, but because his dominating side aroused her so fiercely, she didn't know where to draw the line. The sense of being controlled coiled inside her, undecided if it should spring. Pushing past her hesitation, she unclipped her black lace bra and eased her matching panties over her hips, stepping out of them when they reached the floor.

"Sei bellissima," he whispered before she had time to worry about being so utterly exposed.

He pressed his lips against hers, and then kissed his way down her body, licking the hollow of her collarbone, the swell of her breasts. He teased her nipples with his tongue and teeth as he cupped and squeezed her breasts in his warm hands.

Outside, the New York Dolls' "Personality Crisis" segued into The Stooges' "Search and Destroy." Brooms vibrated against the wall and cans and bottles danced lightly on the shelves.

Luca stripped off his T-shirt, and Gabrielle's gaze slid down his body, taking in the scars from his bullet wound, his magnificent tattoo, his pecs and chiseled abs, and the holsters across his body.

"You carry a lot of weapons." He had two guns holstered behind his back, and a knife on each side. "Is there something I should know about the restaurant business?"

"It's a dangerous world out there." His eyes crinkled at the corners as he undid his belt. "People are uncompromising when it comes to good Italian food."

She licked her lips when he unzipped his jeans, and

released his cock from its restraint. "It's a dangerous world in here."

Luca gave a low growl of satisfaction. "You like what you see, *bella*?"

His shaft was huge and thick from base to the plum-shaped head. Perfect. She wanted that, wanted him, wanted to end this slow tease and feel him deep inside her. "Yes."

Something primal and possessive flared in his eyes. "Touch me."

She wrapped her hand around his cock, smooth skin over rigid steel. He was a very confident lover, crude, and utterly in control. She hungered to get him at her mercy just once and drive him as wild as he drove her.

"Harder."

Warmth pooled in her belly as she pumped up and down his hardened length, imagining him inside her.

"You're gonna take me, angel." He tangled his hand in her hair, tugged her head back. "All of me inside that hot little cunt. I'm going to make you ache inside so every time you move tomorrow you remember I was inside you."

Desire coursed through her, setting her blood on fire. "God, I love it when you talk dirty."

"That's because you're a naughty angel, and underneath all that sweetness, you're as dirty as me." He eased her hand away from his cock, and knelt before her, teasing the soft roundness of her belly with his tongue before he moved lower to blow a hot breath over her mound. Gabrielle tensed in anticipation of his mouth moving where she wanted him to go, but he skipped over her throbbing clit and ran his tongue along her inner thigh.

"No." She threaded her hand through the thickness of his hair, parted her legs without embarrassment or shame. "Lick me."

"Shhh, angel." He held her labia open, and ran his finger around her entrance, sliding it slowly toward her clit. "You're not in charge here."

She groaned in frustration, her hands fisting his hair. Luca kept his gaze on her as he slicked one finger up one side of her clit. Her inner muscles tightened as he slid his finger down the other side. No one had ever paid so much attention to her pussy, and she'd never been on the edge for so long.

"Giorno e notte sogno solo di te."

Oh God. Electricity sizzled under her skin, making the sensations he was creating down below so intense she could barely breathe. "I told you not to speak to me in Italian. I'm already too turned on."

"I'm not speaking to you." He lifted her right leg, placing it over his shoulder, opening her to him. He kissed the soft crease behind her knee and then traced a warm, wet path up her inner thigh with feather-light flicks of his tongue. He murmured again in Italian, and then pushed one thick finger inside her.

"Ahhhh." So good. Need coiled deep in her belly, and she leaned back against the wall. "Luca Rizzoli. You were not just speaking to my pussy."

"I plan to do many things to your pussy." He withdrew his finger and replaced it with two. "Even pussies need attention."

With one arm wrapped around her hip, holding her still, he plunged his fingers deep inside her as he teased her clit, licking around the tender bundle of nerves but never where she needed him to go.

"What did you say?" she whispered, as the need to come grew to a crescendo, cresting and dipping in time to the lazy flicks of his tongue over her clit.

"Secret between me and your pussy." He murmured

again in Italian, the vibration of his lips and tongue sending ripples of desire through her core.

She clutched his head, moving against him, trying to get just one lick of his hot, wet tongue directly on her clit. "I don't like secrets."

"Some secrets keep you safe." His rough fingers dug into her ass, holding her in place, as he teased her in the most intimate way.

Luca had secrets. Even after the time they'd spent together, she knew very little about him. What other businesses was he involved in? Who were his friends in the restaurant and why didn't he talk about them? And who were the guys he was with now? Why did they call him 'boss'? How did a restaurant owner afford a Maserati and a penthouse in one of the fanciest areas of the city, and how did he get the owner of Glamour to give him her address?

She pushed those thoughts aside, determined to enjoy this time with him. The law had a term for a situation in which suspicion was aroused to the point where a person saw the need for further inquiry but deliberately chose not to make those inquiries so as to keep herself unaware: willful blindness.

And in the semi-darkness of the broom closet in Red 27, with her lover's tongue between her legs, the darkness in her heart replaced with warmth and light, sweet oblivion within reach, Gabrielle chose to be willfully blind.

"Oh God, Luca. Make me come," she whispered as her body trembled.

"Io sono tua, bella. Per te farei di tutto."

"Translate," she demanded.

His mouth, hot and wet, closed over her clit, catapulting her into orgasm. She fisted his hair, and her guttural moan rang in her ears as exquisite pleasure washed over her in wave after wave of intense sensation.

"I am yours, *mio angelo*." He pressed a soft kiss to her mound. "I would do anything for you."

He didn't know where to look, wanted to memorize every detail. Her plump glistening lips. Her beautiful blue eyes. Her swollen breasts topped with rosy nipples. Her hot, pink, wet cunt.

Unable to wait a second longer, he dug a condom from his wallet and sheathed himself as he stood.

"Ready for me, *bella*?" He curled his hands around her ass and lifted her to his hips. She locked her legs around him, bracing herself against the wall, her forearms on his shoulders. He didn't realize she had taken over until it was too late. As soon as he felt her soft, slick entrance glide over the head of his cock, he was done. With a soft groan, he canted his hips and plunged deep inside her.

Dio mio. She was so hot. So tight. So wet.

Her head thrashed, her long hair streaming over her shoulders, covering the scar on her chest. Sweat beaded on his forehead, and he sucked in a breath of the stifling air. He had fought his desire so long, he wouldn't be able to hold back, and he wanted her with him. Again. He was greedy for her moans of pleasure. He wanted to feel her pussy clenching around him, wanted to hear her scream.

"Oh God. Fuck me, Luca."

Giving in to his primal need, he pounded into her, slamming her against the wall, alternating thrusts with firm strokes of his fingers over her clit. He heard footsteps in the hallway, felt the vibration of the bass as Green Day's "Welcome to Paradise" pounded through the speakers, breathed in the scent of sex and the wild-flower fragrance that was now inextricably tied with her. Paradise, indeed.

He fucked her in a frenzy, rutting like an animal, nuzzling her neck, biting her shoulder, desperate now for the climax that hovered just out of reach. He was out of control, his vision blurred, his entire body focused on the exquisite, sensual woman in his arms.

"Don't stop. Don't stop."

No, he wouldn't stop. Couldn't stop. Even if Frankie yanked open the door and put a gun to his head, he wouldn't let this woman go. He pumped in and out, harder, deeper, faster. But it was the ripple of her pussy against his cock that sent him over. Sensation coursed through his body. His cock jerked violently inside her. His balls lifted, tightened, and he threw back his head and groaned as pleasure erupted from his spine, tremor after tremor until the pressure relented.

He leaned his forehead against hers, panting his breaths. He had fucked many women, many ways. But he had never fucked like this—furious, desperate, caught in a maelstrom of emotion. He wanted her in his bed and in his life, loved and hated that she was a cop, wished that there was a way they could be together that didn't end with him at the bottom of Lake Mead wearing a pair of Frankie's special cement shoes.

Pushing his dark thoughts aside, he brushed his lips over hers, needing something more, some connection. She whimpered softly, and he slipped his tongue into the welcoming heat of her mouth.

"I liked that," she said softly, pulling away. "I like it rough."

"Like" seemed too mild a word for wild, rough closet-shaking sex. Intoxicating, maybe. Addictive.

She was addictive. And all he could think about as he released her was: When could he have his next fix?

"I need some air." Clothes straightened, hair roughly combed, Gabrielle closed the closet door. Although the hallway was much cooler than their naughty hideaway, she needed a few minutes to come down after yet another mind-blowing illicit encounter.

"This way." Luca clasped her hand and led her down the narrow hallway. He pushed open the Exit door, holding it open with one hand as he pulled out his phone and texted with the other. "Just letting the guys know where we are," he said when she raised a curious eyebrow.

She instantly felt guilty for not doing the same, but before she could dig her phone out of her purse, she heard Nicole's voice out in the alley.

"I was just talking to him, Clint. It was nothing."

"You wanted him. You wanted to fuck him. I saw it." Clint's angry voice sent a shiver down Gabrielle's spine. "You're a fucking slut."

Gabrielle froze behind the partially open door, holding back Luca with one hand, not wanting to intrude, but wary about leaving Nicole alone with Clint in a rage.

"I only want you, baby." Nicole's voice rose to a pleading whine. "Let's go back inside and have a drink."

"You humiliated me out there," Clint snarled. "You need to learn not to do it again. You need to learn who you belong to. Now I'm gonna have to punish you. You know I don't like to do it, Nic. Why do you always make me do it?"

"I don't know. I'm sorry. Please just don't hit me where my friends will see."

Bile rose in Gabrielle's throat. Not just at the thought

that Clint was about to strike her best friend, but at the sound of Nicole's voice—a totally uncharacteristic defeated whimpering that made her question if it was even the Nicole she knew.

"Please . . ."

"Shut the fuck up. You know you deserve this."

Gabrielle was moving even before she heard the crack of flesh on flesh. Slamming the door open she ran into the alley only to see Nicole stagger back against the wall from the force of Clint's blow. How long had this been going on? Why hadn't Nicole told her? What kind of friend was she that she hadn't known?

"No, *bella*." Luca called out behind her, but nothing could stop her now, not even the damn heels that were clacking on the pavement stained with spilled beer, vomit, cigarette butts and gum.

"You fucking bastard," she shouted. "Don't you dare touch her again." Gabrielle smashed her fist into Clint's jaw. Clint had at least eighty pounds and four inches on her, but she'd taken down guys bigger than him when she worked the beat, and Clint was no hardened criminal used to life on the streets. Her strikes were hard and focused, designed to incapacitate him quickly and with minimal effort, but when he dropped to his knees, she couldn't stop. Anger and frustration, and her own self-loathing that she had been so wrapped up in her own pain she hadn't realized Nicole was suffering, demanded more.

"Stop." Luca came up behind her, wrapping his arms tight around her body, pinning her arms to her sides. "He's down. You need to back off."

"Get the fuck off me." She twisted in his grasp, but he held her fast.

"You're a police officer. You can't do this. This isn't your way." The urgency in his voice pierced through the

veil of anger that sheeted her vision. She blinked, saw
Clint groaning on the ground, blood dripping from his
nose. Horror replaced anger when she realized she'd lost
control. Horror, and a betraying sliver of satisfaction.

She shuddered in Luca's arms. "He hit her. He hit
Nicole. And this wasn't the first time. He's going to jail
for this. I'm going to make sure he feels the full force of
the law."

"Look after your friend." He released her. "I'll take
care of him."

Gabrielle ran over to Nicole and helped her to sit.
Blood trickled from the side of Nicole's mouth, and Gabrielle dug through Nicole's purse for a tissue to dab it
away. "God, honey. Are you okay?"

Nicole gave a bitter laugh. "I guess you know now I'm
used to it."

"I'm so sorry." She knelt beside Nicole and pulled her
into a hug. "I've been so wrapped up in David's death
and hunting for his killer, I wasn't there for you. But I'm
here now. I'm going to arrest him and get a squad car
here to take him to the station. He'll face a Battery Domestic Violence charge not just for tonight but—"

"I don't want that." Nicole shook her head. "I don't
want him to go to jail. He was just upset. He'll calm down,
and everything will be fine. He's always so sorry after it
happens. Things will be good if I don't mess up again."

Gabrielle froze, her pulse pounding through her ears.
As a beat cop, she'd dealt with many cases of domestic
abuse. She understood the cycle of violence. After an
abusive incident like this, there would be a making-up
period in which the abuser apologized and promised to
stop. Following that, there was a period of calm until the
tension built up again. Nicole had only been with him
for a year. She could break out of the cycle. She just
needed help.

"It's a misdemeanor. He might spend a few days in jail and he'll get a fine, community service, and he'll have to go to counseling . . ."

"He'll be so angry," Nicole whispered. "He'll hurt me worse than before."

"We can get a protective order."

"You don't understand . . ." Tears trickled down her cheeks. "He won't care. He loves me. He'll want to be with me."

"Gabrielle." Luca pulled Clint off the ground, holding him immobile with one arm twisted behind his back. "She's right. Fines, counseling, and community service—the solutions the law offers won't stop him. I know men like this, and there's only one way to deal with them. Your friends are my friends. I'll make sure he understands that no one fucks with my friends."

Gabrielle pushed to her feet. "That's not how this works. There's a process, a system in place. He'll be arrested and charged. He'll have to face a judge in court. He'll get a criminal record. The counseling and community service will help him understand that what he's done is wrong and hopefully he'll be deterred from doing it again."

She tasted the lie as the words dropped from her mouth. In Battery Domestic Violence cases, rarely did theory meet practice. She'd been called again and again to the same homes where she'd arrested men for domestic abuse. Luca was right. Most abusers didn't stop. Once they had that taste of power, not even the threat of jail would deter them.

"Do you not want to protect her?" he asked.

"Of course, I do. Protecting people is my job. But I have to work within the law to see justice done."

His gaze dropped to Nicole and his eyes softened. "We see justice in very different ways.

If it was up to me, this bastard would suffer ten times more than he made her suffer, and he would learn that there are no second chances."

"It's not up to you." Gabrielle folded her arms across her chest. "And vigilante justice is not the way to handle this. I'd be grateful if you could hold him until the police arrive, but that's all I want you to do."

His jaw tightened, but he held Clint down while she called the police. Part of her understood his anger. Only a few minutes ago, she wanted more than anything to beat Clint the way he'd beat Nicole. She wanted to see him broken and whimpering on the ground. She wanted the kind of justice Luca had offered—the justice she had truly been seeking when she entered the warehouse looking for David's killer.

Justice that had nothing to do with the law.

THIRTEEN

With a Monday-size cup of coffee in her hand, Gabrielle opened the first of dozens of new case files on her desk. Weekends were the peak time for lost and stolen property, and the other investigators in the cell-phone crime ring case had picked up a few leads. She stared at the page, unseeing, her mind drifting back to Friday night. Luca and his friends had left just as the police arrived, and Cissy had come out to lend her support when Nicole gave her statement. Back home, after much gentle prodding, Nicole had finally opened up about Clint and his abuse, making Gabrielle even more determined to get her the help she needed and ensure Clint was prosecuted to the fullest extent of the law.

Unable to focus, Gabrielle walked down the hallway to check in with the detectives handling the investigation into the shooting at her house. The lead detective was a good friend of David's, and they'd socialized often with him and his wife. After David died, she'd cut herself off from everyone that reminded her of their happy times together, and she realized now how isolated she had become. Maybe this fling with Luca was just about her finding her place in the world again by exploring the extremes.

Luca was extreme. He was almost the total opposite of David and the other police officers she knew. And yet, she felt good when she was with him. Happy. Alive. Awake. He had given her a reason to get out of bed in the morning that had nothing to do with revenge and everything to do with seeing the world through different eyes.

Did it matter that he had "friends" who he would rely on more than 911? Or that his friends were all Italian, called him 'boss,' and looked like they could crush boulders in their bare hands? Did it matter that he always knew how to find her or that he carried an arsenal of weapons or that he had offered to teach Clint a lesson that she knew in her heart Clint would never learn at the hands of the law? Did she want to dig too deep? The investigator in her warred with the woman who didn't want the fantasy to end.

She reached the door to the Investigation office, just as Jeff came barreling through, almost knocking her over.

"Gaby!" He grabbed her shoulders to stop her from falling. "I was just coming to see you. They found the guys who shot up your house!"

She frowned at his odd choice of words. "Found? As in someone knows where they are and is planning to arrest them? Or have they been arrested?"

"No. Found as in they're dead and a trucker found their bodies at the side of the road in the desert."

A shiver ran down her spine, and she gently eased out of his grip. "How did they know it was them?"

"The investigation team got a plate number from one of your neighbors that they matched to a tire print they found outside your house. Traffic cameras caught the shooters heading east from your house, and their car showed up again in the video surveillance feed of a gas station about twenty blocks away. The crime lab put the ID together. The gun residue on their hands was consistent with the bullets that were found at your house, and the crime lab even traced some of the dirt in their shoes to your lawn. Those guys really kick ass."

Her stomach twisted in a knot. "Was Garcia behind it?"

He shook his head, folded his arms, pulling his blue shirt tight over his broad chest. "No. Well, maybe. The investigation team sent the pictures around internally and the guys in Organized Crime recognized the shooters. They were Albanian hit-men who worked on a for-hire basis."

"So you think Garcia hired them for a hit on me?"

"Gaby . . ." He reached out and tucked a loose strand of hair behind her ear. His overfamiliarity made her uncomfortable, especially after she'd made it clear where she stood regarding their friendship, and she pulled away.

"There's a complication," he said, reaching for her again. "Organized Crime has taken over the case."

"I thought OC just dealt with Mafia stuff."

"The Albanians weren't just dead." Jeff said, his face taut and hard. "They were beaten, and . . ." He hesitated, filling the silence with a dramatic shake of his head. "What was done to them is something you only see from the Mafia."

"Don't sugar coat it for me," she snapped. "What happened to them?"

"OC has pictures. I don't think words could do it justice."

She had a sick feeling in her stomach, and glanced down the hallway to the safety of her cubicle. Police work had been Patrick's dream, not hers. Working the beat had been tolerable only because she'd thought she could change the world, and it gave her something to share with David. Narcotics had been a means to an end. But she had discovered that the intricate problems involved in investigation work were much like the puzzles she enjoyed. And this was a puzzle that was begging to be solved.

"Well, let's go see them." She followed Jack into the OC war room and greeted the detective in charge. Whiteboards filled with charts and diagrams covered the walls, and stacks of files and a few ancient computers sat on the tables in the center of the room.

"There are so many criminal organizations in the city, we had to request a room to keep track of them all," the detective said, leading her over to a whiteboard on the far wall. "This board is for the Italian mafia. A lot of people think the death of Anthony Spilatro marked the end of the Italian Mafia's long run in Vegas, but that's not the case. About twenty years ago, the big New York families all sent out guys to start up new factions to get a foothold in the city again, and they're all now into the second generation."

Jeff put what she assumed to be a comforting hand on her shoulder. She gritted her teeth, not wanting to annoy him and lose the opportunity to get information she wasn't sure she really wanted. The detective in charge was a friend of Jeff's, and he was spending the time explaining the situation as a favor to Jeff and not her.

"There are three big Italian crime families in Vegas—the Falzones, the Cordanos, and the Toscanis," the detective explained. "Each Vegas family is a faction of a much larger New York family. The Toscanis, for example, are part of the Gamboli crime family. The three Vegas families have been in a fight for control of the city for years, but it really heated up this year when some-one shot the three family dons and left the families in a power vacuum. The Toscanis have split into two factions with two cousins, Tony and Nico Toscani, fighting it out to take over, so effectively there are four crime families now."

Gabrielle breathed a sigh of relief. No Rizzolis. Maybe her imagination was just working overtime.

"Hey, you okay? I guess this isn't what you came to see." Jeff moved to walk away and she grabbed his arm.

"No. It's very interesting. I'd like to hear more."

"We have the structure set out here," the detective said pointing to a chart on the whiteboard. "The New York boss and his administration are ultimately in charge of the faction, but each faction has the same structure. The *don* is in charge, followed by his underboss and his *consigliore,* who is usually a senior advisor, and then beneath them are the *capos*, who are usually referred to as 'boss.' Each *capo* has a number of soldiers working for him, and the soldiers have associates, who are the only ones in the organization who aren't made men. It's like a pyramid with associates doing the bulk of the work, everyone kicking up a percentage of their earnings, and the bosses reaping the rewards."

Gabrielle studied the chart. "You have a lot of question marks at the top levels."

"That's because everything was all shaken up by the triple homicide." He pointed to a list of names on the side of the whiteboard. "We're not sure who is in what role now. We had an undercover agent in the Toscani crime family for ten years, feeding us information, but he disappeared about two months ago."

Question marks were good. She liked question marks. And she didn't see Luca's name anywhere on the board. Just because Luca was Italian, had friends who called him boss, and was a believer in vigilante justice didn't mean he was in the Mafia. In this day and age, she shouldn't be making generalizations about people based on their ethnic heritage.

"You want to see those pictures now?" Jeff asked.

Gabrielle swallowed hard. "Um. No. I don't think I could stomach them."

The detective laughed. "Well if you change your mind about the pictures, make sure you see them on an empty stomach. The victims had been out in the desert a couple of days before a trucker found them on Friday night."

"So . . ." Her mouth went dry. "They were killed on Tuesday?" The night Luca had stood her up for "business" reasons.

"Give or take a day."

"You don't look so good, Gaby." Jeff brushed his knuckles over her cheek. "They're dead. You don't have to worry about them anymore."

You don't have to worry.

I would do anything for you.

We see justice in very different ways.

She needed to see Luca. Willful blindness only worked until the blinders came off.

"I'm dyin' over here. On the floor. Dead."

"Ma. I'm sorry." Luca groaned into the phone and gestured to Mike to knock on the Glamour's door again. Little Ricky hadn't been seen after his last visit to Jason, and Luca wanted to check it out to make sure Jason wasn't playing games.

"You missed church on Sunday and family dinner." His mother heaved a sigh. "My friends, my family, even the priest, they came up to me and asked if you were dead. But now I hear you, I know you're not dead. I just have a son who doesn't have respect. You don't pray; you don't come to church. When did you make your last confession?"

"If I stepped into the confessional, I'd be there for a year." Luca mouthed at Mike to shoot the lock. No one was around this early on a Wednesday morning, and he was too on edge to waste time breaking down the door. His brief altercation with Gabrielle outside Red 27 had opened his eyes to the fact that they approached what they saw as a threat in two very different and irreconcilable ways. She was a cop. He was in the Mafia. Even if they weren't participating in what was essentially a forbidden relationship, they were on opposite sides of the law.

And yet, when he was with her, it didn't matter. She worked as a cop, but her job didn't define her. There was so much more to Gabrielle than the badge she carried; she had strength, courage, and determination. He'd been deeply moved by how fiercely she defended her friend. She'd rescued Max, cared for her elderly neighbor, and she'd set aside her own dreams to give her father something to live for and to save other families from suffering. She was a protector, just like him, and it didn't come from her badge, but from her heart.

Luca had never considered having a relationship with any woman after Gina, nor had he ever imagined wanting anything more than proving himself worthy of the Toscani family's trust and restoring the family honor. But he'd never imagined a woman like Gabrielle.

As a man of action, he had no words to describe what she'd done to him, how deeply she had embedded herself into his heart. All he knew was that the risk of being cut off from the mob—his friends, his livelihood, the culture that defined his life—paled in comparison to the risk of losing her.

"Where's Paolo?" Mike asked, pulling out his gun.

"I'm giving him some time to settle down." He didn't know why Sally G's late arrival had sent Paolo running, but he hoped he hadn't scared the kid away for good. "You go ahead to Jason's office. I'll be there when I'm done with Ma."

"Luca?"

"Yeah, Ma. Sorry. I was talking to Mike." He covered the receiver to hide the sound of the gunshot as his mother continued to chatter—something about his soul and Hell, and forgiveness for his sins. But there was no forgiveness for a man with blood on his hands, even if the lives he'd taken were the worst of the worst, criminals who deserved their fate. Maybe that's why Gabrielle hadn't contacted him all week. Maybe she'd finally realized who he was and that cops and Mafia didn't mix.

"I said Matteo missed you on Sunday," his mother said over the phone as they pushed the door aside. Mike went ahead to Jason's office while Luca secured the door so it wasn't visibly open to anyone on the street.

"He was very sad not to see his Papa," she continued. "You need to spend more time with him."

Jesus Christ. His mother knew just how to push his buttons and turn up the guilt-o-meter. But then she was Catholic, and guilt ran in her blood. "Ma, I spent all Saturday afternoon with him."

Guilt surged inside him when he thought about how excited Matteo had been to see him, even though he'd shown up hours late, and how sad he was when Luca brought him home early. At the time, he'd told himself a few hours wouldn't make a difference. Matteo needed to learn how to grow up strong and independent. He needed to settle down with his nonna and stop wishing he had a regular dad who would take him to ball games or biking in the park or throw a ball around with him.

Luca had never had any of those things, and he'd turned out all right.

Now, however, he just felt like the shit dad he was. And added to that was all the guilt and fucking anxiety about the secret he was now hiding from Nico and the rest of the family. He should just walk away from Gabrielle. Even if he could reconcile the cop/Mafia thing and somehow get Nico to bend the rules, he was bad for her, just as he was bad for Matteo, and just like he'd been bad for Gina. He wasn't capable of love. Gina had turned to drugs because he didn't love her. He didn't want the same for Gabrielle.

Porca miseria! He scraped a hand through his hair. He was back on the goddamned rollercoaster again. Should he stay or should he go?

"Friday night," she said. "You need to pick Matteo up at four."

"I'm working, Ma. Fridays and Saturdays are our busiest nights at the restaurant."

"So you're going to look after other people and not your son?" Her voice rose in pitch, and he had to hold the phone away from his ear. "Is that how I raised you? To abandon your family? Did I abandon you when your father left us? I'm getting my nails done with Josie on Friday and then I'm going out with the girls. Your boy needs you. He wants to be loved. He wants to see his father."

"Okay, Ma." Luca sighed. He was a senior Mafia capo. He had a crew of over fifty guys working for him. Last month he killed a couple of Albanian drug dealers and threw them into a lake. Every week he beat up guys who didn't pay their loans or were trying to muscle in on his territory. But he was afraid of his mother.

"Don't be late," she warned. "It's Josie's night off. Her husband's out playing poker with his friends."

Although Luca respected his mother, he often tuned out when she started talking about her friends, but something about Josie niggled at the back of his brain. "Is she the one who married a cop?"

"She was a cop," his mother said. "In a time when there weren't many women in the police. Her husband, Milo, was a capo in New York. Big scandal. It was a forbidden love. He almost died for her. You should ask her about it. The way she tells the story. So romantic."

A man almost dying for engaging in a forbidden romance didn't sound romantic to Luca. "Why wasn't Milo whacked?"

"He was chased," she said, referring to the fairly merciful punishment in which a wiseguy was banished from the Mafia and forbidden from doing business with any made guys, rather than being killed. "I don't know how he convinced the boss to spare him, but he did."

Luca let out a long breath. So it was possible, but at a cost of his Mafia ties, the family honor, and the business enterprises—all Mafia owned—that supported his mother and son and his drug-addicted brother.

He ended the call, promising to pick Matteo up on Friday, and pushed open the door to Jason's office where he found Mike with a thick arm around Jason's neck.

"Jason says Little Ricky was here yesterday to pick up the weekly nut." Mike tightened his arm and Jason's face turned red. "I tried phoning Little Ricky again, but no answer. You want to cut off one of Jason's fingers, see if he's telling the truth?"

"Let him talk."

"I'm not lying." Jason wheezed out a breath. "He was here. I gave him the money. He took off."

Luca studied Jason. The dude was a weasel. No doubt about that. Luca had checked him out and discovered that he'd been convicted on fraud charges five times, declared bankruptcy twice, and had a bad reputation with the local loan sharks. It was a wonder he still had his legs. But Luca was damned sure he wasn't lying about giving the money to Little Ricky. "Did you see where he went after he got the money? Or did he say anything to you?"

Jason shrugged. "He said he was gonna go across the street and have a meal. He asked if I wanted to go with him, but I had a supply truck coming in."

A warning shiver slid down Luca's spine, and he stood, feigning a calm he didn't feel in the least. "Mike will give you his number. You contact him if Little Ricky shows up again or you hear anything about him. We don't find him, you'll owe us the money."

"But I paid," Jason protested.

"I'll tell you what I'm gonna do." Luca patted Jason on the back. "I'm gonna forgo the protection payment and take a small piece of the action instead. How about that?"

Jason gave him a dubious look. "How small?"

"For you, *stronzo* . . ." Luca smiled. "Tiny."

FOURTEEN

"I'm going to be in the Mafia, like you." Matteo beamed as Luca opened the front door to Il Tavolino. He hadn't stopped talking since Luca told him he was going to let him sleep over tonight to make up for last Saturday. Luca blamed Gabrielle. She had cracked the walls he'd put up around his heart and made him believe he was capable of feeling. Now all sorts of emotions were pouring out. Uncomfortable emotions, including guilt.

Matteo might not be his biological son, but in every way that mattered, and in the eyes of everyone who knew them, Luca was his dad. He needed to start showing the boy some love because he didn't want him to end up bitter and angry like Gina.

"I'm going to wear suits and carry guns and ride in fancy cars and people are going to give me respect and call me Don Rizzoli."

"I own a restaurant," Luca said evenly, struggling to walk the fine line between truth and lies. "Don't tell people otherwise. I know it's more exciting to think that because we're Italian, we're part of the Mafia, but not every Italian is a Mafioso."

"But you are," Matteo said excitedly. "And Paolo wants to be a Mafia man, too. He told me he wants you to be proud of him."

Luca threw a questioning glance over his shoulder at Paolo. They'd picked him up after lunch to help with the search for Little Ricky and he'd been almost hyper where Luca had expected him to be contrite. He wasn't sure if the kid was overcompensating because he was worried he'd screwed up or just happy to see them after the week Luca had given him to cool off.

Not that he cared right now. It had now been three days since anyone had seen Little Ricky. His crew had checked hospitals, jails, bars, and restaurants, as well as friends and family. His car was still parked behind the restaurant, his apartment was untouched, and no one had called to ask for ransom. Little Ricky had never failed to bring in a payment, and Luca had discounted the possibility that he had gone on the lam. He was a good soldier and one of the most loyal members of Luca's crew. That left two options: he was a rat and had gone into witness protection or he'd been whacked.

Luca sent Paolo to his office, and led Matteo to the kitchen. The restaurant opened mid-afternoon on Fridays, giving him just enough time to have a talk with Paolo and make a final inspection before the customers arrived.

"We don't talk about family matters outside the family," he warned his son.

"*Omertà*," Matteo said in perfectly accented Italian. "I know about it. Nonna says it means silence. We have to keep everything secret. I'm good at keeping secrets, Papa. I didn't tell anyone Nonna lets me watch *The Godfather* with her. It's her favorite movie. She likes the part when the man pets the cat."

Luca made a mental note to have a word with his

mother about appropriate movies for six-year-olds and settled Matteo on a seat beside Mike. "Say hi to Cousin Louis. You're gonna have lunch with him while I'm busy talking to Paolo. Make sure he doesn't eat everything in the kitchen."

"How come you call Cousin Louis 'Mike', and I have to call him 'Louis'?"

"Because that's how it is." He didn't want Matteo knowing the wiseguys by their nicknames. Matteo didn't have Rizzoli blood, and although Luca would be a father to him, he didn't want Matteo involved in his world. He was a civilian, and he needed to lead a civilian life.

"Is it because Mike is his Mafia nickname?" Matteo asked, demonstrating that he was far more aware of what was going on than Luca had suspected. "Like Virgil 'The Turk' Sollozzo in *The Godfather*?"

Christ. His mother had a lot to answer for. "Mikey Muscles is his nickname," Luca said, scrambling for an explanation that didn't reveal too much. "He got it 'cause he never misses a day at the gym. Lots of guys go by nicknames, especially if they don't like their real name. Cousin Frankie's real name is Rocco, but when he moved to Vegas he wanted a new name, and he got stuck with Frankie Blue Eyes because the guys found out he likes to sing Frank Sinatra songs."

"What if I want a new name?"

Luca frowned. It was traditional for a made man to name his first son after his grandfather. As a result, he had followed tradition and named his son Matteo. Gina hated the name, and in the end, she had her revenge. No true first-born son of Rizzoli blood would bear his grandfather's name. "What's wrong with Matteo?"

"I like it, I guess," Matteo said. "But it's not cool like Mikey Muscles."

Mike grinned and bumped fists with Matteo before

they headed to the refrigerator to get down to the business of eating. Luca checked his phone as he headed to his office. Still no message from Gabrielle. He had texted her a few times since the Red 27 incident but she hadn't texted back, and he hadn't pursued her for a response. The altercation in the alley had highlighted a fundamental difference between them—one that he needed to think his way through if they were to be together.

Assuming she wanted to be together. Maybe she felt their differences were irreconcilable and this was her way of brushing him off.

"What's up, boss?"

What's up, boss? What the fuck was wrong with Paolo? "Get your fucking feet off my desk and sit up straight. Next time you speak to me, you do it with respect or I'll tell Mike to take you out back for a couple of lessons.

Luca took a seat across the desk and stared at his now contrite wannabe associate. "We need to talk about what happened last week. Whacking guys is not something most of us enjoy. That's why we've got guys like Frankie. *Cosa Nostra* takes in guys like him and beats the fucking empathy out of them until there is nothing left but a cold, hard shell. But sometimes we gotta get our hands dirty. When someone messes with what's yours, you have to make it right, especially if it's your family or your girl."

"It won't happen again, Mr. Rizzoli."

"Maybe it will; maybe it won't," he said, not quite buying the apology given Paolo's body language—slouched in the chair, arms folded behind his head like they were discussing the weather. "Who knows? Sometimes the body has a fucking mind of its own, but in this family, no matter how bad things get, we don't run away. From anything. We face our enemies as we face our fears. Head on. Remember that for next time, and think before you act."

"Will do, boss."

Something wasn't right. Usually Paolo turned red whenever he was chastised, and he folded in on himself. He was always desperate to please and became almost inarticulate when he'd done something wrong. The kid in front of him said all the right things, but he was so nonchalant the words didn't ring true.

He leaned forward, about to press the issue, when Lennie knocked on the door.

"I'm heading out, Mr. Rizzoli, but you got a visitor. A lady. She was here a few weeks ago with her friends. She says her name is Gabrielle."

Gabrielle.

She must have come to apologize for ignoring his messages. He made a token effort to pretend she was just another of the many women he'd fucked who had come begging for more, that he would easily be able to turn her away with sweet words and murmured apologies, and that nothing could ever come between him and his crime family. But his dick wasn't listening. And neither was his fucking heart. She owned him, and if anyone was going to be begging for more, it was him.

He sent Paolo to the kitchen, and said good-bye to Lennie, taking the time to slow the pounding of his heart. But the effort was wasted the moment he walked into the restaurant. His blood roared when he spotted her standing near the entrance. She wore skintight jeans tucked into long black high-heeled boots, a tight red tank top and a leather jacket that just skimmed her waist. Her long blonde hair was loose and tumbled over her shoulders in a golden waterfall that sent his mind back to their night in the closet at Red 27 when he'd fisted her hair and . . .

"I need to talk to you." She brushed back her hair, and he had a vivid image of that golden loveliness spread across her back as he fucked her over his desk.

"Of course, *bella*. We can talk in my office." There. He could do it. Cool, calm, disinterested. The first step in detaching himself if the price of forbidden love proved to be too high and she had come to say farewell.

She closed the distance between them until he could feel the heat of her body, smell the fragrance of her perfume. Sweat beaded on his brow, and he clenched a fist by his side so he didn't put his arm around her and pull her in for a kiss.

"I just came to let you know that the two guys who shot up my place have been found," she said bluntly. "They're dead."

He had no trouble keeping his face smooth and even. He'd lied to the cops before, and he could do it again. "I'm glad to hear they won't bother you again."

Her lips pressed together. "They were Albanian hit men."

"Interesting."

"Jeff thinks they were hired by someone else . . ."

Luca's eyes narrowed at the word "Jeff" and he didn't process anything she said after the bastard's name dropped from her lips. "You were with Jeff?"

"We work together. Well, not on the same team, anymore. He's still in Narcotics and now I'm in Theft. But we're both on the same floor."

Mine.

A tidal wave of anger crashed through him at the thought of Jeff anywhere near Gabrielle. Not only that, Jeff saw her all day every day. Jeff probably thought about all the things he wanted to do to her in bed while they had lunch together. When she walked down the hallway, he would be looking at her beautiful ass, the way her hair swung down her back, her lush curves, and her long legs. And if she turned around, Jeff would look where only Luca's gaze should fall . . .

And that was the end of cool, calm, and fucking disinterested. He'd given her space for a week and now Jeff was moving in on his territory. To hell with the rules and the risks. To hell with the Mafia's ten commandments. He wanted her and he would find a way to make it fucking work where they would have a happily forever ending and no one would wind up dead.

"Do you know anything about how the Albanians wound up on the side of the road?" she asked. "They were wearing Sicilian—"

A thin, high-pitched scream cut her off. Luca's heart pounded and not just because of the question he wasn't prepared to answer.

"Matteo!" He ran for the kitchen, and pushed open the swinging door, pulling up short when he saw Matteo standing in front of the walk-in meat freezer, face white, eyes wide. Mike and Paolo were standing behind him in a similar state of shock.

"Dad!" Matteo ran to him, flung himself into Luca's arms. Luca lifted his son, holding the trembling boy against him as he walked over to Mike.

"What's in the freezer?" he murmured.

"Little Ricky." Mike's voice wavered. "He's been hung upside down, naked, throat slit, letter G carved into his fucking chest. I already called Frankie."

Bile rose in Luca's throat when he glanced into the meat freezer, and even he staggered back.

He had considered the possibility that Little Ricky had been targeted for the money he'd picked up at Glamour, but this wasn't the work of an ordinary thief, and it wasn't about money. This was personal.

"What's going on?" Gabrielle asked from the doorway.

"It's nothing." He waved her away. "You go to my office. Paolo will take you there. I have something I need to deal with." He glanced over at Paolo still frozen in place. "Paolo, show Gabrielle to my office. Take Matteo with you and get him a soda and some biscotti, the chocolate kind he likes." He tried to set Matteo down, but his son clung to him and wouldn't let go.

"He's dead." Matteo's thin body shuddered in his arms.

When was the last time he'd held his son? Soothed him? Wiped away his tears? *Christ*. He was a shit dad.

"Papa, there's a dead man in the freezer."

Luca didn't like to lie to Matteo, but there was no way a six-year-old boy could handle that kind of trauma. "What month is it Matteo?"

"October."

"And what special time is in October? What are you looking forward to where you get to dress up?"

"Halloween."

Luca nodded. "And what you saw is just a Halloween trick Cousin Louis was testing out for a Halloween party. Do you remember the party Auntie Angela had last year? The one where there were skeletons and ghosts and pretend chopped off arms and legs? This is just like that. It's made of plastic."

Matteo gave a relieved shudder. "It was scary, Papa. It looked real. Even Paolo was scared."

"Cousin Louis is good at the pranks, but he shouldn't have used Papa's meat freezer, should he? Now I'll have to miss taking you to the park because I have to clean up. The health inspectors don't like it when there is anything other than meat in the freezer."

"Is Cousin Louis gonna be grounded?"

"No." Luca hugged Matteo tight. "I'll make him help me, and I think I'll tell him not to bring that toy to Auntie Angela's party. You stay with Paolo and drink your soda, and I'll call Auntie Angela to come and take you home."

Finally, Matteo loosened his grip. "I thought I was going to stay with you."

"We'll have to do the sleepover another time. This is going to take me a while to sort out."

"Please, Papa." Big fat tears rolled down Matteo's cheeks. "What if I remember it when I'm trying to sleep? What if I'm scared? Please. Please let me stay with you. I packed my bag and everything. I brought all my super-heroes and Transformers and books for story time and Nonna bought me new Spiderman pajamas. Please Papa."

He could almost feel the now-weakened walls crack-ing around his heart. Matteo had done this before, but Luca had never felt guilt like he felt now. Dammit. Be-fore Gabrielle, he'd never really felt anything, and now his emotions were out of control. "Okay. Okay. You go with Paolo and Gabrielle, and when I'm done I'll take you to my place."

He should have known Gabrielle wouldn't leave with them. She wasn't a woman who was easily dismissed. And as a cop, she had a nose for crime.

"What's in there?" She pointed to the meat freezer.

"Nothing you need to see." He edged in front of the freezer, blocking the door.

"Was that your son?"

Luca nodded. "Matteo. He's six."

"He said someone was dead."

Fuck. She wasn't going to let up, but he couldn't let a cop see a dead body in the freezer. She'd call it in and he'd have police swarming all over his restaurant. There would be questions, and eventually someone would put two and two together and get 'Mafia' as an answer.

"Kids." He tried to shrug it off, wary of giving her information that would put her in a conflict situation.

"You're a terrible liar." She pushed past him and walked through the door. "If someone is dead, I need to—" She choked off her words and gasped. "Oh my God."

"Come, *bella*. You don't need to see this." He put a hand on her shoulder, and she slapped him away.

"Don't tell me what I do and don't need to see," she snapped, her voice so raw and thick with emotion he almost didn't recognize it. She yanked her weapon from beneath her leather jacket and spun to face him.

"We need to clear the restaurant."

"Gabrielle, come sit down outside. You're in shock—"

"I'm not in shock." Her voice tightened. "I know who did this. He might still be in the building."

Luca and Mike shared a curious glance. "Who do you think did this?" Luca asked.

"A drug lord named Garcia. And I know because he killed David exactly the same way. I found David like this except he was hanging from our second story railing over the living room, and there was blood . . ." Her voice hitched, giving him the first indication that her cold, abrupt tone wasn't anger, but pain. "So much blood."

His rage went from a dull roar to a full-blown crescendo, pounding through his veins. "Was that your case? The one they pulled you off? You were after Garcia?"

"Yes."

Jesus fucking Christ. What kind of fucking police force would send a woman after one of the most vicious, violent, and ruthless drug lords on the West Coast. Stupid fucking police. The only good thing they'd done was pull her off the case.

"Got your message." Frankie walked into the kitchen. "Paolo let me in. I was only a few blocks away. What's up?"

Crap. He'd forgotten Mike had called Frankie, which was the right thing to do under normal circumstances. But Frankie was the last person he wanted to see right now. He had been raised in the old-school ways, and once he found out about Gabrielle, there was no way he would let her walk out of here if he wasn't one hundred percent sure she wouldn't betray them.

"In the freezer." Mike directed him. "And . . . uh . . . Luca's girl is here."

"Why's she got a piece?"

Mike shrugged. Even if he now knew that Gabrielle was a cop, he would never betray Luca. No one on his crew would. And especially not to Frankie.

Frankie headed to the freezer, and Gabrielle's hand shot out, blocking his way. "You can't go in there. It's a crime scene."

"You watch too many crime shows, honey." Frankie took another step, and Gabrielle stepped into his path.

"I said, don't go in."

"Luca, get your woman under control." Frankie's voice was tight with warning.

"Come, *bella*." Luca held out a hand and gestured her forward. "We'll let Frankie and Mike deal with this."

"Are you kidding?" Her voice rose in pitch. "Except for the tip about the warehouse, we haven't had a break in this case for the last two years. There might be evidence in this freezer that leads us straight to Garcia."

Frankie let out a long, low breath. "Holy shit. Is she a fucking cop?"

"I'm calling 911." Gabrielle holstered her weapon and pulled out her phone.

Luca held up a warning hand. "If the police come, they'll start asking questions. Rumors will get out. People will talk. The health inspectors will come by. The restaurant will get a bad reputation and that's bad for business."

"She's not going anywhere," Frankie said, reaching for his weapon. He would have no issue getting rid of a witness. Once the police came to investigate, they wouldn't stop until they'd established a connection between Garcia and the dead man in the freezer, and that connection would drag in the crime family Frankie had sworn to protect.

"Christ, Frankie," Luca spat out. "You don't need the fucking piece. No one is calling the cops. I'll take Gabrielle home, and we'll deal with this situation our way." And then terror would rain down on Garcia like he'd never seen before. The Mafia did not tolerate the execution of a made man. Garcia was looking at a long, painful, and very public death, and every member of *Cosa Nostra* would be looking for him.

"You can't." Gabrielle's voice wavered, and Luca could see the tremendous effort she was putting into maintaining her composure in light of the brutal reminder of her husband's death. "Interfering with a crime scene is a criminal offence. The evidence we need to catch Garcia could be in that freezer. All I've wanted for two years is make him pay for what he did to David, and now your friend has died because I failed and Garcia is playing games with me."

Luca's protective instincts grabbed him by the throat and he placed a firm hand on Gabrielle's wrist, forcing her to lower the gun. When he felt her yield, he stepped in front of her, shielding her in case Frankie drew his weapon and keeping her out of sight of the body in the freezer. He cupped his hand around her nape and dropped his forehead to hers. "This has nothing to do with you."

"It does." Her body trembled. "Why else would he be here? Garcia is after me. He came to my house. He knows we're together. He killed your friend the same way he killed David. This is a message for me."

"I got involved," Luca said, reluctantly. "This is payback, and it was directed at me."

Gabrielle stiffened in his arms. "What did you do?"

"Is she gonna be a problem?" Frankie was already behind her, his hand under his jacket where his gun was holstered.

Luca reached for his own weapon. If Frankie pulled on Gabrielle, he didn't know what he would do. Frankie was a made man. Nico's key enforcer. His friend. He couldn't shoot a made man without Nico's permission, and if he whacked Frankie, Nico would whack him, and Matteo would have no dad. But he couldn't let him hurt Gabrielle. She was his to protect.

Mine.

The word rang in his mind. Regardless of the risks, and his fierce desire to restore the family honor, his future did not involve him walking away. He let that certainty settle in his soul as he crossed a mental threshold with only the faintest sliver of hope his mother had given him as a guide. A cop and a wiseguy had hooked up before. It could happen again.

"No, she won't be a problem," he growled. "Stand the fuck down."

"Women are nothing but fucking trouble," Frankie muttered, dropping his hand. "With a fucking capital T. And cops—"

"I can give you what you want," Luca said to Gabrielle, thinking quickly. "You want Garcia. I can make it happen." She was an intelligent woman, a police detective. She'd started asking questions about him already. But now, Little Ricky was hanging butchered in his meat freezer, and no one was planning to call the cops. He had no doubt she would find her way to the truth about who he was and what he did.

"The way you were going to make sure Clint didn't hurt Nicole again?"

"Yes."

She twisted her lips to the side, considering. "Clint only spent twelve hours in jail," she said finally. "He was fined two hundred dollars and he has to do some community service. No counseling. No anger management. He's walking around and Nicole still has bruises, not to mention the damage inside that no one can see. I saw it all the time when I worked the beat. We were called to the same houses again and again. It never bothered me before, but it does now."

"Your system doesn't always work." He kept his gaze on Frankie as he spoke. The enforcer had his own methods when it came to protecting the family, and Luca had no doubt he would shoot first and deal with the repercussions later if Gabrielle said anything that caused him concern.

"I thought it did. I thought I could make a difference. But it seems the harder I fight, the faster I fall." The resignation in her voice and her defeated tone speared through him, ramping up a fear that she didn't care anymore if she lived or died. But he cared. So much that he didn't know if he could recover if he lost her. He'd cared about Gina, but this longing for something impossible, a forbidden love, was a tidal wave compared to the tear she'd left behind.

"Not if we work together."

She studied him for a long time, biting her lower lip.

"Do you know what you're asking me to do? If I give you classified information or if they find out we're together, I could go to jail. If I cross that line, I can't go back."

And he could find himself in Lake Mead wearing a pair of Frankie's cement shoes for sharing Mafia secrets with her. It was a one-way road for him as well. But he wasn't about to tell her that. Now that Frankie knew about them, their only way forward was together, and he could buy some time if he could convince Frankie and Nico that they needed her to find Garcia.

"Nor can I." That night he'd met her in the hospital, he never would have imagined six weeks later they would be together and he would be offering to do the one thing that could destroy his chances of ever restoring the family honor.

Her eyes widened ever so slightly and then she squared her shoulders. "I want Garcia any way I can get him. For your friend, and for my David, and for all the families who have lost someone to the drugs he's bringing into our city."

He felt a small stab of disappointment that their relationship, such as it was, didn't factor into her decision. But her fierce determination to win at all costs just made him want her even more.

"She's on our side," he said to Frankie, who had turned away to check out Little Ricky. "She's spent two years learning everything there is to know about Garcia. She has access to information and resources we can't get, and she's willing to help."

"You really think she wants to help?" Frankie spat out. "You think she's gonna throw her whole career away over a fucking drug lord? More likely, after we hand her Garcia on a golden platter, she's going to hand us over to the cops. We've been betrayed before. There's only one fucking solution here, and we both know what it is."

Gabrielle turned to face Frankie, her hands on her hips. "Six weeks ago, I didn't know any of you, and I would never have imagined I would be throwing away my career and working on the wrong side of the law to bring Garcia down. My life was black and white. People were good citizens if they obeyed the law and criminals if they didn't. And then I met someone I care about, someone I trust who made me see things in a different light . . ."

She cared about him. Luca felt a curious tightening in his chest. She cared, and she wasn't ashamed to tell Frankie. Even more than before, he wanted to be worthy of her trust, worthy of her affection. He wanted to protect her and watch her fly at the same time.

"I don't give a damn what you believe," she continued. "I have more to lose by telling the police about your friend in the meat freezer than I do by keeping my mouth shut. I'm tired of following the rules. I'm tired of keeping quiet. I joined the police so I could make a difference. Now I'm stuck behind a desk, and Garcia is on the loose. I trust Luca, and I'm willing to help him despite the risks. If you don't believe me, then shoot me. Either way it will end my pain."

"It's not just you I'm gonna—"

"No." Luca cut Frankie off, interposing himself between Gabrielle and Frankie. "It's not your call," he warned. "It's up to Nico. Gabrielle can wait in my office while we deal with Little Ricky, and then she'll stay with me until Nico makes a decision."

"What decision? Gabrielle looked from Luca to Frankie and back to Luca.

"Whether he lives," Frankie said, turning away. "Or whether he fucking dies."

FIFTEEN

Paolo carefully poured a small bump of cocaine onto a stolen credit card in *Il Tavolino's* restroom. Even with the bathroom door locked, he could hear Mr. Rizzoli and Gabrielle arguing about where she was going to spend the night. He hoped they kept arguing for a few more minutes. Just enough time for him to get his fix.

He'd forgotten how good it felt. After that first bump of Pink Label on Thursday night, all his fear and humiliation had faded away. He picked up a new phone from Crazy T's friend at a bargain basement price, and then they'd all gone out to party. Riding the high, he was funny and outgoing, charming all the girls and impressing the guys. The night lasted forever, and when dawn finally cracked the darkness, he sat on his front steps and drank in the beauty of the morning.

The next day he'd woken up feeling like he'd been hit by a truck. So he did another bump, and another, and then he called up Crazy T for more. It was good stuff. Better than anything he had tried before. This was what he needed to make it in the Mafia world. Cocaine was the secret to defeating the shame of self. He would ride the incredible high of self-confidence to the day he became a made man.

He carefully balanced the credit card on the edge of the sink and pulled out his straw. At the back of his mind he knew there would be no forgiveness if Luca caught him this time. The Toscani crime family had a no-drugs policy, and doing drugs in a *capo*'s bathroom was the ultimate in disrespect. But he had no choice. He was weak and stupid, just like his father said. He just needed a little boost, something to give him the confidence he needed to gain respect. Just look how he'd handled that meeting with Mr. Rizzoli. He'd been cool and calm. Mature. Mr. Rizzoli had been impressed. He could tell.

He inhaled deeply, felt the burn in his sinuses and down his throat. Within seconds, he was in heaven. He flushed the toilet in case anyone came in and checked his nose on his way out. Damn he was good-looking. If Mr. Rizzoli didn't need him tonight, he'd text Michele Benni, and ask her if she wanted to watch Netflix and chill. He Snapchatted her a picture of himself looking in the mirror to get her warmed up and headed back into the restaurant where Mr. Rizzoli and Gabrielle were facing off in front of an anxious Matteo.

"I'm not staying with you, Luca. I have a life. I have work. I have a best friend alone in that house and Max to look after, too."

"Hey, kid." Paolo bent down beside Matteo, whose crumpled face registered his distress. "You want another biscotti? I think Lennie keeps an extra jar over by the cake display. Go take a look."

"Papa's angry at the lady," Matteo said. "I thought we had to be nice to girls."

"He is being nice," Paolo said quietly. "He wants to keep her safe. She just doesn't understand. Go on. I won't tell anyone."

Mr. Rizzoli glanced over and gave Paolo the briefest nod to acknowledge his thanks for sending Matteo out of earshot. Paolo nodded back as he'd seen the other made men do. Of course, he knew enough to get Matteo away. He was a smart guy, very observant. And he was happy Mr. Rizzoli had noticed.

"Frankie doesn't trust you," Luca said quietly to Gabrielle. "And that means the crew doesn't trust you. They need assurances you're not talking to the cops, and that means we need to stick together." He trailed off and kissed her forehead. "I don't doubt your competence, but it would make life a hell of a lot easier if I only had to protect you from one person and not two."

It was as close to a please as Paolo had ever heard from Mr. Rizzoli. He must really be tight with Gabrielle. Not that Paolo blamed him. She was hot, and dressed the way she was dressed today, she was smoking. If they broke up, he'd make a play for her. He'd heard older women were good in bed, and how could they resist a dude as good-looking as him?

"I need to text Cissy. I don't want Nicole to be alone. And Max . . ."

"You can bring Max to my place," he said. "I promised Matteo he could stay with me tonight, and I think they would get on well."

Gabrielle stared at him aghast. "Matteo's going to be there? I can't do that, Luca. I'm not good around children."

"He's a good boy," Mr. Rizzoli said. "He won't be any trouble."

Paolo followed Gabrielle's gaze to Matteo over by the biscotti jar. She almost looked afraid of him, but who could be afraid of a six-year-old boy whose face was smeared with chocolate? Paolo had few good memories of his childhood, but his mother sneaking him chocolate was one of them. His father didn't want her wasting money on treats for Paolo, but sometimes she'd save just enough to buy him a candy bar, and slip it into his lunch kit on his way to school.

"No. I can't." Gabrielle's voice was strained, her face tight.

Did she hate kids? Some women did. Matteo's mom, Gina, hadn't seemed to care for her son too much. Paolo knew this because sometimes she'd call Paolo to look after him when she went out in the afternoon and Paolo would find Matteo in his crib wearing a soiled diaper and crying because he was hungry and thirsty. On the other hand, Paolo's mom had cared too much. So much that she'd lost everything trying to protect him.

Gah. That wasn't something he wanted to remember right now. He pushed the memory away and relaxed into his high.

Paolo's phone buzzed and he checked the screen. Michele wanted to meet up. Hallelujah. She must have liked the picture he sent. He was also waiting to hear from Crazy T who was setting up a time for Paolo to meet his boss. Once that happened, Paolo would be on his way to becoming the youngest guy ever to formally join the Toscani crew.

"Hey, Mr. Rizzoli. You need me or can I split? I got a hot date tonight." He figured this was a good time to hit the road since Mr. Rizzoli had Gabrielle in his arms and they seemed to have worked things out.

Mr. Rizzoli's eyes narrowed, and fear sliced through Paolo's gut bringing him crashing to the ground.

"Or not," Paolo said quickly. "I'm here if you need me." He wiped his nose with the back of his hand, realizing too late that the simple gesture might give the game away.

"Getting a cold," he mumbled. "Cold medicine's fuzzing my brain."

"Go help with Little Ricky." Mr. Rizzoli's voice held none of the friendliness Paolo was used to hearing. Maybe he was annoyed because Paolo had interrupted when he was about to kiss his girl. Why else would he give him the one job guaranteed to make him lose his lunch all over again? And in front of Frankie. That cold bastard didn't miss anything. He'd need another bump just so he didn't piss himself when Frankie scowled.

"I'll just go wash up first so I don't spread any germs." He regretted the stupid words as soon as they left his lips, but hey, maybe Mr. Rizzoli would find it funny.

His phone buzzed again as he entered the small bathroom. Relief surged through his body when he saw Crazy T's code word.

"Yeah. It's Paolo. Where are you? I need another couple of—"

"Crazy T's gone." The voice on the other end of the phone was deep, slightly accented, and totally unfamiliar.

"Who is this? How did you get his phone?" He locked the bathroom door and pulled out his credit card. The pain was already starting to kick in. Damn, it hadn't taken long for his body to get used to the smaller bumps he'd been using and demand something more.

"Crazy T worked for me. He recommended you. Said you were looking to make some money and you were going to help him out. Now he's gone, and I'm looking for a replacement. You still interested? You buy from me, keep what you earn, and you get all the product you want for free."

Paolo's head was buzzing for a fix, but he didn't hesitate to answer. No one became a made guy without setting up his own business. He could make a lot of money as a dealer and as long as he paid up to Mr. Rizzoli, no one would ask too many questions. Plus, he'd get an unlimited supply of the good stuff.

"I'm in." Tucking his phone under his chin, he emptied the last of his coke on the credit card and pulled out his straw. You got a name?"

"Ray. Looking forward to doing business with you, Paolo."

Paolo snorted and closed his eyes at the burn. His life was finally on the rise. "Yeah, me too."

Fucking heaven.

SIXTEEN

Gabrielle leaned over the toilet, emptying the contents of her stomach into the shiny porcelain bowl. The intensity of her delayed emotional reaction had taken her by surprise. She'd felt curiously calm when she left the restaurant with Luca and his son. Even when they went to collect Max and she caught a glimpse of David's picture on the dresser, her locket draped over the frame, she felt nothing but an ache in her chest.

But it was all coming out now. And in Luca's fancy marble bathroom, all shiny white counters and tiles, gray walls and accents, and the stomach-churning smell of puke.

Her body lurched again and she heaved, more liquid splashing into the toilet. She heard the door open, soft words, and then warm hands gently pulled her hair back, securing it with an elastic so it didn't fall in her face.

"I've got you," Luca said.

"Please go away." She leaned against the cool porcelain, feebly batting at the air between them. "I don't want you to see me like this."

"I would worry if I didn't see you like this." He held

a washcloth under the cool water and leaned down to wipe the tears and snot from her face. "Especially after you told me you'd seen a man killed that way before."

"David." She gagged, leaned over the toilet and threw up again while Luca's warm hand stroked up and down her back.

"Shhh, *mio angelo*. It's okay. You're safe here with me."

"I loved him." She sobbed in a breath. "I had been so lonely for so long, and then I had him, and Garcia took him away."

"He was a lucky man to have had your love." He kneeled on the floor beside her, his hand never losing contact, soothing the tight muscles in her back.

She drew in a shuddering breath. "At least you know what it's like to lose someone you love."

His hand paused. "I know what it's like to lose someone I care about. But not someone I love. I married Gina because it was the right thing to do. She was pregnant. Our families are both very traditional. She was Italian and was familiar with our culture and customs. Neither of us was under any illusions as to why we were getting married. We had no expectations of each other except to raise a good son. She led her life, and I led mine."

"It sounds lonely."

"I didn't realize how much until she died." He wiped her face again. "I found out she'd been doing drugs when I was out—cocaine mostly. She was an addict, and to hide it from me she used her body as payment."

Gabrielle emptied her stomach again and rested her forehead on the porcelain bowl, trying to push her sad memories away. "I can't imagine how hard that must have been for you. It was terrible dealing with my brother's addiction, but your wife . . ."

He gave a bitter laugh. "That is my guilt to bear. She said I drove her to it because I didn't love her, and I have to see it every day in Matteo's face. He looks like her."

She turned her head and frowned. "He looks like you."

"He looks like Gina." He leaned against the giant claw-foot bathtub, pulled her against him. Gabrielle sighed, letting her body melt into his.

"Maybe if she looks just like you, but when I look at him I see you, but with dark hair. He gestures like you, walks like you. Basically, he's your mini-me."

"He doesn't look like me," he said curtly. "And when he laughs, he laughs like her."

Gabrielle took his harsh tone as a warning not to pursue the discussion. She rested her head against his bare chest. He was wearing only a pair of pajama pants, although she'd been unaware of anything but her roiling stomach until now. "I would give anything to hear David laugh again."

He pressed his lips to the top of her hair. "Do you still love him?"

She took a moment to consider his question before answering. "I thought I did. I thought I'd never be able to let anyone into my life again because my heart was full of David. But I think what I love is his memory because what happened that night changed me, and I'm not the person I was when we were together."

Luca had lit a flame in the darkness inside her, but even that wasn't enough to beat away the shadows. Losing David had been horrific, but the miscarriage had been just as bad.

"I think I'm okay now." She pulled out of his hold and he helped her to her feet. "I'm sorry for this. I know you lost a friend today. I didn't mean to intrude on your grief." She went to the sink and grabbed her toothbrush and toothpaste from the toiletry bag she'd packed when they stopped by her place to pick up Max.

"I've lost a lot of friends, *bella*. Holding you gives me more comfort than I've ever had."

Everything in her ached to open her arms, to let him fully in, to share her most secret pain, and the truth about why she was uncomfortable around children. But there was more standing between them than shared grief. The body in the freezer had stripped away the last of her willful blindness. They stood on opposites sides of the law. And although they had come together to find Garcia, she didn't know how they could build a future when their worlds were diametrically opposed.

"I need a shower." Vomit clung to the strands of hair that had fallen down her cheeks before he tied her hair back, and her nightshirt was damp with cold sweat. She turned on the water in the pristine walk-in shower, and undressed, expecting that Luca would return to his room. Instead, he stripped off his pajama pants and joined her under the hot water.

"You don't have to do this."

"Not leaving you alone. Matteo's sleeping, and I'll hear him if he has a bad dream." He wrapped his arms around her and pulled her against his hard, powerful body. Skin to skin they stood under the warm water, hearts pounding together, chests heaving together, joined by sorrow in the silence.

"Mio angelo," he whispered, pressing a kiss to her shoulder. And with his tender words, the last of her walls came down.

"It happened in the shower." She spoke so quietly that at first she didn't think he could hear her, but when his arms tightened around her, she soaked in his strength and continued. "I was at Cissy's place. We were getting ready for the funeral and she sent me to take a shower. I looked down and I saw blood."

Luca held her so tight she almost couldn't breathe, but she felt safe—protected in the warm circle of his arms.

"I still wasn't thinking straight so at first I thought David's blood was still on me even though a few days had passed since I found him. There had been so much. The entire living-room floor was covered in blood. We'd just put in a white carpet and it was red. When I first walked in, I couldn't go to him because part of me shut down and all that was left was my police training and I was assessing it as a crime scene. But when the first responders arrived and cut him down, I stopped thinking and just sat on the floor and held him in my arms." Her voice hitched, and for a moment she thought she couldn't go on.

"*Cristo santo.*" Luca gave a pained growl and cupped her face in his hands. Murmuring in Italian he kissed all her tears away, giving her the courage to finish her story.

"I was pregnant." She gave up trying to be strong and sobbed. He'd already seen her throwing up; it couldn't get worse than that. "The doctors at the hospital said sometimes extreme shock can induce a miscarriage. And it hurt. All of me hurt. It was like he was being torn out of my body. It was all I had left of him, of our life together, of the child I wanted so desperately to have. I wanted to give her all the love in the world, all the love my mom gave me. David died in a pool of blood, and that night so did I."

"No, *bella.*" He stared down at her, his handsome face so fierce it almost shocked her tears away. "You didn't die that day. You suffered a terrible, tragic loss in the most horrific circumstances. But you survived. You soldiered on. You became a detective. You forged a new path. Your strength humbles me. I have seen men break and crumble when they've lost someone. I've seen them turn to drink and drugs to numb the pain. They gave up. You didn't. You became the beautiful, courageous woman I adore. You brought light into my life, and into the lives of all the people you have helped as an officer of the law. You made me feel when I thought I would never feel again. I will do everything in my power to help you have your vengeance, but you need to look to the day Garcia is gone, at the new life you've created for yourself, at the new person you've become. You are still weighed down by the past. You need to let it go."

"Take the pain away." She slid her arms around his neck. "Make me feel good, Luca. I want to feel you. Only you."

"Sei l'unica per me, tesoro mio," he murmured in Italian. *"Sei tutto per me."* And then he switched to English. "Because I know you will ask, it means you are the only one for me, you are everything to me. I am yours. Anything you need, anything you want, I will give you." He kissed her softly, and then he grinned. "But first we'll get you clean."

Turning her to face the wall, he squeezed out a handful of shower gel and smoothed his hands down her back, massaging the slippery soap into her skin, over hips, her thighs, and her calves. The fresh, spicy scent filled the shower, the scent of him.

He slipped one finger into the cleft of her buttocks and then between her legs, making her gasp. But just as her arousal sparked, his hand moved away, and he turned her to face him, giving her a perfect view of his taut, muscular body, and his thick, hard cock jutting out from its nest of curls. He was solid, utterly present, a lifeboat in a storm.

She reached for him, managed one firm stroke, before he eased her hand away.

"This is about you. I want to ease your pain."

His warm, slick hands smoothed down her arms, his thumbs rubbing her muscles, hitting pressure points that she didn't even know she had. She leaned back against the wall as he washed her, his hands never stopping, never missing an inch of her warm, wet skin. He paid perfunctory attention to her breasts, molding and cupping them only briefly, before he turned his attention to her waist and hips, her stomach and thighs. Water sprayed down on him, dancing on his skin like diamonds, carving rivers through the soft hair on his chest.

She widened her legs, drew his hand down to the apex of her thighs. "You missed a spot."

Luca chuckled. "I miss nothing. But if I touch you there now, and find you wet for me . . ."

"The two of us naked in a shower together . . . What did you expect to happen?" She pressed his palm against her clit, his fingers over her folds.

"I didn't expect anything. You're hurting, and I want to take your pain away."

She pushed one of his fingers deep inside her. "This will take my pain away."

He gripped his cock with his free hand, stroked his length so hard and fast she thought it had to hurt. But his shaft grew thicker, longer, the head glistening with a bead of moisture. Gabrielle watched him with fascination. She'd never watched a man pleasure himself before and she couldn't take her eyes away.

"You like watching me?"

Her cheeks burned that she'd been caught staring. "Yes. It's incredibly hot."

"Next time we can watch each other. I can't think of anything I'd like better than watching you make yourself come, except doing it myself." He gave his cock a final pump and kneeled down in front of her. Steadying her with one hand on her hip, he lifted her left leg and placed it on his shoulder. "Hello, pretty pussy."

Gabrielle dug her hands into his hair, tugged him forward, desperate to satisfy the ache inside her, fill the emptiness of loss with intimate connection. "Luca . . ."

"Shhh, *bella*. Let me play." His thumbs slid over her vulva, parting her folds, exposing her so intimately she couldn't help but blush. Her nipples were already hard and aching, so sensitive that the gentle stream of water made her shudder. But he just dipped his head and licked through her fold, scraping his teeth over her clitoris until she cried out, desperate for release.

"Oh God. I need to come."

"Not yet." He dragged a finger through her labia. When he brushed it ever so gently over her throbbing nub, she fisted his hair so hard it had to hurt.

"No more teasing."

He looked up, his hazel eyes so dark they were almost black. "Ask me. Use the dirtiest words you know. I want to hear words a cop wouldn't say. I want to hear you, Gabrielle. The real you."

Her body heated despite the cool water trickling over her skin. She'd never been one for dirty talking, but she was past caring, past worrying about what a police officer should and shouldn't do. If she went after Garcia with Luca, she would be walking a very fine line between right and wrong. So why not practice walking that line with a man who wanted nothing more than to give her pleasure and soothe her pain?

"Lick my pussy. Suck my clit. Fuck me with your fingers. Make me come." She shuddered as the last words slid over her tongue. It felt good to voice her desires. To own her pleasure. To break the rules.

"Ai tuoi ordini, cara." He cupped her ass and lifted her to his hot, wet mouth. The first stroke of his tongue

made her shudder, and when he pushed two fingers deep inside her, she let out a guttural moan. He licked and sucked, his tongue teasing around her clit as he pumped his fingers, all while murmuring in Italian, beautiful words that she didn't understand.

Gabrielle tilted her hips, ground against his soft lips, totally uninhibited in her desire for release. When she thought she couldn't take any more, when her head fell back and she clutched his head, he added a third finger, stretching her, filling her as he swept his tongue closer and closer to her swollen clit. "Come for me, dirty girl," he said, switching to English. "I want you to come in my mouth. I want to hear you scream."

He drove his fingers deep inside her as he sucked her clit into her mouth. Her climax pummeled her body, making her thrash and twist under the relentless stream of water as it washed her pain away until she could see a future, glistening and bright. A future with this man. A man who had made her see her own strength, who showed her that she wasn't defined by her pain, and that there was no obstacle she could not overcome. She wanted that future. Wanted him. She stretched out her hand, reached for it, found his heart beating strong beneath his chest. "Luca. O God. Yes."

There was nothing like watching Gabrielle cry out his name in the throes of an orgasm he had given her.

Nothing.

He withdrew his fingers and stood, hands braced against the shower wall as he took her mouth in a demanding kiss. He wanted her so badly he could barely think for the ache in his cock, but more than that, he wanted this to be about her.

His thoughts scattered when she dropped to her knees in front of him and licked those very same lips that had just screamed his name.

"Your turn."

"You don't need . . ." But his protests died in his throat when she leaned forward kissed the head of his cock.

"*Cristo Mio.*" His hand dropped to her head. "I don't do this easy, *cara*. I'm rough and I'm hard and I take what I need."

"Sounds perfect for a dirty girl like me." She ran her tongue along the underside of his shaft and then flicked her tongue over the crown.

Luca was a visual man, a sexual man. And the sight of his beautiful angel on her knees, water streaming over her lush body, her mouth swollen from his kisses, was too much to bear. With a low growl, he dragged the head of his arousal over her wet lips. "Open for me."

She parted her lips, and he pushed inside with a groan.

"I run this show. You understand?" He twisted his hand through her hair, jerking her head back. She nodded, and her hands slid up his hips, curling around his ass. Fuck, that felt good. He rolled his hips forward, pushing his dick to the back of her throat. She gagged, and he pulled back, giving her a moment before he pushed forward again.

"Dirty girl giving me her dirty mouth." He yanked on her hair, forced her to look up at him, her eyelashes glittering with water drops. So beautiful. Too beautiful. He couldn't take her like this, even if she wanted it, even though he was desperate to fuck her sweet mouth and he'd never seen a more erotic sight. He didn't want to dirty his angel. Not tonight.

Without warning, he released her. Shock, then surprise flickered across her face, but before she could speak, he pulled her up, spun her around and pressed her against the glass. "I want you like this." He kicked her legs apart, covering her with his body, his hardness against her softness, her cool skin against his heat. "I want you to feel me." He grabbed his cock, eased it into her deliciously wet pussy. "Feel my strength, my power. Know you are safe with me. Even when you are at your most vulnerable, you are safe with me." He thrust inside her hard and fast, one hand dropping to her soft, slick breast, the other braced against the wall.

Gabrielle moaned. "God, that feels good."

"Fuck. You have the sweetest, tightest, wettest pussy." Unable to hold back any longer, he pounded into her, his back bowing with the effort, hips rocking, muscles straining. He dropped one hand and rubbed the pad of his thumb over her clit, fast and rough, until her body tensed and she climaxed with a groan, her cunt clenching and tightening around him.

"Luca."

"Say it again," he growled. "That's the only name you're going to say when you come. Because you're mine. Mine to hold. Mine to pleasure. Mine to protect."

"Luca," she whispered.

With a low growl, he leaned down and pressed his teeth against her soft, warm flesh, his control replaced with a primal urge to mark her. He licked the wound then drilled into her, rocking her body against the glass until his balls lifted, tightened.

"Fuck. What you do to me." His muscles locked and pleasure shot down his spine, erupting from his cock in wave after wave of ecstasy.

With his heart still pounding, he pressed a soft kiss to her nape.

Gabrielle looked over her shoulder, her lips tipped up at the corners in a satisfied smile. "I think I'm clean. Let's go to bed."

"What the fuck, Gina?" Luca threw the packages of white powder across the room. "What the fuck is going on? How long has Matteo been in his crib? He's soaked and covered in shit and it's leaking down his fucking legs. He was starving, and so desperate for something to drink, when I walked into his room all he could do was point at his empty bottle and cry."

Gina leaned, languid, against the pillows in the huge bed she'd insisted they needed when they furnished the house. "I don't know."

"You don't know?" His voice rose to a shout. "I come home to spend some time with my son, and discover he's been abandoned by my wife so she can fuck her lover in our bed. Not only that, you're doing fucking drugs in my house. And all I get is 'I don't know.' You can do better than that." He kicked the body at his feet, his vision still hazy with rage. He had no idea who her lover was or how he had wound up battered and unconscious on the floor, the world having turned red the minute he opened the bedroom door.

"You're over-reacting." She sighed and wrapped her silk bathrobe around her slim frame. Why hadn't he noticed how thin she'd gotten? Or the dark circles under her eyes? Or the constant sniffing and reddened nostrils? How had he not known she'd been with another man?

"Over-reacting?" He grabbed a vase from the dresser and smashed it against the wall. "I gave you fucking everything. Everything you asked for. And all I wanted in return was for you to raise our son and do what a wiseguy's wife is supposed to do."

"*You didn't give me love.*" Her bottom lip quivered. "*You didn't love me.*"

"Jesus Christ." He grabbed the faux-Baroque clock—a gift from her mother that he had never liked—and threw it across the room, feeling nothing when it smashed against the wall. "I thought we had an understanding. I never lied to you, Gina. When you told me you were pregnant, I laid it all out on the line. I gave you a choice. If you didn't want this kind of marriage, I would have supported you and Matteo. Love wasn't part of the equation. We both got what we wanted out of it. This is how our world works. You knew I'd have a goomah. You knew why. And you knew that taking a lover would be unacceptable for you."

She leaned back on the pillows, curiously unmoved by his anger or the fact her lover was now unconscious on the floor. "As unacceptable as raising another man's child?"

The world slowed, narrowed, his lungs constricting until he could barely take a breath. "What did you say?"

Gina gave him a cruel smile. "Matteo's not yours. I was sleeping with other men before we had our night together. Many men. When I got pregnant, I figured you could give us the best life so I told you the baby was yours. I thought we'd grow to love each other. But you didn't love me. You spent every Friday with Marta and the rest of the week you didn't come home, and when you did, it was only for Matteo." She held up a packet of white powder. "I needed something to make it bearable, but I couldn't let you find out. You are so strict with the money. So I found another way to pay the dealers."

With nothing left to throw and an unbreakable rule about hitting women drilled into him since birth, he smashed his fist into the family picture that they'd had *taken shortly after Matteo was born. The glass shattered and the picture tumbled to the floor.* "Get out."

"You just need some time to cool off. I'll take Matteo—"

"You're fucking high, Gina. You abandoned him all day. It makes me sick to think about how many other days he spent crying, dirty, hungry, and alone in his crib. He might not have my blood, but my name is on his birth certificate and I've been part of his life since the minute he was born. Until you clean yourself up, and I know he'll be safe with you, you can't have him. Pack up your own stuff and get the hell out."

She gave a bitter laugh. "Are you going to look after him? By yourself?" She leered, swayed on her feet as she stood. "He's not your son, Luca. You've been raising another man's child."

He took a deep breath and then another. In his entire life, he'd never felt rage like this, never felt so totally and utterly betrayed. "Five minutes. If you're not out of here, I'll throw you out. And consider yourself divorced."

"You can't divorce me." She smirked. "Cosa Nostra won't allow it. We're together for life, Luca, darling."

"Gina, for fuck's sake. Do you really think they'll hold me to a marriage after what you've done? There is nothing more important in our family than a son. The family business is handed down from father to son. It's our name. It's our bloodline. It's what a father can give to his boy. I'm calling Charlie Nails as soon as you're out the door." *Charlie Nails was the Toscani crime family's attorney, a legitimate lawyer who had no issues working for the mob.*

Her face fell, and for the first time since he'd burst into the room, he saw a hint of emotion. She'd played her best hand and lost because she didn't understand the rules of the game. "Don't be rash, Luca." She dropped her voice to a soft, soothing tone. "We have a good thing going here. Look at our beautiful house, our nice cars, the shows we attend, the parties we throw. No one will know you're not Matteo's father. And if you've got a problem with the drugs, I can stop any time. I won't say anything about Marta." Her gaze flicked to the man on the floor. "And I guess he's not an issue any-more. Please don't take it all away. I made a mistake. Forgive me, caro."

Jesus Christ, he'd married a cold-hearted bitch. She didn't even seem sad that her lover might be dead. She wasn't sorry for neglecting their son. Only the thought of losing the lifestyle he'd given her made her beg.

"Out." He roared so loudly that the window shook. "Mike will come and get you. I don't want to see you ever again."

Unable to be in the room with her one second lon-ger, he headed down to the kitchen and called Mike, in-structing him to make sure she had somewhere safe to go. Then he called Frankie to deal with the trash on the bedroom floor. The only reason he hadn't killed the bastard then and there was because he didn't want Gina to witness the crime. She was no longer trustworthy, and given her vindictive nature, he wouldn't put it past her to go to the police. Frankie would handle it. Drug dealers were his special treat.

Luca opened a bottle of whiskey, and did shot after shot, barely tasting the bitter liquid as it burned its way to his gut.

He heard the wheels of Gina's suitcase squeaking over the tiled floor. She paused by the kitchen, but he didn't look up until he heard the front door close.

Even if he'd known what she was going to do later that night, he wouldn't have said good-bye.

Luca startled awake, his heart pounding. Instinctively, he reached for his nightstand. Ever since the Toscani civil war had started, he never slept without his gun. But the room was still and quiet. Gabrielle slept peacefully beside him, her golden lashes fanned out over her creamy cheeks. Her hand rested on his chest just below the wings of his tattoo of a crowned skull and roses. He'd been inked when he became a made man and the world was full of hope and promise.

His tension eased and he lowered his arm. It was the nightmare that had woken him—the last night with Gina that haunted his dreams. The taste of guilt lingered on his tongue, washing away the sweetness of Gabrielle's kisses. He couldn't go through that again, wouldn't survive that kind of betrayal. Maybe the dream was a warning, that he had let her get too close.

Carefully, he pulled away. Matteo was sleeping in the guest room. He could go and lie with him, get some distance as he figured out a way to put the brakes on the runaway train that had stolen his heart.

"Luca?" Half asleep, Gabrielle reached for him. "Are you okay?"

Are you okay?

He froze, half in and half out of bed. Women didn't ask if he was okay. Gina had never asked about his silences on the days he lost a friend, never patched his cuts and bruises, never understood that he felt regret every time he had to pull the trigger. And the women who came after her wanted only his money or his cock or the illicit thrill of sleeping with a man who shared nothing about his life.

"Baby?" Her eyes fluttered open, and his heart squeezed in his chest.

Baby. Although he was anything but, the term of

endearment touched him deeply—a balm for a soul he thought forever tainted by his choices in life.

"Shhh." He eased back down on the bed, and rubbed his knuckles over her cheek. "Turn over, *bella*. Go back to sleep."

She turned, sighed softly when he curled his body around her, threaded his fingers through hers, and held her tight.

Warmth suffused his body, and he was swept up in a fierce wave of emotion like nothing he'd felt since the day he first held Matteo in his arms.

Love.

This was love.

He closed his eyes and gave himself over to the rush, letting it flow through his body, filling the emptiness inside him, turning the darkness to light, making him strong again—strong enough to envision a future where a devil and an angel could make a life together.

Love had found him worthy.

But was he worthy of love?

SEVENTEEN

"Are you getting up?"

Gabrielle woke to find Max licking her cheek and the curious face of Luca's mini-me only inches away.

"Yes." Her stomach tightened and she felt the familiar pang of longing as she studied the little boy who would be about five years older than her child if she had lived.

"When?"

"Um . . ." She glanced at the clock. 9 A.M. When had she ever slept in so late on the weekend? David had been an early riser, and she'd gotten used to early starts and early finishes. "Now."

"Papa says we can't eat until you get up. He says you need to sleep, but I don't like cold pancakes."

"Neither do I." She gave Max a pat. "How about you take Max out, and I'll get dressed so your pancakes don't get cold."

He clutched Max's collar and turned, his face intense. Were children his age always so serious?

"Hurry."

Gabrielle turned in the bed, resting her hand on her

elbow as the soft morning light flickered through the window blinds. Her night with Luca hadn't ended in the shower, and she felt deliciously sore. She was also naked and had to wait until Matteo was gone before she could slip out of the sheets.

She felt lighter this morning, unburdened. The darkness had retreated, and in its place was a curious shade of gray.

After showering and dressing, she finger-combed her hair and made her way to the kitchen where Luca and Matteo were talking over a glossy gray-and-white granite breakfast bar.

"Sorry to keep you waiting." She moved toward the kitchen, and Luca's arm shot out.

"Guests on that side. Cooks on this side."

"I can help out," she protested.

"I'm sure you can." A smile tugged at his lips. "But I do have some experience in the kitchen."

"I thought you just ran the restaurant. I didn't know you also cooked." She took a seat on the bar stool while he dished out plates of pancakes and bacon along with a fresh fruit salad and steaming mugs of coffee.

Luca snorted. "You can't run a restaurant if you don't know how to cook. And I learned from the best. Our family practically lives in the kitchen, and my mother teaches as she cooks."

"I need to feed Max, too."

He glanced over at Max, sitting beside Matteo's stool like he belonged there. "Max has been fed and walked. He and Matteo had a great time together."

"I told Papa I want a dog just like him," Matteo said. "He likes to run, and I like to run. We could run in the park together."

"You have to discuss the dog with your nonna," Luca

said gently. "She's the one who would have to look after it."

"Why can't I live with you, Papa? Then we could have a dog and look after it ourselves." Matteo's lips turned down at the corners, and Luca's face tightened.

"We've discussed this before. I'm never home, so I can't look after you the way your nonna does."

"But why?"

Tension thickened the air between them, and Gabrielle picked up her fork, thinking frantically of a way to avert what looked like an oncoming storm. "This looks so good, I don't know where to start. What do you think, Matteo? What's best?"

"Start with the pancakes," Matteo said. "Papa makes them special for guests."

Gabrielle tamped down an unexpected surge of jealousy. Of course, Luca would have had other women over for the night. She'd met one of his exes at the restaurant, and she was sure there were others. How could there not be? He oozed sex appeal.

"I'm sure they're very good." She focused on her pancake, not wanting to look up and see the truth in Luca's eyes while she tried to get a handle on her emotions. But dammit, he was hers.

"Best pancakes ever." She savored the sweetness of pure maple syrup soaked into the light fluffy pancakes.

Matteo beamed. "She likes them, Papa."

"Now we know what to make tomorrow."

"Tomorrow? I just came for one—" She cut herself off when Matteo tugged on her hair.

"You have nice hair. It's soft and golden."

"Thank you."

He touched her cheek. "You're pretty, too. And your eyes are very blue like the sky."

Her lips quivered with a smile. "I see your father is teaching you all sorts of nice things to say to girls."

Laughing, Luca opened his hands. "It's part of the culture."

"And very effective in setting him up to be a master of seduction when he grows up."

Luca's phone buzzed on the counter and he excused himself to take the call. Left alone with Matteo, Gabrielle's heart pounded and her mouth went dry. She sipped her coffee, struggling with a maelstrom of emotion. She'd tried to avoid being around children for the last two years so she wouldn't be reminded of what she had lost. And now that she was alone with Luca's son, the pain started to resurface. She had always assumed her baby would be a girl. But what if he'd been a boy? Would he have looked like David, the way Matteo looked like Luca, or would he have looked like her?

"You're not eating," Matteo pointed out.

"I was just thinking about something, and it took my mind off the food." She speared another piece of pancake.

"Papa didn't know if you liked pancakes. One lady who stayed over only drank coffee for breakfast." He shoved a pancake in his mouth, smearing syrup on his cheek.

She didn't want to know, but she did. "Does he have a lot of friends stay over?"

"I don't know. He's never let me stay here before, but he told me about the coffee lady. Do you get to stay here again tonight? Do you think Papa will let me stay, too?"

Gabrielle put down her knife and fork and reached for his napkin. "I was just here for one night. I have some things to do this weekend, and on Monday I have to go to work."

"Where do you work?"

"I'm a police officer." She dabbed at his cheek, wiping the syrup away.

Matteo's eyes lit up. "That's cool. None of Papa's other friends are police officers. Do you have a gun?"

"Yes."

He dropped his knife and fork and jumped off his chair. "Can I see it?"

"Well, I don't know if your dad would like that." She tucked into the crispy bacon and finished it in two mouthfuls. There were advantages to sleeping with a man who knew how to cook. "How about we ask him when he's done his call?"

Matteo hung his head and his shoulders slumped. "He'll say no. Papa doesn't like guns."

She snorted a laugh and grabbed a napkin to hide her smile. "Well, that's very sensible. Guns are dangerous. We use them only if we have to."

"What about a police car?" He climbed back on his seat. "Do you have a police car? Can I go for a ride and turn on the siren?"

"I don't use one anymore. Only patrol officers use police cars. I'm a detective now."

He gave an exaggerated sigh. "What about a badge or a uniform? Do you have those?"

"I do have a badge with me. I can show it to you after breakfast." She smiled, realized that she'd been talking to Matteo for at least ten minutes and she hadn't had any flashbacks, and the sadness had retreated under the constant barrage of questions.

Matteo beamed. "None of my friends know a police officer in real life. I'm going to tell them about you." He hesitated, a piece of bacon half in and half out of his mouth. "Are you Papa's girlfriend?"

She opened her mouth and closed it again. What were they? Definitely more than a casual hook-up. Friends?

With benefits? They'd never talked about what they had between them, but after last night when they'd opened up to each other, she felt closer to him than anyone she'd ever known except her mom—closer even than David. "I guess we're friends."

"Gabrielle is Papa's girl."

She looked up, saw Luca standing in the doorway, leaning against the doorframe like he'd been there for a long time. His arms were folded over his chest, highlighting the bulge of his biceps beneath the sleeves of his white T-shirt.

"His only girl." He added, lifting an eyebrow to let her know he had, indeed, heard most of the conversation.

"Woman," she corrected. "And I'm not your—"

Luca chuckled, cutting her off. "Get over here then, woman, and give your man a kiss."

She glanced over at Matteo and gave a warning shake of her head, but Luca just crossed the kitchen and pulled her into his arms. "He's been raised in an Italian household, *bella*. We're affectionate people. Everyone kisses, and he's seen this kind of affection between my sister, Angela, and her boyfriend, and my brother, Alex, and the many girlfriends who have shown up at the breakfast table, only to be replaced the next week. If you're going to be with me, you need to get used to it."

Was she "with" him? Certainly, they were working together to catch Garcia. But could they be more? He seemed to have made a unilateral decision about their relationship status, and if he'd been a normal guy in a normal job, she would have been happy to know he wanted them to be together. She cared about him deeply, and the more time she spent with him, the more she found to like. He had been respectful and caring when she told him about her past, and he had never shown any jealousy or resentment about her relationship with David.

He was fiercely protective, funny, and charming; he clearly loved his mother and siblings and was adored by his son. So unlike the stereotype of a typical mobster.

And yet that's exactly what he was. Although he'd never said the words, she knew he was in the mob. How did he think their relationship would work? His friends and family wouldn't trust her. And what if he told her he'd done something illegal? She'd be in a conflict position, her knowledge making her an accomplice to the crime. Of course, conflicts would be the least of her worries if Agent Palmer found out she had shared police information and joined forces with the mob to hunt down Garcia.

Although she'd boldly claimed she was willing to take the risk of going to jail to catch Garcia, she hadn't thought it through. Yes, she was willing to risk her career to catch him, but she wasn't prepared to risk her freedom. The night she met Luca was the first time she'd thought that maybe there was something else to live for, and now, as he wrapped his arms around her in his sunlit kitchen, in the kind of idyllic scene she had never allowed herself to imagine since David's death, there was another.

Of course, he didn't just peck her on the lips. No. Matteo was treated to a full-on, full-mouth, tongue-in-all-the-wrong places (if you were being avidly watched by a six-year-old), hands-on-the-ass (thank God, he couldn't see behind her) kiss.

"You taste sweet," she said licking her lips.

"You taste like sex," he murmured in her ear. "If Matteo wasn't here, I'd tie you to the table, pour syrup all over you and lick it off until you were begging to come."

Her eyes widened and mouth went dry. "Why does everything have to be about sex with you?"

"I'm a sexual man."

"Yes, you are." Heat pooled between her legs. "I'm

suddenly very glad we're not alone and we have your mini-me to take down the heat. You two are so alike it's scary."

Luca stiffened and pulled away. "I told you. We are nothing alike."

"Yes, you are." Puzzled, she stroked a soothing finger along his jaw. "You have the same shape of face, the same curve to your eyebrows, same eyes and nose. His hair has the same wave as yours, although it's dark. You both have hazel eyes—"

"Gabrielle." Luca snapped, his voice slicing through the room. "I know you have good intentions, but you are seeing things that aren't there. He looks like Gina. He doesn't look like me. It's not possible that he looks like me. Why the fuck do you keep bringing it up?"

She glanced over at Matteo who had frozen in place, a piece of pancake hanging from his fork inches away from his mouth. Her heart went out to him, just as it had gone out to Max when she'd seen him that first day in the shelter, cowering in the corner. She understood better than anyone what it was like to lose someone but to burden Matteo with his issues wasn't right.

"Excuse us please, sweetheart." She smiled at Matteo so he wouldn't think anything was wrong. "I'm going to steal your dad away for a second. I think Max would be happy to taste that pancake on your fork." She shoved Luca hard toward the bedroom.

"I need to speak to you. Alone."

If she hadn't been so angry, Luca's shocked expression would have been almost comical, as was his uncharacteristic obedience.

"Don't swear at me." She poked him in the chest after closing the bedroom door behind them. "And get over yourself. I don't know what your problem is, but it's not that beautiful, sweet little boy out there who absolutely adores you and wants desperately to feel a connection with the father he loves. Maybe he has some of Gina's features. So what. Just because she wasn't the perfect mom, doesn't make him any less your son."

Luca swept his hand over the dresser, smashing a vase against the wall. Shards of pottery tumbled over the floor like purple rain. "My relationship with Matteo is my business. You don't know anything about me. You don't know anything about him. He doesn't need you to defend him. He's perfectly happy. He understands why things are the way they are."

Gabrielle stared at him, trying to understand what had set him off. She'd touched this nerve last night and backed off, but after talking to Matteo this morning, hearing the longing in his voice, and seeing his shock and pain when his father refused to acknowledge their resemblance, she had to say something. She wasn't the same woman who had sat for two years in an office pushing paper while a monster roamed the city taking innocent lives. She had a voice, and Matteo needed someone to speak for him, someone who wasn't afraid to push back against the two hundred pounds of angry alpha male now glowering at her from across the room.

"What about the mole on his ear?"

"Gabrielle." His voice thundered through the room. "Leave the subject the fuck alone. It's none of your business."

Even when you are at your most vulnerable, you are safe with me.

She closed the distance between them and leaned up to press a soft kiss behind his left ear. "You have a mole here," she said softly. "Matteo has the same one, in the same place. They're hereditary. The one I have on my earlobe is the same as my mother's and her mother had it, too."

His face smoothed to an expressionless mask and he took a step away. "We've talked enough about this. Don't bring it up again."

"Well then, I guess Max and I will get going," she said. "Because there's a little boy out there who is desperate to spend the day with his dad. And I think his dad needs to spend a little less time being an ass and a little more time with him."

"Gabrielle." He called to her as she walked away, but for once he didn't follow.

EIGHTEEN

"Get in the car."

Luca pulled his SUV over to the side of the road with a loud screech. Damn woman storming out of his apartment. Did she not realize Frankie and his crew were on the street just waiting for an opportunity to prove she couldn't be trusted? He'd already explained to her that they needed Nico's approval to move ahead with the plan to catch Garcia. What he hadn't explained was that it was also up to Nico whether he lived or died. He'd broken the rule about associating with a cop, and by now Nico would know about his relationship with her and would have made a decision about what to do.

Gabrielle ignored him and continued to walk down the residential street with Max sniffing bushes by her side.

Sweat beaded on his forehead as the midday sun blasted into the car. "Gabrielle. You can't walk all the way home. It's too far. And I told Frankie you would stay with me until the meeting with Nico." He gritted his teeth at the hint of pleading tone in his voice. *Capos* didn't plead. He didn't plead. But dammit, she'd left him no choice. Although tempting, picking her up and tossing her in the car wasn't an option, especially if he ever wanted to have another kid. She wasn't the kind of woman who would go for his jugular if he tried to manhandle her; she would get him where it would hurt the most.

Max looked over and barked, but when he tried to pull Gabrielle over to Matteo, now waving from the back window, Gabrielle tugged him back.

"Don't tell me what I can and can't do."

How had he fucked this up so badly? One minute they were kissing in the kitchen, and the next Gabrielle was walking out the door.

"I think she's mad at you," Matteo said from the back seat. "She sounds like Nonna and Auntie Angela when they're mad. Maybe it's because you shouted at her."

"I didn't shout." He tightened his grip on the steering wheel, cursing himself for losing his temper. Gina seemed to have that power over him even from the grave.

"You were very loud, Papa. And you were angry. I'm sorry I don't look like you."

Fuck. He'd hurt Matteo, too. He'd forgotten how kids picked up on everything. He was usually very careful about saying or doing anything that would make anyone think Matteo wasn't his son. But Gabrielle had a way of getting past all his walls and exposing his vulnerabilities.

Just because she wasn't the perfect mom, doesn't make him any less your son.

His son. Unlike many of the wiseguys he knew, he had been there when Matteo was born, held him, changed him, and fed him. He'd heard his first word, seen his first tooth, and caught him when he'd taken his first step. He sat up with Matteo at night when he couldn't sleep, and read him countless stories. Thinking back, he'd actually spent more time with Matteo than Gina, who was always sick or tired or out with her friends. It was only after Gina died that he'd stopped being a proper dad.

Did it really matter if they had a blood tie? No one knew the truth. Matteo was a great kid, and he couldn't even contemplate sending him to live with Gina's parents. Three lives would be devastated if he ripped the family apart—Matteo's, his mother's, and his. He might have built a wall around his heart after Gina died, closing off his ability to grow his love, but Matteo was already safe inside.

And an angel had climbed in there with him.

"I think you're right, Matteo," he said, looking over his shoulder. "Papa said things he shouldn't have said. And I think we do have things in common. We are both Italian, aren't we?"

"*Si*, Papa!" Matteo's face lit up, and Luca felt it right in his goddamn, fully exposed, heart.

"And we both like our cars to go fast, don't we?"

"*Si*, Papa! Go fast. She's getting away." Matteo pointed down the road and bounced in his seat.

Luca put his foot on the gas, and caught up to Gabrielle, screeching to a stop yet again.

"*Tesoro mio . . .* " He leaned out the window, prepared do anything or say anything to see her smile. She was the woman he'd always dreamed about. She'd changed his life. And he wanted her always by his side. He thought about telling her in English, but he knew Italian was her weakness, and there was no better way to convey what was in his heart than the language of love. "*Sei la donna dei miei canzoni. Mi hai cambiato la vita. Ti voglio sempre al mio fianco.*"

Gabrielle stopped on the sidewalk and sighed. "Everything you say in Italian sounds beautiful and you sound sincere, but if you want to apologize, do it in English."

"Papa says he dreams about women, you should be different, and he wants you to be on the sidewalk," Matteo called out from the backseat.

Luca groaned and made a mental note to tell his mother to find a new Italian tutor.

"Sono innamorato di te." He told her he loved her, knowing she wouldn't understand, but he wanted to say the words that were truly in his heart the best way he knew how.

"Is that an apology?"

"Of a sort."

She walked up to the passenger side window and smiled at Matteo. "Do you know what your Papa said?"

"Yes." Matteo beamed. "It was nice."

"What do you think? Was it a good apology?"

Matteo's gaze flicked to Luca and then back to Gabrielle. *"Molto bene!"* he said, making his Papa proud.

"I'm still not speaking to you," Gabrielle said, after she and Max were both in the vehicle. "I looked up the Italian word for sorry on my phone and you didn't say it. But I have been playing around with an app for learning Italian and I know the word 'innamorato' so I think you said something especially nice, and since it's blazing hot, I'll take the ride."

Twenty minutes later, Luca parked the SUV in front of his mother's Spanish-style home in Mira Villas. He would have preferred not to bring Gabrielle to meet his family just yet, but Matteo had baseball practice and he was already late bringing him home. Introducing a woman to his mother was akin to a marriage proposal, and having only just realized the depth of his feelings for her, he wasn't quite ready to take that next step.

"I just have to drop Matteo off with my mother." He hesitated. It would be impolite to ask her to stay in the car, but bringing her inside would be a full-blown formal affair involving a meal and an interrogation for which she would be ill-prepared.

"I'll stay in the car with Max," she said. "He can be a handful when I take him someplace new."

He let out a relieved breath. "If you want . . ."

"It's okay." She reached over and squeezed his hand. "I understand."

Dio mio. Could she be any more perfect? He kissed her cheek. "I'll be back in five minutes."

After Matteo said good-bye to Gabrielle and Max, Luca brought him inside and went to find his mother. He'd bought the two-story, four-bedroom home for her and his siblings, after she'd agreed to raise Matteo, and she spent most of her time in the high-end kitchen with its black granite countertops, sleek white cabinets and stainless steel appliances.

"Ma?"

"We're in the living room," she called out. "We have company."

Luca's pulse kicked up a notch, and he reached under his jacket for his gun as he walked through the house. His mother never entertained anywhere other than the kitchen, and the waver in her voice told him something was wrong.

"Frankie." His stomach twisted as he greeted the Toscani enforcer, who was sitting beside his mother on the plastic-covered couch. He had known Frankie would come for him, either to take him to Nico for judgment, or for a ride from which he would never return. When he held Gabrielle last night, he'd wondered how long he would have and if they'd give him a chance to say good-bye. Running wasn't an option. Not only because it would show a lack of honor, but also because there was nowhere he could go that the mob wouldn't find him.

"Frankie came to visit." His mother's lips pressed in a thin line. She knew who Frankie was, and she also knew he didn't make social calls. "I wanted to make him a little something, but he said he was just here looking for you. And when Alex told him you would be bringing Matteo home for practice, he said he'd wait."

Fucking Alex should have known better than to give any information to Frankie, but his brother never did think straight when he was high.

"Matteo's upstairs, Ma. Why don't you go get him ready for baseball? Frankie and I have business."

His mother shot him a worried look as she left the room. There was only one kind of business that would bring Frankie to the house, and it wasn't good.

"I had to get your mother out of the kitchen," Frankie said. "She kept offering to make me a little something that involved chopping things with big knives. I think she woulda stuck me if I turned my back on her."

"She's a strong woman. Very protective. There's no one I respect more."

"Woulda liked to know how that felt." He gestured to the door and pushed to his feet. "Let's go."

Talk wasn't necessary. Luca knew he was being called to account for breaking the rules and getting involved with a cop. Today he'd face judgment and if he couldn't convince Nico of the benefit of his alliance with Gabrielle, this was the last time he would see his mother and Matteo.

"Gabrielle's in the car."

"She's coming, too."

Luca froze. "She's not part of this. We don't involve women in our affairs."

Frankie made an impatient gesture toward the door. "We do if they're cops who might have been given information they shouldn't have had."

"I didn't tell her anything she didn't already know."

"Papa?" Matteo came down the stairs with his mother. "Can you come and watch me play ball?"

"I have to do some work with Cousin Frankie. Give me a hug good-bye." He held Matteo in his arms, kissed his little cheeks, his forehead, his nose, ran a hand through his dark hair, which his mother had let grow too long. "Be a good boy. Listen to your nonna." He kissed Matteo's ear, fought the urge to check to see if he had the same mole. It didn't matter. Matteo was his son. If today was his last day, he wanted to die believing that was true. He wanted to die with hope.

His mother reached up and grabbed his cheeks, kissing him as he'd kissed Matteo. *"Polpetto,"* she said, using a nickname he hadn't heard for years. He had no idea why she'd started calling him meatball when he was younger, but he knew why she was saying it now. He gave her a hug and she shuddered in his arms.

"Bye, Ma." He gave her one last hug and walked away, not daring to look back.

Frankie snickered as they left the house. *"Polpetto?* You're never gonna live that one down."

Luca thought it an odd thing to say if his life was going to end in the next hour or two, but then Frankie wasn't a normal man.

"You drive." Frankie gestured to Luca's SUV. "Sally G's already in the back with your girl."

Luca slid into the driver's seat and turned to look at Gabrielle, buckled in beside bald and portly Sally G. Nico's oldest capo was wearing his favorite bowling shirt with dress pants and lots of bling. Of all the wiseguys Luca knew, happily married Sally G was probably the least likely to suffer from wandering hands when seated beside a beautiful woman, but he was still a guy and Luca fixed him with a warning stare before reassuring Gabrielle.

"It's okay, *bella*."

"Like fuck it is," she bit out, while Max growled softly in her lap.

"Who do we have here?" Frankie looked over from the passenger seat.

"Max." She glared at Frankie. "He's a rescue dog and afraid of men, so this ride is going to be hard for him."

"Yeah?" Frankie's face softened, and he held out his hand to Max. Minutes passed as man and dog stared at each other. No one moved. It was the strangest thing Luca had ever seen. Finally, Max sniffed Frankie's hand. Then he licked Frankie's fingers and rubbed his head in Frankie's palm.

"You a dog whisperer now?" Sally G asked.

Frankie patted Max's head and turned around without saying anything. Maybe he had an ounce of heart after all.

They drove in silence to the Toscani family clubhouse, located at the back of an abandoned garage just off the 95 in the outskirts of North Las Vegas. A black Chrysler 300C followed behind them, no doubt containing members of Nico's crew. At least they weren't driving out into the desert. Usually when the mob intended to whack someone, they would have the victim drive to an isolated area and shoot him from the backseat of the car.

Luca checked in the rear-view mirror when they hit the 95. He didn't like the idea of Sally G alone in the backseat with his girl. Gabrielle had changed into a pair of frayed, cut-off jean shorts before she stormed out of his penthouse and they drew attention to her perfect heart-shaped ass, the curve of her hips, and her long, lean legs. Her form-fitting black tank top was cut low in front—too low for Luca's liking—and advertised his favorite brand of whiskey. Despite his anger, he'd been hard when she walked out of the bedroom for breakfast, but when she put on a pair of cowboy boots on her way out the door, he'd seriously considered throwing himself on the floor and begging for forgiveness.

"Get your fucking eyes off my girl." He speared Sally G with a glare through the rear-view mirror.

Sally G laughed. "She sure doesn't look like a cop. If I thought they were all so hot, I'd have boned one, too, back in the day."

Luca yanked the steering wheel to the side, intending to pull the vehicle off the road and beat the fucking shit out of Sally G.

"Shut it, Sal," Frankie barked over the seat. "You gonna join him for breaking the rules? Apologize and look the fuck away."

"Sorry. No offence." Sally G lifted his hands in apology and turned his head to the window.

Twenty minutes later, they arrived at the clubhouse and parked around the back. Most of the buildings in the area were vacant or run down, and the property was completely enclosed by bushes and wire fencing.

"Luca. Sally G. You come with me." Frankie looked over his shoulder and drew his gun. "Gabrielle, stay in the car with Max."

"*Bella* . . ." Luca tried to find words to say as he stepped out of the vehicle, an expression of love, a lasting good-bye. He had a strong feeling this wasn't going to go as badly as he'd originally thought simply because no one would ever do a hit in broad daylight at the clubhouse where it might attract attention. But he liked to be prepared, and he'd once heard that adversity brought people together.

Steeling himself for Gabrielle's tears, he was brought up short when he met fury instead.

"I cannot fucking believe this," she spat out.

"*Mio angelo . . .*" He tried again, but she cut him off with a raised hand.

"Save it for when I'm interested in listening and not busy trying to think of a way to get us out of this."

"There is no way out. It's up to Nico."

As if on cue, the door to the clubhouse slammed open and Nico stepped out into the sunshine. Five members of his crew filed out behind him, men Luca had known for years, and all of whom he called friend.

Luca swallowed hard as he walked across the parking lot, preparing for a showdown he had little hope of winning.

"Apparently, we have a problem." Nico met him halfway, impeccably dressed in his usual tailored suit, silk tie, and Italian leather shoes. Luca felt underdressed in his jeans and T-shirt, but he'd left his penthouse in a hurry to catch up with Gabrielle, and hadn't given the usual attention to his attire.

"Only problem is my girl being here. Let her go."

"You're the fucking problem," Frankie spat out. "Millions of girls out there, and you gotta stick your dick in a cop."

Luca was right in Frankie's face, chest to chest, fists raised, before his brain even processed he had moved. "Respect, *paisano.*" They were evenly matched in height and weight, but Frankie had been raised as a hitman, a trained killer. Luca was under no illusion about how quickly Frankie could kill him or how little remorse Frankie would feel when the deed was done.

"You break the rules; you don't get our respect," Frankie said. "You and your old man are exactly the same. Always in fucking bed with the cops. The Rizzolis have no honor."

Luca's stomach tightened in anger. Nico and Frankie were like brothers to him. They knew him. They knew he would never do anything to endanger them or the Toscani crime family. He'd eaten at Nico's table. Hell, he'd taken a bullet for Nico, and their total and utter lack of trust was like a blade through his heart.

Apparently, Nico remembered that night in the casino, too, because he held up a hand, cutting Frankie off. "Don't be so quick to judge. Luca almost gave his life for me. It doesn't make sense that he would betray us now."

"Men don't think straight when women are involved," Frankie said coldly. "Even you know that."

Nico's expression darkened at the veiled reference to the risks he had taken when he first met Mia. At the time, she was the daughter of his greatest enemy and their relationship was almost as dangerous as Luca's relationship with Gabrielle. "You're out of line."

"On my honor, I haven't betrayed you," Luca said quickly, turning Nico's attention back to him. Nico was more likely to go easy on him if he wasn't riled. "Gabrielle is after Garcia. He killed her husband. She's willing to help us to catch him, and she's prepared to risk her career to do it by giving us access to all the classified information the police have on him."

Frankie snorted. "We can't trust the fucking police. And we can't trust a fucking Rizzoli."

Luca bit back a growl. One day he would make Frankie pay for that disrespect. He'd spent years proving his loyalty, fighting to restore the family honor. "Garcia is the key to everything," he reminded Nico. "Without him, Tony doesn't have access to the cash flow he needs to control the city. Not only that, what he did to Little Ricky is an attack on us all."

Nico stepped into the shadow of the building, leaving Luca to roast in the sun. Spawned in hellfire, Frankie stood close to Luca and didn't even break a sweat.

"My sources have confirmed Garcia was behind the hit on Little Ricky," Nico said. "But who was the message for? Did Little Ricky owe them money? Was it a message to you? Or to us? Or was it payback because you whacked two Albanians who possibly worked for Garcia?"

Of course, Nico knew about the Albanians. He knew everything because Frankie knew everything. And when Frankie knew something, he knew all the details, so there was no point talking around the truth. "They shot up Gabrielle's house when we were inside. I didn't fucking care who hired them, but when we asked they didn't know. They were told to scare her as a warning, but not kill her. She doesn't have any other enemies, so she was pretty sure Garcia was behind it."

"Fair enough." Nico nodded. "They got what was coming to them. But I'm trying to figure out if they're connected to Little Ricky's death, or if these are two separate incidents. Why were they after your girl?"

Luca's tension eased the tiniest bit. Nico seemed more interested in fact-finding than putting a bullet through his head. Maybe he would walk out of here alive after all. "She's got sensitive information about Garcia because she's been tracking him for two years, although we don't know why he sent his goons to her house after she'd been pulled off the case. She already took a bullet when someone—she thinks it was Garcia—ambushed her in a warehouse during a raid and shot her."

"It's you," Frankie spat out. "You're the fucking connection. Garcia wants to shut the cop up because she knows too much. He tries to kill her and misses so he hires the Albanians to warn her to keep her mouth shut. Luca pops the Albanians and Garcia gets pissed so he offs Little Ricky because he knows Little Ricky works for Luca. Boom. Mystery solved."

Luca shook his head, resisting the urge to pull out a tissue and wipe the sweat off his brow. Any movement of his hand toward his jacket would be seen as a threat and Frankie would shoot first and apologize when Luca was lying in his grave. "It doesn't make sense," he said. "Why try to kill her and then try to warn her? And why try to warn her after she's been pulled off the case and has no new information since she was shot?"

Nico folded his arms across his chest. "Maybe she's not being honest with you and there's more going on than you know. This could be a set-up or a trap."

"A honey trap," Frankie added. "And you're stuck right the fuck in dick first. That's why we have rules against associating with cops."

"We also have rules against going to the bar, and you were there the other night," Nico countered, jumping to Luca's defense. "And I believe a rule was also once waved about looking at another wiseguy's woman, so let's put aside our concern about rules for now and focus on the problem at hand."

"Rules are fucking rules." Frankie's face hardened and he looked away. Luca didn't know much about Frankie's life before he joined the Toscani crime family, except that most of the wiseguys who were sent from New York were in Vegas as punishment for some wrong. Had cold-hearted Frankie slept with a boss's wife or daughter? He couldn't imagine a woman falling for a guy who had no soul. But if Frankie had broken the rules, why wasn't he trying to restore his adoptive family's honor the way Luca was trying to restore his?

"The rules are a guide," Nico said. "Not law. And here in Vegas, we have a certain freedom to interpret them as we will."

Hope flared in Luca's chest. Nico had split the family because he was the kind of leader who wasn't afraid to break the rules. Few *capos* would have dared to refuse Tony's claim to head the family and fewer still would have set up their own family faction to challenge him.

"The way I see it," Nico continued. "The rules are there to protect the family. Given Luca's loyalty, his pledge of honor, and the debt I owe him, I trust him to keep our secrets until we catch Garcia. Little Ricky's death gives us yet another reason to go after him. The benefits outweigh the risks. Once Garcia has been eliminated, however . . ." He sucked in his lips and gave Luca a sympathetic look. "The relationship can't continue. It looks bad for you, it looks bad for the family, and in the end we will have to answer to the Gambolis in New York, and their solution will be unacceptable to me. I don't want to lose a friend."

In other words, Luca could have her until they caught Garcia, and then he would have to let her go. For a moment, he couldn't believe what he'd just heard. He and Nico had been friends since they were fifteen years old. They'd risen through the Mafia ranks together, broken legs together, built crews and businesses, and partied in Nico's penthouse suite at the casino until Nico met Mia and became a changed man. He couldn't believe Nico, of all people, didn't understand that love wasn't a choice, and once you found it, you couldn't let it go.

He knew he should be grateful. He should, right now, be thanking Nico for his mercy, but just as the New York family's solution would be unacceptable to Nico, so Nico's solution was unacceptable to Luca. He wasn't prepared to lose Gabrielle. There had to be another way.

But this was not the time to argue.

"*Grazie, Don Toscani.*" He used formal language to show his appreciation for Nico's decision not to put a bullet through his brain.

Nico nodded, and then his eyes turned hard. "Now there is a matter of punishment for hiding the affair instead of coming to me in the first place. "On your knees. Hands behind your head. Frankie, he's all yours."

"Can you believe this?" Gabrielle smashed her fist on the window as she watched Luca drop to his knees and put his hands behind his head. Max scrambled off her lap, unused to her anger, and she gave him a soothing pat. "This is not happening to me again, Max. I am not going to lose another man I care about."

She pulled her weapon from beneath her jacket. Although she struggled for acceptance as an equal in the police department, she wasn't averse to taking advantage of the fact that men often underestimated her. If she'd been in control of this whole ridiculous scenario, she would have ensured that the prisoner left behind in the vehicle was at least unarmed, and at best guarded and secured. But they'd clearly assumed she was no threat, and she was pretty damn sure that was because she was a woman.

Big. Fucking. Mistake.

With one hand on the vehicle door, she checked out the parking lot. The tall, dark haired guy in the suit had to be the boss, Nico. She remembered the name from the briefing she'd had during her visit to Organized Crime, and his resemblance to the photograph taped to the whiteboard. He had an air of authority around him, a sense of command. There were five men standing behind and around him. Frankie was to his right. Another guy stood to his left, tapping a baseball bat over his palm. Sally G was a few steps in front of the car. He was a big guy, but he was short, probably no more than an inch taller than her. Perfect for what she had in mind.

Everyone's attention was focused on Luca on his knees in the gravel. The sight grated on her. A man like Luca should never be on his knees. Even in front of the boss.

Taking a deep breath, she opened the door just enough to slip out on the shadowed side of the vehicle. Running into the fray with her gun blazing would only get her killed. She'd looked into Frankie's eyes, and although he had some connection with Max, she knew he wouldn't hesitate to pull the trigger. She needed a hostage. And Sally G had just volunteered for the job.

She rose to a crouch, counted to three, and ran full speed ahead.

Frankie's head jerked up. But she was behind Sally G and moving fast. She ran into him, knocking him to his knees. Recovering quickly, she wrapped one arm around his thick neck and pressed her gun to his temple. Taking a deep breath, she shouted loud enough for everyone to hear. "Let Luca go or I'll shoot."

There was an almost comical moment of stunned silence as the mobsters just stared.

"Luca. Get up. Come on. Move it." She prayed no one put her to the test. She'd never shot anyone in her life, and she didn't think she'd be able to pull the trigger on Sally G. She could feel his heart pounding against his ribs, hear the rasp of his breath. In the car, he'd talked about his beautiful wife, his golden lab, his two kids and how proud he was that they were going to college.

Luca lowered his hands. He made a bizarrely apologetic gesture to Nico and shrugged his shoulders. She couldn't understand why he was moving so slowly. The next move in this game was for someone to pull a gun on Luca and then they'd wind up in a standoff that no doubt would end with her and Luca dead. But Frankie didn't move. And Nico just watched as Luca ambled over to her and Sally G like he was out for a morning stroll.

"Get up." She tugged on Sally G's arm, indicating that he should stand. "Walk backwards." Still holding her gun to his head, she walked him back to the driver's side door where Luca was waiting.

"Luca!" She tipped her head to the passenger side. "Get in over there. I'm not going to drag him around."

"I'm letting you rescue me," he said curtly. "If I don't at least drive out of here, you might as well shoot me now."

"Fine," she snapped. "I'll get in the back. We're going at the count of three. One. Two. Three." She shoved Sally G forward, ran for the vehicle and threw herself in the backseat beside Max. Luca slammed his door and they peeled out of the parking lot, leaving the mobsters, still motionless, behind them.

"We made it!" She sat up in the seat and gave Max a hug. "I've never done anything like that before. It's kind of liberating to pull my gun and not think I'll be spending the next two days doing paperwork, or second guessing whether I needed to pull it or not. And I actually feel like I accomplished something. I saved you. I didn't think it would work. Frankie is pretty sharp. He doesn't miss anything."

"Enough."

She startled at Luca's abrupt tone. "You're supposed to say thank you. Or you could be more effusive and add, 'for risking your life to save me.' Or even just 'great job, Gabrielle'."

"You should have stayed in the car. I didn't need to be saved." He turned onto the 95 and headed south, out of the city.

"Where are we going?"

"Don't talk. You've done enough damage for one day."

Her stomach twisted in a knot, and she couldn't hide the sarcasm in her tone. "Oh, sorry. I must have misunderstood when they made you get to your knees and put your hands behind your head like they were going to execute you."

"Jesus Christ. When you burst out of the car waving your gun . . ." His voice hitched. "Shouting at them to let me go. Threatening to shoot them . . ." He thudded his hand on the steering wheel. "And taking Sally G hostage?" He yanked the steering wheel and turned down a side road. Gabrielle stared back at the dusty horizon, watching the last of the urban sprawl disappear.

"Why are we leaving the city?"

His shoulders shook, and he made a noise that sounded suspiciously like a chuckle.

"Are you laughing?"

Luca shook his head and Gabrielle glared at the partial glimpse she had of his face in the rearview mirror. "Did I miss something? Is there something funny about the fact they were going to beat you with a baseball bat and then shoot you in cold blood?"

Without answering, Luca turned in to an abandoned chemical plant. Giant iron tubs covered in peeling white paint dotted a gravel-covered field, and a small corrugated-iron shack creaked in front of them. Out in the desert with no shade to protect them, the sun was fiercely hot, and Gabrielle began to sweat almost as soon as she followed Luca out of the car.

"Luca?"

He walked away, past the shack and over to a giant bin that rocked gently on four wobbly legs as the wind blew hot around her. Wary of the heat, she left him to work off his anger, and went to cool off beneath the awning of a shack that looked like it had been boarded up long ago.

"I'm never going to live that down," Luca said, coming up to her a few minutes later.

"What?"

He curled his hand around her nape and pulled her close, until their noses touched. "I was just rescued by a female police officer from a beating I deserved."

Her breath left her in a rush. "They weren't going to kill you?"

"No. Not today." His hand tightened around her neck. "And after that performance, if they change their minds, they'll probably send a few more men to do the job. You were fucking magnificent."

Her mouth opened and closed again. She'd prepared herself for yet another fight about putting herself in danger stemming from his overprotective nature, but was he finally accepting what she did? Not only that, had he just complimented her?

"I was just doing my job."

"Your bureau is wasting their best asset sticking you behind a desk." He pressed a kiss to her forehead.

Still stunned by his seemingly abrupt change of attitude, she stammered. "You aren't angry? Usually you rant about how it's the man's job to protect the woman and I shouldn't put myself in danger, blah, blah, blah."

His lips twitched at the corners. "You are mine, and your safety is a matter of honor. I would rather die with honor, than to have you hurt trying to save me. But you've made me rethink my views, and when you can have my back without putting yourself at risk, then I'll accept your help."

Gabrielle bit back a laugh. His overprotectiveness was still there, but between the lines she read respect and no small amount of pride.

"Although it was not necessary," he continued. "And I will have to go back as a matter of honor, I am indebted to you."

Gabrielle frowned. "I won't let you go. I would rather have an unharmed dishonored Luca than a beaten honorable one."

"Honor is not something to be taken so lightly," he said, his smile fading. "Without honor, you feel like someone has taken a chunk of your flesh. My father dishonored our family. He got involved with the drug trade and turned rat instead of going to prison when he was caught. But the family found out." His voice tightened. "I've spent my life since trying to restore the family honor, trying to show that I am not my father's son, to make myself whole . . ."

Her heart squeezed in her chest. "I'm sorry about your dad, but I couldn't just sit in the car and let them hurt you, even if I had understood your concept of honor. That's not who I am." She sighed as the last of her adrenaline faded away. "I'm probably the most wrong woman on the planet for you. How can you restore your family honor when you're with a police officer?"

His gaze never left her face. "You can't help who you love. You are the perfect woman for me."

It took a long moment before his words sunk in.

He loved her.

Even though she was bitter and broken, and they were on opposite sides of the law, and even though their love was forbidden and the risks of being together were astronomically high, he loved her.

"I don't know what to say." She couldn't say it back because she didn't know if she was capable of loving someone again. She liked him, enjoyed spending time with him, and cared about him deeply. But she had never let herself consider a future with Luca, never thought there was a way they could be together except to hunt Garcia down, never dared to open herself to love.

"You don't need to say anything," he said. "It is what it is."

She didn't see him coming. One moment he was five feet away, and the next she was in his arms, his body hot and hard against her. "You're mine, Gabrielle. You were mine from the moment we met. Nico wants me to end our relationship after we find Garcia, but we will find a way to make it work, even if I have to leave the family." He claimed her with a kiss, fierce and demanding, so passionate her knees went weak and she had to clutch his shoulders to stay upright.

She wanted to believe him, but it seemed an impossible task. From what she understood, there were only two ways out of the Mafia: death and witness protection. And after what he'd just told her about his father, there was no way she could let him make the choice that would mean losing the one thing he'd been struggling for all his life. She didn't want Luca without that chunk of flesh. She wanted him whole.

"What were they going to do to you?"

"Hurt me. Maybe break a few bones."

"Because of me," she said bitterly.

"Because I broke the rules." His rough hand cupped her cheek, his thumb brushing lightly over her jaw. "*Mio angelo.* I would endure any hardship for you. I will welcome the pain because it gives us time to be together.

Every extra day I get to spend with you is worth a dozen bruises."

"Luca." His name was a prayer on her lips. She had lost David. She wasn't going to lose Luca, too. There had to be a way for them to be together that didn't involve him getting killed or beaten with a baseball bat or losing the honor that was such an important part of his life. "I think I just showed you I would make the same sacrifice for you."

"And you will be punished for it." He wrapped his arms around her so tight she could barely breathe.

"Punished?"

He buried his face in her neck, nuzzled behind her ear, his five o'clock shadow a sensual burn over her skin. "I will give you more pleasure than you can bear."

Gabrielle swallowed hard and all her awareness suddenly centered on the pulse of arousal between her thighs. "I want you to be rough."

"I'll be rough."

"I want you to tear me apart so you understand that how you feel about me is how I feel about you. How your pain is my pain. How I couldn't sit there and watch you suffer."

He drew in a ragged breath. "I will break you and then I will put you together again. I will mark you so that every time you look in the mirror you think of me, and every man who dares look at you knows you are mine."

"I want to be yours, Luca," she whispered. "And I want you to be mine."

"*Sei mia per sempre, anima e cuore. Senza di te non vivo piu.* You are mine forever," he translated for her. "Body and soul. Without you, I couldn't live."

She surrendered to him, unable to do anything but

feel as he feathered kisses down her neck to the sensitive juncture of her throat and shoulder.

And then he leaned down and bit her so deliciously hard she screamed.

NINETEEN

Paolo couldn't see anything through the blindfold covering his eyes. Not a sliver of light, not even a shadow. Fear wrapped around him, insulating him from the frigid air.

"Where are we?" He clutched Ray's arm as he stepped out of the vehicle, his feet hitting a solid, flat surface. Ray had picked Paolo up in a black sedan outside his apartment building just after the sun set, blindfolding him before they started their drive through the city no more than half an hour ago.

"I told you before. No questions. Move fast." With a firm hand on his shoulder, Ray pushed Paolo forward.

"Did Crazy T have to go through this to meet the boss, too?"

Ray cuffed him on the side of the head. "You aren't meeting the boss. He only meets with his biggest customers. Now, shut the fuck up and walk."

"Can I ask one more question? What happened to Crazy T?"

"Overdosed." Ray pulled Paolo to a stop. "Wait here."

Paolo drew in a deep, calming breath and smelled

freshly cut grass, a rarity in the inner city where he lived. They had to be out in the burbs, somewhere nice where they had the time and money to water and cut the grass. He heard the beep of a security panel, and the distant hum of a lawnmower. Definitely a residential area, and this was a bungalow or ranch house since there were no steps.

He heard the creak of a door and felt a blast of cold air as Ray pushed him forward. He thought about Crazy T coming here to buy his dope, and how Crazy T was gone. He had to be careful not to make the same mistake. It was easy to get addicted and hard to quit. But Paolo was smart. He would limit himself to just one bump a day, maybe two if he had an important job to do. Just enough to keep him going, but not enough that Mr. Rizzoli would ever notice, or to push him into addiction.

Ray gave a satisfied snort as he pulled off Paolo's blindfold. "That shut you up."

Paolo blinked as his eyes adjusted to the light. He was standing in the living room of what appeared to be a middle-class family home. Tan leather couches were positioned in front of a wall-mounted TV, separated by fancy tables holding ornate lamps that cast the room in a soft glow. Behind thick curtains, Paolo glimpsed the slats of closed blinds. Pictures of landscapes decorated the wall, and framed photographs filled the mantelpiece above the fireplace.

Unnerved by the incongruity of a drug dealer hiding out in an average family home, he hesitated in the hallway. "Maybe we should take off our shoes."

His mom had always made him take off his shoes before he walked into the house. He only forgot once, and his mother had suffered his lapse when his father got home to find her on her knees trying to get the stains out of the carpet.

"What? Are you shitting me? No one takes off their shoes." Ray led Paolo over to a table covered in clear packages of white powder.

"Is this the boss's place?" Paolo opened the bag he'd been instructed to bring to carry the dope.

"You think I'm gonna tell you anything about the boss?" Ray snorted a laugh. "I've seen what he does to guys who piss him off, and I've got no interest in being treated like a piece of meat."

Paolo's heart thudded in his chest. This was almost as bad as the mob. One day he would have a job where mistakes weren't punished with torture and death.

"We've got five locations in the valley," Ray said, lifting one of the bags. "Three in the northeast, one in the southwest, and one in Henderson. Once we know you can be trusted, you'll be given directions to one of the locations to pick up your supply. After today, you're responsible for your own transport. If you need anything other than coke, we've got heroin and meth."

Paolo stared at the bag. "Do you give it to me like that?"

"*Pendejo!* I thought Crazy T set you up with his label."

Paolo didn't know much Spanish, but he figured Ray had called him something equivalent to an idiot. "I haven't seen him in a week. Maybe he was planning to do it before he died."

Ray let off another stream of invective. "You buy it from me, you package it up, and you sell it. Crazy T had lots of customers who knew his Pink Label brand. They knew he could be trusted, and he sold good quality stuff. If I were you, I'd take over his brand. He had a good business going until he snorted it away. He was charging twenty dollars for an eight ball. You do the math."

"Not really my strong suit." Paolo dug into his pocket

and pulled out all the money he had earned in the last few months working for Mr. Rizzoli.

"He was getting $160 per gram, and he paid us $60. He was more than doubling his money."

Paolo's eyes widened and he pointed to the packages. "In that case, I'll take one."

Ray doubled over with laughter. "You really are bad at math, unless you got forty grand in that bag."

"I've got one thousand dollars." And no way to pay his rent or buy food if Mr. Rizzoli didn't pay him before he got this racket going.

"You come up with another four hundred and ninety-nine thousand, and you get to meet the boss, even sit down with him for a drink," Ray said. "For one thousand, you get to entertain yourself while I measure it out."

"Sure." Paolo's shoulders slumped. So now he'd have to try and find a way to duplicate Crazy T's label. He couldn't remember what he'd done with the empty packets, although he knew where Crazy T lived because they'd gone to his place after the party and met his girlfriend.

He wandered around the room as Ray carefully measured the powder on a digital scale. Was this one of the dealer's houses? Or was it just a front in case of a police raid? The pictures on the mantle looked real enough. He studied the photos of a family—a man, woman, and child, all with the same dark hair and complexion as Ray—in front of the "The Castle" of Chichén Itzá, in Mexico. There were pictures of the family on a beach, in front of a huge church, and another of them eating ice cream in a park.

Paolo felt a pang of longing for the days before his mother died and the rare occasions his dad wasn't in a hitting mood. The mob was the closest he'd ever come to having a real family since his mother was injured. If they ever found out what he was doing . . .

"Are these pictures real?" Paolo knew he wasn't a smart guy, but even he wouldn't have put up pictures of himself in a drug house for anyone to see.

Ray shrugged. "Dunno. They've always been there. I just go where I'm told to go. We move around a lot to throw off the cops." He held out a baggie. "Here you go. This is what your one grand buys. Be smart and you can double, even triple your money. Be stupid and you'll wind up like Crazy T."

Paolo reached for the bag, hesitated. "You said I'd get all the coke I wanted for free. That was part of the deal."

"I just gave you a bag of coke with a street value of almost two grand and you just paid one thousand." Ray grinned. "You wanna snort it all yourself, you're practically getting it for free."

Paolo's hand tightened around the bag. A deal was a deal. If someone broke a deal with the mob, they wound up with bruises and broken bones, if they were lucky, or dead if they weren't. But he didn't have the mob behind him to enforce the deal. He was physically no match for Ray who looked to be in his late thirties and had about eighty pounds of muscle on him. Hell, he didn't even have a gun.

"We had a deal," he muttered, shoving the baggie into his backpack.

"You're nothing," Ray said, not unkindly. "You're the lowest of the low. Bottom feeder. The boss doesn't even know you exist. When you have big money, then you're in a position to start asking for favors. Then we listen." He held out the blindfold. "Ready to roll? You've got my number. Get in touch when you need to top up. I've got guys on the street who will tell me how you do. I get a good report, then I'll send you an address. But you gotta move fast to secure the territory. Everyone wants a piece of the action: street gangs, Triads, Russians, Albanians, even the fucking Mafia. They all want a piece of the pie."

"The Mafia isn't involved in the drug trade." He shuddered when the blindfold went over his eyes. Sometimes, when his dad was in a really bad mood, his mother used to hide him in the linen closet and close the door. Even now he associated darkness with the scent of laundry detergent, a sense of suffocation, and abject fear.

"Sure, they are." Ray tied the blindfold tight. "They're our biggest customers."

TWENTY

"Wake up. It's time for church." Luca slapped Gabrielle's ass beneath the bedclothes, jerking her out of a delicious dream where she'd been slathered in chocolate sauce and he'd been licking it off.

"Church?" Gabrielle looked up from the comfort of Luca's massive bed. "I don't go to church."

"You do today." He ripped the bedclothes off her, and the freezing air sent a wave of goosebumps rippling across her skin.

"Hey. Give me the covers back. Sunday is my sleep-in day. And I'm tired. Every time I tried to sleep, I was manhandled into some twisted sexual position, poked, and prodded—"

"Poked?" Luca gave an indignant sniff. "I do not poke. I pleasure."

"Fine." She pulled the pillow over her head. "I was pleasured. Again and again and again. Now I need the pleasure of sleep."

"Once I left you on your back," he reminded her.

"Oh yes." She reached behind her, feeling for the sheet. "That was the time I woke up with your cock pressed against my lips. You're lucky I wasn't dreaming about biting into something."

"You liked it when I fucked your face." His voice dropped to a sensual purr. "You were very, very wet."

Gabrielle was glad of the pillow that hid the sudden burn in her cheeks. She was still not used to his dirty talking, but man, did it ever turn her on.

The bed dipped, and his hand smoothed down her back and over her ass. "You have to stop this, or we won't get out of here."

"I'm not doing anything except trying to sleep."

He idly traced patterns on her skin, sending a ripple of desire down her spine. "I've been up for hours reading the notes you made last night about the Garcia investigation. You have an incredible memory for detail."

"That case was my whole life for two years." She sighed. "It's strange, but I felt like I knew him, although he rarely went out in public so we never got a physical description. Because I was the most junior detective on the case, I read and filed every piece of paper and every digital file. I knew everything, but no one was interested in what I had to say. Every time I told them I knew where he would be, they said it wasn't a good time. I started thinking someone was thwarting the investigation, or there was some higher political agenda at work."

"Not all cops are good cops." His warm lips brushed up her spine, licking over the mark he'd made yesterday afternoon when he fucked her in the desert as an appetizer for what he had planned when he got her home.

"Any ideas about how to find him?" she asked, her mind snapping into work mode. "I don't know what happened after the raid. I thought he might leave the city until things cooled down."

"Frankie has sources that confirmed he's here, but underground."

"I guess that makes sense. We thought he had some connection to the city," she said. "Or it just might be that Vegas works best as a central hub for his distribution chain."

"Or he might have forged a new, very powerful alliance and needs to be here to make it stick." He shifted on the bed, rolling closer. His hand slid between her legs, and he slicked a finger through her labia.

Gabrielle moved restlessly against his questing finger. "Do you know who he's allied with?"

"Yes."

"But you can't tell me?" She tried to turn, and he pressed her back down to the bed. "That could be our way in, Luca."

"That route is closed to us."

Gabrielle sighed. "If we could get our hands on some money . . ."

His finger stopped its gentle torment. "Why do you need money?"

"He only meets in person with powerful people—the ones who are major distributors of his product. The figure we heard was $500,000. If you happened to have that much money kicking around, and a few underworld connections, we could arrange a meeting."

"We?"

She looked back over her shoulder. "We're doing this together. Remember when you told me I was magnificent when I rescued you? I will be even more magnificent when I capture Garcia and throw him in jail."

"Perhaps I shouldn't have been so free with my praise," he muttered. "It seems to have gone to your head."

"You like girls with guns," she reminded him. "You said that when I saved your ass from the Albanians who shot up my house." She cut herself off, suddenly remembering why she'd gone to the restaurant yesterday. In all the confusion, she'd never asked him the question that had sent her to him in the first place. But when he pressed a kiss to the scar on her back, the exit wound of the bullet that had brought them together, she decided she didn't want to hear the truth.

"I was covering you while you saved Max." He dropped his weight from his elbows, pinning her to the bed.

She laughed, straining against him. "Are you going to squish me until I agree?"

"I'll fuck you until you agree." He nuzzled her neck, his breath warm on her skin. "And Garcia won't be going to jail. He'll be coming with me to pay for what he did to Little Ricky."

"No." She pushed herself up, only to be flattened on the bed by the weight of Luca's body as he moved to lie on top of her. She shivered at the brush of his cool shirt on her back, the press of the buckle of his belt, the hard shaft pressed against the cleft of her ass. "He has to answer for his crimes in a court of law," she continued, trying to keep her arousal in check. "He'll be tried, and no doubt he'll be found guilty and he'll spend the rest of his life rotting in jail."

"That's not justice. Sitting in jail eating three meals a day, continuing to run his drug empire from behind bars while Little Ricky and David are no longer on this earth? That's a travesty. Justice means he suffers the way he made your husband suffer, the way he made Little Ricky suffer, and countless others. Justice means he sits naked in a cold, dark room not knowing where the next blow will fall or how long he will scream. Justice means a long, slow painful death."

"I can't." She buried her head in the bedspread. "I can't condone that."

"But you want it." His breath was hot temptation in her ear. "Deep down in your very heart, you want the kind of vengeance only I can give you."

"No."

"Yes, *bella*. You are not the straight-laced cop you pretend to be. Beneath your uniform beats a rebel heart. That's how we found our way together. You didn't break with the police when you decided to work with me to find Garcia. You broke with them the day you went rogue and got shot—the day we found each other."

She squirmed to get away, but he was too heavy, too warm, his stubble an erotic burn, his breath a whispered promise, his cock too tantalizingly hard, for any serious effort. Yes, she wanted it. In her most secret heart, she wanted more than a prison sentence. She wanted Garcia to taste the kind of pain she had gone through when she lost David and her unborn child. She wanted justice. Mafia style.

"He's too dangerous to go after without back-up," she said as the last threads of her resolve faded away beneath the pounding of her newly awakened rebel heart.

He huffed out an indignant breath. "I'm dangerous. My friends are dangerous."

"You're dangerously sexy." She wiggled her ass against him to let him know that for now, the discussion was over. They didn't have the money or the information to get close to Garcia. So why not turn her attention to something else she wanted . . .

Luca's body tensed and he growled. "You're sexy, showing me your sexy body, reminding me of last night, saying sexy things . . ." He hooked his knees between hers and shoved her legs apart. "Open for me," he demanded.

"Not again." Her arousal kicked up a notch at the sharp edge to his voice. "How can you be hard again? It's only been an hour."

"Because it's you." He pushed her head down to the mattress, baring her nape to the heated slide of his lips.

She'd never experienced Luca like this—forceful, aggressive, and more dominant than he'd ever been before. His urgency was unsettling, and a thrill of fear shot through her body.

Kneeling behind her, he lifted her ass, positioning her on her knees with her head and shoulders pinned to the bed. He thrust his hand between her legs, and roughly shoved her knees apart. "I'm going to fuck you hard," he growled softly in her ear. "And you're going to lie there and take my cock as deep as it can go. You will not move. The more you struggle, the rougher I'm going to be, and when you come, you're going to scream my name."

She heard the clank of his belt buckle, the whisper of fabric, and then the thick head of his cock circled her wet entrance.

"Brace yourself, *bella,* because I'm going to fuck you until you understand that I will let nothing and no one hurt you." He entered her in one hard thrust. "And then I want you to come to church and meet my mother."

Gabrielle squeezed Luca's hand as they made their way down the aisle of the Sacred Heart Church, trying to ignore the curious glances and whispers around her. Her mother had taken her to church on Sundays when she was a little girl, but the visits had ended with her mother's death. After her family moved to Nevada, Sundays were either spent watching her brothers play sports or in hospital as Patrick wrestled yet again with his addiction.

She smoothed down her dress, mauve with cap sleeves, a crew neckline, suede strip waist accents, and a pleated, A-line skirt. She didn't own many dresses, so Nicole had lent her the relatively modest outfit when she'd returned home to change. Nicole hadn't been in contact with Clint since last Friday night at Red 27, but she'd been in good spirits, picking up extra shifts at the casino and updating her profile on online dating sites with Cissy.

"We'll sit here." Luca gestured her to a pew a few rows from the back. "It's not right to join the family until you've been formally introduced."

"It's also not right to have marked up your girlfriend so much that beneath her dress she looks like she was attacked by a wild animal," she whispered, testing out the word "girlfriend" to see how he would react.

Luca gave a satisfied rumble. "I like my marks on you."

"You're making this sound very serious."

"If it wasn't serious," he said, squeezing her hand. "We wouldn't be here."

A few people stopped to talk to Luca as they passed by, and she was greeted with hugs and kisses. Although unused to so much affection, she swallowed her discomfort and forced a smile for the cousins, friends, aunts, and uncles who were clearly intrigued about her relationship with Luca. When she finally had a chance to sit down, she spotted Matteo near the front beside a woman with short, dark wavy hair.

"That's Ma," he said following her gaze. "She doesn't want to look old so she gets my sister, Angela, to dye her hair. Every week it's a different shade, sometimes red, sometimes brown, once it was jet black. Angela is on her left. She's a hairdresser. She's a blonde like my mother, but she's dyed her hair brown. Alex, my younger brother, is beside her." He gave a wry smile. "Normal hair color."

"It's a beautiful church." She studied the giant stained-glass windows behind the altar and in the vestibules along the sides of the church. Light and airy, with highly polished floors, and modern pot lights in the ceiling, it had a relaxed, welcoming feel.

"Ma thinks it's too modern. Some very generous benefactors funded the renovation a few years ago. I think it's a huge improvement."

"Is she very traditional?"

Luca laughed. "Only when it comes to family, food, and religion."

After the service, everyone gathered outside, huddling in the shade of the trees planted along the walkway. Luca tugged her through the gauntlet of well-wishers toward his family but they were intercepted by Matteo before he could introduce her.

"Papa!" He ran and threw his arms around his father. "You're here. You're here."

Laughing, Luca swept him up and into his arms. "It's Sunday. Of course, I'm here."

"You never come to church." Matteo looked over at Gabrielle and smiled. "Hi Miss Gabrielle."

"Hi, Matteo." She ruffled his hair. "I see you're wearing a suit just like your dad. You look very handsome."

He beamed and patted his little suit jacket. "Nonna bought me a tie just like Papa's."

Gabrielle looked up and caught Luca's mother watching them. She smiled, but Luca's mother didn't smile back.

Oh God. She'd had a good relationship with David's parents, although they lived in Florida and didn't visit often. They had both been warm and welcoming and as supportive as they could be after David's death.

"Ma!" Luca kissed his mother on both cheeks while holding Matteo, and they spoke briefly in Italian.

Gabrielle clutched her purse and tried to calm the frantic thudding of her heart. She'd faced down hardened criminals almost every day on the beat, survived two shootings, and stalked a vicious drug dealer in a dark warehouse. So why was she scared of Luca's mother?

"Ma. I want you to meet Gabrielle Fawkes."

"It's very nice to meet you, Mrs. Rizzoli." Gabrielle smiled again and dutifully leaned down so Luca's mother could kiss her cheeks.

"Are you Italian?" Luca's mother asked. "You don't look Italian."

"No. I'm half Irish, and half a mix of English, Scottish, and a little Swedish."

His mother's face fell and she looked up at Luca, who towered over her five-foot-three-inch frame. "She's not Italian."

"No, Ma." He put his free hand on Gabrielle's shoulder and gave her a reassuring squeeze. "But it's not the end of the world."

"And she's too thin," Luca's mother said to him, as if Gabrielle wasn't standing right there. "Look at her. You own a restaurant. Don't you feed her?"

"Ma. She's perfect."

"Bring her for dinner. I'll feed her. Everyone's coming over. Gino's coming over. Daniel's coming over. Josie's coming cover. Donna's coming over and bringing all the kids . . ."

"She's coming over."

That settled, Gabrielle was quizzed about where she lived and who she lived with, what she drove, who her family was and where they had lived over the years. She answered questions about her mother and her father, her stepmother, and her stepbrothers. She even mentioned Patrick, although not how he died.

"What do you do?" his mother asked.

Gabrielle looked to Luca for help and he shrugged.

"I'm a police detective," she said quietly.

Luca's mother stared at her for a long time and then her gaze flicked to Luca. "Nico?"

There was more to the question than Gabrielle understood because Luca's smile faded and he shook his head. His mother's face softened, and then she huffed out a determined breath.

"She should meet Josie." She gave Gabrielle's arm a firm squeeze. "Come for dinner. Meet Josie. You have a lot in common."

"We have to get going, Ma. I'm going to pick up Paolo and bring him over so he gets a good meal, and the deli is on the way. You need us to pick up anything?" Luca put Matteo down and clasped Gabrielle's hand.

"I need more mozzarella," she said. "The wet one. Alex goes through it like water. And don't forget your laundry."

Gabrielle looked over, amused. "Your mother does your laundry?" she asked in a low voice.

Totally unembarrassed, Luca shrugged. "It makes her happy."

More kissing. More hugs. While Matteo played on the grass, she met Luca's sister, Angela, who greeted her warmly, and his brother Alex who seemed detached and ill-at-ease, and acted so very much like Patrick she was sure he was high. After being introduced to a dizzying array of relatives, they went to collect Matteo for the ride home.

"You all have the same scowl," she said when Matteo

kicked up a fuss about being dragged away from his friends. "You, your sister, your mum, and Matteo. I didn't get to see Alex frown, but you all get a funny crease in the center of your forehead and you all narrow your eyes the same way. It makes me laugh."

"Everyone's forehead creases when they scowl," he said tightly.

"But everyone doesn't get this V." She traced gently on Matteo's forehead, and he forgot about his tantrum and grinned.

"You have it, too." She reached up and Luca clasped her hand and drew it away. Gabrielle cringed inwardly, realizing she'd broken the unwritten rule about comparing him to his son and braced herself for the storm.

"I think that went well." Luca said, as if their unspoken altercation hadn't happened.

"She hated me."

He put an arm around her shoulders. "She doesn't know you."

"I don't want to cause trouble for your family. Maybe I shouldn't come for dinner."

"You have to come over." Matteo bounced along the sidewalk beside them. "You're Papa's girl. You have to be there."

"That's right." Luca stopped and pulled her into his arms. "You go where I go."

Sensing an opportunity, she leaned up and whispered in his ear. "I'm going to hold you to that."

"Except if I'm going after Garcia," he said quickly. "Then where I go, you don't go."

She gave him a smug look. "Too late. You can't change the deal."

Luca scowled. "I can do anything."

"Can you make five hundred thousand dollars appear

out of thin air? Because if you can't, then this discussion is irrelevant."

Luca stilled, his face growing thoughtful. "Actually, I can."

TWENTY-ONE

Paolo flushed the toilet and snorted. Mr. Rizzoli's mother's bathroom was, by far, the nicest bathroom he'd used to indulge his new habit. Mr. Rizzoli had paid for renovations to the house after he brought Matteo to live with his mother, and now the kitchen and bathrooms had granite counters, shiny tiled floors, and rich wood cabinets. He slumped on the floor and stared up at the pot lights twinkling in the ceiling like stars, waiting for the first crest of his high.

One day, he would have a bathroom like this, and not a dark hole-in-the-wall with rusty fixtures and brown water coming through the pipes. But he needed to get his ass in gear. He'd dropped by Crazy T's place after picking up his supply, and the dealer's girlfriend had been happy to give him the last of Crazy T's labels and his label-making supplies. She'd even thrown in the plastic packets and some baggies and mumbled something about keeping Crazy T's name alive.

Paolo didn't know about Crazy T's name, but he sure as heck wanted to keep the Pink Label brand going. He'd spent the morning repackaging his dope and then walked the streets of his neighborhood trying to figure out how to tell if someone was looking for "something special." Was that guy really waiting for the bus or was he looking to score? Were those two girls giggling outside the convenience store needing a little something for a party they were going to tonight? Paolo didn't know. People were a puzzle he couldn't figure out the way he could figure out a lock, and he'd wished for a moment that he could make a living solving the puzzles of cold, hard steel.

He finally felt the rush he'd been waiting for, and peeled himself off the floor. After checking the mirror for telltale signs of his illicit activity, he smoothed down his hair, and opened the door.

"Alex." He startled when he saw Luca's brother leaning against the wall in the hallway. Although Alex was only a few years older than him, they'd never really hit it off. Alex was a serious drug addict, and Mr. Rizzoli had done everything he could to get Alex clean. He'd paid for a couple of stints in rehab, and even sent some of his crew out to shake up Alex's regular dealers. But for every dealer who disappeared, another took his place. Just like Paolo had taken over for Crazy T.

Paolo fingered the packet in his jeans pocket. He didn't need to guess whether Alex would want to buy it. Alex would take anything. And he could count on Alex's discretion. No one wanted to endure Mr. Rizzoli's wrath. But dealing in Mr. Rizzoli's mother's house to Mr. Rizzoli's drug-addicted brother was all kinds of wrong.

"Um . . . Bathroom's free." He took a step, and Alex moved to block his way.

"You missed some."

Boom. Paolo's body turned into a fireball, and sweat sizzled on his skin. He put his hand up to his nose, realizing his mistake only when Alex grinned.

"Oldest trick in the book. Plus, if you've been around as long as me, you can smell another user as soon as he walks in the door." He walked forward, herding Paolo down the hallway and into his bedroom. Taking a quick look behind him, he closed the door.

"You got a bump to share?"

Paolo swallowed hard. Was this a trick? Was Alex setting him up? If Paolo admitted to bringing drugs into the house, would Alex call in Mr. Rizzoli?

Alex sighed. "Christ. You gotta work on the game face. Everything you're thinking is right there. No, I'm not going to tell Luca. Or any of his crew. Or my mother. And I'm not gonna blackmail you either. My dealer's out of town and I'm running low, and then you walked in the door and my radar went beep. This guy's like me. He's gotta have something on him because these Sunday dinners are a frickin' bore."

"I . . . uh . . . I'm dealing now." He pulled the packet out of his pocket. He'd brought one "just in case," although at the time he hadn't thought through what "just in case" might be.

Alex looked at the packet and frowned. "You're Pink Label? What happened to Crazy T?"

"You know him?"

"I know everyone."

"He overdosed." Feeling more confident, Paolo straightened his spine. "I've taken over his territory."

"You?" Alex laughed. "Crazy T has been working that part of the city for years. People know him. He has a reputation, respect. You think you're just gonna step into his shoes? You think anyone's gonna trust a skinny kid like you?"

"Ray didn't have a problem with it."

Alex's head jerked up, and his smile faded. "You met Ray?"

"Yeah." Sensing a tiny bit of respect in Alex's tone, he straightened even more. "Ray took me to a drug house. We shot the shit while I bought my supply. He's giving me a good deal. I'll be able to double my money."

Alex looked thoughtful. "Crazy T must have vouched for you. Ray is the line to some of the best quality shit in the city. Not many people get to meet him."

Boastful now. "I have his number. When I run out of product, I just have to call him and he'll tell me where to go to get some more. I'm going to be rich. He says as soon as I make good money, I get to meet the boss and have a drink with him."

Paolo had fantasized about meeting the big boss all night long—the Lamborghini he was going to drive, the suits he was going to wear, the nightclubs that he'd walk into as a VIP with Michele Benni on his arm, shooting the shit with the boss as his crew packed his kilos into bags. He had also fantasized about the beautiful rest home his mother would live in and the warm clothes he would buy her that no one would steal. He was going to be someone. He was going to have respect. Only the sick feeling he got when he thought about how he was betraying Mr. Rizzoli tainted his dream.

"Garcia's never gonna meet with you." Alex snorted a laugh. "He only meets with big guys. Like really big. We're talking Dragon Head of the Triad, Pakhan of the Russian Mafia, leaders of street gangs, and *Cosa Nostra* bosses who are willing to bend the rules about getting involved with drugs, like Nico's cousin Tony. He wants to meet guys who can spread his product as far as it can go. People with power."

"Garcia?" Wasn't Garcia the guy who had killed

Little Ricky and sold the lethal dope to Sally G's soldiers? The same guy who was now allied with Mr. Toscani's cousin, Tony? Paolo had heard talk about Garcia at the clubhouse. He was the dude Mr. Toscani and Mr. Rizzoli were after. The man no one could find.

Alex shook his head and sighed. "Fuck. You don't even know who you're working for? Yeah, Garcia heads up the Fuentes Cartel. They bring cocaine, meth and heroin up from Mexico and distribute their product across the country. With all the visitors that come to Vegas, it's big business here, and Garcia has been trying to get a foothold in the city for years, but there's been too much competition. When he became the focus of a police investigation, he had to go underground. His alliance with Tony Toscani fills the gaps. He gets territory and enforcement. Together they're gonna wipe the competition and dominate the market. Ray is one of his top lieutenants."

"Fuck." Paolo sat on Alex's bed, scrubbed his hands through his hair. He had an in to the guy who killed Little Ricky, but how could he tell Mr. Rizzoli? If he did, he'd have to tell him he'd broken he rules, and Mr. Rizzoli had already warned him that there were no second chances when it came to breaking the rule about drugs.

"You okay, kid?"

"Yeah." He needed to think, and right now his mind was still buzzing from his last hit. "Do you . . . and Mr. Rizzoli talk? I mean about business stuff. Like what he's doing and what you're doing and who you know that he might know? That kind of stuff?"

Alex shrugged. "All he wants to talk about is me getting clean. Other than that, we have nothing in common. I'm not the perfect son like him. I was never good at sports or at school. I wasn't interested in joining the family business. I don't have his talent with the ladies, and I've got no interest in marrying a Mafia princess and popping out the usual heir and a spare. My drug habit disgusts him, and he's never held back sharing his thoughts about that."

"His wife died because of her drug habit," Paolo reminded Alex. "Maybe he doesn't want the same thing to happen to you."

Alex waved his hand vaguely in the air. "It's too late for me. And what the fuck else am I going to do with my life that's gonna measure up? I was supposed to join the family business, but you know what? I can't stand the sight of blood. The first time my dad took me out on a whack job, I puked all over the road. Humiliated myself. My father wouldn't talk to me all the way home except to tell me Luca didn't throw up his first time. Luca got right in there, beating the guy down. Luca made him proud." He sighed and waggled the package of Pink Label. "How much? I need to get those bad memories out of my head."

"Twenty bucks."

Alex dug out his wallet and threw a twenty on the bed. "You sure this is the path you want to take? You want to wind up like Crazy T? Or me? Luca's said good things about you. He thinks you've got a future with his crew once you get your head on straight. He says no one knows locks like you do."

Nooooo. He didn't want to hear that Mr. Rizzoli had said good things about him. It made what he was doing seem even more of a betrayal. There was a reason Mr. Rizzoli had joined the only *Cosa Nostra* faction in Vegas that didn't deal in drugs, and it wasn't just because of his close friendship with Mr. Toscani. Drugs had killed Mr. Rizzoli's wife and Little Ricky, and drugs were killing his brother.

"Yeah." Paolo grabbed the money and headed for the door.

"Think carefully," Alex called out. "Everyone who gets involved in his business winds up dead."

TWENTY-TWO

"What are we doing here?"

"Shh, *bella*." Luca led Gabrielle into Il Tavolino's kitchen. Although everyone had gone after a quiet Monday night, the air was still warm and smelled deliciously of tomato sauce. Luca loved his kitchen at night, the metal counters gleaming, copper pots hanging from hooks above the gas stove, cans and jars neatly stacked on the shelves. It reminded him of home, and sneaking into the kitchen for a late-night snack, only to have his mother walk in and prepare a meal for him no matter what time it was. They'd had some of their best conversations in the quiet of the night.

"When a man is hungry, *bella*, he needs food." He also wanted to cheer her up. Although she tried to hide it, she'd been very down when he picked her up after work, and he missed her smile.

"You know what's funny? It's the same for women. Isn't that crazy? Hungry women need food, too." She lifted an eyebrow in censure. "We could have gone to my place where I could kick back and relax after a long, incredibly boring Monday sitting in the Theft bureau calling people about missing phones. Although I'm not a professional cook like you, I do have food and a microwave in which to cook it. I also have a comfy sofa, comfy clothes, a TV that will be showing my favorite game show, and a dog who likes food, sofas, and game shows, too."

"You also have a roommate to look after Max." He opened the fridge and surveyed the contents.

"Well . . . yes." She sat on Mike's favorite stool and when she leaned forward to rest her chin on her hands, he got a perfect view of the crescents of her breasts. What he had planned tonight was something they definitely couldn't do with Max and Nicole around.

"What are you going to make?"

"I'm not going to make anything. We're going to play." He pulled out a cucumber and she gave a horrified gasp.

"Luca Rizzoli. We are not playing with food."

Well, that was unexpected. His kitchen was a world of culinary possibilities of the most sensual kind. Maybe she didn't understand the kind of pleasure he wanted to give her.

"I see you looking at the fridge." She glared at him. "I know how your mind works. And just in case you get any ideas, nothing is going inside my vagina that is meant to be consumed." Her hands found her hips and Luca tried not to frown.

How were they going to have fun with all these rules? How would he demonstrate his sexual prowess? Show her he was an adventurous lover? He had everything he needed right here. His last shipment had included eggplants, some smooth-skinned cucumbers, summer squash, zucchini, and for extra sensation, corn-on-the cob.

"*Bella . . .*" He opened his hands, used his most cajoling tone of voice.

Gabrielle shook her head and crossed her hands in front of her pussy. "Sorry. This right here is a no-vegetable zone."

"Meat?" He asked hopefully. He had an abundance of pepperoni, sausage, and hot dogs, although he suspected the hot dogs wouldn't do the trick after she'd had the pleasure of his substantial girth.

"I'm particular about my salami," she said dryly. "I'd feel like I was cheating on you."

He looked around the kitchen, assessing the limited options now available to him. An empty kitchen was an opportunity not to be missed, and with the cleaners coming in the morning to ensure everything was up to hygiene standards, he could indulge one of the fantasies he'd had when Gabrielle first walked into his restaurant. An idea grew in his mind and the mental image made him hard.

Rounding the counter, he pulled her gently up from her stool.

"What if I kissed you here?" He feathered kisses down her neck to the hollow at the base of her throat, inhaling the lingering fragrance of his body wash on her skin. After his mother's dinner last night, he'd taken her home and almost made her late for work this morning because he couldn't get enough of her soft, lush body.

Her face softened. "Yes, I suppose that would be okay."

"And here?" He moved lower, kissing his way down the V of her T-shirt to the crescents of her breasts.

"Yes."

"Your clothes are in the way." Sliding his hands under

her shirt, he eased her T-shirt over her head, then removed her bra and tossed her clothing on the counter.

"Better." Without warning, he descended on her left nipple, licking and sucking the bud into a tight peak. Her breath caught and he could see the pulse quicken in her neck.

"Luca."

He loved hearing his name on her lips. After giving equal attention to her right breast, he knelt before her, pressing kisses over her stomach as he tugged her jeans and panties over her hips. "And here, *bella*?" He kissed the soft down at the apex of her thighs. "Can I play here?

Her hands dropped to his head and she fell back against the counter as he helped her step out of her clothing. "Yes."

Luca smiled as he stood. "Close your eyes," he whispered.

"What are you going to do?"

"Trust me."

Her eyelashes fluttered closed and he cupped her ass in his hands, lifting her easily to sit on the stainless steel counter.

"Open your legs for me."

She swallowed hard and parted her legs, giving him a tempting glimpse of her pussy.

"Now, lean back on your elbows, arch your back, and offer me your beautiful breasts." He stripped off his clothes as she got in position. God, she was a beautiful. Too fucking much. He wrapped his hand around his cock and pumped to relieve some of the pressure.

"What are you doing?" Her eyes flew open and he almost came all over his hand when her gaze dropped down to watch as he stroked himself.

"That's not fair," she moaned. "You promised you'd let me watch."

"Not this time. And now I'll have to blindfold you for being such a bad girl." He grabbed a length of cheese-cloth from the drawer and tied it carefully around her head. "Can you see?"

"No." Her lips turned down in a frown. "I'm not sure I like not being able to see you."

"Shhh. No talking." He wandered around the kitchen gathering supplies for what promised to be a sensual feast.

"Luca?"

"You keep disobeying me, *bella,* and I'll have to find something for that mouth to do."

She laughed softly. "You think that's going to put me off?"

Fuck. His hand tightened around the basket of straw-berries he'd just taken from the cooler as mental images of his sweet little cop on her knees assailed him. With purposeful strides, he crossed the kitchen and stood between her parted legs. "Open up, naughty girl. Tip your head back."

She did as he asked, and he dangled the strawberry above her mouth. "Lick."

Her tongue came out, and she licked at the strawberry as he moved it lower. "Bite."

"Strawberry." She bit the soft flesh from the stem, and he watched, fascinated as the juice turned her lips red. Unable to resist, he leaned down and kissed the juice away, savoring the burst of sweetness on his tongue. His cock pressed against her pussy, sliding over her moist heat.

"Again." He fed her another strawberry, watched the glide of her tongue, the sensual movement of her lips.

This time when he leaned in to kiss her, he pulled her up and thrust his tongue into her mouth, tasting as she tasted.

He left her to prepare the rest of the food he'd collected and returned with his fingers sticky and wet.

"Lick." He pushed a finger in her mouth and she sucked and licked it until he groaned. No way was he going to last long enough to get through the cornucopia of delights he had on the plate beside him.

He lifted a piece of cantaloupe and held the sweet-smelling fruit to her nose. "Can you guess what it is?"

She sniffed, shook her head and he rubbed the soft flesh over her lips.

"Now?"

Her little pink tongue darted out touching, tasting. "Melon?"

He pushed the fruit between her lips and watched her bite, then fed her fruit after fruit, pausing to lick the juice from her lips and her chin. He'd chosen cantaloupe, mango, and papaya for their sweet smell, and their soft texture; figs and avocados for their irresistible creaminess and aphrodisiacal properties. Not that either of them needed an aphrodisiac. His cock was hard, aching; her nipples were taut, and moisture glistened between her thighs.

Gabrielle swallowed a fig and he watched her throat tighten. He'd been with many women, done many things, but he'd never experienced anything as erotic as the full sensory, sexual overload of feeding Gabrielle, naked, in his kitchen.

He fed her one last strawberry, but when a drop of juice dropped to her breast, he'd had enough.

"Back on your elbows. Heels on the counter. Legs wide." She dropped back with a moan and he slicked a finger along her slit, making her shudder.

"You're soaked." His voice was thick, husky with need. "It seems you like food games."

"No more games. I need you."

"One more." He searched around the counter, grabbed the last item he had collected.

"What goes well with strawberries?"

Gabrielle tipped back her head and moaned, her head still buzzing from the maelstrom of sensation. He'd murmured in Italian as he fed her, his deep voice stroking that empty space inside her that was getting smaller every day. Her skin was warm, sticky with juice. She could still smell the strawberry, the lingering traces of the other fruits he'd fed to her. And the sweetness of it all lingered on her tongue. It was unbearably erotic to eat from his hand, to have him lick her clean, to have her mouth plundered after every bite, as if he wanted to devour her. The darkness had made the experience more intense, forcing her to focus on her other senses, the hard counter beneath her, the ache between her thighs, the warmth of his lips when he sucked on her nipples, and the stroke of his finger through her labia.

"I asked you a question, Gabrielle. Unless you want a hot pepper next, I want an answer."

"Cream?"

He gave a satisfied rumble. "That's right. Now don't move."

A shiver ran down her spine as the first splash hit her throat, and then a soft trickle ran between her breasts, and over her stomach. Luca's fingers slid over her mons, parting her labia to expose her clit just as the stream crested her mound.

Gabrielle sucked in a breath as cool liquid streamed

over her clit, a gentle, insistent tickle, enough to make her pussy ache but not enough to bring her to release. "Oh God. Luca." Her inner muscles tightened, and she bucked her hips against the soft, relentless erotic trickle that was nothing more than a tease.

"So fucking hot." His hungry mouth licked along the creamy trail, sending erotic shivers up and down her spine.

She heard the soft thud of a carton. Another stream of liquid slid over her skin, so cold it took her breath away. "What is that?"

"Ice water."

When the first burn of water hit her clit, she gasped, the change of sensation sending her shooting to the edge of climax. "No more, Luca. I need you. Now."

Finally, the water stopped. Blood rushed downward to warm her cool skin, making her clit pulse and throb.

"You are beautiful," he whispered. *"Mio angelo."*

She'd never been so exposed, lewdly displayed, totally and utterly out of her comfort zone, and yet he made her feel worshiped, adored, loved.

His rough hands cupped her breasts, and he circled his thumbs over her nipples as his hands squeezed and plumped her flesh. Gabrielle arched her back and he teased her nipples with light flicks of his tongue, followed by deep pulls that she felt deep in her core.

"Did you enjoy your meal?"

"Yes."

He curled his hands around her face and kissed her breathless. "Do you want to come, *bella*?"

"Yes. Oh God. Yes."

"Ask me for what you need."

Her body trembled, her sex so wet and aching she didn't hesitate. "Make me come, Luca. Please."

"Promise me you will tell me next time when you're

feeling down, or lonely, or ill, or you have a bad day at work, and I will try to make you smile again. If you are hungry, I will feed you. If you are sad, I will comfort you. You may not always want me to protect your body, *bella,* but I will always protect your heart."

"I promise." He had a way with words that made her feel like he was speaking to her very soul.

She heard his sexy rumble of pleasure, and then his hand dove between her thighs, his palm gently pressing down on her clit.

Gabrielle jerked, ground her hips shamelessly against him. Teeth encased her nipple and he bit down as he thrust two fingers inside her and pumped hard.

The firm press of his hand, the sting of his teeth, the rasp of his breath, the forceful glide of his fingers inside her coalesced into a blaze of white-hot heat. Bombarded by erotic sensation, she dropped her head back and screamed as the orgasm hit her, sparking fire through every part of her body.

"Fuck. You're so hot." Luca clamped his hands on her hips and yanked her forward. The thick head of his cock breached her entrance and he plunged his shaft deep inside her.

Without a chance to come down, she felt need rise again as his fierce thrusts shook her body. He was so thick, so hard, filling her so completely that she spiraled up quickly, and when his fingers dug deep into her hips, she climaxed again, her pussy tightening around his rigid cock as his heat filled her to the erotic sound of his groan.

He tugged off the blindfold and dropped his body over hers, his heart pounding against her ribs. "Worth it," he murmured, half to himself.

Gabrielle lay back on the cool counter, wrapped her arms around him and pulled him down. It hadn't been easy to wear the blindfold, to give up her control after so many years of struggling to hold up the walls that kept her despair at bay. She hadn't trusted herself to open up and let go for fear of losing herself to the darkness again. But then she'd never met a man she trusted to catch her when she fell. She felt curiously free, empowered. She'd opened herself up, and he'd rewarded her trust with the most erotic experience of her life. "What's worth it? Naughty sex in the kitchen? Being saved from my cooking?"

"You." He stood, pulled her up and into his arms. "You are worth any risk. You make me want to be a better man, a better father. I want to be worthy of you. I want to give you what I couldn't give Gina. A better life than the one I live. A future. I want to give you everything, *bella*. And tomorrow, I will give you Garcia."

TWENTY-THREE

Walking beside Luca through Casino Italia in a low-cut Donna Karan dress that draped over her breasts and hugged her hips so tight she'd had trouble hiding her weapon, Gabrielle was fairly certain they were being watched. Not by the cameras or casino staff, but by someone who made her skin prickle and the hair on her neck stand on end.

"Maybe we should go to a different casino." She pulled on Luca's sleeve, trying to make him stop. The expensive fabric of his tuxedo hugged his body to perfection, highlighting his broad chest, wide shoulders, and powerful thighs. And yet the slight curl to his hair, the thick, rebellious waves that didn't sit just right, hinted that he wasn't quite what he seemed.

"We need the money to come from a legitimate source," he said. "You never know who is watching. And we won't get better odds anywhere than here."

Gabrielle shook her head wondering yet again why she had agreed to Luca's crazy plan. She was thinking as a police officer, he'd said when she gave him more information to review. Why waste time reading notes and going over files in the hopes of finding something that might lead them to Garcia, when they could buy an audience with the big man himself for only half a million dollars? How hard could it be to come up with the money when they lived in the city where dreams came true? He just needed one hundred thousand dollars up front and they would be good to go.

He clasped her hand and gave it a squeeze as they made their way to the entrance of the high-limit gaming room. "Don't worry. After Gina died, I spent a year playing craps, trying to lose myself and forget how I'd failed her. It became an addiction. I would still be playing now if my friends hadn't pulled me out, slapped some sense into me, and got me . . ." He hesitated. "Working again."

She now knew his "work" involved much more than running the restaurant, but she was glad not to know the details. It was safer for him, and no doubt safer for her.

They walked through the high-limit room, looking for Nicole and Cissy. Luca had suggested inviting them to keep her company while he played so they could all have a bit of fun. She had reluctantly agreed to call them, knowing that Cissy, in particular, was going to rake her over the coals for giving Luca all the money she'd received from the sale of David's house as a buy-in, although he'd matched her fifty thousand with his own.

"There they are." She waved to her friends, who were sipping drinks in the fancy lounge, all dressed up and ready to party.

"Oooh. You look amazing." Nicole gave Gabrielle a hug. "This is so exciting. I've never been in a high-limit room, not even at work." She spun around, showing off her navy floral bodycon dress. "Do I look like I belong?"

"*Bellissima.*" Luca kissed Nicole's cheeks and she blushed.

"I have to say, I do like the whole Italian thing," Cissy whispered to Gabrielle. Her sleeveless black lace appliqué cocktail dress was more conservative, but suited her style.

Luca ordered a round of drinks and left them to watch the action at the tables. Although the atmosphere in the high-limit room was more subdued than on the main casino floor, the undercurrent of energy and excitement lifted Gabrielle's spirits and took the edge off her reservations about Luca's plan.

"He's so into you," Cissy said. "He didn't take his eyes off you. Not even when that Sophia Loren lookalike walked in the door. How was your weekend?"

"Um . . ." She decided to skip finding out he might have killed the two men who shot up her house, discovering the body in the meat freezer, throwing up in Luca's bathroom, her visit to a Mafia clubhouse, and filthy morning sex interspersed with divulging confidential information about the Garcia case. "I met his son, we went to church, and he introduced me to his mother and family."

"It's serious when they bring a girl to meet the mother," Nicole said. "Very—"

"Wait." Cissy waved a hand, cutting Nicole off. "Who cares about his mother? He has a son? How did you forget to mention that to us? Give us the details."

Gabrielle shrugged. "His son is six and lives with his mom. She's very traditional, an amazing cook, and still does Luca's laundry. I think she hated me, but she introduced me to her friend Josie who was in a . . . similar situation to me." Josie had been understandably reluctant to speak to her, but she had given Gabrielle hope that there was a way for a good girl and a bad boy to be together without anyone dying or winding up in jail.

Nicole groaned and leaned back in her chair. "Of course, she hated you. He's a mama's boy, and you're trying to take her son away."

"He's not a mama's boy." Gabrielle gritted her teeth in annoyance. "He's very loving and respectful to her, but he made it clear he does what he wants to do. She didn't like the fact I'm not Italian, and in the nicest and most respectful way, he told her he didn't care."

But Nicole was right. She was trying to take Luca away. The more time she spent with him, the more she wanted. They worked well together, complemented each other. Although they approached things in different ways, they always seemed to be able to find a middle ground. They were stronger together than apart. Not only that, she could be herself with him, whether it was wearing heels and lace panties or waving a gun around.

"I didn't think I could care for anyone after David, and I almost feel like I'm betraying him having feelings for someone else. But Luca is different, exciting . . ."

"Maybe David was who you needed when you met him," Cissy said to Gabrielle. "Someone stable and caring who could give you the love and attention you never got after your mom died and everyone was focused on Patrick's addiction. But Luca is who you need now. Someone wild and exciting who makes you want to live life to the fullest because you know just how short it can be." Cissy sipped her drink and frowned when she caught Nicole and Gabrielle staring. "What?"

"Where did that come from?" Nicole asked. "Have you been hiding a psychology degree in your pocket?"

Cissy blushed and made a dismissive gesture. "I must have read it somewhere. So what's going on tonight? I don't usually party on a Tuesday night, but I've got a bit of down time between trials and when you said 'exciting casino night,' I couldn't resist."

"I could resist." Nicole sighed. "Every night is an 'exciting casino night' for me. My new idea of fun is sitting in a dark room in absolute silence."

"But you came." Gabrielle gave her a warm smile. "You're always there for me."

Nicole grinned. "It's because I'm such an awesome friend."

Gabrielle looked around to make sure they couldn't be overheard and beckoned them close. "Luca is trying to help me raise half a million dollars to get an audience with the drug lord who killed David. He says he can make that much playing craps in one night with a one hundred thousand dollar buy-in. So we get to watch him turn one hundred thousand dollars into half a million."

"That's a lot of money to gamble with." Nicole frowned. "His restaurant must be doing very well."

For a moment, Gabrielle considered lying to her friends, but she couldn't do it. Not to the two women who had pulled her out of the darkness that had almost claimed her life. "I cashed in the bonds I bought after selling David's house and gave him fifty and he's put up the rest."

Cissy choked on her drink. "You gave him fifty thousand dollars to gamble with? Are you crazy?"

Gabrielle's smile faded. "No, I'm not crazy. This is what I've wanted since David died. And since I was pulled off the case, this is my only option. Luca has the connections to get the drug lord's attention. We just need the money to show him we're serious."

"There are so many things wrong with what you just said, I don't know where to start." Cissy thumped her drink down on the table. "First, what connections does he have that could get you an audience with a drug lord? Second, what the hell are you thinking trying to meet with a drug lord anyway? Wasn't that the same guy who brutally killed David, shot you and arranged to have two guys shoot up your house? And third, how well do you really know Luca? What if he runs off with your money or loses it? It happens all the time. Rich widow is seduced by charismatic, charming, handsome young man. He convinces her to give him her money and POOF he disappears."

"It's his money, too," she said defensively, now regretting her decision to tell Cissy and Nicole her plan. Without knowing about Luca's mob connections, there was no way they could understand that the risk wasn't as high as it appeared to be. "And we're going to meet him together. Luca knows his way around a weapon. As for connections, he knows people who know people. He's not into drugs."

Nicole shook her head. "I see this every day. Desperate people putting up their life savings, or the last of their money, thinking they are going to win big and all their problems will be solved. And guess what happens? They lose. This is a casino like every other casino. It doesn't matter how badly you want it or need it or if the stars are aligned or your horoscope says it's your lucky day. It doesn't matter if you have a lucky rabbit's foot in your pocket or even if your life is in the toilet and you deserve a break. It's a mathematical fact that unless you cheat, the odds are against you. What if he loses it all, Gabrielle? What will you do?"

"What if he wins?" Gabrielle bit out, losing her patience. Luca had assured her over and over again that he would win, although he couldn't tell her why. But listening to Nicole she wondered if he was just saying the words every gambler said before entering a casino.

"He won't."

"I'm willing to take the risk," she said finally. "And if he does lose it, so what? I'm happy where I am. I have

David's pension, his life insurance, my savings, and my job. I don't need designer clothes or handbags. I'd rather lose that money and feel that I did everything I could to avenge David than spend the rest of my life regretting that I didn't take this chance."

"Why don't you let David go?" Cissy said quietly. "You've changed since you met Luca. It's like you came out of your shell. You sparkle. You smile. You laugh. You take risks. You have fun. I've known you forever, and I've never seen you as happy. You've met a great guy who adores you and makes you laugh. Isn't that enough? Why don't you give up the quest for revenge and grab your happily ever after? With all the work you did on that case, you know the drug lord will eventually be caught. Meantime, you can get on with the business of living your life, which you haven't really done since David died. Take that money and invest in the future. If you go after that drug lord, you might not have a future at all."

"For the last two years, revenge is all I've lived for." Gabrielle curled her hand around her glass so her friends wouldn't see her trembling fingers. "It was the reason I got out of bed in the morning. It pulled me out of a depression that almost cost me my life. I feel like I have to pay it back. I have to finish what I started. I promised David I would avenge him."

"You know he wouldn't want that," Cissy said softly. "He was good man. He would want you to be happy. And we can both see that Luca makes you happy. You just need to see it, too."

Gabrielle looked away, trying to hide how much Cissy's words had shaken her. Not once had she ever second-guessed her goal. But was revenge really worth losing the love she had never imagined she could have again— the love she had just found?

"It's time," Luca said, coming up to them. "The table is clear. Let's go have some fun. I need my angel by my side to blow on the dice and bring me luck."

"I'm not a lucky person, Luca," she said, following him to the craps tables.

"You're the luckiest woman on the earth." He looked over his shoulder and gave her a cocky grin. "You caught me."

Luca joined a rowdy table and bought a stack of chips. As soon as he hit his point number, everyone began to bet. The game moved so fast that Gabrielle couldn't keep up, even with her fledgling knowledge of the rules. Luca rolled double sixes, hard fours, snake eyes, and every possible winning combination of the dice. Some people called out requests, and he managed to fulfill them. Players from the high-limit slot machines and blackjack tables came over to watch, and then came the casino executives, men and women with stern faces and dark suits.

"Why are there so many?" Gabrielle whispered.

Luca barely spared them a look. "They're looking for controlled shooting. They think I'm setting the dice." He rolled another double six and the crowd cheered.

"Are you?"

He gave her a sideways glance. "Let's add that one to the questions-that-shouldn't-be-asked-because-they-won't-be-answered category."

She felt a disturbance in the air, a ripple of breath. The crowds behind Cissy and Nicole parted and the man she now knew as Nico appeared behind them. Every inch the mobster, he wore a dark suit, crisp white shirt, and red tie. He spoke briefly to a few of the casino executives and Gabrielle frowned.

"He acts like he runs the place."

"He does. This is his casino."

Suddenly it all made sense. Luca's insistence that he had to play at Casino Italia, his confidence that he would win big tonight . . . Whatever Luca was up to, Nico was in on it, and she was just along for the ride.

Gabrielle glared at Nico and fought back the urge to slap that smug expression off his face. Despite his involvement in their plan, he had intended to hurt Luca, and she would never forgive him for that.

"Stop scowling at him, *bella,* or you'll make him laugh."

"I'll give him something to laugh at." She curled her hand into a fist. "If he still plans to go through with that beating, he'll have to get through me."

Luca threaded his hand through her hair and angled her head back for the searing heat of his kiss. "He's given me a pass until we deal with Garcia. And yes, it will happen. I broke the rules and I have to pay. Now, stop threatening him under your breath because it's turning me on and I can't concentrate." He nipped her earlobe in warning and gave a soft growl.

"Luca!" Embarrassed by his very overt display of affection, she pulled away.

"Shhh. It's time you understood what it means to be mine."

"It means I get ravaged in public?" she muttered, while Cissy and Nicole shot her amused glances from the other side the table.

"You get ravaged all the time." He held the dice under her lips. "Blow, sexy girl in her sexy dress that I'm going to tear off as soon as we get out of here."

Mollified by his sweet words, Gabrielle blew on the dice for the luck Luca didn't need.

Maybe Cissy was right. She'd been on this path so long she couldn't see the exit sign staring her in the face. She hadn't had anything to live for when she vowed to avenge David. But now she'd found Luca and in opening herself up to him, she'd found herself. Was revenge worth losing everything?

She glanced down at the pile of chips in front of him. "Are you close to making the target? Maybe we should just call it quits."

Luca laughed and pulled her into his arms. "We have everything we need. The last fifteen rolls have been for fun. Let's go cash out."

He was right. She had everything she needed, right here in her arms. In her darkest despair, she'd never imagined her salvation would come in the form of a high-rolling mobster with a sensual smile. As soon as they were alone, she would tell him she didn't want to go through with the plan. She wanted a life unburdened by revenge. A future with the man she loved.

The casino manager and a hospitality executive escorted them to the cashier where Luca cashed out his chips, and took his winnings in cash in a complimentary black leather bag. They returned to the high-limit room where they enjoyed champagne with Cissy and Nicole while Nico talked nearby with his casino manager.

Gabrielle glared at Nico from beneath her lashes to Luca's obvious amusement. When she muttered something quietly under her breath about betraying friends, Luca leaned down and quieted her with a soul-searing kiss.

"We'll go to my restaurant after we're done," he said quietly. "I'll put the money in the safe, and then I have something to show you in the kitchen. A new dish."

"What dish?"

"Gabrielle à la mode."

She laughed, but her smile faded when three dark-haired uniformed police officers appeared in the doorway. One of them talked to the security guard and he pointed in their direction.

"We're looking for Luca Rizzoli," the tallest police officer said, walking toward them.

Nico moved to stand in front of Luca while the casino manager ushered the curious crowd away. "I'm the owner of Casino Italia. We didn't call for the police."

"Someone did." An officer with short jet-black hair and a round face pulled a set of handcuffs from his belt and pointed at Luca. "Are you Luca Rizzoli?"

"Yes." Luca stepped out from behind Nico, his face an expressionless mask.

"Hands behind your back. You're coming with us."

Gabrielle's police training finally overrode her shock and her brain kicked into gear. "I'm Detective Fawkes from the Theft Bureau of the LVPD." She pulled her badge from her purse and held it up as the officer started to read the Miranda Warning. "What are you charging him with?"

The tall officer laughed as if she'd make a joke. "You should know, Detective Fawkes. You called it in."

"Jesus Christ." Nico's face twisted in anger. "You set him up?"

She stared at him aghast. "No. Of course not. I had nothing to do with this."

"Did you want to get him out of the way so you could make the arrest yourself?" Nico snarled. "Was it about the glory? Or was it the money you were after? Or did you want to see him behind bars all along? Was he your target from the beginning?"

"No." She stared at him in horror. "I didn't call anyone. I promise."

"Get her out of here." Nico gestured to one of his security guards. "Her friends, too."

"No." She tried to twist away when one of the guards grabbed her arm. "Wait. Let me talk to the police officers again. I need to understand what's going on. I want to help sort this out."

"You've done enough," Nico spat out. "Now go."

"Luca." Gabrielle called out as the police officers led him away. "I'll come down to the station. I'll get to the bottom of this."

He hadn't said anything since the police arrived, and he didn't even turn when she called. She felt sick at the thought that he might believe she had betrayed him, and even worse about the niggle in her mind that maybe he had actually done something wrong. She had never asked him about the bodies of the two Albanians who had shot up her house or about the work he did outside the restaurant.

He was in the Mafia.

She was a police officer.

They were, and would always be, on opposite sides of the law.

TWENTY-FOUR

"Hey, Gaby. You doing okay?" Jeff leaned over Gabrielle's partition only moments after she'd had her first sip of her morning coffee. "You look tired."

"Yeah. Just . . . didn't sleep well last night." Now that was an understatement. She'd spent the entire night trying to find out which police agency had Luca, and which station or jail he'd been taken to. She'd never realized just how many agencies there were in the LVPD or how hard it was to track an arrest.

"You don't sound so good."

"I must be coming down with a cold." Or maybe she'd talked herself hoarse on the phone asking the same questions again and again.

"You want to go for lunch? The deli down the road makes great chicken noodle soup."

"No, thanks. I'm not hungry. Did you need something?"

"I have good news." His face brightened, and he held up a phone. "I got a lead on the guy who vandalized my car. I had charged up his phone to see if I could crack the password and someone called and asked for Paolo."

"Paolo?" Her blood chilled and she stared at the phone. Luca's young associate was named Paolo. He had looked after Matteo when they found the dead body, and he'd ridden with them in the car to Mrs. Rizzoli's house for Sunday dinner. "Any last name?"

"No, he hung up when I asked who he was, and the damn phone wouldn't let me access the contacts or any information without the password. But I've got his number. I'm going to reverse track it to see if I can get an address or some kind of record. Maybe I'll be lucky and it was someone calling on a landline. But if that doesn't work, I've put a tracer in the phone. Next time someone calls, I'll trace the number and use the friend to find him."

Gabrielle clenched her hand in a fist on her lap. It couldn't be a coincidence that a guy with the same name as Luca's associate had been at her house the same night Luca showed up. Paolo was young, and he seemed like a nice kid, although why he threw a rock at Jeff's car window, she didn't know. She needed to warn him, or better yet, she needed to get her hands on the phone. "That's a lot of effort to find a car vandal."

"He owes me two thousand dollars for the repairs because the rock hit the hood and damaged the paint. I think the time spent will be well worth it when I catch him."

She glanced down at the files on her desk, almost laughed to see the solution literally staring her in the face. "You've come to the right place," she said, smiling. "Missing phones are my specialty. I'm looking into a crime ring that buys them up and ships them overseas, so I've got copies of all the missing phone reports filed in the city. Why don't you leave it here? I'll go through the paperwork and see if anyone reported it."

"Thanks, but I think I'll track this guy down myself."

Damn. She scrambled to think of another way to get her hands on the phone. "Well, at least let me take down the serial number and I can run it through the database. With those old models, the number is engraved on the SIM tray."

"Good idea." Jeff gave her the phone and she used a paperclip to remove the SIM tray from the side of the device. After copying down the number, and replacing the chip, she returned the phone. She could only hope Paolo could use the number to shut it down.

Jeff tucked the device in his pocket. "I need to keep it on me in case one of his friends calls again," he explained when she lifted a querying eyebrow. "No way am I going to miss a call. Some jobs you just have to do yourself."

Gabrielle stared at the files on her desk and sighed. "That's what I thought, and then I got shot and now everyone is hunting for Garcia except me."

Jeff patted her back. "Are you feeling sorry for yourself?"

"I suppose I am a bit. I'm back to where I started. Sitting at a desk, pushing paper while he's out there killing people and selling drugs that destroy lives. I just wanted to stop him from hurting people."

"I thought you wanted revenge," Jeff said, leaning on her partition. "Have you given that up?"

"Yes." The word slipped out before she could catch it, but it felt right. Revenge was a cold, empty, lonely place without joy or love or happiness. Luca had shown her that there was something else worth living for. He had made her look forward not back, at a world new and exciting and filled with hope and possibility—a world worth fighting for. She still wanted Garcia caught, but not for David. She wanted him off the streets so little boys didn't walk into their daddy's restaurant and see a man hanging in a meat freezer, and so people didn't destroy their lives with drugs and leave their families to suffer.

"I still want justice," she continued. "I'll keep my fingers crossed that Agent Palmer and his team find him soon so he can spend the rest of his life in jail. I just wish I was involved."

"Hey, there." Jeff mocked a downturned smile. "You know it's for the best. You were wasting your time chasing after a guy who is never going to get caught. Now, instead of banging your head against the wall, you can focus on something positive. There are lots of thieves out there just waiting for you to catch them. I know you're disappointed to be off the case, but you don't always make the best decisions, so it's good Agent Palmer finally took you in hand."

"What do you mean I don't make the best decisions?"

Jeff shrugged. "Look at the fling you had with that mobster."

Her blood chilled. "What mobster?"

"The guy I met at your house. Luca Rizzoli. He's Italian. Violent. Runs a restaurant downtown. He had mob written all over him. I mean, come on, Gaby. You're a police officer. Weren't you even suspicious when he showed up at your house and only a few hours later two guys arrive with AKs and start shooting? Did you not make the connection?"

No, she hadn't made the connection. She had always assumed Garcia sent the shooters and they were after her. Maybe she was wrong. And if she was wrong about that, she could have been wrong about other things, like just how involved Luca really was in the Mafia world.

"And then he attacks me?" Jeff continued, his voice rising in indignation. "A police officer? You were risking your career for what? Was he really that good in bed?"

"Jeff, you're out of line." She stood, folding her arms across her chest, a bolder, stronger, more assertive version of herself. "He owns a restaurant. And he's never told me he's in the mob."

"He can't. He's bound by *omertà*—a blood oath of silence. He'll die before he tells anybody anything. Although with the right incentive, you can make anyone talk."

"I don't know anything about Luca being part of the mob, and I'm uncomfortable having this discussion with you." Despite the small seed of doubt he had planted in her mind, she was beyond angry with Jeff. He had well and truly gone too far. "It's one thing to be jealous. Something else entirely if you're accusing him of being a criminal." Her stomach clenched at the irony. Luca had just been apprehended on criminal charges and here she was defending him.

"Sorry." He held up his hands in mock defeat. "I just worry about you. I don't want you to get hurt again. Guys like that make a lot of enemies and they wind up dead. You need someone stable in your life. Someone who will always be there for you. Someone you know and trust."

"Gabrielle Fawkes?"

She looked up just as the internal courier placed an enormous foil-wrapped bouquet on her desk. "Are those for me?"

"Even bigger than the last bunch. Someone really cares."

Her heart skipped a beat as he walked away. Luca must be out on bail and trying to apologize. She pulled open the foil and her nose wrinkled at the bold, gaudy colors and garish arrangement. The flowers were the opposite of anything she would ever have picked for herself. Even the scent was overpowering, thick and sickly like stale perfume. She thought Luca knew her, but maybe she'd been wrong about him in more ways than one.

"You don't look happy," Jeff said, frowning.

"They're not really . . ." She trailed off, not wanting to say anything bad about Luca in front of Jeff.

Fighting to hide her distaste, she tore open the card.

Miss you. Let's start over. Jeff.

"Jeff?" She stared at him in shock. "You sent these? They're . . ." *Garish. Ostentatious. Inappropriate. Unsettling.*

"Beautiful. I know. And different from what you're used to, but different is good." He leaned in and kissed her cheek. "Beautiful women should have beautiful flowers especially at the start of what's gonna be a great week. Tomorrow I'm going to make dinner for you. I'll cook a special Mexican dish and bring it to your place with a bottle of wine. And on Wednesday, I have another surprise . . . a sparkly one."

"Jeff. I don't . . ."

"I do a great *cochinita pibil*," he called out as he walked away. "Almost as good as my mother used to make. I'll see you tomorrow at seven. And this time I won't take no as an answer."

Luca jerked his hands, testing the steel cuffs around his wrists. The chain attaching them to the metal table in the room clattered, jangling nerves already raw from being knocked unconscious after he was secured in the back of the police van. Talk about police fucking brutality.

And what the hell kind of police interrogation room was this? No two-way mirror. No cameras as far as he could see. The ceiling tiles were stained and cracked, revealing sagging beams, rusty piping, and exposed electrical wires. A single bulb cast a stark glow over the cinderblock walls. It looked like someone's basement. Where the fuck was all his tax money going? The police department needed updating in a very bad way.

Well, he wouldn't be here long. No doubt Charlie Nails or one of the other Toscani crime family lawyers would be on his way to bail him out, and then they'd go to court and deal with whatever charges had been laid against him. He still didn't know why he was here, although if he had to guess they had probably tied him to the Albanians who shot up Gabrielle's house, or maybe Jason Prince had squealed, or had someone figured out the scam he and Nico had pulled to get five hundred grand out of the casino?

Someone like Gabrielle.

Christ, she'd betrayed him just like Gina had betrayed him. How had he miscalculated just how badly she wanted revenge? Was she out there right now getting ready to buy her way into a meeting with Garcia and putting herself in danger all over again?

Fuck it. He didn't give a damn. He was ice. Cold. Hard. Dark in a way he hadn't been after Gina's betrayal, because only love could rip out your heart and leave it bleeding on the fucking floor. He hadn't loved Gina. But he loved Gabrielle. Loved her so much he'd been blind.

But it didn't make any sense.

The door opened, and Gabrielle's cop friend, Jeff, walked in, flanked by two of the police officers who had apprehended him in the casino. One look at Jeff's face and his gut clenched in warning. This was about to get personal in a very painful way.

"Nice to see you again, Rizzoli." Jeff sprawled on the

chair across the table. "You seem to always be where trouble is at."

"I'm not talking without my lawyer."

"I guess I'll have to do the talking then." Jeff smirked. "So, first we have two Albanians who are running a protection racket for a drug lord named Garcia that includes a convenience store and a nightclub both on the same street as your restaurant. And then one day they disappear. Where do you think they went?"

"Maybe they went back to fucking Albania."

"I don't think so. And neither does Mr. Prince, the nightclub owner who pays you money every week to protect him. He says you told him they'd gone on a permanent swimming vacation."

Fucking Prince was about to lose the remaining interest he had in his business as well as a couple of limbs. But Luca wasn't worried. Prince didn't have any concrete evidence tying him to the crime.

"Extortion is against the law, Mr. Rizzoli."

"Glad to hear you passed that exam in police school. And why the fuck are you involved? I thought you were in Narcotics."

Jeff lifted his ankle to his knee and leaned back in his chair. "I have a diverse range of interests including arresting people who try to fleece casinos for cash. As for the Albanians, I think they were operating on territory that you thought was yours."

"My territory is a restaurant plus ten yards for outdoor tables and ten parking stalls out back. I pissed in all the corners so everyone knows it's mine."

Jeff's nose wrinkled slightly in disgust. Good. He wanted a reaction because he was beginning to suspect Jeff had nothing on him, although how did he know to talk to Prince?

"And then there were the two guys who shot up Gabrielle's house when you were there. They were Albanians, too. Again, tied to Garcia. He must be very upset that someone has been taking out his workforce. We found them in the desert, by the way. They'd been beaten so badly their faces were pulp. But they didn't die from the beatings. They died from being hogtied in a very special way. You know what that is?"

"I'm in the restaurant business, not the pig business. Can't say I do." Sweat trickled down his back. He fucking hated being toyed with. If Jeff had something on him, he wanted to know.

"It's very ingenious and a painful way to die," Jeff continued. "When they struggled to escape, they strangled themselves." Jeff shifted his weight. "Did you know only the Mafia use that kind of hogtie?"

Luca shrugged. "Then I guess you'll be looking for some mobsters."

"Or I could be looking for a particular mobster who might want these Albanians dead. Say, for example, someone who was angry that they shot up his girlfriend's house while he was fucking her inside."

Luca's hand tightened into a fist by his side. Those last four words told him everything he needed to know. Jeff was pissed that Gabrielle had chosen Luca over him, and he was going to use the law to get his revenge.

Don't react. Don't react. But it was so damn hard.

"I think any man would get angry if he was interrupted while he was fucking his girl," he said evenly. "But I guess you wouldn't know about that."

Fuck. He needed to control his mouth, but everything about Jeff pissed him off, from his smarmy face to his supercilious attitude, and from the fact he was a cop to his fucking blatant desire for Gabrielle.

Mine.

Seemingly unaffected by Luca's little dig, Jeff folded

his arms across his chest. "I think you punished the Albanians for shooting up Gabrielle's house, and you handled it the way all mobsters deal with these things— with a total lack of respect for both the law and the people who might be hurt by your actions. You're lucky Garcia didn't find you first. I can't imagine he would let four deaths go unpunished. Incidentally, murder is also against the law."

"I get it." Luca faked a laugh. "I'm Italian so I must be in the mob. Well sorry to disappoint. I own a restaurant. I pay my taxes. You want to see my books or take a tour of my kitchen, I'm happy to oblige." Luca was so fucking done with this. "You got any other interesting stories you want to share with me? More things you learned in police school? I've got a call I'm entitled to."

Jeff's face tightened and he pulled a phone out of his pocket. "There's one last thing. Someone vandalized my car outside Gabrielle's house. Again, you were there. I picked up his phone. Managed to get a name. Paolo. You know any Paolos?"

"I know lots of Paolos," he said carefully. "It's a common Italian name."

"Of course, it is." Jeff tucked the phone away. "I'm just waiting for someone to call him again. I've got a tracer on the phone. I'm going to find his friend and then I'm going to find him. Nothing pisses me off more than someone damaging my car." He hesitated. "Actually, there is one thing that pisses me off more and that's someone fucking my girl."

"There it is." Luca laughed for real this time. "Why don't you just be a man and admit that's really why I'm here? You obviously have nothing on me or you wouldn't be throwing shit around about Albanians and mobsters and hoping something sticks."

"Actually, I've got the girl." Jeff smiled. "She's having dinner with me tomorrow night. She loves Mexican food and I'm making her something very special. Too bad you won't be able to join us and expand your culinary repertoire. But, thanks to Gabrielle, you'll be spending some time in a very special cell where men like you pay for their crimes, and I think food will be the least of your concerns during your stay."

So Gabrielle had betrayed him? It didn't make sense. First, except for the unfortunate situation with Little Ricky, and the unintentional visit to the clubhouse, he'd been careful to keep his mob-related activities quiet so she would never be in a conflict situation. She didn't have any knowledge of the crimes Jeff had accused him of committing. Second, she wasn't the betraying type. Although she'd decided to work with him to find Garcia, her motives were altruistic. At heart, she was a good person, a protector who was always putting others before herself. Why risk her life to save him at the clubhouse if she planned to have him arrested? And third, she loved him. Although she'd never said the words, he saw it in her eyes, heard it in her voice, felt it when they were together. Love had ripped her apart, and she was afraid to embrace it again, but the feelings were there just the same.

So how the fuck did he wind up here?

"What crimes?" he asked Jeff. "What evidence do you have? What the fuck are you charging me with?"

A slow smile spread across Jeff's face. "Crimes of the heart."

Gabrielle drove down her street, squinting into the late-afternoon sun. Unable to focus after Jeff's visit, she'd taken the rest of the day off to visit every police station, detention center and jail, trying to find Luca. There was no record of his arrest in any database, which meant he hadn't been processed or charged, and since she couldn't find him in any waiting room, holding center, or interrogation room, she had to conclude that he'd been released shortly after the police apprehended him and he was too angry to call.

Why did the officers think she'd called in a tip about Luca? She'd tried to find them, but no one remembered three officers coming in to any detention facility last night with a man of Luca's description, and the beat cops who covered the Freemont Street Experience, where Nico's casino was located, had not been informed about the arrest. Well, she wasn't going to give up. She'd texted Luca and left him voice messages, and she'd keep texting until he answered.

She pulled up in front of the house and groaned when she saw Clint's truck parked at an angle in the driveway. Goddammit. He shouldn't be here. Nicole had obtained a protection order against him and he was prohibited from coming to the house or going to her casino.

She reached for the phone to report his breach of the order, and then pulled back. Clint knew about the protection order. His presence here was deliberate, and she had a strong feeling he hadn't come to apologize and profess his love. He clearly didn't care about his recent conviction or the fine he had to pay or even the repercussions of showing up at the house. Calling the police last time hadn't made a difference. Why would it make a difference now?

Luca would have made a difference. She was pretty damn sure Clint wouldn't be here if he'd spent ten minutes in a dark alley with Luca.

Or with her.

You were magnificent.

Damn right. And although she still believed in the

law, Luca had made her see that the world wasn't black and white; there were shades of gray where mobsters and cops could be together and bad deeds could be punished with justice of another kind.

Fuck Jeff and his garish flowers and his platitudes. He wasn't her friend. Friends didn't break your door or insist you owed them because they'd been there when you needed them. Friends gave and expected nothing in return. Friends saw into your heart and told you the truths you needed to hear.

Fuck Agent Palmer and the pile of cases on her desk. She was no paper pusher. She didn't want revenge, but she did want justice. She'd worked damn hard for it and no one was going to take it away.

Fuck Luca who refused to answer her calls. She hadn't done anything wrong. And if he wouldn't come to her, she would go to him. She loved him and she was damn well going to let him know.

Her rebel heart pounded in her chest as she tucked her badge under the seat and stripped off her holster and gun. If Clint was inside on his knees begging forgiveness, she would leave him be. But if he'd hurt Nicole in any way, he would learn the lesson he should have learned in the alley. The lesson she'd learned from the mafioso who had stolen her heart.

No one fucked with her friends.

Heart pounding, she crossed the drive and opened the front door. She could hear Max barking in the back yard, something he would never do if all was well. Taking a deep breath she walked into the living room, still smelling of fresh paint and sawdust. Clint had his back to her as he slammed his fist into Nicole's face.

"Stupid, ugly, fucking bitch," he snarled. "This is what you get for calling the fucking cops. You deserve this, Nic. You asked for it. You and that cunt who got in the way. I don't give a damn that she's a cop. I'm not afraid of her."

"You should be," Gabrielle said from the doorway. "You should be very afraid."

It took her three minutes to teach him a lesson he would never forget, and two minutes to drag his limp body out the door. Although she would have liked to go full Mafia and dump him in the desert, she wasn't strong enough to lift an unconscious two hundred pound man into a pickup truck, even with Nicole's help. But she did roll him down the steps and call the police to report an assault, and the paramedics to report an accidental fall.

No doubt he would be charged with assault and breaching the order, but she knew that wasn't what would keep him away. It was the fury of her fists, and the heat of her anger. It was her refusal to recognize limits, and her willingness to take risks and break rules. And maybe, just maybe, it was the fear she put into his heart when she told him what would happen if he ever came near Nicole again. Something about . . . neckties.

Luca would have been proud.

TWENTY-FIVE

Paolo shoved his fist into his mouth to stifle a moan as Frankie swept the Toscani clubhouse for bugs using a small, handheld surveillance detector.

This was bad. Very bad.

Mr. Rizzoli missing. That damn cop with his phone. His body wracked with the pain of withdrawal. His face still smarting from Michele Benni's punch when he'd been high during their date and let his hands roam free.

He needed a bump so bad. One snort and the pain would go away. He would feel that blissful numbness that made life as a loser so much easier to bear. But how would he help Mr. Rizzoli if his mind was fucked up? He wanted a hit, but he wanted to help Mr. Rizzoli more, and that wasn't going to happen if gave in to the craving.

"It's clear," Frankie yelled. "Don Toscani can come in."

Frankie was a cold-hearted bastard who'd never had a kind word for Paolo, but if Paolo could pick a job in Mr. Rizzoli's crew, it would be to do one of the jobs Frankie did. Not his work as an enforcer—Paolo didn't have the stomach for violence—but his work as a bodyguard. Paolo had enjoyed looking out for Matteo before Mr. Rizzoli's wife died. And he'd felt good when he threw the stone to protect Gabrielle. He hadn't been able to protect his mother, but he could make it up to her by protecting other people. Problem was he didn't have a bodyguard body and he was getting thinner every day because when he was high he forgot to eat.

Paolo hadn't had many opportunities to see Don Toscani in action and he'd never been formally introduced to the big boss. Introductions were never made until you became a soldier, or a highly trusted associate. One day, maybe, he'd get to shake Don Toscani's hand, but for now his job was to stay on the fringes of the room during this important meeting until one of Luca's soldiers needed him.

"Bring me up to speed." Don Toscani's voice echoed around the clubhouse. Tall, broad shouldered and heavily muscled, he dominated the room through the force of his presence alone.

"Luca is still missing," Frankie said. "We've checked hospitals, medi-centers, his apartment, his mother's house, the restaurant, and the bars and clubs where he likes to go. His car is still at the casino. Charlie Nails checked the City of Las Vegas Jail and the Clark County Detention Center. He's also been to the detention centers in Henderson, Las Vegas, and North Las Vegas. He's tried the online Inmate Search databases, and hit up every one of our contacts in the local police stations. There's no record of Luca's arrest, and no one remembers seeing him brought in."

Silence.

"What about Gabrielle?" Don Toscani asked.

"Paolo knew where she lived so he took me to her place," Mike said. "She was at work, but I talked to her roommate, Nicole. Someone beat Nicole up pretty bad and I'm gonna find the fucker and make him pay. Anyway, she said Gabrielle has been looking for Luca, too, without any luck. Seems strange if she was involved in his arrest. But who knows how cops think?"

"You think he ratted us out and went into witness protection?" Sally G asked.

"I think it's a possibility." Frankie pulled out a pack of smokes. "He broke the rules to be with Gabrielle, and he knew once we had Garcia it was over between them. It was her or us. Maybe he made the wrong choice, and he's run off with her. Or maybe he left her behind, too, like his old man did. You can't trust those Rizzolis."

Don Toscani's face tightened. "I don't think you understand how deeply his father's betrayal cut him. His whole life since then has been about restoring the family honor. He has given his life for the family—he almost gave his life for me. He would die rather than do what his father did. This thing with Gabrielle . . . it's not the same. It comes from the heart."

Bang. Bang. Bang. The front door shook. Frankie and Don Toscani's bodyguards rushed to surround the don.

"Paolo," Frankie barked. "Go check the surveillance cameras."

Conscious of all the eyes on him, Paolo ran to the check the surveillance monitors in the alcove by the door.

"Holy shit! It's Gabrielle."

"Shoot the bitch," someone yelled.

Paolo looked back over his shoulder and Frankie shook his head. "She's not welcome here. Tell her to fuck the hell off."

"I'm looking for Paolo." Gabrielle's voice was loud and clear through the steel door. "And if Luca's there, I've got something for him."

"She doesn't know where he is," Paolo said, half to

himself. "How can she not know where he is if she arranged to have him arrested? Or if she put him in witness protection? Or if she was going with him?"

"Luca!" She shouted through the door. "If you're in there, you'd better come out or I'll call 911 and report a fire in your damn clubhouse. You are not going after Garcia alone."

Paolo turned. "She said . . ."

"We heard what she said." Don Toscani's lips quivered, amused. "Frankie, go open the door."

Frankie gave a violent shake of his head. "Nico . . ."

Don Toscani held up his hand, cutting off Frankie's protest. "I want to get to the bottom of this. She was genuinely shocked when the police showed up to arrest Luca, and horrified that we thought she was involved. I don't think she would betray him. I saw them together. Love is blind, but it is also hard to fake."

Jaw tight, eyes hard, his disapproval etched in every line of his body, Frankie opened the door. Gabrielle stepped inside and held her arms out at her sides. She wore tight jeans, a form-fitting green tank top and a black leather jacket that matched her knee-high black leather boots. Her long blonde hair tumbled over her shoulders and Paolo's mouth watered. She was so hot he thought he might melt just from looking at her. And then he remembered the rule about looking at a made man's woman and cooled himself off by staring at Frankie instead. Damn enforcer had to be made of stone to show no sign of being affected by the bold, beautiful woman standing in the doorway.

"You'll want to disarm me," she said. "I've also got a .22 in my left boot, and a knife in my right. The rest you'll have to find yourself."

Cursing in Italian, Frankie patted her down and relieved her of her weapons. Paolo definitely wanted bodyguard duty if it meant he got to feel up hot chicks. Although maybe not ones as dangerous as Gabrielle. After Frankie finished disarming her, Paolo counted three guns, one Taser and two knives.

Gabrielle handed another knife to Paulo. "There's a cop at my office who has your phone and he's looking for you. Warn your friends not to call your old number because he's planning to track them down to get to you."

Fuck. Yet another mistake coming back to haunt him.

"I've got two more weapons on me." She challenged Frankie with a stare. "But I don't think Luca will be happy if you go looking for them. They aren't in readily accessible places."

"*Cristo mio*," Frankie spat out. "He bought himself a shitload of trouble with you."

Gabrielle shrugged. "He's a man who likes a challenge. Now, where is he?"

"We don't know." Don Toscani leaned against the pool table, arms folded over his chest. "We thought you might."

"I called everywhere and went to visit every station and detention center. No one has a record of an arrest, there are no police reports about him being apprehended, and he isn't in the system for the jails. He hasn't answered my calls or texts, so I figured either he thinks I had something to do with what happened at the casino, or he's taken the money and gone to see Garcia on his own." Her brow creased with worry. "Maybe he's there. Maybe Garcia got him."

"I have the money," Nico said. "So it's unlikely he went after Garcia. The only other realistic possibility is that Garcia has him. He may be trying to even the score. He's down three men to our one."

Paolo's stomach twisted in a knot. He hadn't even considered the possibility that Garcia might have kidnapped Mr. Rizzoli. What if Paolo went to the restaurant and found Mr. Rizzoli hanging in the meat freezer like Little Ricky? Mr. Rizzoli was like a father to him, and what had Paolo given back? The last time he'd been at the restaurant, he'd been high and disrespectful.

Paolo's hand fisted by his side, and he was almost overwhelmed with the urge to throw his remaining drug supply in the toilet. What the fuck was he doing with his life? There was no one he respected more than Mr. Rizzoli and if he were dead, Paolo's last memories would be tainted with the guilt of dealing drugs to Mr. Rizzoli's addicted brother in his mother's house and putting his damn feet on Mr. Rizzoli's desk.

Gabrielle reached into her purse. At least eight guns left their holsters and pointed in her direction. Alarmed, Paolo moved to her side. She was still under Mr. Rizzoli's protection and since no one else from Mr. Rizzoli's crew was coming forward, the burden of protecting her fell on him.

Gabrielle gave an exasperated sigh. She didn't really seem to be afraid of the wiseguys or the guns. She had balls of steel. Paolo wanted to have balls like her.

"Although it's flattering to think you're all so terrified of me that you need multiple weapons pointed in my direction," she said. "I was just trying to get my phone so I could share the information I have on Garcia and we could work together to find him."

"We don't work with fucking cops." Frankie glared at Gabrielle. Paolo shivered. No one wanted to be on the wrong end of Frankie's scowl.

Except, it seemed, Gabrielle. She scowled at Frankie, and her hands found her hips. "You're working with one today because if Luca is with Garcia, you're not going to find to him without my help."

"We don't need your help."

"Yeah?" She faced off with the formidable Frankie. "So what's your plan? Are you going to call up Garcia on his personal line and say hey, buddy, did you kidnap one of my friends? Can you do me a solid and drop him off with his arms and legs intact?"

A shiver ran over Paolo's skin as he sensed where this was headed. He took one last look around the clubhouse, remembering the first time he'd walked inside, his dreams of becoming a wiseguy and how excited he'd been to tell his mom that he was going to make real money at last.

"We've got the money," Frankie retorted. "We'll stick with Luca's plan."

"Garcia knows who we are," Don Toscani said. "Tony will have given him all our details. That's probably how he found Little Ricky. And if he has Luca, he'll be expecting us to show up if he hasn't whacked him already. We need to find another way."

Paolo winced at Don Toscani's harsh words. Mr. Rizzoli couldn't be dead. He was a good man. An honorable man. He looked after his mother and his son. He had tried again and again to help Alex. He had taken a bullet for Don Toscani. He had protected Gabrielle. Paolo wanted to be worthy of his mentor. He'd made a huge mistake with the drugs. He just needed a second chance . . .

Or he could take it.

His heart leaped in his chest. Mr. Rizzoli had given him a dream. He'd given Paolo hope, and he'd given him forgiveness. Now, Paolo was going to pay it back. For once in his life he would do the right thing. He would be worthy. Even if it meant his dream was lost forever.

"I can do it," he said. "I have a way in to Garcia."

TWENTY-SIX

Even though Luca was expecting the beating, the first blow came as a shock, the smack of flesh on flesh a harsh echo in the room. He jerked in the cuffs that bound his hands over his head, and almost lost his footing on the cold cement floor. His new cell was much like the other, except this one had chains on the ceiling and bloodstains on the floor.

Jeff laughed. "Not so tough now without your mob friends around."

"I own a restaurant." And soon a nightclub after he got his hands on Prince. Bracing himself for what was to come, Luca drew in a deep breath inhaling the fetid air curiously laced with the sweet smell of laundry detergent. He had figured out pretty fast that he wasn't in an ordinary jail. No, this appeared to be Jeff's own personal torture chamber, which meant no one knew where he was and no one would be coming for him.

"Italian food." Jeff smashed his fist into Luca's jaw, sending Luca's head jerking to the side. "Much too heavy. I'm making Gabrielle a *cochinita pibil* tonight. Very light. Very tasty. I've paired it with a bottle of Tarapaca Gran Reserva 2009 Cabernet Sauvignon. Gabrielle loves her reds. After two glasses, she becomes very affectionate. Usually, I'll just cuddle with her on the couch—such a bore—but tonight I think we're ready for the next step. She's obviously gotten over David's death if she's been fucking you." He delivered two more blows, each more painful than the next, but the physical pain paled in comparison to the rage he felt at the thought of this sick bastard anywhere near Gabrielle.

"Just think," Jeff continued. "You'll be here, hanging from the ceiling. And I'll be there, making her mine." He moved to the side and delivered a powerful punch to Luca's kidney, sending a wave of nausea through Luca's gut. "Actually, she's always been mine. It just took her a while to realize it."

"Fuck you."

"Actually, fuck her." Jeff moved again, punching Luca with abandon. Luca grunted, but didn't give in to the pain. As far as beatings went—and he'd been through a few—this wasn't so bad.

"That's what I'll be doing. Unless, you tell me you're in the mob . . . Then I have to rethink how this ends. Even I don't want a *Cosa Nostra* vendetta on my head. I'll have to be more careful with disposal. I hear Lake Mead is very deep."

"I own a restaurant." Nothing would ever make him break *omertà*. He would die before he admitted he was in the Mafia.

"Right now you own a restaurant. But when I'm done with you, I have a feeling you'll tell me something else." Jeff tipped his neck from side to side, bounced up and down like he was in a boxing ring or sparring at the gym. He'd clearly dressed for a workout in his LVPD T-shirt and sweat pants, giving him free range of movement for the roundhouse kick that sent Luca rocking in his chains.

"Either way, I win," he continued, huffing his breaths. "If you admit you're in the mob, I get the girl, scoop up all your friends and associates in a career-boosting arrest, and I'll finally get the promotion David stole from me."

Luca didn't care about Jeff's jealousy toward David but talking about it seemed to distract him from the beating, so he kept his mouth shut and imagined all the different ways Jeff was going to suffer when he got out of here. He couldn't figure out if this was just about Gabrielle or if there was something more, but it was clear that Jeff had come unhinged.

"She was always supposed to be mine." Jeff switched sides, delivered a brutal kick to the kidney he'd just punched. Luca gritted his teeth and focused on breathing through the pain.

"We both taught her classes," Jeff said. "I met her first, but I couldn't ask her out because of the damn rules about dating academy recruits. David knew I wanted her. We used to go for drinks together at the end of the day and he'd listen to me talk about her." He glared at Luca as if Luca was the one who had stolen his girl. But then, in a way, he was.

"The day she graduated I went to buy her flowers," he continued. "She loves flowers. But the line was so damn long, and by the time I got there, it was too late. David got to her first. He asked her out after she walked off the stage, and she said yes." He slammed a fist into Luca's gut and Luca's vision blurred.

"What kind of friend does that?" he shouted. "He knew I was going to buy flowers. He knew why. He knew I wanted her. He fucking betrayed me. I did everything to get her back. I sacrificed everything so I could have more money, a bigger house, a better car . . ."

Luca already knew how the story ended. Gabrielle

wasn't that kind of woman. She put her heart into everything she did, and when she gave her heart, she gave it all. He had no doubt that she'd loved David deeply, and far from feeling jealous, it just made him want her even more. He was grateful for every day David had spent with her. Not only because it meant she had truly been loved, but also because he had saved her from this monster.

"I didn't have a chance," Jeff spat out. "Not even with all the money. He was so fucking perfect."

With a roar, he launched himself at Luca, pummeling him with fists and knees. Luca's body bowed under the force of his blows, his brain fuzzing with the pain, until all he could think was *thank God David got to her first.*

"She doesn't care for you." Jeff dropped his arm and panted his breaths, his T-shirt dark with sweat. "She ratted you out. That's how my officers knew where you were last night, how I knew about the Albanians. It was all a set up. She told me everything about you."

Far from destroying him, Jeff's words gave Luca strength and hope. Gabrielle hadn't told Jeff anything. Luca knew it in his heart, as much as he knew the words for a lie, because he'd never told Gabrielle about the Albanians. She hadn't even asked. Gina had fooled him because he didn't really know her. But Gabrielle was part of his soul.

Luca's stomach churned when Jeff picked up a multitailed whip from a collection of torture implements on a table by the wall and walked behind him where Luca wouldn't be able to see to prepare for the blows.

Cristo Santo. If he made it out of here alive he was going to confession, no matter how long it took.

Pain sheeted across his back like a thousand stinging bees. Jesus Christ. He had no idea where he was, but he wasn't at a police station where he might have hoped someone would intervene. He might not trust the legal system, but there were at least limits to what a police officer could do under the law. Unless, of course, he was a dirty cop.

"Did you seriously think I'd let you have her?" Jeff asked. "After all the work and time I put in? I gave up everything for her. I did things I never imagined I would do. I waited two years for her to get over David's death, and then you waltz in and try to steal her away."

Another crack of the whip. Another line of searing pain. Despite his resolve, Luca grunted at the sheer agony and grounded himself by focusing on staying alive to save Gabrielle from the monster that lurked beneath the surface of the man she thought of as a friend.

"And then I find out you're messing with my fucking business, too."

The blows came faster, searing across his back, and it became harder to focus on Jeff's words as he struggled to contain the pain.

"Everything . . . Sex . . . Flowers . . . Casino . . . Ironic . . . Church . . . Your mother . . . Pathetic . . . Son."

A pause. Blood pounded his ears, drowning out everything but the frantic thud of his heart.

"Are you fucking listening to me?" Madness tinged Jeff's voice and Luca sagged in his chains, shuddered. He'd endured torture and beatings, bullets and broken bones. But he'd never endured anything like this.

"Jeff."

Luca lifted his head in the direction of the unfamiliar voice. They weren't alone. Sometime during the beating someone had come in, and he didn't even notice. He was losing it, and he needed to get his shit together or Gabrielle would never be safe.

"Take it down a notch," the visitor said. "You'll kill

him, and if he is in the mob, that's signing a fucking death warrant for us all."

"Shut the fuck up," Jeff snarled. "I'm not afraid of the fucking mob. We just have to be more careful when we get rid of his body."

Luca's heart kicked up a notch. He heard footsteps. The click of a door.

Jeff picked up a bullwhip.

Then he heard himself scream.

"Cristo santo. Look at you. Luca's gonna fill me full of lead for letting you meet Garcia dressed like that."

Gabrielle tugged down her tank top under Frankie's appraising stare. Posing as Paolo's eighteen-year-old girlfriend had its disadvantages, namely the ultra-tight clothes that made it difficult to conceal her weapon. Paolo had shown her a picture of the girl he was dating and Gabrielle had done her best to dress the same, squeezing into a pair of ultra-tight worn denim jeans, a white tank top decorated with big pink jewels, pink UGG boots and a black-and-white letterman-style jacket sporting a giant pink G. After she'd added a black wig, pink ball cap, pink sunglasses and chunky pink jewelry, Paolo had pronounced her "cute."

"Just tell him I didn't give you a choice," she said to Frankie.

Frankie laughed. "If you were any other woman, I wouldn't get away with that excuse. But you . . . I might just get off with only a few broken limbs. If they do have him and he gets a look at you, we won't have to bust him out. He'll break down the fucking walls."

"I'll take that as a compliment." She leaned against his Chrysler 300C while the rest of the crew parked around them in the tourist lookout above the city.

"At least you'll keep the guys inside distracted," Frankie said. "I did a couple of drive bys after Paolo got the address for the meet. There's not much to the place. Looks to be about a four thousand square foot rancher with a basement in a middle-class suburban neighborhood. He's got cameras around the perimeter, and a guard on each door. We shouldn't have any problem getting inside to look for Luca if you provide the distraction. It's a strange set up. If I was him, and I was wanted by the police, and I kidnapped a guy like Luca, I wouldn't be hiding out in plain sight."

"It's a very effective strategy." Gabrielle twirled one of her fake braids. "He's very good at blending in, which is why we had so much trouble finding him. And no one has ever seen his face. Even when we caught high-level dealers who had managed to get a personal audience, they couldn't give us a description. He's like a ghost."

"And I'm a fucking ghostbuster." Frankie cracked a rare smile.

"What does that make me?"

"Dunno." He pulled out a packet of cigarettes. "Haven't figured you out yet. I don't trust you. Don't get why you're risking your career by wanting to be part of this. You coulda gone back to the police station, rounded up your police pals and raided the place once Paolo gave you the address. Something goes wrong tonight, you could wind up dead, or even in jail if they think you're working for the wrong side."

"They would have made me stay behind," she said. "They think I'll go off half-cocked like I did before. But I don't want revenge anymore. After I met Luca, I realized it had left me empty inside. There is more to life. There's the future. And I want him in it. This time I'm here for Luca, and if we manage to catch Garcia while we're at it then I'll be happy with whatever kind of justice you want to dish out."

"I got some ideas . . ." He pulled out a cigarette. "How are you going to protect yourself while we search the house? Paolo's your ticket inside but he's going to be next to useless in a fight. You packing?"

"It wasn't easy, but I managed to get a .22 behind my back." She plucked the cigarette out of his hand and tossed it in a nearby garbage bin.

Frankie's smile faded. "What the fuck?"

"It's an addiction, and it will kill you. My uncle died from lung cancer, and my brother was a drug addict and he died, too. Life is short, Frankie. I learned that the hard way. Don't waste it doing something that's going to make it even shorter."

"Maybe I want it to be short." He pulled out another cigarette and lit it. "Maybe I found my reason for living, and lost it, so there's nothing to look forward to except the odd fucking cigarette and the hope it will bring the end that much faster." Pain flickered across his face so fast, she wondered if she'd seen it.

"So what are you going to do with Garcia when we catch him?" she asked, taking the hint that she should drop the topic of his health.

"You don't want to know, but I promise you'll have your justice."

Gabrielle sighed. "There's a certain appeal to the way you do things. You get a tip where Garcia might be. Don Toscani orders a raid. Boom. Ten guys show up in less than an hour all ready to go and we're on the road. No weeks of planning. No meetings and endless discussions. No politics. No paperwork. No warrants. No due process—"

"No law."

"No law." Gabrielle watched him puff on his cigarette, his hard, muscular body at ease as he leaned against the car. "What about Luca? What will happen to him?"

Frankie shrugged. "That's Nico's call, but you gotta understand you can't be together. It's an unbreakable rule."

Gabrielle toed the cement with her bright pink boot. "Do you know Luca's mother's friend, Josie?"

"Everyone knows Josie."

"She used to be a police officer."

Frankie lifted an eyebrow. "Used to be. Operative words. And she wasn't a normal cop. She was a renegade back in the day." He gestured for her to get in the car with Paolo. "Kinda like you."

"You think I'm a renegade?"

Amusement flickered across his face and for a moment she thought she saw a hint of the man beneath the beast. "You're here. Pretty much says it all."

Twenty minutes later, Paolo parked his vehicle in front of a tidy ranch house in the upper-middle-class suburb of Henderson. Gabrielle followed him up the walk, skirting around the underground sprinkler soaking the lush green lawn. She was taking a big gamble that Garcia wouldn't recognize her. From what she knew, he hired out his dirty work, and the only reason she'd thought different in the warehouse was because the tipster had assured her Garcia would be there.

"I think this is the place Ray brought me the first time we met," Paolo said, pushing the buzzer below the security panel. "I was blindfolded, but it feels the same. No steps. Smell of grass. Quiet. After that first meeting, I picked up my stuff at Commercial Center."

"It was brave of you to let everyone know about your connection to Garcia." She squeezed his hand. "I know what that means for you. I just hope you can stay clean.

I know how hard it is and if you need someone to talk to, I've been through it all with my brother."

"I'm gonna try. I quit cold turkey last time and I'd been using for almost six months. This time it's only been a few weeks."

"Paolo." A short, dark-haired dude wearing army fatigues and an army-green T-shirt opened the door. Two tall guys with barrel chests and thick necks stood behind him.

"This the girlfriend you told me about?"

"Yeah. This is Michele." Paolo put his arm around Gabrielle's shoulders. He was a few inches taller than her, which helped with the charade. "This is Ray and his friends."

"Ray." Gabrielle nodded, dialing up the young, hip vibe. Ray looked like he'd gone a few rounds in the boxing ring and broken his nose every time. He had a broad chest and huge biceps that she had a feeling didn't come from steroids. He was big-time enforcement, if she had to guess, which meant it was time to get serious.

"Michele won the money at the casino, so she insisted on coming along." Paolo shifted his weight, and Gabrielle groaned inwardly. He was so nervous he might give them away.

Ray frowned. "How old are you, sweetheart? You don't even look legal to be in a casino."

"My daddy owns the Casino Italia," she said, thinking fast. "He taught me how to play and he kinda looks the other way when I want to game. He let me into the high-limit room for my birthday last week, gave me a bunch of chips and told me to go wild. I think he might have had something to do with my big win, but I'm not complaining, and neither are all my friends who are excited that Paolo's gonna keep us well supplied with the good stuff."

"The boss is gonna get a kick out of you." Ray checked the street one more time and sent the two guards out to keep watch while Gabrielle and Paolo were in the house.

"Gotta do a pat down." Ray said after he closed the door. His gaze traveled up and down Gabrielle's body, making her cringe. "You first."

She lifted her arms and twirled around with a giggle, praying that he wouldn't touch her because he would easily find the .22 and there was no way she could meet Garcia unarmed. "You think I could hide anything in this outfit. I could barely get it on. And Paolo gets crazy jealous when other guys touch me. Don't you, baby?"

Paolo's eyes widened and he swallowed hard. "Yeah. Don't touch her. She's my . . . girl . . . friend."

Ray's lips tipped up at the corners, and he winked at Gabrielle. "Okay, sweetheart. You go in, and I'll check Paolo out."

After he'd given Paolo a thorough pat down, he led them over to a tan leather couch positioned in front of a wall-mounted TV. Gabrielle wasn't surprised Garcia was distributing from a residential home. The Narcotics bureau had caught dozens of dealers operating the same way. Some of them lived normal middle-class lives, selling their product while their children were at school.

Gabrielle dumped the bag of money on the coffee table and wandered around the room as Ray counted the stacks of bills under Paolo's watchful eye. She couldn't see much beyond the living room although she could smell something delicious coming from the kitchen.

"Will Garcia come in here to meet us?" She checked out the family pictures on the mantelpiece, all of a couple and their young son. Was Garcia that brazen? From the clothes the couple were wearing and the woman's hairstyle, she figured the pictures had been taken about twenty-five years ago, and although Narcotics had little information on Garcia, they had been certain he was under forty.

"He meets people in a special room that we set up for preferred customers like yourselves. No one sees his face."

"Why?" Paolo blurted out.

"He was scarred in an explosion at a meth lab," Ray said casually. "He had third-degree burns. His face almost melted off. Now, he doesn't let anyone see him."

Paolo's face twisted in horror. "I didn't think faces could melt."

"Yeah, they can, and if you saw him, you'd think twice about doing your own manufacturing."

"That's why we came to you," Gabrielle said. "We're happy to pay a little extra so we don't have to get involved with that side of the business."

"You want something to eat or drink while you're waiting?" Ray paused his counting. "Garcia likes me to treat our special customers right. We got all types of booze, chips . . ."

"What smells so good?" Gabrielle asked. "I wouldn't mind having some of that."

"It's *cochinita pibil*. But the boss made it for a private dinner."

Cochinita pibil? Wasn't that the dish Jeff was making for her tonight? What a coincidence. Or maybe not. Could Jeff be working for Garcia? No. That would be crazy. She'd known him as long as she'd known David. He was a good guy, a good detective, a good friend, although he'd been a little off kilter the last few weeks.

Paolo cleared his throat and glanced over at Gabrielle, then away. "I'll have . . . uh . . . a beer."

"Sure." Ray wrote his count on a piece of paper. "How about you, Michele?"

"Just water, thanks."

As soon as Ray disappeared down the hallway, Gabrielle crossed the room to look down the hallway opposite to the one Ray had taken. If Luca was being held here, he would most likely be in the basement. She just had to find the stairs.

"Gabrielle!" Paolo called after her in a horrified whisper. "We're supposed to stay here while Frankie and the others check the house."

"I'm sure you can handle the distraction on your own." She turned the handle on the nearest door, but it was locked.

"I can open it," Paolo said. "Locks are my thing." He pulled what looked to be a metal wire from his pocket, and within a few seconds the locked clicked open.

"Handy skill to have," Gabrielle said, checking out the very ordinary linen closet. "I'm going to search the rest of the house. You stay here and tell Ray I went to the bathroom. If they find me somewhere I shouldn't be, I'll pretend I got lost."

Paolo's eyes widened in alarm. "Don't leave me."

"I'm not sitting around playing giggly girlfriend while Luca is in danger. If he's here, I'll find him. We're depending on you, Paolo. Time to show us what you're made of." She drew in a breath, inhaled the delicious smell from the kitchen again. Ray had said Garcia had made the dish for a private dinner. Jeff was bringing his meal over to her house tonight . . .

No. She was jumping to conclusions. She'd been to Jeff's place and this wasn't it. He lived in a two-bedroom condo only a few blocks from the station, and she and David had visited him many times. Why would he cook a meal here instead of at home where he had all his fancy pans and special ingredients? Jeff was an excellent cook and he'd treated them to many delicious meals. And Ray had revealed that Garcia hid his face because he'd been disfigured in an explosion. Jeff was a good-looking guy with not a scar on his face.

Still, she couldn't ignore the warning niggle in her mind. On the off chance that her intuition had picked up on something that her mind couldn't accept, she pulled out her phone and sent Jeff a quick text to tell him she was looking forward to dinner. But before she could even tuck her phone away, she heard the unmistakable sound of a Harley-Davidson engine . . . Jeff's ringtone.

Her heart thudded so hard she thought it might break a rib. She sent a second text and a third, gesturing for Paolo to come as she followed the sound to a locked door down the hall. "Open it."

Paolo quickly picked the lock and opened the door. Pulling out her .22, she edged inside. Jeff's phone lay on the dresser, still lit up from her messages. His suit was lying on the bed, along with his LVPD-issue holster and his empty gym bag.

"Jeff is here," she whispered.

"Hey! What are you doing in here? This room is off limits."

Gabrielle startled at Ray's shout. Taking a deep breath, she turned and played as innocent as she dared. "I was looking for the bathroom."

"Together?" He glared at Paolo who had turned sheet white.

"He just came to tell me I was going the wrong way when I heard the sound of a motorcycle and opened the door. I love motorcycles. I thought maybe it was the door to the garage and I wanted to take a peek." She crossed the floor to Ray and put a gentle hand on his arm. "Sorry. I shouldn't have been so nosy, but the door was unlocked."

He grunted, but didn't pull away. "No motorcycles here. It's a ring tone."

"It's the coolest ring tone ever. It went on and on." She gave his arm a squeeze, guessing he had a soft spot for eighteen-year-old girls in tight pink clothes. "Is it yours?"

"No." He grabbed the phone off the dresser and closed the door behind them on the way out, ushering them back to the living room. "Stay in there." He pointed to the tan leather couches. "I'm just gonna take this downstairs, and I'll be right back."

"On the floor." Gabrielle gestured Paolo down after Ray left. "Listen where he goes. I'm going to text again. Tell me when you hear an engine roar."

TWENTY-SEVEN

Thump. Thump. Thump.

Luca barely registered the sound of a fist hitting the door. He didn't know how long he'd been hanging here, but time had stood still since Jeff grabbed the bullwhip and he'd been lost in an eternity of pain.

"*Qué chingados!* They know I'm not to be disturbed during my workout." Jeff stalked across the room and yanked open the door.

"Ray. What the fuck do you want?"

Luca heard a murmured apology and something about a phone message. He tried to lift his head to see who Ray was, but his neck wouldn't obey.

"Our special guests have arrived," Ray said. "They've got the money. The girlfriend is so fucking cute. Can't be more than eighteen or nineteen and her dad owns one of the casinos downtown so she's got to be loaded. She wants our new guy to supply all her friends."

Jeff let out a long breath. "Good job setting that up. I wanted to finish up here, but I'd better go meet them. A casino owner's daughter can give us a line in to a new tier of the city. Get the room ready. I'll see you upstairs."

Luca sagged in the chains, thanking whatever guardian angel had just spared him the agony of being whipped again with ten feet of thick, braided leather.

Jeff collected his implements and laid them neatly on the table, before grabbing a towel from his gym bag to wipe himself down. "I won't be back tonight," he said. "I plan to fuck Gaby until the sun comes up. But I'll leave instructions for my men to come down and keep you company."

Luca heard the unmistakable roar of a Harley-Davidson engine. For a moment, he thought he'd passed the point of no return, but when he forced his head up he saw Jeff smiling at his phone by the open door.

"It's Gaby," he said in delight. "She's texted four times in the last hour about our dinner tonight. She's really looking forward to it." He slid his thumb over his phone. "Do you notice how quickly she came to me when you disappeared? You were nothing to her. A fling. And once you were gone, she came back to me."

His phone rang in his hand, the unmistakable sound of "This Life" by Curtis Stigers & The Forest Rangers.

"Gaby!" He looked back over his shoulder with a satisfied smirk as he answered the call. "I just got your texts."

Christ. Gabrielle was going to spend the night with this monster? Luca yanked on the chains but the thick metal cuffs were tight around his wrists. Maybe after a few hours' recovery, he might be able to swing his body in the direction of the table—

"That's great news! I'm on my way." Jeff ended his call and turned to face Luca, an almost fanatical gleam on his face. "I've got him! Gaby found the fucker who vandalized my car. I thought it was you, but she tracked him down through the serial number on his phone, and she's watching him right now at a Mexican restaurant

in Harlingen. This day is just getting better and better."
He scooped up his gym bag and towel. "I might be in a
very good mood when I come back. Vengeance and
fucking in one night. You just might get to die easy."

Luca shook in his chains. "You touch her and the
things you've seen the Mafia do to people that piss them
off will be nothing compared to what I do to you."

Jeff laughed. "You're hardly in a position to make
threats, and if you think you're going to be rescued,
think again. No one knows where you are. As far as anyone is concerned, you were taken to jail by a couple
of LVPD police officers. Except there is no record of
your arrest, and no way of tracing you here. You've disappeared, and you'll never be seen again."

"Fuck you."

"Fuck her. And I will. Again and again and again
until she doesn't even remember your name." He turned
as he pulled the door closed. "Now if you'll excuse me,
I've got a business meeting to attend, a vandal to arrest,
a dinner date with a hot little cop, and then a little pussy
for dessert."

"He's coming." Paolo leaped up from the living room
floor. "I heard a door close, and now I can hear footsteps.
I think the basement stairs lead into the kitchen."

"Damn. He can't see me." Gabrielle looked around
frantically just as Ray came down the hall.

"Something the matter?"

"Bathroom." She bounced up and down as if she were
desperate. "I really need to go."

"Down the hall," Ray said pointing in the opposite
direction to the door where they'd found Jeff's clothes.
"And Garcia will be ready for the meeting in about five
minutes."

"Thanks." She blew him a kiss and hurried down the hall, noting the kitchen to her left. Keeping Ray sweet was an insurance policy she couldn't afford to pass up.

Once in the bathroom, she texted Frankie with an update, alerting him to the fact that she'd just discovered that one of her colleagues, Jeff, was a dirty cop working for Garcia, but would be leaving shortly to hunt down an imaginary car vandal.

Frankie: Get out. Hi-Tech electric fence around perimeter. Can't give you back up.

Gabrielle: Text me when Jeff leaves. We'll find Luca.

Frankie: Two new guards on site. Total of four outside. Stand down.

Gabrielle: Man up. I'm going in.

Frankie: WTF? I say leave. You leave.

Gabrielle: Sorry. Bad service. No texts getting thru. Going to find Luca.

Frankie: PITA

Gabrielle: Bad service again. Text garbled. Was that THX? You're welcome.

Frankie: Someone just came out. Tall. Stocky. Dark Hair. Jeff?

Gabrielle: I hope so.

When she emerged from the bathroom, Paolo and Ray were chatting with one of the guards in the living room. Heart pounding, she slipped into the kitchen, taking in the warm terracotta tiles, colorful hand towels, frilly curtains, and what she assumed was the *cochinita pibil* cooling on the stove. The incongruity of the domestic scene with what was going on in the house was unsettling, but not as much as the dried blood on the floor outside the basement door.

Cautiously, she made her way down the carpeted stairway to a vast basement with crisp white walls, soft white carpet, and gray leather furniture. She checked out the doors along the walls, stopping at one that had a set of keys hanging on a hook near the hinges. Gabrielle grabbed the keys and unlocked the door. Then she prayed.

Creak. Swish.

Luca's head jerked up as a rush of cool air brushed over his body. Jeff hadn't even been gone five minutes and he was fading already.

The door opened, just a crack and then wider. Luca tensed. Had Jeff decided to come back for round two?

"Luca!"

Luca stared. Maybe he was hallucinating. There were no angels where he was going when he died. So why had an angel come? A sexy angel. Dressed in pink. With long dark hair. She reminded him of Gabrielle. Maybe if he hallucinated Gabrielle, the pain would go away.

"Oh, my God, baby. What did they do to you?"

Hmmm. She sounded just like Gabrielle. And she called him baby. He liked that term of endearment, although he didn't want to hear it from anyone except the woman he loved.

"Calm. Calm. He's okay. Breathe." Muttering to herself, she pulled out her phone and thumbed the keys. Was she sending a text? Did angels text? Was this the modern version of Judgment Day? Would God text back with "Heaven" or "Hell"?

"Okay. I'm going to get you out of here," she said, tucking her phone into her fancy pink purse. "Frankie is going to arrange for a distraction and Paolo will come down and pick the locks on those cuffs. I didn't see any other keys outside."

Frankie. Paolo. He knew those names. His mind cleared, but not enough to understand why this angel looked and sounded like Gabrielle.

"Are you going to be able to walk when I take you down?" She touched his face, stroked a very gentle finger over his cheek. "If not, I'll carry you out. You're not spending another minute in here."

Dio mio. It wasn't a hallucination because the moment she touched him, he could feel her in his soul.

"Gabrielle?"

"Yes, it's me. We came to rescue you. Me and Paolo."

And that woke him right the hell up. "Paolo? You brought Paolo? What were you—?"

A loud crash outside cut him off. Moments later Paolo dashed into the room.

"Frankie got a guy to drive his truck into one of the cars parked outside. It's not going to keep them busy for long." He reached up and used a nifty little wire to open Luca's cuffs.

"You should give Paolo a raise," Gabrielle said, sliding under Luca's shoulder to take his weight. "I've never seen anyone who can pick a lock like him."

Paolo eased under Luca's other shoulder, and although Luca balked at having to rely on their assistance, he knew it would take at least a few minutes before he could walk on his own. His back felt like it was on fire, every breath hurt from what he suspected were broken ribs, his arms were next to useless from lack of circulation, and his legs shook with every step.

Gabrielle glanced over at his back and her breath caught. "Who did this to you? Was it Garcia?" She pulled a .22 from under her jacket, holding it in front of them with her free hand.

"Jeff."

"Jeff?" She froze, but before she could ask any questions, footsteps thudded across the floor above.

"Jesus Christ!" Jeff's voice echoed down the stairwell. "My fucking car. They destroyed my fucking car. How the fuck am I supposed to get across the city now? Don't just stand there staring at me. Someone get me another vehicle. And find out who owned that piece of shit truck. Where's the kid and the fucking girl you wanted me to meet?"

Luca gritted his teeth and forced his unsteady legs to take his weight. "Give me the fucking gun."

That was it? A five-minute diversion?

Gabrielle bit back a howl of frustration. How the hell did Frankie think they'd rescue Luca, get out of the house, clear the yard and get past the electric fence all in five minutes? Luca could barely walk, and if they were spotted on their way out, he wouldn't be able to run.

Emotion welled up in her chest as she took in the extent of Luca's injuries. His back was a mess of angry red stripes, blood and bruises, his body was slick with sweat, and from the way he held himself she was sure he had a few broken bones. She'd always considered Jeff a friend, but now she wondered if she even knew him at all.

They waited for footsteps, but when the voices faded away, Gabrielle tugged Luca toward the stairs. "He must have changed his mind. Let's go."

"Give me the gun," Luca said again.

She gave an exasperated sigh. "You can have the gun if you can walk."

He took a step, leaned so heavily on her that she

staggered to the side. There was no way they'd get him out like this.

"I'm going to create another distraction." She propped Luca up against the wall and slid out from under his arm. "Hopefully that will give Frankie enough time to take down the four guards outside and get through the electric fence so he can give us a hand. Paolo, you stay with him. Do you have a gun?"

"Frankie gave me one." Paolo pulled out a Sig Sauer P320. "I've only been out to the shooting range once, but I was pretty good."

"Take good care of Luca. Gentle with the trigger." She couldn't believe she was entrusting Luca's safety to a boy who'd only ever fired a gun at a paper target, but she had no choice.

"Fuck." Luca gritted his teeth. "I'm not letting you go up there alone. Jeff is out of control."

"I can handle Jeff." She felt a rush of confidence she would never have imagined feeling two months ago when she'd been shot and kicked off her case, her quest for revenge at an apparent end. But then she'd met Luca and discovered a core of strength she never knew she had, and a side of herself that was willing to break the rules. Her quest to see justice done the legal way had given her a reason to live, but it had also held her back. Luca had shown her another path, a way forward. He had opened her heart and freed her from the past. Jeff would pay for what he had done. And if the law wouldn't step up to punish him, then she would.

She heard the thud of footsteps, the creak of a door.

"Find them," Jeff shouted. "They have to be around. Who leaves half a million dollars behind?"

Heart pounding, she walked up the stairs listening as Jeff barked orders. How long had he worked for Garcia?

David would have been devastated if he'd known. She was almost glad he wasn't alive to find out that the man he thought of as a brother had betrayed everything he believed in.

She pushed open the door and walked boldly into the kitchen as if she had every right to be there just as Jeff turned the corner.

"Gabrielle?" If their situation hadn't been so dire, she would have laughed at the total and utter shock on Jeff's face. But it gave her a few precious moments she could turn to her advantage.

"Jeff." She barked out his name, holding her gun down by her side and out of sight. "What the hell is going on here? We need to talk." Before he could speak, or even react, she swept past him and marched down the hall toward the bedroom where she'd found his clothes, and as far away from Luca and the basement stairs as possible.

"Gabrielle."

She made it to the room just as Jeff's heavy palm landed on her shoulder, and she spun around to face the man who had been David's best friend.

"What are you doing here?" His eyes narrowed, and she gritted her teeth against the tidal wave of fear crashing through her body.

"I got a tip that Garcia was here. You know me. I couldn't resist. Do you like my disguise?" She lifted one of the black braids as she checked out the bedroom, furnished solely with a king-size bed in dark wood and matching dresser. If things got rough she could lock herself in the ensuite bathroom, or maybe escape out the window hidden behind the heavy navy blue curtains.

"How did you get in?"

"Ray."

His face darkened and he pulled the door closed behind him, sending her pulse skittering. "What the fuck is going on?"

"Why don't you tell me?" She was playing her "offense is the best defense" card but it was starting to wear thin. "Are you working for Garcia?"

"No. I'm not working for Garcia." He took a step toward her, and something dangerous flickered in his eyes. "Garcia's dead."

Hope flared bright in her heart. "You killed him?"

"Yeah." His voice softened. "I did. For you." He pulled his damp T-shirt over his head, tossed it on the floor, as if they were two friends having a casual conversation and he hadn't just beaten Luca half to death downstairs in the house of the drug lord she'd been chasing for the last two years.

Stunned, she just stared. "Where is he? Why didn't you call anyone?"

"Put down the gun, Gaby," he said softly, holding out his arms. "Come and give me a thank you hug. You know I would never hurt you."

Gabrielle stared at his open arms as she tried to make sense of the surreal situation, of what she knew and what she'd seen, of the facts that still weren't adding up.

"If he's dead, why was Ray going to take me to see him?"

He lifted an eyebrow. "You were the new customer?"

"I needed a way in."

"Agent Palmer didn't give you half a million dollars to buy a meet." His sucked in his lips as he stared at her, considering. "Where did you get the money?"

She shrugged. "Casino."

He snorted a laugh. "Aren't you a lucky girl!"

Gabrielle wasn't feeling particularly lucky at this moment, trapped in a room with a friend who had become a stranger, and who had a dark side she couldn't even begin to comprehend. "I don't understand what's going on."

He walked over to his dresser, pulled open a drawer. "I think it's better that way. I don't want anything to come between us, and Garcia will."

"What are you doing here, Jeff?"

He pulled a fresh black T-shirt over his head and sighed. "Put down the gun, Gaby. We had a nice evening planned, and I spent most of the afternoon preparing dinner. I'll pack it up, and we'll go to your place, eat, have a little wine, then we can cuddle and talk on the couch for a bit before we go to bed. Unless you were actually being honest about finding the guy who threw the rock at my car, and then we might take a detour first."

She heard the slightest waver in his voice, realized he wasn't as calm and collected as he appeared on the surface, and if she didn't play this right, he might just explode "I wasn't lying. I know it's important to you. I was staring right at him when I called."

"Fuck." He thudded his fist on the dresser. "I want that guy so fucking bad. It was fucking rude. That's what really got to me. There was no reason to break my windshield. It wasn't even like he was after my spare change."

"He thought you were threatening me when you broke my door." She had talked to Paolo briefly in the car about the night he lost his phone and he'd explained that he was trying to protect her.

"You talked to him?"

"Yes." She shuddered, wondering what she was going to do when he asked how she had talked to him on the phone while looking at the car vandal when she was here and not on the other side of the city.

Myriad emotions crossed his face, and his eyes softened. If he'd pieced her lies together, he hid it well. "I would never hurt you, Gaby. You know that. I was just frustrated that night. I'd been waiting for you for so long." In two strides, he closed the distance between them and leaned down to kiss her cheek. "Let's go and have that nice evening we planned together."

Was he crazy? He had just tortured a man in his cellar, and killed Garcia. He was clearly here without Agent Palmer's authorization, and the house was in chaos. He had to know she wouldn't have come alone, and instead of suggesting they bring in her backup or call the police, he wanted to go for dinner? "Jeff . . ."

He reached for her hand. "I said, 'Let's go.'"

But she couldn't move. Every instinct screamed danger, and her mind was desperately trying to put all the pieces together to come up with a picture that made sense. This was his room. His clothes were on the bed and in the drawers. He had cooked a meal in the kitchen. He tortured people downstairs. But this was also where Paolo had been told to meet Garcia. Ray seemed to think Garcia was alive and had talked to him after she and Paolo arrived. And only four days ago, a not-dead Garcia had killed Little Ricky and left him hanging in the meat freezer as a warning.

"When did you kill Garcia?"

Jeff sighed and returned to the dresser. "You're going to ruin our evening with all these questions. Sometimes, Gaby, it's better not to know."

"I want to know," she demanded.

"How about we talk after dinner? We can turn on those terrible game shows you like to watch and curl up on the couch . . ." He trailed off when she shook her head.

"Are you crazy? We're not having dinner. We're not watching TV. You're working with Garcia, Jeff. You have to know it ends here."

He leaned a casual arm over the top of the open

drawer and laughed. "What are you saying? You're going to call Agent Palmer? I'll tell him I came here looking for answers, the same as you. What evidence do you have linking me to Garcia? None. I found the drugs on the table when I got here. The men I've got with me are all LVPD officers and will back me up. You're so desperate to find Garcia, you're grasping at straws."

Maybe a few weeks ago she would have second-guessed herself, but not any more. Anger lit a flame inside her, giving her the strength to challenge him. "So you came here looking for Garcia, killed him, put your clothes in the drawers, cooked dinner, and then changed into your gym clothes so you could go and beat on the man you kidnapped downstairs?"

When he spoke, even the tone of his voice was stark. "You saw him."

"Yes, I saw him. I saw what you did to Luca." Her hand shook as she raised her gun. "I want to understand, Jeff. I may not have had the same feelings for you that you do for me, but you've always been a good friend. I never imagined you could do what you did to him. I almost didn't believe him when he told me it was you. We've shared so much, not just together, but with David, and now I feel like I never really knew you."

"David." His face curdled as he spat out the name. "Always fucking David. You think you didn't know me? You knew nothing about him."

"He was my husband," she said indignantly. "I knew him very well."

"Did you know he stole you away from me? He stole everything. I'm standing here now because of him." He clenched his hand on the edge of the dresser.

"Tell me," she said quietly, seeing an opening to get him to talk. "Tell me what he did to you, and then we'll go for dinner and talk."

"We both got into Narcotics together." Jeff shook out his hand. "That's when I met Garcia. I pulled him over for a traffic violation and found drugs in his car. He was just small-time then. He gave me a little something to keep quiet and we became friends. He told me I could make more in a week with him than I did in a year with the police."

Gabrielle felt sick inside. It was a familiar story. Good police officers, struggling to make ends meet on low pay, were seduced by the lavish lifestyle of the criminals they were supposed to apprehend.

"I said no." Jeff dropped his hand over the drawer again, a seemingly casual gesture that wasn't casual at all. She stared at the drawer, wondering if he had a weapon hidden inside.

"Can you believe it?" He continued. "My friendship with David was more important and I knew he would never forgive me. We had planned to move up the ranks together. Sergeants, then lieutenants, captains, and commanders. We were going to change things for the better. David always had high ideals. He was so fucking perfect. The perfect cop. The perfect friend . . . at least until he stole you away. He knew I wanted you, and the day you graduated I was going to ask you out. I told him I was going to do it. I trusted him. I went to buy you flowers and when I came back it was too late."

She remembered that day. The thrill of having fulfilled Patrick's dream. The disappointment that her father hadn't come. David asking her out. Jeff uncharacteristically quiet . . .

"I don't remember you giving me flowers."

"I didn't. David told me he'd already asked you out when I got back, so I threw them away. I would never have risked our friendship by pursuing you after that." His pulse throbbed in his neck, and she dipped her head, making another quick search of the room, planning her escape route. Jeff wasn't the man she thought he was, and she didn't know who lay behind the mask.

"You were a good friend to him." She tried to soothe him with a calm, quiet voice, although her heart was pounding in her chest. "Even though he did you wrong."

"I told myself it was for the best," he said. "You never looked at me the way you looked at him, and I figured I probably never even had a chance because I didn't come from a rich family like him. I decided I was never going to lose out because of money again. I'd had enough of that growing up with a foster family on social assistance. So, I called up Garcia. Told him I'd get involved. He had expanded his operation, and he needed protection when his shipments arrived. I got some like-minded guys together from the department and we realized the shiny beacon on top of the squad car was the path to easy money. We targeted Garcia's rivals, putting what we took back on the street and taking the cash. We were rolling in it, and then Garcia decided he wanted a piece of our action."

A chill ran through her body. "What did you do?"

"I took him out," he said flatly. "He had become the weak link, and we didn't need him anymore. But he had one hell of a reputation. He could do deals based on his name alone. He'd been disfigured in a meth-lab explosion and he never showed his face, so I figured why not keep his name alive? I got rid of all the guys who worked for him and got my own boys on board. All cops. All disillusioned with a system where the criminals are riding around in luxury cars and the good guys are just scraping by."

She froze in absolute shock, her mouth hanging open as she stared at him aghast. "You're Garcia?" All these years chasing after David's killer and he was right under her nose, sitting in her living room watching TV, walking with her in the park, and holding her during her darkest days.

"I couldn't have done it if we didn't share the same heritage," he said proudly. "All our product comes from Mexico, and I have to do a lot of negotiating over the phone with the cartel bosses, none of whom speak English. They don't know that Garcia has been dead for years or that they've been dealing with me. We had a great thing going. We'd flash the cherry, confiscate the drugs, and sell them under Garcia's name. It was perfect."

Something niggled at her brain. An unbearable, impossible, sickening thought.

"How long has Garcia been dead?"

"Three years."

"You're lying," she said, making a quick mental calculation. "He's been active over the last two years. I have reports, witness statements. And I was pretty sure it was Garcia who shot me in the warehouse."

The faintest flicker of remorse crossed his face. "I shot you."

Her heart skidded to a stop. "You?"

"You were endangering yourself, Gaby." He sighed and ran his hand through his thick, dark hair. "You were obsessed and losing yourself. All you talked about was Garcia and getting revenge. I needed to get you out of the bureau so you could move on with your life. A life with me in it."

"No. Jeff. Please tell me you didn't."

"I did," he said firmly. "I set the whole thing up. I called in the tip, nudged you just enough by repeatedly expressing my concern that Garcia might get away. I knew you'd jump the gun. I just knew it. You wanted Garcia so badly you couldn't think straight. But I was very careful where I placed the shot. I didn't want to hit any internal organs and I wanted you to recover quickly. I knew they'd pull you off the case for that. I thought it would be enough to scare you off Garcia for good. I even arranged for your transfer to Theft so we could be on the same floor."

Her hand came to her mouth. "Jeff. How could you?"

"To save you from yourself. To save us. We were meant to be together. I saw you first, Gaby. You just never gave us a chance."

"I loved David."

He snorted. "David didn't love you. If he did, he wouldn't have threatened me when he found out what was going on. He would have known what I would have to do. He chose to leave you alone, Gaby. But I didn't. I could have given myself up and gone to jail when David confronted me. But I chose you."

TWENTY-EIGHT

"Give me the gun." Luca held out his hand for the gun hanging loosely in Paolo's grip.

Paolo shook his head. "With all due respect, Mr. Rizzoli, you can barely stand, and you can't even wiggle your fingers. How are you going to pull the trigger?"

Luca shook his arms, trying to restore his circulation. He could hear footsteps above them, shouts from outside. He had to get out of this damn basement. If only he could get his feet to move. "I'll hold it in my fucking teeth if I have to. That bastard is upstairs with Gabrielle and he's fucking obsessed with her. I can't imagine what he's gonna do now that she knows he's connected to Garcia."

He trailed off when he heard gunshots. A shout. A scream. "Fuck. That's going to bring the cops. We have to get Gabrielle out of here. Let's go." Luca gritted his teeth and staggered across the carpet to the stairwell. Forcing his fingers to curve around the railing, he heaved his body up the first step. Fire screamed through his ribs and sweat trickled into his open wounds, the sting so fierce he could barely breathe. *Christ.* How the fuck would he make it to the top?

He felt Paolo's shoulder under his own. Without speaking, Paolo half dragged, half carried Luca up the stairs, his slim body bending under Luca's weight.

Good man. Paolo had really proved himself today. If Luca got out of this alive, he'd make Paolo an associate. Put him in charge of locks. The kid was strong, too. He could even be a bodyguard for Gabrielle.

Like that was going to happen.

With Paolo's help, Luca made it up the last few stairs, fighting back a wave of dizziness when they reached the top. Goddamn drug dealers destroying his goddamn life all over again. When he got out of here he was going on a mission to clean up the damn city.

Paolo pushed open the door to the kitchen and a bullet whizzed over his shoulder thudding into the stairwell wall. "Get back, Mr. Rizzoli!"

Blocking Luca's body with his own, Paolo lifted his gun and shot randomly through the door.

Silence.

Luca pushed open the door a crack and spotted a uniformed cop lying facedown on the floor. "Good shooting, kid."

Paolo stared at the man in horror. "I shot a cop." Then his face creased in a frown." How did I shoot him in the back of the head?"

"You didn't," Frankie said from the kitchen doorway. "But you did hit just about everything else in the kitchen."

"Where's Gabrielle?" Luca didn't have time for conversation. He needed to find Gabrielle like he needed to breathe.

"I haven't seen her," Frankie said. "We gotta get

out of here. Sally G reported cops only a few minutes away."

Luca shook his head. "I'm not leaving without her."

"You killed David." Gabrielle stared at Jeff in horror, the sickening image of David hanging from the balcony sending a wave of nausea through her gut.

"He'd already taken you," Jeff said. "I couldn't let him take my business away from me, too."

As if a dam had opened, anger poured from her in violent waves that shook her to the core. He had murdered David, betrayed them both. And then he had dared comfort her when he was the reason for her pain. He had touched her with hands forever stained with David's blood and the blood of her unborn child.

"You sick, twisted, fucking bastard," she shouted as her vision turned red with rage. "Thank God David asked me out that day. He loved you like a brother, trusted you. And you stole his life away."

"A *brother* doesn't steal his friend's woman," Jeff snarled. "He doesn't listen to him talk about her for months and then ask her out on the very day he knows his *brother* intends to do it. He doesn't try to arrest his *brother* for making a little extra on the side. That's not brotherhood or friendship, in any sense of the word. And he paid the price."

"The price?" She took a small step toward the door, wary of the man who was so cavalier about the murder of his best friend. How had she never seen the monster hidden beneath his smooth charm? "Going to jail is a price. A few bruises after a fistfight is a price. You didn't just murder him, you butchered him in the home we bought together—a home where you were always welcome as a friend."

She took another step, her gaze shifting to his hand dangling casually over the dresser. His fingers dropping a little bit too far. No doubt about it, he had a gun in the dresser, and if she didn't get her emotions under control and bite her tongue, he would kill her as easily as he had killed David.

"Always the fucking friend," he muttered. "I thought when David was gone, we would finally be together. But no. You had to go and spread your legs for that fucking mobster." His face turned ugly, the handsome features curling in a scowl. "Always interfering in my business. Always in the wrong place at the wrong time. I hired the Albanians to give you a scare, and when I came to look after you, there he fucking was. But he got his pay-back. I killed his friend as a warning, and tonight I'll finish him"

Gabrielle's heart squeezed in her chest. She had imagined this moment over and over after David died. The satisfaction of finally having answers. The release she would get by venting her anger and pain. The re-lief she would feel when she pulled the trigger. But she felt none of those things, and she felt no desire to become the monster he was, and spend the life she had only begun to live again in jail. Instead, sorrow gripped her by the throat. She felt heartsick that David would have died knowing his closest friend had betrayed him, and that Jeff had let jealousy, greed, and anger destroy him in this terrible, twisted way.

"I only ever wanted to be with you," Jeff said bitterly.

Her hands closed into fists and she forced her words out past the lump in her throat. "I was pregnant. Three months. We had planned to tell you that weekend. We were so excited. David had bought your favorite cham-pagne. I was going to make a cake and write Uncle Jeff on it. Then he was dead, and the trauma was too much.

I had a miscarriage. You took them both from me. You took everything."

His face smoothed to an expressionless mask. "I'm sorry," he said, his voice as bland as his face. "Really, I am. But that's what happens when you make the wrong choice. And you made another wrong choice when you chose that mobster over me."

"No. I'm sorry." She was only a few steps from the door now, but crossing the threshold would put her directly in his line of fire. "Even after you took everything, I found something you'll never have. Love."

"Love?" He gave a bitter laugh. "Look what love gave me. A friend who betrayed me. A woman who rejected me. All I've got now is this life I created out of the ashes. I can't let you take this away from me, Gaby. It's all I've got."

He pulled a gun from the dresser and the world stood still.

"Now." Frankie shouted, kicking in the door.

With the last of his strength, Luca rushed inside. He took in the scene in a heartbeat.

Jeff. Gun. Gabrielle.

He threw himself between them just as the gunshot cracked the air.

Pain seared through his chest and he crashed to the ground.

Fuck.

Not again.

TWENTY-NINE

Heaven.

He had to be in Heaven.

There were angels in Heaven. Angels with beautiful smiles.

Luca couldn't remember the last time a woman had smiled at him the way the angel on the adjacent bed was smiling right now.

Well, except for Gabrielle. But she'd been unhappy in the ambulance on their way to the hospital, and unhappier still when the emergency room staff had whisked him away to the operating room.

Would she smile now that he was in Heaven?

His hand drifted to his chest where the doctors and nurses had attached various tubes and wires beneath his hideous gown in an attempt to save him. He had tried to explain that he could not maintain *la bella figura* when his boxers were on display, and he required something more appropriate to his dignity than a hospital gown. Even Gabrielle had agreed. Her face had been wet with tears when his trousers were cut off and the gown draped around his person. He wished he could have seen her smile one last time. He also wished he could have died wearing his clothes.

Miss you.

He blinked to clear his vision, and focused his gaze on the angel who sat on a hospital bed across the room. Her eyes were the blue of the endless sky, and her hair the gold of the sunlight as it streamed through the stained-glass windows of his mother's church.

Someone must have put in a good word at the Pearly Gates because he would definitely remember if he'd spent a year in confession.

"Devo essere morto ed ora mi trovo in paradiso perchè è proprio un angelo quello che vedo di fronte a me."

He heard the murmur of voices, and then the angel's smile broadened. "Your mother is on the phone. She told me I had to call the minute you woke up. She heard you and she says that roughly translates as, 'I have died and gone to heaven. I see an angel.' She's on her way now with a little something for you to eat. I think she's also angry that you got shot again, but I haven't learned many Italian curse words so maybe she was shouting for joy."

And didn't that just wake him up. When his mother was angry enough to curse, people suffered.

But he still saw an angel.

On a hospital bed.

"Gabrielle? Are you hurt?" He tried to push himself up, but pain lanced through his chest and he sank back on the pillow.

"I'm fine. I just wanted to stay with you so you didn't wake up alone." She slid off the bed, and walked over to him, then stroked a soft finger along his jaw. "You were in surgery for hours and then you slept for an entire day. I was very annoyed that you threw yourself in the path of Jeff's bullet, but Don Toscani came by and he said it's a habit of yours."

"Don Toscani saw me in the hospital gown?"

"Everyone saw you. Your mother saw you, Angela saw you, Alex saw you, Matteo saw you, your crew saw you, and Frankie, Mike, Paolo, and Sally G . . ."

"Enough." He held up his hand. "Where are my clothes? I must dress."

"You didn't have a shirt on when you decided to try and stop a bullet with your chest, and the medics cut off your pants because they were worried you had kidney damage from the beating. So the gown is all you've got. Suck it up."

He lifted an eyebrow in response to her disrespect, but she just laughed. And it was a beautiful sound.

"You weren't hurt?" He covered her hand, pressing it against his cheek.

"No, thanks to you. But Jeff is dead. Frankie shot him after he shot you. I'm good with that. I didn't need revenge to fulfill me anymore. And I don't think I could have handled taking a life—especially his life. I think justice was served, and David is at peace."

"Poor *bella*." He squeezed her hand. "So much loss."

"Good things came of it," she said. "The FBI rounded up all the members of his operation, and we've cut off a major drug supply into the city."

"Your department must be proud of you."

She twisted her lips to the side. "Well . . . I've actually been suspended for going rogue. I broke a lot of rules doing what I did. Apparently using information that was accessed without authorization from the police database to hunt down a drug lord and break into his house to save your boyfriend from being tortured is frowned upon, even if the drug lord is a dirty cop. Good thing I didn't mention my boyfriend's crime connections or the half a million dollars of dirty money that Paolo thought to scoop up before the police arrived."

"The boyfriend is pleased that you went rogue to save him," he said. "Not so pleased you put yourself and your job at risk."

"I think I always had a bit of rebel in me. You just helped me see it. It may also have come out when I found Clint beating on Nicole at our house. Not that he'll ever report my use of excessive force. He moved away after our altercation. I don't think he'll bother Nicole again."

Luca couldn't help but smile. "I wish I'd seen that."

"You probably would have told me it was dangerous and tried to stop me."

He turned his head to kiss her palm. "I love you, Gabrielle. I will always want to protect you, whether it's having your back or being by your side." But what was he going to do now that Garcia was out of the picture? Leaving her as Nico had directed was not an option, but *Cosa Nostra* would never let him go, and the penalty for breaking the rule against associating with cops . . .

Dare he believe in miracles?

"What will happen with your job?" he asked.

Her eyes sparkled, and he felt a quiver of excitement in her hand. "I've only talked about this with my commander on the phone, but because everything turned out well, it looks like I'll be given a choice of leaving on good terms or staying to face disciplinary charges."

Luca steeled his face to a neutral expression. He didn't want to push her one way or the other. Regardless of her decision, he would find a way for them to be together. But if she did leave . . .

Gabrielle's lips quivered with a smile. "Stop looking at me like that."

"Like what?"

"Like you don't know what I would choose."

Hope flared in his chest. "What will you choose, *mio angelo*?"

She leaned over and pressed a soft kiss to his lips. "I choose you."

THIRTY

EPILOGUE

Six months later

"Papa!" Matteo burst into the house and ran full tilt
at Luca with Max hot on his heels.

"Slow down, *cucciolo*. What's going on?"

"It's a party! At Nonna's house. She says everyone's
going to be there. Don Toscani is coming, his wife, Mia,
is coming, Cousin Frankie is coming, Cousin Louis is
coming, Cousin Sal is coming, Gabrielle's friends are
coming—"

"I get it," Luca said. "You are sounding more like
your nonna every day."

"Is that bad?"

"No, of course not. But what is bad is little boys going
to their nonna's house without a grown-up."

"But she lives right across the street," Matteo whined.
"I can see her house from my bedroom window. It's not
far, Papa. And I always look both ways. Gabrielle said
it was okay."

Luca looked over at Gabrielle, who was pretending
not to listen to the conversation as she sorted through

her papers on the dining-room table of their new home, purchased, in part, with his winnings from the casino. Nico had generously allowed Luca to keep some of the money if he promised never to play human shield ever again.

Gabrielle had just obtained her private investigator's license and had joined a PI office in partnership with two other ex-cops. Luca was happy that she was excited about her new career. Not so happy about her working with two men, and even less happy about her going into potentially dangerous situations alone. Not that he dared raise the issue of her safety. But he did plan to have a discrete discussion with her partners about what might happen to them if Gabrielle were ever injured at work, maybe mention that he knew they both wore size 11 shoes.

"I thought we decided that important decisions about Matteo should be made together," he said. He wanted Gabrielle to be a part of Matteo's life even if they had not yet formalized their commitment to each other. He understood her hesitation to get married. Hell, he'd been through a bad experience, too. But marriage meant something to him. Not just as a statement to the world that they belonged to each other, but as an assurance to her that he would always be there for her, to love her and protect her, that she owned him body and soul.

He glanced down at the paper in his hand. Yep. Those were the words he had written. He just hoped he remembered them when he went down on one knee this afternoon.

"Crossing the street to his nonna's house isn't an important decision, especially if she's standing on the other side of the street shouting at everyone to get out of the way." Gabrielle looked up from her papers. "Who is the party for?"

The party was for their engagement, but he wanted it to be a surprise.

"My mother loves parties," he said, dissembling. "She throws them for the smallest of occasions. Maybe she's celebrating the opening of my new nightclub, or your new job, or maybe that Alex has been clean for six months, or that Paulo is now an associate in my crew, or that your friend Nicole is dating one of my soldiers, or it might be just because Angela finally found a hair color that looks real. Who knows?"

"Hmmm." She stared at him as if she could see right through his lies to his very soul.

"What does 'hmmm' mean?"

She lifted a suggestive eyebrow. "It means can you send Matteo back to your mother's place so I can show you something upstairs?"

Show him something upstairs? Oh yeah. He was all over that. Not that their "upstairs" activity was lacking in any way, but when his woman wanted to go upstairs in the middle of the day, who was he to refuse?

"Matteo! Take Max to your nonna's house," he shouted, sending his mother a quick text so she would be there when he crossed the street. "Look both ways and don't run."

"Come, *bella*." He held out a hand. "Show me something . . . upstairs."

She snorted a laugh. "Why do you always think everything is about sex?"

"Because it's you."

He followed her to their bedroom and closed the door. But when he moved to pull off his shirt, she held out a warning hand. "Clothes on. Sit on the bed."

He didn't like the "clothes on" idea, but maybe she wanted to tease. Luca sat on the edge of the bed, puzzled when she sat beside him with an envelope in her hand.

"I did something bad," she said.

Considering how he lived his life, 'bad' was a relative term. "What did you do, *bella*?"

"From what you said, and the way you reacted whenever I mentioned any similarities between you and Matteo, I figured out that Gina told you Matteo wasn't yours. So I sent DNA samples for you and Matteo to a friend at a crime lab. You look too much alike for it to be a coincidence, right down to the mole you both have behind your ear. He even walks like you."

Luca stared at the envelope in her hand. "I told you it doesn't matter. He's my son, whether he has my blood or not."

She opened the envelope and placed the letter on his lap. "Yes, he is your son. The DNA matches. She lied to you."

Luca stared at the letter. His eyes blurred, and he couldn't make out the patterns on the page. All he could see was the word, "match."

"My blood."

"Your blood, Luca. Your son."

His throat thickened, and he had no words. She had given him back his son, breached the walls around his heart, and showed him how to live again.

"I have something else for you." She placed another envelope on his lap.

Luca stared at it warily. "Something bad?"

"Something good."

He tore open the envelope, stared at the white stick inside.

"I'm pregnant." Her hand shook as she turned it over to show him the pink cross. "I didn't think I could get pregnant after what happened, but I guess if you spend every waking moment when you're not at work or with family having sex without protection, chances are pretty good."

"Our blood," he murmured.

"I expect this will take your protectiveness to a whole new level," she said, smiling.

Luca cupped her beautiful face between his hands. "*Mio angelo.* You have no idea."

THE END

Read on for an excerpt from the next book by

Sarah Castille

ROCCO

Coming soon from St. Martin's Paperbacks

She was being watched.

Grace looked over her shoulder yet again, but couldn't determine who or what was causing the hair on the back of her neck to stand on end, only that it was the same feeling she'd had in the cemetery earlier this afternoon when she thought she saw someone in the shadows.

She briefly considered asking one of her father's bodyguards to check it out. Her father's visit to Vegas was not without danger, given that the two cousins who had split the Toscani crime family would do anything to seize control. Although an underboss was considered untouchable—his death could be approved only by the don himself—it was not uncommon for a powerful capo to seize the reins of power by whacking everyone who stood in his way, and to hell with the consequences.

"Is something wrong?" Mia followed Grace's gaze to the back hallway.

"No. I just . . . It's nothing." She smiled at Nico Toscani's unconventional wife, dressed in punk clothes, with a pink streak in her dark hair. Although they had both been brought up in Mafia families, they couldn't have been more different. Mia was confident and outgoing, her disregard for the traditional role of a Mafia wife apparent in everything from her appearance to her attitude. A shrewd businesswoman, she ran her own cybersecurity firm, and seemed to have no issue with taking on clients from the mob.

By contrast, Grace had dressed in her usual boho-chic—a burgundy lace crochet mini swing dress, antique jewelry, knee-high black boots, and a black fedora which she had tucked in her oversize crochet bag when they sat down to dinner. Far from running her own business, she had been drifting since finishing her psychology degree, working part-time for a non-profit, and singing with a jazz band in the evenings. And as for working with the mob . . . forget about it. Ever since she was sixteen and had discovered who her father was and what he did for a living, she wanted nothing to do with the Mafia, and after they destroyed the first man she'd ever loved she'd left New York and moved to Vegas.

Of course, personal wishes only took you so far. When your father, who was second-in-command of the most powerful Mafia family in the US, came to Vegas for a visit and asked you to meet a "nice boy"/attend a funeral/join him for dinner with the self-appointed boss of the Las Vegas faction of the family, you met the boy, went to the funeral, and choked down your dinner with a smile on your face. The smile was because she loved her father. She just didn't like what he did for a living.

Grace.

She heard—no, felt—her name whisper over her skin, and a shiver ran down her spine. Unsettled, and determined to seek out the cause of the curious sensation that had dogged her since the funeral this afternoon, she excused herself to get some air and walked through the restaurant toward the front door.

"Can I help you, Grazia?"

Luca Rizzoli, the owner of *Il Tavolino*, and one of Nico Toscani's senior capos, intercepted her after she'd made her way through the crowded tables and past the stage where a small jazz band was setting up for the evening show.

"It's just Grace. My father is the only person who calls me Grazia. He's pretty old school."

Luca laughed. "I didn't want to offend and possibly lose a few fingers. My wife wouldn't be very happy. Our baby is due in a few weeks and she's keeping me busy getting the house ready."

"Your first?"

"Second. We have a son, Matteo. He's six."

"He must be excited." She felt a tug in her heart, remembering how excited she'd been at the same age when her brother, Tom, was born. She had always imagined herself with at least two kids, but Rocco and his father had destroyed that dream.

Rocco. Her first. Her last. Her only love. It had been ten years. Why was she thinking about him now?

"Not as excited as me." A smile spread across his handsome face and she felt inexplicably jealous of the woman who had a man like Luca with whom to share her life.

"I was just going to step outside," she said by way of explanation for her wandering. "That was quite a feast you cooked for us."

"It's quieter out back." He pointed to a narrow hallway beside the kitchen. "Frankie's keeping watch by the door so you have nothing to worry about."

"Sounds perfect."

He glanced around, and his voice dropped almost to a whisper. "I overheard you telling Mia you're in a jazz band."

Grace's blood chilled. If her father found out her internship had ended a year ago and she still didn't have a permanent job he would drag her back to New York. "I don't . . ."

"It's okay," Luca said, raising a placating hand. "I won't tell anyone. I only mention it because I've got a friend who just opened a new jazz club only a few blocks away, and she's looking to hire. Are you interested?"

"I'm always interested in new gigs."

Luca pulled a card from his breast pocket and handed it to her. "Address is on the card. Ask for Sam. Tell her I sent you."

"Thanks." She tucked the card into her bag and followed his directions to the back hallway with a curious sense of anticipation. Grace's mother and nonna and all her female relatives on her mother's side were firm believers in a sixth sense that was passed down through the women in the family. No one laughed if someone "felt" something. Coincidence was explained by karma. Portents and omens were taken seriously. Close calls and brushes with death were the work of angels.

Although no one could explain why that sixth sense, and all the angels in heaven, couldn't save her mother when Jimmy "The Nose" Valentino burst into Ricardo's Restaurant on the corner of Mott and Grand and sprayed the restaurant with bullets after finding out that Ricardo was having an affair with his wife.

Her heart pounded although there was nothing unusual in the hallway. Two kitchen doors with glass windows. Broom closet, door ajar. Storage room, also open. Men's restroom on the left. Women's restroom on the right.

She reached for the exit door and her skin prickled in warning.

Turning, she saw a man in the shadows behind her. Tall. Dark. Dressed in a leather jacket, faded jeans and a worn pair of boots. She blinked, trying to make out his face, as she reached into her purse for the weapon her father had bought her before she moved to Vegas.

"Grace."

That voice. Deep and dark, like the brush of velvet over her skin. So familiar.

A name worked its way through the barriers in her mind. A name she had wiped from her thoughts as well as her heart.

Rocco.

No. It wasn't him. It couldn't be. Last she'd heard he was still in New York with his psychopathic father, doing what he'd been trained to do. The beautiful dark-haired boy she had fallen in love with had become the Gamboli crime family's most feared enforcer, causing the kind of trauma she had dedicated her life to heal.

He took a step forward and she saw his face.

"Rocco?" She didn't need to ask the question, but the shock of seeing him again after so many years stole her rational thought away. The years had not been kind to Rocco De Lucchi. His lean angled cheeks and firm square jaw were lined and scarred, his once-thick hair cut military short. Gone were the softness from his face, the roundness of his cheeks, and the dimple at the corner of his mouth. But his sculpted lips were still full and sensual, and gold flecks glittered in the whiskey-brown eyes that had once seen into her soul.

The soft beat of Otis Redding's, "These Arms of Mine" drifted from the restaurant as the band began to play, and the sound brought up far too many memories, ones she had buried long ago.

They had connected through music. Shared through music. Loved through music.

She drew in a ragged breath, inhaling the scent of him, whiskey and leather, and something so familiar a wave of heat flooded through her veins, shocking her with its intensity. How could he affect her so deeply after all this time, and after everything that had happened between them?

Grace swallowed hard, forcing her throat to work. "What are you doing here?"

He didn't answer and she had nothing else to say. It had been ten years since they last saw each other. Ten years since she had discovered what kind of man Rocco truly was. Ten years since he had destroyed a friendship and a love that had grown slowly over time.

His gaze raked over her, stopping at the bare expanse of thigh between the hem of her dress and the top of her knee high boots, before returning to her face. She trembled beneath his scrutiny. This man who had been her friend, her soulmate, her lover. Her first.

"Fuck."

Of all the things he had imagined he might say if they ever met again, 'fuck' was not it, but the harsh word jarred her out of her shock at seeing him again.

"Is that all you have to say, Rocco?"

"Frankie. They call me Frankie here."

"Frankie?" She pushed back all the memories associated with that name. "You work for Nico now? In Vegas?"

"Yeah."

"I've been living here for three years. It's hard to believe we never met."

He reached for her, his fingers gently brushing back the hair that she always wore down to hide the scar on her cheek. His touch set off a cascade of images in her mind. Ten years of beautiful and ten minutes of horror.

His hissed intake of breath startled her, but when she jerked back, he gripped her jaw with a rough hand and turned her head to the side to inspect the long silvery scar. "I did that to you."

Pain that she had locked away clawed at her insides, ripping open the emotional scars that had never truly healed.

He shuddered and a sound escaped his lips, a cross between a growl and moan. "I never meant for you to get hurt."

"Then you should never have given me that ride." She covered his hand, intending to draw it away, but instead, she pressed his hand to her cheek. Despite the surreal situation, the past that could never be changed, and the future that would never be, she wanted just for a moment to feel the warmth of the connection that had flared to life the first day they met.

"You were at the cemetery, weren't you?" she asked softly as their hands dropped.

He nodded, stared at their parted hands as if he could will them back together.

"I knew you were there. I felt you." She wasn't embarrassed to tell him. He knew everything about her. At least he did until she turned eighteen.

"I've never stopped feeling you, Gracie."

Gracie. No one had ever called her that except him. She closed her eyes as memories flooded her senses. Beautiful and bittersweet.

The first time she saw him.

The day he gave her that ride.

"Rocco." She whispered his name.

But when she opened her eyes, he was gone.